About the Author

Born in Toronto in 1903, MORLEY CALLAGHAN is a graduate of the University of Toronto and of Osgoode Hall law school. He was called to the bar in 1928, the same year that his first novel, *Strange Fugitive*, was published, but he never practised; his part-time work as a cub reporter on the *Toronto Star* had infected him with the ambition to be a full-time writer.

Although he has travelled widely, and lived for some time in Paris during the golden years of Hemingway and Fitzgerald, Callaghan has spent most of his life in Toronto quietly producing a stream of novels and short stories that have gained him admiration around the world. In Canada he has won a host of honours, including the Governor General's Award for Fiction. In late 1982 he became a Companion of the Order of Canada. In 1983 his acclaimed novel *A Time for Judas* became a major best-seller, and his novel *Our Lady of the Snows* was published in 1985.

MACMILLAN PAPERBACKS

Morley Callaghan's Stories

Macmillan Paperbacks 13

Macmillan of Canada

A Division of Canada Publishing Corporation
Toronto, Ontario, Canada

Canadian Cataloguing in Publication Data

Callaghan, Morley, date.
  Morley Callaghan's stories

(Macmillan paperbacks ; 13)
ISBN 0-7715-9247-7

I. Title.

PS8505.A41A159 1986   C813'.52   C85-099900-6
PR9199.3.C34A15 1986

Originally published in hardcover 1959 by The Macmillan
Company of Canada

First softcover edition 1967, Laurentian Library 5, ISBN
0-7705-0250-4 (later ISBN 0-7715-9716-9)

Reprinted 1970, 1972, 1975, 1979, 1983

First Macmillan Paperbacks edition 1986

Printed in Canada

The Stories

To the way it has been with us

Many other stories I have written might have been included in this book, but these are the ones that touch times and moods and people I like to remember now. Looking back on them I can see that I have been concerned with the problems of many kinds of people but I have neglected those of the very, very rich. I have a story that begins, 'Once upon a time there were two millionaires,' but I haven't finished it yet.

Morley Callaghan

All the Years of Her Life

They were closing the drugstore, and Alfred Higgins, who had just taken off his white jacket, was putting on his coat and getting ready to go home. The little gray-haired man, Sam Carr, who owned the drugstore, was bending down behind the cash register, and when Alfred Higgins passed him, he looked up and said softly, 'Just a moment, Alfred. One moment before you go.'

The soft, confident, quiet way in which Sam Carr spoke made Alfred start to button his coat nervously. He felt sure his face was white. Sam Carr usually said, 'Good night,' brusquely, without looking up. In the six months he had been working in the drugstore Alfred had never heard his employer speak softly like that. His heart began to beat so loud it was hard for him to get his breath. 'What is it, Mr. Carr?' he asked.

'Maybe you'd be good enough to take a few things out of your pocket and leave them here before you go,' Sam Carr said.

'What things? What are you talking about?'

'You've got a compact and a lipstick and at least two tubes of toothpaste in your pockets, Alfred.'

'What do you mean? Do you think I'm crazy?' Alfred blustered. His face got red and he knew he looked fierce with indignation. But Sam Carr, standing by the door with his blue eyes shining brightly behind his glasses and his lips moving underneath his gray moustache, only nodded his head a few times, and then Alfred grew very frightened and he didn't know what to say. Slowly he raised his hand and dipped it into his pocket, and with his eyes never meeting Sam Carr's eyes, he took out a blue compact and two tubes

1

of toothpaste and a lipstick, and he laid them one by one on the counter.

'Petty thieving, eh, Alfred?' Sam Carr said. 'And maybe you'd be good enough to tell me how long this has been going on.'

'This is the first time I ever took anything.'

'So now you think you'll tell me a lie, eh? What kind of a sap do I look like, huh? I don't know what goes on in my own store, eh? I tell you you've been doing this pretty steady,' Sam Carr said as he went over and stood behind the cash register.

Ever since Alfred had left school he had been getting into trouble wherever he worked. He lived at home with his mother and his father, who was a printer. His two older brothers were married and his sister had got married last year, and it would have been all right for his parents now if Alfred had only been able to keep a job.

While Sam Carr smiled and stroked the side of his face very delicately with the tips of his fingers, Alfred began to feel that familiar terror growing in him that had been in him every time he had got into such trouble.

'I liked you,' Sam Carr was saying. 'I liked you and would have trusted you, and now look what I got to do.' While Alfred watched with his alert, frightened blue eyes, Sam Carr drummed with his fingers on the counter. 'I don't like to call a cop in point-blank,' he was saying as he looked very worried. 'You're a fool, and maybe I should call your father and tell him you're a fool. Maybe I should let them know I'm going to have you locked up.'

'My father's not at home. He's a printer. He works nights,' Alfred said.

'Who's at home?'

'My mother, I guess.'

'Then we'll see what she says.' Sam Carr went to the phone and dialed the number. Alfred was not so much ashamed, but there was that deep fright growing in him, and he blurted out arrogantly, like a strong, full-grown man, 'Just a minute. You don't need to draw anybody else in. You don't need to tell her.' He wanted to sound like a swaggering, big guy who could look after himself, yet the old, childish hope was in him, the longing that someone at home would come and help him. 'Yeah, that's right, he's in trouble,' Mr. Carr was saying. 'Yeah, your boy works for me. You'd better come down in a hurry.' And when he was finished Mr. Carr went over to the door and looked out at the street and watched the people passing in the late summer night. 'I'll keep my eye out for a cop,' was all he said.

Alfred knew how his mother would come rushing in; she would rush in with her eyes blazing, or maybe she would be crying, and she would push him away when he tried to talk to her, and make him feel her dreadful contempt; yet he longed that she might come before Mr. Carr saw the cop on the beat passing the door.

While they waited – and it seemed a long time – they did not speak, and when at last they heard someone tapping on the closed door, Mr. Carr, turning the latch, said crisply, 'Come in, Mrs. Higgins.' He looked hard-faced and stern.

Mrs. Higgins must have been going to bed when he telephoned, for her hair was tucked in loosely under her hat, and her hand at her throat held her light coat tight across her chest so her dress would not show. She came in, large and plump, with a little smile on her friendly face. Most of the store lights had been turned out and at first she did not see Alfred, who was standing in the shadow at the end of the counter. Yet as soon as she saw him she did not look as Alfred thought she would look: she smiled, her blue eyes never wavered, and with a calmness and dignity that made them forget that her clothes seemed to have been thrown on her, she put out her hand to Mr. Carr and said politely, 'I'm Mrs. Higgins. I'm Alfred's mother.'

Mr. Carr was a bit embarrassed by her lack of terror and her simplicity, and he hardly knew what to say to her, so she asked, 'Is Alfred in trouble?'

'He is. He's been taking things from the store. I caught him red-handed. Little things like compacts and toothpaste and lipsticks. Stuff he can sell easily,' the proprietor said.

As she listened Mrs. Higgins looked at Alfred sometimes and nodded her head sadly, and when Sam Carr had finished she said gravely, 'Is it so, Alfred?'

'Yes.'

'Why have you been doing it?'

'I been spending money, I guess.'

'On what?'

'Going around with the guys, I guess,' Alfred said.

Mrs. Higgins put out her hand and touched Sam Carr's arm with an understanding gentleness, and speaking as though afraid of disturbing him, she said, 'If you would only listen to me before doing anything.' Her simple earnestness made her shy; her humility made her falter and look away, but in a moment she was smiling gravely again, and she said with a kind of patient dignity, 'What did you intend to do, Mr. Carr?'

'I was going to get a cop. That's what I ought to do.'

'Yes, I suppose so. It's not for me to say, because he's my son. Yet I sometimes think a little good advice is the best thing for a boy when he's at a certain period in his life,' she said.

Alfred couldn't understand his mother's quiet composure, for if they had been at home and someone had suggested that he was going to be arrested, he knew she would be in a rage and would cry out against him. Yet now she was standing there with that gentle, pleading smile on her face, saying, 'I wonder if you don't think it would be better just to let him come home with me. He looks a big fellow, doesn't he? It takes some of them a long time to get any sense,' and they both stared at Alfred, who shifted away with a bit of light shining for a moment on his thin face and the tiny pimples over his cheekbone.

But even while he was turning away uneasily Alfred was realizing that Mr. Carr had become aware that his mother was really a fine woman; he knew that Sam Carr was puzzled by his mother, as if he had expected her to come in and plead with him tearfully, and instead he was being made to feel a bit ashamed by her vast tolerance. While there was only the sound of the mother's soft, assured voice in the store, Mr. Carr began to nod his head encouragingly at her. Without being alarmed, while being just large and still and simple and hopeful, she was becoming dominant there in the dimly lit store. 'Of course, I don't want to be harsh,' Mr. Carr was saying, 'I'll tell you what I'll do. I'll just fire him and let it go at that. How's that?' and he got up and shook hands with Mrs. Higgins, bowing low to her in deep respect.

There was such warmth and gratitude in the way she said, 'I'll never forget your kindness,' that Mr. Carr began to feel warm and genial himself.

'Sorry we had to meet this way,' he said. 'But I'm glad I got in touch with you. Just wanted to do the right thing, that's all,' he said.

'It's better to meet like this than never, isn't it?' she said. Suddenly they clasped hands as if they liked each other, as if they had known each other a long time. 'Good night, sir,' she said.

'Good night, Mrs. Higgins. I'm truly sorry,' he said.

The mother and son walked along the street together, and the mother was taking a long, firm stride as she looked ahead with her stern face full of worry. Alfred was afraid to speak to her, he was afraid of the silence that was between them, so he only looked ahead too, for the excitement and relief was still pretty strong in him; but in a little while, going along like that in silence made him terribly aware of the strength and the sternness in her; he began to wonder what she was thinking of as she stared ahead so grimly; she seemed to have forgotten that he walked beside her; so when they were passing under the Sixth Avenue elevated and the rumble of the train seemed to break the silence, he said in his old, blustering way, 'Thank God it turned out like that. I certainly won't get in a jam like that again.'

'Be quiet. Don't speak to me. You've disgraced me again and again,' she said bitterly.

'That's the last time. That's all I'm saying.'

'Have the decency to be quiet,' she snapped. They kept on their way, looking straight ahead.

When they were at home and his mother took off her coat, Alfred saw that she was really only half-dressed, and she made him feel afraid again when she said, without even looking at him, 'You're a bad lot. God forgive you. It's one thing after another and always has been. Why do you stand there stupidly? Go to bed, why don't you?' When he was going, she said, 'I'm going to make myself a cup of tea. Mind, now, not a word about tonight to your father.'

While Alfred was undressing in his bedroom, he heard his mother moving around the kitchen. She filled the kettle and put it on the stove. She moved a chair. And as he listened there was no shame in him, just wonder and a kind of admiration of her strength and repose. He could still see Sam Carr nodding his head encouragingly to her; he could hear her talking simply and earnestly, and as he sat on his bed he felt a pride in her strength. 'She certainly was smooth,' he thought. 'Gee, I'd like to tell her she sounded swell.'

And at last he got up and went along to the kitchen, and when he was at the door he saw his mother pouring herself a cup of tea. He watched and he didn't move. Her face, as she sat there, was a frightened, broken face utterly unlike the face of the woman who had been so assured a little while ago in the drugstore. When she reached out and lifted the kettle to pour hot water in her cup, her hand trembled and the water splashed on the stove. Leaning back in the chair, she sighed and lifted the cup to her lips, and her lips were groping loosely as if they would never reach the cup. She swallowed the hot tea eagerly, and then she straightened up in relief, though her hand holding the cup still trembled. She looked very old.

It seemed to Alfred that this was the way it had been every time he had been in trouble before, that this trembling had really been in her as she hurried out half-dressed to the drugstore. He understood why she had sat alone in the kitchen the night his young sister had kept repeating doggedly that she was getting married. Now he felt all that his mother had been thinking of as they walked along the street together a little while ago. He watched his mother, and he never spoke, but at that moment his youth seemed to be over; he knew all the years of her life by the way her hand trembled as she raised the cup to her lips. It seemed to him that this was the first time he had ever looked upon his mother.

A Country Passion

The paper was not interesting and at the end of the column he did not remember what he had been reading, so he tossed the paper on the porch, and slumped back in the chair, looking over into Corley's back yard.

A clump of lilac trees prevented him from seeing directly through the open door to Corley's kitchen. Jim Cline, sitting on the porch, could see two wire bird-cages on Corley's back veranda. The faint smell of lilacs pleased him.

Jim got up, leaning over the porch rail and sucked in his upper lip. The moustache tickled him, and he rubbed his hand quickly across his bearded face. Ettie Corley came out and sat down on the back steps. Ettie was sixteen but so backward for her age she had had to quit school. Jim was twenty-nine years older than Ettie. In two days' time Ettie was to go away to an institution in Barrie. Jim had wanted to marry her but the minister, who had reminded him that he had been in jail four times, would not marry them, so he had come to an agreement with her anyway.

Jim rubbed the toe-cap of his right boot against the heel of his left. His boots were thick and heavy. He repaired them himself and could not get the soles on evenly. His brother Jake came out and picked up the paper. Jake saw Jim's forehead wrinkling and knew something was worrying him. One of the canaries in a cage on Corley's veranda started to sing and Jake looked over and saw Ettie.

'It ain't no good, Jim.'

'Eh?'

'What's the matter?'

'Aw, lay off, Jake.'

'Heard up town today they're thinkin' of ropin' you in on somethin' pretty bad.'

'They roped me in a few times before, didn't they, Jake?'

'Well, it's done you no good.'

'Awright, it's done me no good.'

'It'll be serious.'

'Who's going to touch me around here?'

Turning away in disgust he looked through the lilac leaves. Jake thrust his hands in his pockets, then drew out the right one and examined the palm attentively.

'The sun's hitting the porch,' Jim said suddenly. 'I think I'll go in.' The sun shone on his thick neck. He turned around, shaking his head, and blinked his eyes in the sun.

'Didn't I buy Corley's coal last winter? Where'd Ettie be now if it weren't for me? Where's her sister gone, running around like a little mink somewhere?'

He went in the house, right through the kitchen to the hall and out to the front steps, and looked around, surprised to find himself facing the street so unexpectedly, then he stared down at a broken picket in the walk. As he looked at the one broken picket in particular, he wondered how he could fix things up with Ettie. Stepping down to the walk he pulled the broken picket from the scantling and tossed it out to the road. Dust formed in a small cloud and drifted toward the green grass on the other side of the road.

He walked across the front of the house and stood at the corner, waving his hand at Ettie. She saw him and came out to the sidewalk and down to Cline's veranda.

'What do ya want, Jim?'

'What's up, do you know?'

'I'm kind of scared. They got it out of me.'

'They won't do nothin'; that's all right.'

'Can't we beat it, Jim?'

'No use, you can't beat it.'

She was a big girl for her age, and her mouth was hanging open, and her dress was four inches above her knees, and her hair uncombed. Jim didn't notice that her hair wasn't combed. He was so eager to explain something to her, an idea that might be carried to a point where everything would be satisfactory, but words wouldn't come readily. It was a feeling inside him but he had no words for it. He felt himself getting hold of a definite thought. Last winter he had wanted to give her some underwear after discovering she had made some herself out of sacking but she had protested strongly against such extravagance.

'I'm going to give you something to wear before you go 'way, Ettie.'

'Aw no, Jim.'

'I'm going to get the car out and we'll go down-street and get some.'

Half grinning she wiped away a strand of hair from her face. She looked worried, moistening her lips, and she leaned against the thick poplar tree while he went around the house to get the car. He had a slouchy stride, his wide shoulders swinging as he walked.

The car rocked and swayed coming up the driveway. Ettie got into the car. Passing Corleys', Jim drove slowly without looking at Ettie. Mrs. Corley came out to the sidewalk, wiping her hands in her apron, shaking her head jerkily. She watched the car turn the corner, then went into the house quickly, her loose shoes scraping on the steps.

At the Elton Avenue bridge Jim stopped the car while Noble's cow crossed, its tail swishing against the rear mudguard. Tommie Noble, following a few paces behind, glanced at Jim and Ettie, then turned his head away. 'Co Boss,' he said, cutting at the cow with a gad. The car jerked forward, Ettie bounced back, her head hitting Jim's shoulder.

They drove down Main Street and Jim parked the car outside Hunt's dry-goods store. Until the car stopped in front of the store Jim had imagined himself going in with Ettie, but he merely took hold of her by the wrist, giving her an idea of the things he thought she should buy. Ettie giggled a little till Jim took seven dollars out of his pocket and counted it carefully. 'Aw gee, Jim, you'd be good to me,' she said.

She got out of the car and walked timidly across the sidewalk to the store. The door closed behind her and Jim fidgeted to get a more comfortable position, one foot thrust over the car door, his eyes closed. Ettie would just about be talking to a clerk, he thought, and imagined the woman taking down from a shelf many flimsy articles for a girl. He hoped Ettie would not buy the first shown to her instead of taking time to pick out pale blue, or cream, or even pink, which would be a nice colour for a girl. Jim opened his eyes, looking down the street. Three kids, swinging wet bathing-suits, were coming along the street.

Smiling prettily, Ettie crossed over to the car and Jim kicked the door open with his heel. She had the bundle under her arm. 'Oh, boy,' she said, climbing into the car. Jim looked at her, her cheeks flushed, eyes bright, and grin-ning. He started the car. She would become a fine woman later on, he thought.

'We'll be getting along,' he said cheerfully.

'Ain't it too bad we got to go home?'

'Aw hell, Ettie.'

The car turned out to the middle of the road, and backed up, and Jim saw the sheriff, Ned Bickle, getting out of a car at the curb. Jack Spratt and Henry Tompkins were with him. The three men, walking alertly, approached Jim's car.

'Get out of the car, Jim,' the sheriff said.

'What's the matter, Ned?' Jim said suspiciously, though appearing very friendly. Ned had arrested him three times, twice for stealing chickens, once when he had got into a fight at Clayton's blind pig, but it had required at least three men to hold him. The sheriff weighed two hundred and twenty-five pounds. His hard hat was pushed well back on his head, a two-days' growth of hair was on his face. Jim did not look directly at either Tompkins or Spratt, though aware of them as if they had been just a few feet from him many times before.

'Now Jim, there's a couple of charges against you. You know how it is, Jim.'

'Awright, go on, don't get tongue-tied.'

'Well, it's about Ettie, Jim.'

'What about her?'

'Her old woman's had a lot to say.'

Jim leaned over the steering-wheel, staring at the sheriff, then glancing casually at Ettie, was suddenly disappointed and bewildered. He straightened up, his back erect, resentful, his neck getting red, his moustache twitching till his lower lip moved up and held it. His left foot shot out and the door flew open, catching Tompkins in the middle, forcing him back two or three paces.

Jim jumped out, but tripped on the running-board and lurched forward, bumping blindly against Tompkins and spinning half-way round. Tompkins wrapped his arms around Jim's back and held on as Jim tried to swing him off. Twice he swung his shoulders, and one of Tompkin's arms lost its grip. Only someone had Jim's feet. He yelled and kicked out with his free foot, the boot sinking into something soft, but a huge weight was on his shoulders, forcing him down slowly, his knees bending gradually, his feet stationary, his legs held tightly together. They had him. Jim knew when they had him in such a way he couldn't move. Always they tried to get him the same way. He toppled over on his back and the road bricks hurt his shoulder-blades.

'Just a minute now till I get the cuffs out,' the sheriff said.

The cuffs went on easily. Jim stretched out on the road, twisted his head till he could see Ettie, who was standing up in the car, leaning over the seat, crying and yelling, 'Leave him alone, do ya hear, leave him alone.'

They hoisted Jim to his feet. He walked willingly to the sheriff's car. People who had come out of the stores to stand on the curb now formed a ring around the police car. 'Aw leave the guy alone,' somebody yelled. Ned Bickle pushed Jim into the back seat and got in beside him. Tompkins stepped into the driver's seat. Spratt went over to Jim's car to drive Ettie home.

'This is about the worst you been in yet,' Bickle said to Jim as the car passed the dry-goods store. The sheriff, puffing a little, was smiling contentedly, feeling good-natured.

'Yeah.'

'I'm afraid you'll do a long stretch, Jim.'

'What for? What gets into you guys?'

'Seduction and abduction we're calling it, Jim.'

'Aw lay down.'

Under the maple trees in front of the jail the car stopped.

The leaves of the tree were so low they scraped against Jim's bare head as he stood up to get out. The jail was a one-storey brick building, four cells and a yard with a twelve-foot brick wall. Jim had been in jail three times but had never remained there more than fifteen days.

Tompkins and Spratt followed Jim and the sheriff into the cell and leaned against the wall, very serious while Ned was taking the handcuff from his own wrist, then from Jim's wrist. Jim, rubbing his wrist, looked at the bare walls, many names written there, his own over at the corner, underneath the window.

'Who else is around?' Jim asked.

'Willie Hopkins.'

'What for?'

'Stealing three barrels of wine from old man Stanley's cellar.'

Jim sat down on the bed and they went out, locking the door carefully. He leaned forward, his elbows on his knees, his chin cupped in his hands, staring at three iron bars in the small window. Sitting there on the bed he felt all right till he remembered that an hour ago he had been sitting on his back porch looking at the lilacs. He got up and walked around the room, his thoughts confused, and when he tried thinking slowly his head seemed to ache. He sat down on the bed to forget all about it, stretching his legs out, his arms behind his head. The sun shone through the window, forming barred squares of light on the opposite wall.

A tap on the door aroused him. 'Heh, Jim.' Dannie Parker, the guard, was smiling at him. 'Do you want to take some exercise in the yard?'

'Not now,' Jim said mildly.

'Ain't you feeling well?'

'Awright.'

'Suit yourself then, I thought you'd like to, that's all.'

Jim lay on the bed till Dannie brought him some supper, cold beef, potatoes, and maple syrup. The meat and potatoes he ate greedily, and liked the maple syrup so much he coaxed Dannie to give him an extra saucerful and promised to play checkers after supper.

For fifteen minutes Jim waited for Dannie to return with

the checker-board. Then he heard Dan's voice and another voice. The Rev. Arthur Sorrel, a plump, agreeable little man with a small nose, the minister who had refused to marry Ettie and Jim, came into the cell with Dannie.

'Well, Mr. Cline,' he said.

'Well,' Jim said soberly.

'I thought we might want to talk things over.'

'Maybe I'd better get another chair,' Dan said.

'Don't bother. I'll stand, or perhaps sit on the bed.'

Dan went away. Jim folded his arms across his chest and glared at the minister, who sat down on the edge of the bed.

'I want you to understand, Jim, that I'll do all in my power to help you. I'm not against you.' The minister scratched his head thoughtfully, rubbing his cheek with the palm of his hand. 'But there's not much I can do for you,' he added.

'There's only one thing I want to know,' Jim said.

'What's that?'

'If I'm guilty, what'll I get for it?'

'Oh, I don't know, I'm sure. I mean I can't say for certain but I'm afraid it will be life and lashes. That's the usual thing.'

Jim jumped up. 'Life?'

'And lashes, yes. But I can do all in my power to have them go easy on the lashes.'

'Life, eh?'

'I'm afraid so.'

Jim sat down, then stretched out on the bed, vaguely aware that the minister was talking but not interested in following the words.

'Ettie is going down to Barrie tomorrow and she'll be with the Ladies of Charity and I wouldn't wonder if she grew up to be a decent woman.'

Jim, staring at the ceiling, did not answer.

'Of course she's had the worst home in town and something should have been done about it long ago,' he said.

Jim did not answer.

The minister got up, slightly irritated, and called through the door to Dannie, who let him out.

Turning over on the bed Jim rubbed his forehead on the

pillow. The minister had said he would get life and he had
helped Corleys and bought coal for them last winter.
Everybody in town knew he had bought coal and food and
some men had said the Corley kid would be lucky if he
married her. Jim sat up, feeling uneasy. He had almost hit
upon an idea that would be a solution for everything.
Everybody knew it would be best for Ettie to marry him,
and Ettie wanted to, and he could go to work, but the
people who had arrested him couldn't understand it.
Fiercely indignant, he felt himself getting excited. If he
could get out he could explain his idea to everybody and get
people behind him. Jim walked over to the window, and
looked out over the yard to the tall brick building, the
waterworks.

A key turned in the door. 'How about the checkers now?'
Dannie Parker said.

'I got a headache, Dannie. Can't I go out in the yard a
while?'

'Wouldn't you like a little game first?'

'I feel kinda rotten, Dannie.'

'Did Sorrel bother you?'

'No, I just feel punk.'

'All right, just as you say.'

Dannie left him alone in the yard. It was about half past
seven Daylight Saving Time and the sun was striking the
tops of the trees. Jim walked the length of the yard without
looking at the walls. Walking back, his eye followed the top
line of the wall. He wasn't thinking of anything, just watching the wall. It was very old. He could remember when it
was built twenty-five years ago. Cracks and crevices were
spoiling it. One long crevice ran the full height of the wall.

Slyly he looked around at the jail, though he kept on
walking. Passing the crevice, he saw that there was room
for his boot three feet above the ground.

The second time he passed the crevice he turned quickly,
jammed in his boot, reached up, hoisting himself to the wall
top. He dropped over to the street. No one in sight. He
started to run. As he ran down the street he tried to concentrate on the idea of doing something definite that would

explain his feeling for Ettie, and appeal to the whole town. The idea had come to him back in the cell but it was necessary to get home first. He passed Hanson's grocery store, then the Catholic church, and the caretaker watering the lawn yelled at him.

He ran across the bridge and on to Corley's house. Mrs. Corley was sitting on the veranda. Seeing her, he stopped, shaking drops of sweat from his forehead and pulling his shirt open at the throat. 'Now you keep out of this, do you hear, you old bat,' he said. She stood up, remained motionless, then squealing, ran in the door, slamming it. 'Scared as a rabbit,' Jim said to himself. He laughed out loud. He walked around his own house and in the back way. The evening paper was on the porch.

No one was in the house. In the front room he sat down on the sofa, breathing deeply, fascinated by the heavy beating of his heart. He was ready to go on with the idea of getting people behind him but did not know how to go about it. He stood up angrily, rubbing his forehead. His own head was to blame. There was a way, only he couldn't see it and make use of it.

He stepped into the hall to the telephone and called up the sheriff, Ned Bickle. 'Is that you, Ned? This is Jim Cline. You'd better keep away from me. I'm out and I'm going to stay out.'

Jim didn't hear what the sheriff said. Walking away from the phone he felt much better. He went upstairs to get a Mauser revolver from the bureau drawer. He put it in his back pocket. No one would bother him, but it was better to have it. Downstairs he felt helpless, wondering how it was the idea seemed so simple back in the cell.

A car drew up on the road. Jim heard the car and turned to run out of the back door. He rubbed his chin, assuring himself he should go out of the front door. He opened the door and stood there on the veranda. Ned Bickle jumped out of the car, pointing a gun.

Jim half opened his mouth, getting ready to give an explanation, then looked stupidly at the barrel of the gun He couldn't think of anything to say. Hunching his shoulders, he

resentfully clenched his fists, leaning forward, his forehead
wrinkled. He half turned on one heel, his hand moving toward his hip.

'Stick 'em up, Jim.'

Jim straightened up and let his muscles relax. His mouth
closed abruptly; there was no way of getting people behind
him. Shaking his head he grinned sheepishly, holding out
his hands. Ned slipped on the cuffs.

It was getting dark and crickets were singing along the
road. Jim got in the back seat between two men. 'You ought
to be ashamed of yourself, Jim,' Ned said.

A Predicament

Father Francis, the youngest priest at the cathedral, was
hearing confessions on a Saturday afternoon. He stepped
out of the confessional to stretch his legs a moment and
walked up the left aisle toward the flickering red light of the
Precious Blood, mystical in the twilight of the cathedral.
Father Francis walked back to the confessional, because too
many women were waiting on the penitent bench. There
were not so many men.

Sitting again in the confessional, he said a short prayer to
the Virgin Mary to get in the mood for hearing confessions.
He wiped his lips with his handkerchief, cleared his throat,
and pushed back the panel, inclining his ear to hear a
woman's confession. The panel slid back with a sharp
grating noise. Father Francis whispered his ritual prayer
and made the sign of the cross. The woman hadn't been to
confession for three months and had missed mass twice for
no good reason. He questioned her determinedly, indignant
with this woman who had missed mass twice for no good
reason. In a steady whisper he told her the story of an old
woman who had crawled on the ice to get to mass. The

woman hesitated, then told about missing her morning prayers. . . . 'Yes, my child yes, my child . . . ' 'And about certain thoughts . . . ' 'Now, about these thoughts; let's look at it in this way . . . ' He gave the woman absolution and told her to say the beads once for her penance.

Closing the panel on the women's side he sat quietly for a moment in the darkness of the confessional. He was a young priest, very interested in confessions.

Father Francis turned to the other side of the confessional, pushing back the panel to hear some man's confession. Resting his chin on his hand after making the sign of the cross, he did not bother trying to discern the outline of the head and shoulders of the man kneeling in the corner.

The man said in a husky voice: 'I wanna get off at the corner of King and Yonge Street.'

Father Francis sat up straight, peering through the wire work. The man's head was moving. He could see his nose and his eyes. His heart began to beat unevenly. He sat back quietly.

'Cancha hear me, wasamatter, I wanna get off at King and Yonge,' the man said insistently, pushing his nose through the wire work.

On the man's breath there was a strong smell of whiskey. Father Francis nervously slid the panel back into position. As the panel slid into place he knew it sounded like the closing of doors on a bus. There he was hearing confessions, and a drunken man on the other side of the panel thought him a conductor on a bus. He would go into the vestry and tell Father Marlow.

Father Francis stepped out of the confessional to look around the cathedral. Men and women in the pews and on the penitents' benches wondered why he had come out of the confessional twice in the last few minutes when so many were waiting. Father Francis wasn't feeling well, that was the trouble. Walking up the aisle, he rubbed his smooth cheek with his hand, thinking hard. If he had the man thrown out he might be a tough customer and there would be a disturbance. There would be a disturbance in the cathedral. Such a disturbance would be sure to get in the papers. Everything got in the papers. There was no use telling it to anybody. Walking erectly he went back to the confessional. Father Francis was sweating.

Rubbing his shoulder-blades uneasily against the back of the confessional, he decided to hear a woman's confession. It was evading the issue – it was a compromise, but it didn't matter; he was going to hear a woman's confession first.

The woman, encouraged by many questions from Father Francis, made an extraordinarily good confession, though sometimes he did not seem to be listening very attentively. He thought he could hear the man moving. The man was drunk – drunkenness, the over-indulgence of an appetite, the drunken state. Scholastic psychology. Cardinal Mercier's book on psychology had got him through the exam at the seminary.

'When you feel you're going to tell a lie, say a short prayer to Mary the mother of God,' he said to the woman.

'Yes, father.'

'Some lies are more serious than others.'

'Yes, father.'

'But they are lies just the same.'

'I tell mostly white lies,' she said.

'They are lies, lies, lies, just the same. They may not endanger your soul, but they lead to something worse. Do you see?'

'Yes, father.'

'Will you promise to say a little prayer every time?'

Father Francis could not concentrate on what the woman was saying. But he wanted her to stay there for a long time. She was company. He would try and concentrate on her. He could not forget the drunken man for more than a few moments.

The woman finished her confession. Father Francis, breathing heavily, gave her absolution. Slowly he pushed back the panel – a street-car, a conductor swinging back the doors on a street-car. He turned deliberately to the other side of the confessional, but hesitated, eager to turn and hear another confession. It was no use – it couldn't go on in that way. Closing his eyes he said three 'Our Fathers' and three 'Hail, Marys', and felt much better. He was calm and the man might have gone.

He tried to push back the panel so it would not make much noise, but moving slowly, it grated loudly. He could see the man's head bobbing up, watching the panel sliding back.

'Yes, my son,' Father Francis said deliberately.

'I got to get off at King and Yonge,' the man said stubbornly.

'You better go, you've got no business here.'

'Say, there, did you hear me say King and Yonge?'

The man was getting ugly. The whiskey smelt bad in the confessional. Father Francis drew back quickly and half closed the panel. That same grating noise. It put an idea into his head. He said impatiently: 'Step lively there; this is King and Yonge. Do you want to go past your stop?'

'All right, brother,' the man said slowly, getting up clumsily.

'Move along now,' Father Francis said authoritatively.

'I'm movin'; don't get so huffy,' the man said, swinging aside the curtains of the confessional, stepping out to the aisle.

Father Francis leaned back in the confessional and nervously gripped the leather seat. He began to feel very happy. There were no thoughts at all in his head. Suddenly he got up and stepped out to the aisle. He stood watching a man going down the aisle swaying almost imperceptibly. The men and women in the pews watched Father Francis curiously, wondering if he was really unwell because he had come out of the confessional three times in a half-hour. Again he went into the confessional.

At first Father Francis was happy hearing the confessions, but he became restive. He should have used shrewd judgment. With that drunken man he had gone too far, forgotten himself in the confessional. He had descended to artifice in the confessional to save himself from embarrassment.

At the supper-table he did not talk much to the other priests. He had a feeling he would not sleep well that night. He would lie awake trying to straighten everything out. The thing would first have to be settled in his own conscience. Then perhaps he would tell the bishop.

Watching and Waiting

Whenever Thomas Hilliard, the lawyer, watched his young wife dancing with men of her own age, he was very sad, for she seemed to glow with a laughter and elation that didn't touch her life with him at all. He was jealous, he knew; but his jealousy at that time made him feel humble. It gave him the fumbling tenderness of a young boy. But as time passed and he saw that his humility only added to her feeling of security, he grew sullen and furtive and began to spy on her.

At times he realized that he was making her life wretched, and in his great shame he struggled hard against the distrust of her that was breaking the peace of his soul. In his longing to be alone with her, so that he would be free to offer her whatever goodness there was in him, he insisted that they move out to the country and renovate the old farmhouse on the lake where he had been born. There they lived like two scared prisoners in the house that was screened from the lane by three old oak trees. He went into the city only three days a week and his business was soon ruined by such neglect.

One evening Thomas Hilliard was putting his bag in the car, getting ready to return to the city. He was in a hurry, for the sky was darkening; the wind had broken the surface of the lake into choppy little waves with whitecaps, and soon it would rain. A gust of wind slammed an open window. Above the noise of the water on the beach, he heard his wife's voice calling, rising eagerly as it went farther away from the house.

She was calling, 'Just a minute, Joe,' and she was running down to the gate by the lane, with the wind blowing her short fair hair back from her head as she ran.

At the gate a young man was getting out of a car, waving his hand to her like an old friend, and calling: 'Did you want to speak to me, Mrs. Hilliard?'

'I wanted to ask you to do something for me,' she said.

The young man, laughing, lifted a large green bass from a pail in the back of his car, and he said: 'I caught it not more than half an hour ago. Will you take it, Mrs. Hilliard?'

'Isn't it a beauty!' she said holding it out at arm's length on the stick he had thrust through the jaws. 'You shouldn't be giving such a beauty away.' And she laughed, a free careless laugh that was carried up to the house on the wind.

For a while there was nothing Thomas Hilliard could hear but the murmur of his wife's voice mixed with the murmur of the young man's voice; but the way the laughter had poured out of her, and the look of pleasure on the young man's face, made him tense with resentment. He began to feel sure he had been actually thinking of that one man for months without ever naming him, that he had even been wondering about him while he was packing his bag and thinking of the drive into the city. Why was the young man so friendly that first time he had stopped them, on the main street of the town, when they were doing their week-end shopping, to explain that his name was Joe Whaley and he was their neighbour? That was something he had been wondering about for a long time. And every afternoon when Joe Whaley was off shore in his motorboat, he used to stand up and wave to them, the length of his lean young body outlined against the sky. It was as though all these things had been laid aside in Thomas Hilliard's head, to be given a sudden meaning now in the eager laughter of his wife, in her voice calling, and the pleasure on the young man's face.

He became so excited that he started to run down to the gate; and as he ran, his face was full of yearning and despair. They watched him coming, looking at each other doubtfully. When his wife saw how old and broken he looked, she suddenly dropped the fish in the dust of the road.

'Hey, there! Wait a minute,' he was calling to the young

man, who had turned away awkwardly.

'Did you want to speak to me, Mr. Hilliard?' Joe Whaley said.

'Is there something you want?' Hilliard asked.

'I just stopped a moment to give you people the fish.'

'I'd like to know, that's all,' Hilliard said, and he smiled foolishly.

The young man, who was astonished, mumbled some kind of an apology and got into his car. He drove up to the lane with the engine racing, and the strong wind from the lake whirling the dust in a cloud across the fields.

Speaking quietly, as if nothing had happened to surprise her, Mrs. Hilliard began, 'Did you think there was something the matter, Tom?' But then her voice broke, and she cried out: 'Why did you come running down here like that?'

'I heard the way you laughed,' he said.

'What was the matter with the way I laughed?'

'Don't you see how it would strike me? I haven't heard you laugh like that for such a long time.'

'I was only asking him if he'd be passing by the station tonight. I was going to ask him if he'd bring my mother here, if she was on the night train.'

'I don't believe that. You're making up a story,' he shouted.

It was the first time he had openly accused her of deceit; and when she tried to smile at him, her eyes were full of terror. It was as though she knew she was helpless at last, and she said slowly: 'I don't know why you keep staring at me. You're frightening me. I can't bear the way you watch me. It's been going on for such a long time. I've got to speak to someone – can't you see? It's dreadfully lonely here.'

She was staring out over the choppy wind-swept water: she turned and looked up with a child's wonder at the great oak trees that shut the house off from the road. 'I can't stand it any longer,' she said, her voice soft and broken. 'I've been a good wife. I had such an admiration for you when we started. There was nothing I wouldn't have trusted you with. And now – I don't know what's happened to us.' This was the first time she had ever tried to tell him of her hidden desolation; but all he could see was that her smile as she pleaded with him was pathetically false.

'You're lying. You're scared of what might happen,' he shouted.

'I've known how you've been watching me, and I've kept asking myself what the both of us have been waiting for,' she said. As the wind, driving through the leaves of the trees, rattled a window on the side of the house, and the last of the light faded from the lake, she cried out: 'What are we waiting for, day after day?'

'I'm not waiting any more,' he shouted. 'I'm going. You don't need to worry about me watching you any more. I'll not come back this time.' He felt crazy as he started to run over to the car.

Running after him, she cried out: 'I've kept hoping something would happen to make it different, something that would save us. I've prayed for it at night, just wanting you to be like you were three years ago.'

But he had started the car, and it came at her so suddenly that she had to jump out of the way. When the car lurched up the lane, he heard her cry out, but the words were blown away on the wind. He looked back, and saw her standing stiff by the gate, with both hands up to her head.

He drove up to the highway, swinging the car around so wildly at the turn by the grocery-store that the proprietor shouted at him. He began to like the way the car dipped at high speed down the deep valleys, and rose and fell with him always rigid and unthinking. When he reached the top of the highest hill in the country, the first of the rain whipped across his face, slashing and cutting at him in the way they slap the face of a fighter who has been beaten and is coming out of a stupor. His arms were trembling so he stopped the car; and there he sat for a long time, looking out over the hills in the night rain, at the low country whose roll and rise could be followed by the line of lights curving around the lake through the desolation of the wooded valleys and the rain-swept fields of this country of his boyhood, a gleaming line of light leading back to the farm and his wife.

There was a flash of lightning, and the fields and pasture-land gleamed for a moment in the dark. Then he seemed to hear her voice crying out above the wind: 'I've been waiting for so long!' And he muttered: 'How lost and frightened she'll be alone there on a night like this.' He knew then that he could go no farther. With his heart full of yearning for the tenderness he knew she had offered to him, he kept repeating: 'I can't leave her. I can't ever leave her. I'll go back and ask her to forgive me.'

So he sighed and was ashamed; and he drove back slowly along the way he had come, making up in his head fine little speeches that would make his wife laugh and forgive him.

But when he had turned off the highway and was going down the lane that led to the house, he suddenly thought it could do no harm if he stopped the car before it was heard, and went up to the house quietly to make sure no one else was there.

Such a notion made him feel terribly ashamed. As the car rocked in the ruts and puddles of the dirt road, and the headlights gleamed on the wet leaves from overhanging branches, he was filled with a profound sadness, as if he knew instinctively that no matter how he struggled, he would not be able to stop himself from sneaking up to the house like a spy. Stopping the car, he sat staring at the shuttered windows through which the light hardly filtered, mumbling: 'I've got a heart like a snake's nest. I've come back to ask her to forgive me.' Yet as he watched the strips of light on the shutters, he found himself thinking it could do no harm to make sure she was alone, that this would be the last time he would ever spy on her.

As he got out of the car, he stood a while in the road, getting soaking wet, assuring himself he had no will to be evil. And then as he started to drag his feet through the puddles, he knew he was helpless against his hunger to justify his lack of faith in her.

Swinging open the gate and crossing the grass underneath the oak tree, he stopped softly on the veranda and turned the door-knob slowly. When he found that the door was locked, his heart began to beat unevenly, and he went to pound the door with his fist. Then he grew very cunning. Jumping down to the grass, he went cautiously around to the side of the house, pressed his head against the shutters and listened. The rain streamed down his face and ran into his open mouth.

He heard the sound of his wife's voice, and though he could not make out the words, he knew she was talking earnestly to someone. Her voice seemed to be breaking; she seemed to be sobbing, pleading that she be comforted. His heart began to beat so loud he was sure they would be able to hear it. He grabbed at the shutter and tried to pry it open with his hand, but his fingers grew numb, and the back of his hand began to bleed. Stepping back from the house, he looked around wildly for some heavy stick or piece of iron. He remembered where there was an old horseshoe imbedded in the mud by the gate, and running there, he got down on his knees and scraped with his fingers, and he grinned in delight when he tugged the old horseshoe out of the mud.

But when he had inserted the iron prongs of the shoe between the shutters, and had started to use his weight, he realized that his wife was no longer talking. She was coming over to the window. He heard her gasp and utter a little cry. He heard her running from the room.

Full of despair, as though he were being cheated of the discovery he had been patiently seeking for years, he stepped back from the house, trembling with eagerness. The light in the room where he had loosened the shutter was suddenly turned out. He turned and ran back up the lane to the car, and got his flashlight.

This time he went round to the other side of the house, listening for the smallest sounds which might tell him where they were hiding, but it was hard to hear anything above the noise of the wind in the trees and the roll of the waves on the shore. At the kitchen window at the back of the house he pulled at the shutter. He heard them running out of the room.

The longing to look upon the face of the one who was with his wife became so great that he could hardly think of his wife at all. 'They probably went upstairs to the bedroom. That's were they'll be. I think I heard them going up the stairs.' He went over to the garage and brought out the ladder they had used to paint the house, and put it up against the bedroom window and started to climb on the slippery rungs with the flashlight clutched in his hand, eager for the joy that would be his if he could see without being seen.

The voices he heard as he lay against the ladder were broken with fright; he began to feel all the terror that grew in them as they ran from room to room and whispered and listened and hid in the darkness and longed to cry out.

But they must have heard some noise he made at the window, for before he was ready to use the flashlight, they ran from the room; they hurried downstairs in a way that showed they no longer cared what noise they made, they fled as though they intended to keep on going out of the front door and up the lane.

If he had taken the time to climb down the ladder, they might have succeeded; but instead of doing that, he wrapped his arms and legs around the wet rails and slid to the ground; he got over to the oak tree, and was hidden, his flashlight pointed at the door, before they came out.

As they came running from the house, he kept hidden and flashed the light on them, catching his wife in the strong beam of light, and making her stop dead and scream. She was carrying the rifle he used for hunting in the fall.

With a crazy joy he stepped out and swung the light on the other one; it was his wife's mother, stooped in horror. They were both held in the glare of the light, blinking and cringing in terror, while he tried to remember that the mother was to come to the house. And then his wife shrieked and pointed the gun into the darkness at the end of the beam of light, and fired: and he called out helplessly: 'Marion –'

But it was hurting him on his breast. The light dropped from his hand as he sank to the ground and began to cough.

Then his wife snatched up the light and let it shine on his face. 'Oh, Tom, Tom! Look what I've done,' she moaned.

The mother was still on her knees, stiff with fright.

His hand held against his breast was wet with warm blood; and as his head sank back on the grass he called out jerkily to the mother: 'Go on – hurry! Get someone – for Marion. I'm dying. I want to tell them how it happened.'

The mother, shrieking, hobbled over to the lane, and her cries for help were carried away on the wind.

With his weeping wife huddled over him, he lay dying in the rain. But when he groped with his hand and touched her head, his soul was suddenly overwhelmed by an agony of remorse for his lack of faith in her: in these few moments he longed to be able to show her all the comforting tenderness she had missed in the last three years. 'Forgive me,' he whispered. 'It was my fault – if only you could forgive me.' He wanted to soothe the fright out of her before the others came running up from the lane.

A Cap for Steve

Dave Diamond, a poor man, a carpenter's assistant, was a small, wiry, quick-tempered individual who had learned how to make every dollar count in his home. His wife, Anna, had been sick a lot, and his twelve-year-old son, Steve, had to be kept in school. Steve, a big-eyed, shy kid, ought to have known the value of money as well as Dave did. It had been ground into him.

But the boy was crazy about baseball, and after school, when he could have been working as a delivery boy or selling papers, he played ball with the kids. His failure to appreciate that the family needed a few extra dollars disgusted Dave. Around the house he wouldn't let Steve talk about baseball, and he scowled when he saw him hurrying off with his glove after dinner.

When the Phillies came to town to play an exhibition game with the home team and Steve pleaded to be taken to the ball park, Dave, of course, was outraged. Steve knew they couldn't afford it. But he had got his mother on his side. Finally Dave made a bargain with them. He said that if

Steve came home after school and worked hard helping to make some kitchen shelves he would take him that night to the ball park.

Steve worked hard, but Dave was still resentful. They had to coax him to put on his good suit. When they started out Steve held aloof, feeling guilty, and they walked down the street like strangers; then Dave glanced at Steve's face and, half-ashamed, took his arm more cheerfully.

As the game went on, Dave had to listen to Steve's recitation of the batting average of every Philly that stepped up to the plate; the time the boy must have wasted learning these averages began to appal him. He showed it so plainly that Steve felt guilty again and was silent.

After the game Dave let Steve drag him onto the field to keep him company while he tried to get some autographs from the Philly players, who were being hemmed in by gangs of kids blocking the way to the club-house. But Steve, who was shy, let the other kids block him off from the players. Steve would push his way in, get blocked out, and come back to stand mournfully beside Dave. And Dave grew impatient. He was wasting valuable time. He wanted to get home; Steve knew it and was worried.

Then the big, blond Philly outfielder, Eddie Condon, who had been held up by a gang of kids tugging at his arm and thrusting their score cards at him, broke loose and made a run for the club-house. He was jostled, and his blue cap with the red peak, tilted far back on his head, fell off. It fell at Steve's feet, and Steve stooped quickly and grabbed it. 'Okay, son,' the outfielder called, turning back. But Steve, holding the hat in both hands, only stared at him.

'Give him his cap, Steve,' Dave said, smiling apologetically at the big outfielder who towered over them. But Steve drew the hat closer to his chest. In an awed trance he looked up at big Eddie Condon. It was an embarrassing moment. All the other kids were watching. Some shouted. 'Give him his cap.'

'My cap, son,' Eddie Condon said, his hand out.

'Hey, Steve,' Dave said, and he gave him a shake. But he had to jerk the cap out of Steve's hands.

'Here you are,' he said.

The outfielder, noticing Steve's white, worshipping face and pleading eyes, grinned and then shrugged. 'Aw, let him keep it,' he said.

'No, Mister Condon, you don't need to do that,' Steve protested.

'It's happened before. Forget it,' Eddie Condon said, and he trotted away to the club-house.

Dave handed the cap to Steve; envious kids circled around them and Steve said, 'He said I could keep it, Dad. You heard him, didn't you?'

'Yeah, I heard him,' Dave admitted. The wonder in Steve's face made him smile. He took the boy by the arm and they hurried off the field.

On the way home Dave couldn't get him to talk about the game; he couldn't get him to take his eyes off the cap. Steve could hardly believe in his own happiness. 'See,' he said suddenly, and he showed Dave that Eddie Condon's name was printed on the sweatband. Then he went on dreaming. Finally he put the cap on his head and turned to Dave with a slow, proud smile. The cap was away too big for him; it fell down over his ears. 'Never mind,' Dave said. 'You can get your mother to take a tuck in the back.'

When they got home Dave was tired and his wife didn't understand the cap's importance, and they couldn't get Steve to go to bed. He swaggered around wearing the cap and looking in the mirror every ten minutes. He took the cap to bed with him.

Dave and his wife had a cup of coffee in the kitchen, and Dave told her again how they had got the cap. They agreed that their boy must have an attractive quality that showed in his face, and that Eddie Condon must have been drawn to him – why else would he have singled Steve out from all the kids?

But Dave got tired of the fuss Steve made over that cap and of the way he wore it from the time he got up in the morning until the time he went to bed. Some kid was always coming in, wanting to try on the cap. It was childish, Dave said, for Steve to go around assuming that the cap made him important in the neighbourhood, and to keep telling them how he had become a leader in the park a few blocks away where he played ball in the evenings. And Dave wouldn't stand for Steve's keeping the cap on while he was eating. He was always scolding his wife for accepting Steve's explanation that he'd forgotten he had it on. Just the same, it was remarkable what a little thing like a ball cap could do for a kid, Dave admitted to his wife as he smiled to himself.

One night Steve was late coming home from the park. Dave didn't realize how late it was until he put down his newspaper and watched his wife at the window. Her restlessness got on his nerves. 'See what comes from encouraging the boy to hang around with those park loafers,' he said. 'I don't encourage him,' she protested. 'You do,' he insisted irritably, for he was really worried now. A gang hung around the park until midnight. It was a bad park. It was true that on one side there was a good district with fine, expensive apartment houses, but the kids from that neighbourhood left the park to the kids from the poorer homes. When his wife went out and walked down to the corner it was his turn to wait and worry and watch at the open window. Each waiting moment tortured him. At last he heard his wife's voice and Steve's voice, and he relaxed and sighed; then he remembered his duty and rushed angrily to meet them.

'I'll fix you, Steve, once and for all,' he said. 'I'll show you you can't start coming into the house at midnight.'

'Hold your horses, Dave,' his wife said. 'Can't you see the state he's in?' Steve looked utterly exhausted and beaten.

'What's the matter?' Dave asked quickly.

'I lost my cap,' Steve whispered; he walked past his father and threw himself on the couch in the living-room and lay with his face hidden.

'Now, don't scold him, Dave,' his wife said.

'Scold him. Who's scolding him?' Dave asked, indignantly. 'It's his cap, not mine. If it's not worth his while to hang on to it, why should I scold him?' But he was implying resentfully that he alone recognized the cap's value.

'So you are scolding him,' his wife said. 'It's his cap. Not yours. What happened, Steve?'

Steve told them he had been playing ball and he found

that when he ran the bases the cap fell off; it was still too big despite the tuck his mother had taken in the band. So the next time he came to bat he tucked the cap in his hip pocket. Someone had lifted it, he was sure.

'And he didn't even know whether it was still in his pocket,' Dave said sarcastically.

'I wasn't careless, Dad,' Steve said. For the last three hours he had been wandering around to the homes of the kids who had been in the park at the time; he wanted to go on, but he was too tired. Dave knew the boy was apologizing to him, but he didn't know why it made him angry.

'If he didn't hang on to it, it's not worth worrying about now,' he said, and he sounded offended.

After that night they knew that Steve didn't go to the park to play ball; he went to look for the cap. It irritated Dave to see him sit around listlessly, or walk in circles, trying to force his memory to find a particular incident which would suddenly recall to him the moment when the cap had been taken. It was no attitude for a growing, healthy boy to take, Dave complained. He told Steve firmly once and for all he didn't want to hear any more about the cap.

One night, two weeks later, Dave was walking home with Steve from the shoemaker's. It was a hot night. When they passed an ice-cream parlour Steve slowed down. 'I guess I couldn't have a soda, could I?' Steve said. 'Nothing doing,' Dave said firmly. 'Come on now,' he added as Steve hung back, looking in the window.

'Dad, look!' Steve cried suddenly, pointing at the window. 'My cap! There's my cap! He's coming out!'

A well-dressed boy was leaving the ice-cream parlour; he had on a blue ball cap with a red peak, just like Steve's cap. 'Hey, you!' Steve cried, and he rushed at the boy, his small face fierce and his eyes wild. Before the boy could back away Steve had snatched the cap from his head. 'That's my cap!' he shouted.

'What's this?' the bigger boy said. 'Hey, give me my cap or I'll give you a poke on the nose.'

Dave was surprised that his own shy boy did not back away. He watched him clutch the cap in his left hand, half crying with excitement as he put his head down and drew back his right fist: he was willing to fight. And Dave was proud of him.

'Wait, now,' Dave said. 'Take it easy, son,' he said to the other boy, who refused to back away.

'My boy says it's his cap,' Dave said.

'Well, he's crazy. It's my cap.'

'I was with him when he got this cap. When the Phillies played here. It's a Philly cap.'

'Eddie Condon gave it to me,' Steve said. 'And you stole it from me, you jerk.'

'Don't call me a jerk, you little squirt. I never saw you before in my life.'

'Look,' Steve said, pointing to the printing on the cap's sweatband. 'It's Eddie Condon's cap. See? See, Dad?'

'Yeah. You're right, Son. Ever see this boy before, Steve?'

'No,' Steve said reluctantly.

The other boy realized he might lose the cap. 'I bought it from a guy,' he said. 'I paid him. My father knows I paid him.' He said he got the cap at the ball park. He groped for some magically impressive words and suddenly found them. 'You'll have to speak to my father,' he said.

'Sure, I'll speak to your father,' Dave said. 'What's your name? Where do you live?'

'My name's Hudson. I live about ten minutes away on the other side of the park.' The boy appraised Dave, who wasn't any bigger than he was and who wore a faded blue windbreaker and no tie. 'My father is a lawyer,' he said boldly. 'He wouldn't let me keep the cap if he didn't think I should.'

'Is that a fact?' Dave asked belligerently. 'Well, we'll see. Come on. Let's go.' And he got between the two boys and they walked along the street. They didn't talk to each other. Dave knew the Hudson boy was waiting to get to the protection of his home, and Steve knew it, too, and he looked up apprehensively at Dave. And Dave, reaching for his hand, squeezed it encouragingly and strode along, cocky and belligerent, knowing that Steve relied on him.

The Hudson boy lived in that row of fine apartment houses on the other side of the park. At the entrance to one of these houses Dave tried not to hang back and show he was impressed, because he could feel Steve hanging back. When they got into the small elevator Dave didn't know why he took off his hat. In the carpeted hall on the fourth floor the Hudson boy said, 'Just a minute,' and entered his own apartment. Dave and Steve were left alone in the corridor, knowing that the other boy was preparing his father for the encounter. Steve looked anxiously at his father, and Dave said, 'Don't worry, Son,' and he added resolutely, 'No one's putting anything over on us.'

A tall, balding man in a brown velvet smoking-jacket suddenly opened the door. Dave had never seen a man wearing one of these jackets, although he had seen them in department-store windows. 'Good evening,' he said, making a deprecatory gesture at the cap Steve still clutched tightly in his left hand. 'My boy didn't get your name. My name is Hudson.'

'Mine's Diamond.'

'Come on in,' Mr. Hudson said, putting out his hand and laughing good-naturedly. He led Dave and Steve into his living-room. 'What's this about that cap?' he asked. 'The way kids can get excited about a cap. Well, it's understandable, isn't it?'

'So it is,' Dave said, moving closer to Steve, who was awed by the broadloom rug and the fine furniture. He wanted to show Steve he was at ease himself, and he wished Mr. Hudson wouldn't be so polite. That meant Dave had to be polite and affable, too, and it was hard to manage when he was standing in the middle of the floor in his old windbreaker.

'Sit down, Mr. Diamond,' Mr. Hudson said. Dave took Steve's arm and sat him down beside him on the chesterfield. The Hudson boy watched his father. And Dave looked at Steve and saw that he wouldn't face Mr. Hudson or the other boy; he kept looking up at Dave, putting all his faith in him.

'Well, Mr. Diamond, from what I gathered from my boy, you're able to prove this cap belonged to your boy.'

'That's a fact,' Dave said.

'Mr. Diamond, you'll have to believe my boy bought that cap from some kid in good faith.'

'I don't doubt it,' Dave said. 'But no kid can sell something that doesn't belong to him. You know that's a fact, Mr. Hudson.'

'Yes, that's a fact,' Mr. Hudson agreed. 'But that cap means a lot to my boy, Mr. Diamond.'

'It means a lot to my boy, too, Mr. Hudson.'

'Sure it does. But supposing we called in a policeman. You know what he'd say? He'd ask you if you were willing to pay my boy what he paid for the cap. That's usually the way it works out,' Mr. Hudson said, friendly and smiling, as he eyed Dave shrewdly.

'But that's not right. It's not justice,' Dave protested. 'Not when it's my boy's cap.'

'I know it isn't right. But that's what they do.'

'All right. What did you say your boy paid for the cap?' Dave said reluctantly.

'Two dollars.'

'Two dollars!' Dave repeated. Mr. Hudson's smile was still kindly, but his eyes were shrewd, and Dave knew the the lawyer was counting on his not having the two dollars; Mr. Hudson thought he had Dave sized up; he had looked at him and decided he was broke. Dave's pride was hurt, and he turned to Steve. What he saw in Steve's face was more powerful than the hurt to his pride; it was the memory of how difficult it had been to get an extra nickel, the talk he heard about the cost of food, the worry in his mother's face as she tried to make ends meet, and the bewildered embarrassment that he was here in a rich man's home, forcing his father to confess that he couldn't afford to spend two dollars. Then Dave grew angry and reckless. 'I'll give you the two dollars,' he said.

Steve looked at the Hudson boy and grinned brightly. The Hudson boy watched his father.

'I suppose that's fair enough,' Mr. Hudson said. 'A cap like this can be worth a lot to a kid. You know how it is. Your boy might want to sell – I mean be satisfied. Would he take five dollars for it?'

'Five dollars?' Dave repeated, 'Is it worth five dollars, Steve?' he asked uncertainly.

Steve shook his head and looked frightened.

'No, thanks, Mr. Hudson,' Dave said firmly.

'I'll tell you what I'll do,' Mr. Hudson said. 'I'll give you ten dollars. The cap has a sentimental value for my boy, a Philly cap, a big-leaguer's cap. It's only worth about a buck and a half really,' he added. But Dave shook his head again. Mr. Hudson frowned. He looked at his own boy with indulgent concern, but now he was embarrassed. 'I'll tell you what I'll do,' he said. 'This cap – well, it's worth as much as a day at the circus to my boy. Your boy should be recompensed. I want to be fair. Here's twenty dollars,' and he held out two ten-dollar bills to Dave.

That much money for a cap, Dave thought, and his eyes brightened. But he knew what the cap had meant to Steve; to deprive him of it now that it was within his reach would be unbearable. All the things he needed in his life gathered around him; his wife was there, saying he couldn't afford to reject the offer, he had no right to do it; and he turned to Steve to see if Steve thought it wonderful that the cap could bring them twenty dollars.

'What do you say, Steve?' he asked uneasily.

'I don't know,' Steve said. He was in a trance. When Dave smiled, Steve smiled too, and Dave believed that Steve was as impressed as he was, only more bewildered, and maybe even more aware that they could not possibly turn away that much money for a ball cap.

'Well, here you are,' Mr. Hudson said, and he put the two bills in Steve's hand. 'It's a lot of money. But I guess you had a right to expect as much.'

With a dazed, fixed smile Steve handed the money slowly to his father, and his face was white.

Laughing jovially, Mr. Hudson led them to the door. His own boy followed a few paces behind.

In the elevator Dave took the bills out of his pocket. 'See, Stevie,' he whispered eagerly. 'That windbreaker you wanted! And ten dollars for your bank! Won't Mother be surprised?'

'Yeah,' Steve whispered, the little smile still on his face. But Dave had to turn away quickly so their eyes wouldn't meet, for he saw that it was a scared smile.

Outside, Dave said, 'Here, you carry the money home, Steve. You show it to your mother.'

'No, you keep it,' Steve said, and then there was nothing to say. They walked in silence.

'It's a lot of money,' Dave said finally. When Steve didn't answer him, he added angrily, 'I turned to you, Steve. I asked you, didn't I?'

'That man knew how much his boy wanted that cap,' Steve said.

'Sure. But he recognized how much it was worth to us.'

'No, you let him take it away from us,' Steve blurted.

'That's unfair,' Dave said. 'Don't dare say that to me.'

'I don't want to be like you,' Steve muttered, and he darted across the road and walked along on the other side of the street.

'It's unfair,' Dave said angrily, only now he didn't mean that Steve was unfair, he meant that what had happened in the prosperous Hudson home was unfair, and he didn't know quite why. He had been trapped, not just by Mr. Hudson, but by his own life. Across the road Steve was hurrying along with his head down, wanting to be alone. They walked most of the way home on opposite sides of the street, until Dave could stand it no longer. 'Steve,' he called, crossing the street. 'It was very unfair. I mean, for you to say . . . ' but Steve started to run. Dave walked as fast as he could and Steve was getting beyond him, and he felt enraged and suddenly he yelled, 'Steve!' and he started to chase his son. He wanted to get hold of Steve and pound him, and he didn't know why. He gained on him, he gasped for breath and he almost got him by the shoulder. Turning, Steve saw his father's face in the street light and was terrified; he circled away, got to the house, and rushed in, yelling, 'Mother!'

'Son, Son!' she cried, rushing from the kitchen. As soon as she threw her arms around Steve, shielding him, Dave's anger left him and he felt stupid. He walked past them into the kitchen.

'What happened?' she asked anxiously. 'Have you both

gone crazy? What did you do, Steve?'

'Nothing,' he said sullenly.

'What did your father do?'

'We found the boy with my ball cap, and he let the boy's father take it from us.'

'No, no,' Dave protested. 'Nobody pushed us around. The man didn't put anything over us.' He felt tired and his face was burning. He told what had happened; then he slowly took the two ten-dollar bills out of his wallet and tossed them on the table and looked up guiltily at his wife.

It hurt him that she didn't pick up the money, and that she didn't rebuke him. 'It is a lot of money, Son,' she said slowly. 'Your father was only trying to do what he knew was right, and it'll work out, and you'll understand.' She was soothing Steve, but Dave knew she felt that she needed to be gentle with him, too, and he was ashamed.

When she went with Steve to his bedroom, Dave sat by himself. His son had contempt for him, he thought. His son, for the first time, had seen how easy it was for another man to handle him, and he had judged him and had wanted to walk alone on the other side of the street. He looked at the money and he hated the sight of it.

His wife returned to the kitchen, made a cup of tea, talked soothingly, and said it was incredible that he had forced the Hudson man to pay him twenty dollars for the cap, but all Dave could think of was Steve was scared of me.

Finally, he got up and went into Steve's room. The room was in darkness, but he could see the outline of Steve's body on the bed, and he sat down beside him and whispered, 'Look, Son, it was a mistake. I know why. People like us – in circumstances where money can scare us. No, no,' he said, feeling ashamed and shaking his head apologetically; he was taking the wrong way of showing the boy they were together; he was covering up his own failure. For the failure had been his, and it had come out of being so separated from his son that he had been blind to what was beyond the price in a boy's life. He longed now to show Steve he could be with him from day to day. His hand went out hesitantly to Steve's shoulder. 'Steve, look,' he said eagerly. 'The trouble was

I didn't realize how much I enjoyed it that night at the ball park. If I had watched you playing for your own team – the kids around here say you could be a great pitcher. We could take that money and buy a new pitcher's glove for you, and a catcher's mitt. Steve, Steve, are you listening? I could catch you, work with you in the lane. Maybe I could be your coach ... watch you become a great pitcher.' In the half-darkness he could see the boy's pale face turn to him.

Steve, who had never heard his father talk like this, was shy and wondering. All he knew was that his father, for the first time, wanted to be with him in his hopes and adventures. He said, 'I guess you do know how important that cap was.' His hand went out to his father's arm. 'With that man the cap was – well it was just something he could buy, eh Dad?' Dave gripped his son's hand hard. The wonderful generosity of childhood – the price a boy was willing to pay to be able to count on his father's admiration and approval – made him feel humble, then strangely exalted.

Last Spring They Came Over

Alfred Bowles came to Canada from England and got a job on a Toronto paper. He was a young fellow with clear, blue eyes and heavy pimples on the lower part of his face, the son of a Baptist minister whose family was too large for his salary. He got thirty dollars a week on the paper and said it was surprisingly good screw to start. For five a week he got an attic room in a brick house painted brown on Mutual Street. He ate his meals in a quick-lunch near the office. He bought a cane and a light-gray fedora.

He wasn't a good reporter but was inoffensive and obliging. After he had been working two weeks the fellows took it for granted he would be fired in a little while and were nice to him, liking the way the most trifling occurrences surprised him. He was happy to carry his cane on his arm and wear the fedora at a jaunty angle, quite the reporter. He liked to explain that he was doing well. He wrote home about it.

When they put him doing night police he felt important, phoning the fire department, hospitals, and police stations, trying to be efficient. He was getting along all right. It was disappointing when after a week the assistant city editor, Mr. H. J. Brownson, warned him to phone his home if anything important happened, and he would have another man cover it. But Bowles got to like hearing the weary, irritable voice of the assistant city editor called from his bed at three o'clock in the morning. He liked to politely call Mr. Brownson as often and as late as possible, thinking it a bit of good fun.

Alfred wrote long letters to his brother and to his father, the Baptist minister, using a typewriter, carefully tapping the keys, occasionally laughing to himself. In a month's time he had written six letters describing the long city room, the fat belly of the city editor, and the bad words the night editor used when speaking of the Orangemen.

The night editor took a fancy to him because of the astounding puerility of his political opinions. Alfred was always willing to talk pompously of the British Empire policing the world and about all Catholics being aliens, and the future of Ireland and Canada resting with the Orangemen. He flung his arms wide and talked in the hoarse voice of a bad actor, but no one would have thought of taking him seriously. He was merely having a dandy time. The night editor liked him because he was such a nice boy.

Then Alfred's brother came out from the Old Country, and got a job on the same paper. Some of the men started talking about cheap cockney labourers crowding the good guys out of the jobs, but Harry Bowles was frankly glad to get the thirty a week. It never occurred to him that he had a funny idea of money. With his first pay he bought a derby hat, a pair of spats, and a cane, but even though his face was clear and had a good colour he never looked as nice as his younger brother because his heavy nose curved up at the end. The landlady on Mutual Street moved a double bed into Alfred's room and Harry slept with his brother.

The days passed with many good times together. At first it was awkward that Alfred should be working at night and his brother in the day-time, but Harry was pleased to come down to the office every night at eleven and they went down the street to the hotel that didn't bother about Prohibition. They drank a few glasses of good beer. It became a kind of rite that had to be performed carefully. Harry would put his left foot and Alfred his right foot on the rail and leaning an elbow on the bar they would slowly survey the zigzag line of frothing glasses the length of the long bar. Men jostled them for a place at the foot-rail.

And Alfred said: 'Well, a bit of luck.'

Harry grinning and raising his glass said: 'Righto.'

'It's the stuff that heals.'

'Down she goes.'

'It helps the night along.'

'Fill them up again.'

'Toodleoo.'

Then they would walk out of the crowded bar-room, vaguely pleased with themselves. Walking slowly and erectly along the street they talked with assurance, a mutual respect for each other's opinion making it merely an exchange of information. They talked of the Englishman in Canada, comparing his lot with that of the Englishman in South Africa and India. They had never travelled but to ask what they knew of strange lands would have made one feel uncomfortable; it was better to take it for granted that the Bowles boys knew all about the ends of the earth and had judged them carefully, for in their eyes was the light of far-away places. Once in a while, after walking a block or two, one of the brothers would say he would damn well like to see India and the other would say it would be simply topping.

After work and on Sundays they took a look at the places they had heard about in the city. One Sunday they got up in good time and took the boat to Niagara. Their father had written asking if they had seen the Falls and would they send some souvenirs. That day they had as nice a time as a man would want to have. Standing near the pipe-rail a little way from the hotel that overlooks the Falls they watched the water-line just before the drop, smooth as a long strip of bevelled glass, and Harry compared it favourably with a cataract in the Himalayas and a giant waterfall in Africa, just above the Congo. They took a car along the gorge and getting off near the whirlpool, picked out a little hollow near a big rock at the top of the embankment where the grass was lush and green. They stretched themselves out with hats tilted over their eyes for sunshades. The river whirled below. They talked about the funny ways of Mr. Brownson and his short fat legs and about the crazy women who fainted at the lifted hand of the faith healer who was in the city for the week. They liked the distant rumble of the Falls. They agreed to try and save a lot of money and go west to the Pacific in a year's time. They never mentioned trying to get a raise in pay.

Afterwards they each wrote home about the trip, sending the souvenirs.

Neither one was doing well on the paper. Harry wasn't much good because he hated writing the plain copy and it was hard for him to be strictly accurate. He liked telling a good tale but it never occurred to him that he was deliberately lying. He imagined a thing and straightway felt it to be true. But it never occurred to Alfred to depart from the truth. He was accurate but lazy, never knowing when he was really working. He was taken off night police and for two weeks helped a man do courts at the City Hall. He got to know the boys at the press gallery, who smiled at his naïve sincerity and thought him a decent chap, without making up their minds about him. Every noon-hour Harry came to the press gallery and the brothers, sitting at typewriters, wrote long letters all about the country and the people, anything interesting, and after exchanging letters, tilted back in their swivel chairs, laughing out loud. Heaven only knows who got the letters in the long run. Neither one when in the press gallery seemed to write anything for the paper.

Some of the men tried kidding Alfred, teasing him about women, asking if he found the girls in this country to his liking; but he seemed to enjoy it more than they did. Seriously he explained that he had never met a girl in this country, but they looked very nice. Once Alfred and

Bun Brophy, a red-headed fellow with a sharp tongue who did City Hall for the paper, were alone in the gallery. Brophy had in his hand a big picture of five girls in masquerade costumes. Without explaining that he loved one of the girls Brophy asked Bowles which of the lot was the prettiest.

'You want me to settle that,' said Alfred, grinning and waving his pipe. He very deliberately selected a demure little girl with a shy smile.

Brophy was disappointed. 'Don't you think this one is pretty?' – a colourful, bold-looking girl.

'Well, she's all right in her way, but she's too vivacious. I'll take this one. I like them kittenish,' Alfred said.

Brophy wanted to start an argument but Alfred said it was neither here nor there. He really didn't like women.

'You mean to say you never step out?' Brophy said.

'I've never seemed to mix with them,' he said, adding that the whole business didn't matter because he liked boys much better.

The men in the press room heard about it and some suggested nasty things to Alfred. It was hard to tease him when he wouldn't be serious. Sometimes they asked if he took Harry out walking in the evenings. Brophy called them the heavy lovers. The brothers didn't mind because they thought the fellows were having a little fun.

In the fall Harry was fired. The editor in a nice note said that he was satisfied Mr. H. W. Bowles could not adapt himself to their methods. But everybody wondered why he hadn't been fired sooner. He was no good on the paper.

The brothers smiled, shrugged their shoulders and went on living together. Alfred still had his job. Every noon-hour in the City Hall press room they were together, writing letters.

Time passed and the weather got cold. Alfred's heavy coat came from the Old Country and he gave his vest and a thin sweater to Harry, who had only a light spring coat. As the weather got colder Harry buttoned his coat higher up on his throat and even though he looked cold he was neat as a pin with his derby and cane.

Then Alfred lost his job. The editor, disgusted, called

him a fool. For the first time since coming over last spring
he felt hurt, something inside him was hurt and he told his
brother about it, wanting to know why people acted in such
a way. He said he had been doing night police. On the way
over to No. 1 station very late Thursday night he had met
two men from other papers. They told him about a big fire
earlier in the evening just about the time when Alfred was
accustomed to going to the hotel to have a drink with his
brother. They were willing to give all the details and Alfred
thankfully shook hands with them and hurried back to the
office to write the story. Next morning the assistant city
editor phoned Alfred and asked how it was the morning
papers missed the story. Alfred tried to explain but Mr.
Brownson said he was a damn fool for not phoning the
police and making sure instead of trying to make the paper
look like a pack of fools printing a fake story. The fellows
who had kidded him said that too. Alfred kept asking his
brother why the fellows had to do it. He seemed to be losing
a good feeling for people.

Still the brothers appeared at noontime in the press room.
They didn't write so many letters. They were agreeable,
cheerful, on good terms with everybody. Bun Brophy every
day asked how they were doing and they felt at home there.
Harry would stand for a while watching the checker game
always in progress, knowing that if he stood staring intently
at the black and red squares, watching every deliberate
move, he would be asked to sit in when it was necessary
that one of the players make the rounds in the hall. Once
Brophy gave Harry his place and walked over to the window
where Alfred stood watching the fleet of automobiles
arranged in a square in the courtyard. The police wagon
with a load of drunks was backing toward the cells.

'Say, Alfie, I often wonder how you guys manage,' he
said.

'Oh, first rate.'

'Well, you ought to be in a bad way by now.'

'Oh no, we have solved the problem,' said Alfred in a
grand way, grinning, as if talking about the British Empire.

He was eager to tell how they did it. There was a store in
their block where a package of tobacco could be got for five

cents; they did their own cooking and were able to live on five dollars a week.

'What about coming over and having tea with us some-times?' Alfred said. He was decidedly on his uppers but he asked Brophy to visit them and have tea.

Brophy, abashed, suggested the three of them go over to the café and have a little toast. Harry talked volubly on the way over and while having a coffee. He was really a better talker than his brother. They sat in an arm-chair lunch, gripped the handles of their thick mugs, and talked about religion. The brothers were sons of a Baptist minister but never thought of going to church. It seemed that Brophy had travelled a lot during war-time and afterward in Asia Minor and India. He was telling about a great golden temple of the Sikhs at Amritsar and Harry listened carefully, asking many questions. Then they talked about newspapers until Harry started talking about the East, slowly feeling his way. All of a sudden he told about standing on a height of land near Amritsar, looking down at a temple. It couldn't have been so but he would have it that Brophy and he had seen the same temple and he described the country in the words Brophy had used. When he talked that way you actually believed that he had seen the temple.

Alfred liked listening to his brother but he said finally: 'Religion is a funny business. I tell you it's a funny busi-ness.' And for the time being no one would have thought of talking seriously about religion. Alfred had a casual way of making a cherished belief or opinion seem unimportant, a way of dismissing even the bright yarns of his brother.

After that afternoon in the café Brophy never saw Harry. Alfred came often to the City Hall but never mentioned his brother. Someone said maybe Harry had a job but Alfred laughed and said no such luck in this country, explaining casually that Harry had a bit of a cold and was resting up. In the passing days Alfred came only once in a while to the City Hall, writing his letter without enthusiasm.

The press men would have tried to help the brothers if they had heard Harry was sick. They were entirely ignorant of the matter. On a Friday afternoon at three-thirty Alfred came into the gallery and, smiling apologetically, told

Brophy that his brother was dead; the funeral was to be in three-quarters of an hour; would he mind coming? It was pneumonia, he added. Brophy, looking hard at Alfred, put on his hat and coat and they went out.

It was a poor funeral. The hearse went on before along the way to the Anglican cemetery that overlooks the ravine. One old cab followed behind. There had been a heavy fall of snow in the morning, and the slush on the pavement was thick. Alfred and Brophy sat in the old cab, silent. Alfred was leaning forward, his chin resting on his hands, the cane acting as a support, and the heavy pimples stood out on the lower part of his white face. Brophy was uncomfortable and chilly but he mopped his shining forehead with a big handkerchief. The window was open and the air was cold and damp.

Alfred politely asked how Mrs. Brophy was doing. Then he asked about Mr. Brownson.

'Oh, he's fine,' Brophy said. He wanted to close the window but it would have been necessary to move Alfred so he sat huddled in the corner, shivering.

Alfred asked suddenly if funerals didn't leave a bad taste in the mouth and Brophy, surprised, started talking absently about that golden temple of the Sikhs in India. Alfred appeared interested until they got to the cemetery. He said suddenly he would have to take a look at the temple one fine day.

They buried Harry Bowles in a grave in the paupers' section on a slippery slope of the hill. The earth was hard and chunky and it thumped down on the coffin case. It snowed a little near the end.

On the way along the narrow, slippery foot-path up the hill Alfred thanked Brophy for being thoughtful enough to come to the funeral. There was little to say. They shook hands and went different ways.

After a day or two Alfred again appeared in the press room. He watched the checker game, congratulated the winner and then wrote home. The men were sympathetic and said it was too bad about his brother. And he smiled cheerfully and said they were good fellows. In a little while he seemed to have convinced them that nothing important had really happened.

His last cent must have gone to the undertaker, for he was particular about paying bills, but he seemed to get along all right. Occasionally he did a little work for the paper, a story from a night assignment when the editor thought the staff was being overworked.

One afternoon at two-thirty in the press gallery Brophy saw the last of Alfred, who was sucking his pipe, his feet up on a desk, wanting to be amused. Brophy asked if anything had turned up. In a playful, resigned tone, his eye on the big clock, Alfred said he had until three to join the Air Force. They wouldn't take him, he said, unless he let them know by three.

Brophy said, 'How will you like that?'

'I don't fancy it.'

'But you're going through.'

'Well, I'm not sure. Something else may come along.' It was a quarter to three and he was sitting there waiting for a job to turn up before three.

No one saw him after that, but he didn't join the Air Force. Someone in the gallery said that wherever he went he probably wrote home as soon as he got there.

The Voyage Out

Jeff found himself sitting next to her one night in a movie, and when he discovered that she was neat and pretty, he began to watch her furtively. Though she didn't even turn her head, he felt sure she was aware of him beside her. When she got up to go, he followed her out, and as she hesitated at the theatre entrance, drawing on her gloves, he began a polite, timid conversation. Then they walked along the street together.

He soon found out that her name was Jessie, and that she

worked in a millinery store and lived with her father and mother. Until that night a month later when they were standing in the hall of her apartment house, saying good night in the way they had so often done in the last weeks, he hadn't thought he had much chance of making love to her. They were standing close together, laughing and whispering. Then she stopped laughing and was quiet, as though the shyness which was hidden underneath her warm, affectionate ways was troubling her. She suddenly put her arms tight around him, lifted up her face, held him as if she would never let him go, and let him know she was offering all her love.

'I don't want to go home. Let me go in with you and stay a while,' he pleaded.

'All right – if they're asleep,' she whispered.

As they opened the door and tiptoed into her place, the boldness he felt in her made his heart beat loud. Then they heard her father cough. They stood still, frightened, her hand tightening on his arm.

'We'd better not tonight,' she whispered. 'They're awake. You'd better go quick.'

'Tomorrow night then?'

'Maybe – we'll see,' she said.

Brushing her face nervously against his, she almost shoved him out into the street.

As he loafed over to Eighth Avenue, his nervousness left him. He was full of elation, and he thought, 'Gee whizz, she'll do anything I want now. It came so easy, just like I wanted it to,' and a longing for her began to grow in him. He still could feel her warmth and hear her urgent whispering. He grinned as he loafed along, for he had thought it would take a long time and he'd have to go slow and easy. Lights in the stores, the underground rumble, and the noise of the cross-town buses on Twenty-Third Street seemed to be touched and made important by the marvellous tenderness within him. He wanted suddenly to lean against a bar or sit at a counter, hear men's laughter, and feel his own triumphant importance among them, and he hurried into the restaurant where he had a cup of coffee every night after leaving her.

At this time men from a bakery in the block came in for a lunch, and a smoke, and Jeff, who had got to know some of them, sat at the counter and ordered a cup of coffee and looked around to see who else was in the restaurant. There were two decently dressed girls, sitting at a table talking quietly. When Jeff smiled at the girls without any shyness, because a warm feeling for everyone and everything was in him, they shrugged their shoulders in surprise and laughed at each other.

Then the men from the bakery, with the strong, sweet smell of freshly baked bread on them, and their pants white with flour, came in and sat in a row at the counter and began to order plates of hot food.

Sitting next to Jeff was a big, powerful, fair-haired fellow wearing a little flour-marked cap. The others called him Mike, and Jeff had often seen him in the restaurant. Having finished his plate and wiped his mouth, he winked at Jeff and said, 'Hello, kid. You around here again tonight? What's new?'

'Nothing,' Jeff said. 'I've just been feeling pretty good.' But he looked so happy as he grinned that Mike puckered up his eyes and appraised him thoughtfully, and the two girls at the table were watching him, too. To seem non-chalant, Jeff whispered to Mike, as he indicated the girls with a nod of his head, 'How do you like the look of the blonde doll in the green hat?'

'That one?' Mike said as he turned on his stool and looked at the girls, who were whispering with their heads close together. 'That one, son? She's a cinch. Didn't you see the glad eye she was giving you? She's a soft touch. She'd give you no trouble at all.'

'She don't look like that to me,' Jeff said.

'I guess I can put my finger on them by this time. If you couldn't go to town with her in two weeks, you ought to quit,' Mike said. Then, as if ashamed to be arguing about women with a kid who was so much younger, he added, 'Anyway, she's too old for you. Lay off her.'

But Jeff kept shifting around on the stool, trying to catch a sudden glimpse of the girl in the green hat, so he could see her as Mike had seen her, yet knowing that to him she still looked quiet and respectable and good-natured. When she smiled suddenly, she seemed like any other friendly girl – a little like Jessie, even. 'Maybe Mike could have looked at Jessie and known from the start it would only take a month with her,' he thought. Feeling miserable, he kept staring at the girl, yearning to possess Mike's wisdom, and with a fierce longing growing in him to know about every intimate moment Jessie had had with the men who had tried to make love to her. 'If I had been sure of myself, I guess I could have knocked Jessie over the first night I took her out,' he went on thinking. The elation he had felt after leaving Jessie seemed childish, and he ached with disappointment.

The girls, who had become embarrassed by Jeff's sullen stare, got up and left the restaurant, and when they had gone Jeff said to Mike, 'I get what you mean about the doll in the green hat.'

'What did she do?' Mike asked.

'Nothing, nothing. It was just the way she swung her hips going out of the door,' Jeff lied, and he lit a cigarette and paid his check and went out.

Jeff and his brother, who was a salesman out of work, had a small apartment on West Twenty-Second Street. As soon as Jeff got home, he realized that the sight of the food in the restaurant had made him hungry, and he went to the icebox and got a tomato, intending to cut some bread and make himself a sandwich. He was holding the tomato in his hand when there was the sound of someone rapping on the door.

It was his brother's girl, Eva, a tall, slim girl with fine brown eyes, who was only about two years older than Jeff. She often came to the apartment to see Jeff's brother. She was at home with Jeff, and laughed a lot with him, and never minded him having a cup of coffee with them. But tonight she looked dreadfully frightened. Her eyes were red-rimmed and moist, as though she had been crying.

'Hello, Jeff. Is Bill home?' she asked.

'He ought to be home any minute, Eva. I thought he was with you.'

'He was, but he left me, and I thought he'd be here.'

'Why don't you sit down and wait for him?' Jeff said.

When she had been sitting down a little while and they were talking, Jeff found himself trying to look at her as Mike had looked at the girl in the green hat in the restaurant, looking at the way she held her head, at her legs, at her eyes – with such a strange, shrewd glance that she became uneasy and began to smooth her skirt down over her legs.

'She knew what I was thinking,' Jeff thought, smiling and cynical, and he tried to say with his eyes, 'I know a lot more about you tonight than I used to know. I'll bet if I put my arms around you, you'd snuggle up against me.'

'What's the matter with you tonight?' Eva said uneasily.

Startled, Jeff said, 'Nothing. There's nothing the matter with me.'

'I guess I'm restless. I can't sit still. I think I'll be going,' she said, and with her face flushed, she got up and went out before he could think of anything to say that might keep her there.

When she had gone, Jeff, remembering the look of terror that had been in her eyes when she first came in, grew ashamed of the stupid, leering way he had looked at her. 'I've driven her away. Thinking of Mike made me act like a fool.' He hurried to the open window and looked down at the street, and he could see her pacing up and down, waiting.

He stayed at the window, watching, till he saw his brother coming along the street. Eva ran up to him, and they stopped under the light and began to talk earnestly. Then Bill took her by the arm very firmly and they started to walk toward the corner, but then they turned and came back and stood talking beneath the window.

In the murmur of their voices the words were indistinguishable, but Jeff knew, from the tone, that his brother was apologetic and fumbling. Then the voices rose a little and seemed to be lifted up to him, and there was a desperate pleading in the snatch of words, an eloquent sound Jeff had never heard in a girl's voice before. 'It's all right. I wish you'd understand I'm not worrying and I'll never, never hold it against you.' She stopped suddenly and grabbed at Bill's arm. Then she let him go and hurried along the street, while Bill stood still, looking after her.

When Bill came in, Jeff said, 'Eva was in here waiting for you.'

Throwing his hat on a chair, Bill walked aimlessly toward the bedroom. 'I know she was here. I ran into her outside,' he said.

'What did she want?'

'Nothing important.'

'She was worked up about something, all right.'

'Why are you staring at me? What's the matter with me? What's the matter with you? Do I look funny?' Bill said.

In Bill's eyes there was the same scared expression that Jeff had seen on the face of Eva. He was accustomed to having his older brother dominate him, even bully him a little. Bill seemed years older than Jeff, because his hair had got so thin. And now the worry, the wonder, and fright showing in Bill's eyes made Jeff feel helpless.

'Eva thinks she's going away, but I'm not going to let her,' Bill said. 'I'm going to marry her even if we have to all live here together.'

'Doesn't she want to marry you?'

'She keeps saying it's her fault, and I didn't intend to marry her, and now she's put me in a hole at a time when we can't do anything about it. She wants to go away for a while till everything's all right.' Then Bill, looking straight ahead, said quietly, 'I don't know what I'd do if anything happened to Eva.'

Jeff could still see Eva clutching at his brother's arm on the street – but not in the way Jessie had clutched at his own arm – and he said hesitantly, 'I've got a girl of my own. I wouldn't want to get in the jam you're in.'

'Nobody does. There's no use talking about it,' Bill said, and he went into the bedroom and lay down on the bed.

Jeff knew that he was lying there quietly, fearing for Eva, loving her, and longing to protect her.

As Jeff watched his brother lying inert on the bed, he began to feel all his wretchedness and terror, and he himself grew timid. If he went back to Jessie, it might get for them like it was for Bill and Eva now. Who wouldn't want to duck that?

He sat and pondered and worried about his brother for a long time. Then he knew suddenly that he was no longer even thinking of his brother; without noticing it, he had begun to dream of the way Jessie had held him against her, and he was thinking of them being together and whispering tomorrow night in her place when it was very late. He could see her lifting her ardent face up to him.

He got up restlessly, realizing that neither Mike's wisdom nor his brother's anguish could teach him anything tonight. Standing at the open window, he looked out over the lighted streets where he walked a little while ago, looking over toward Jessie's place, stirred with a longing for more and more of whatever she would be able to give him. It had started now for them and it would keep going on. And then he was filled with awe, for it seemed like the beginning of a voyage out, with not much he had learned on that night to guide him.

The White Pony

It was a very beautiful white pony, and as it went round and round the stage of the village theatre the two clowns would leap over its back or whistle to it and make it flap its ears and shake its long white mane. Tony Jarvis, like every other kid in the audience that summer afternoon, longed to own it, and he wondered if there wasn't some way he could get close to the pony after the show and slip his arm around its neck.

If he could persuade the owners to let him ride the pony down the street, or if he could just touch it or feed it a little sugar, that would be enough. After the show he went up the alley to the back of the theatre to wait for the clowns and the pony to come out. But the alley was jammed with kids – all the summer crowd from the city as well as the village boys – and Tony couldn't get even close to the back door of the theatre. First the two clowns came out, their faces still coloured with bright paint; then a big red-headed man, apparently the trainer, led the pony out. It shook its head and neighed, and all the kids laughed and rushed at it.

The big red-head, in blue overalls and an old felt hat that had the brim cut off, yelled, 'Out of the way, you kids! Go on, or I'll pull the pants off you!' Then he began to laugh. It was the wildest, craziest, rolling laugh Tony Jarvis had ever heard. The man was huge. His red hair stuck out at all angles under the lopped-off hat. He had a scar on his left cheek and his nose looked as if it had been broken. Whenever the kids came close he swung his arm and they ducked, but they weren't frightened – only a little more excited. As he walked along, leading the white pony, a wide grin on his face, he seemed to be just the kind of giant for the job. If the pony started to prance or was frightened by the traffic, the big man would make a clucking noise and the pony would swing its head over to him and lick his hand with its red tongue.

Tony followed the troupe along the street to the old garage they were using as a stable. Then the red-head yelled, 'All right, beat it, kids!' and led the pony inside and closed the door. The kids stood around watching the closed door, wondering if accidentally it mightn't swing open. It was then that Tony left the gang and sneaked around to the back of the garage. When he saw an old porch there, his heart pounded jerkily. He climbed up to the roof and crawled across the rotting shingles to the edge of a big window. At first he could see nothing. Then, when his eyes became accustomed to the comparative darkness, he saw the two clowns. Squatting in front of mirrors which they had propped up on old boxes, they were scraping the paint off their faces. With a pail in his hand and singing at the top of his voice, the red-head was walking over to a corner of the garage. Stretching, Tony could just see the pony's tail swishing back and forth.

He couldn't see the pony, but he knew it would be rubbing its nose in the red-head's hand. At last the clowns finished cleaning their faces. One of them took a bottle out of a coat that was hanging on the wall and the red-head joined them and they all had a drink. Then the red-head began to talk. Tony couldn't make out the words, but he heard the rich rumble of the voice and saw the wide and eloquent gestures. The clowns were listening intently and grinning. Day after day he must have talked to them like that and it must have been just as wonderful every time. And all the while the white pony's tail kept swishing, and Tony could hear the scraping of the pony's hoofs on the floor.

But now it was getting dark and Tony had to get home. When he tried to move, he found his legs were asleep. Pins and needles seemed to shoot through his arms. Afraid of falling, he grabbed at the window ledge and his head bumped heavily against the pane. Before he could dodge away, the red-headed giant came over and stared up at him. 'Get down out of there!' he yelled. 'Get down or I'll cut your gizzard out!'

They were looking right at each other, and then Tony slid slowly off the roof. As he limped homeward, he felt an intimation of perfect happiness. He kept hearing the sound of the voice, kept seeing the swishing white tail.

The next afternoon he went to the theatre with two lumps of sugar in his pocket. At the end of the show, he pushed his way through the crowd of kids and got right up by the door. When the clowns came out, most of the kids started to yell and there was some pushing and shoving, but Tony hung back, keeping well over to one side of the door, ready to thrust the sugar at the pony's mouth before the red-head could stop him.

The big man appeared at the door and you could hear the pony clopping behind. In his hands the big fellow was carrying two water pails, and the rein that held the pony was clutched in his right hand also. This time, instead of going on down the alley through the path of kids, he stood still and looked around. Then he grinned at Tony. 'Come here, kid,' he said.

'What is it, Mister?'

'What's your name?'

'Tony Jarvis.'

Maybe the big man remembered him from seeing his face

at the window, Tony thought. Anyway, the big man's grin was wide and friendly. 'How would you like to carry these pails for me?' he asked.

Tony grabbed the pails before any other kid could touch them. And the big, freckled, crazy, blue-eyed face of the giant opened into a smile.

Tony walked down the alley, carrying the pails. The big fellow walked beside him, leading the pony and grinning in such a friendly fashion Tony felt sure he understood why the pony swung his head eagerly to the giant whenever he made the soft, clucking noise with his tongue. While Tony was going down the street, his mind was filled with how it would be in the garage, making friends with the pony. Even now he might have reached out and touched the pony if he hadn't had a pail in each hand. The pails were heavy because they were filled with water-soaked sponges, but Tony kept up with the big fellow all right, and he held the pail handles tight, for they were like a ticket of admission to the garage.

'I guess the pony's worth a lot of money?' he said timidly to the red-head.

'Uh?'

'I guess a lot of people want to ride him.'

'Sure.'

'I guess a lot of kids have wanted a little ride on him, too,' Tony said. And when the red-head just nodded and looked straight ahead Tony was so stirred up he dared not say anything more. It was understood between them now, he was sure. They would let him hang around the garage and maybe even have a little ride on the pony.

When they got to the garage he waited while the red-head opened the door and gave the pony a gentle slap on the rump and sent it on ahead. Tony was so full of pride he thought he would choke as he started to follow the pony in.

'All right, son, I'll take the pails,' the red-head said.

'It's all right. I can carry them.'

'Here, give them to me.'

'Can't I go in?' Tony asked, unbelieving.

'No kids in here,' the red-head said brusquely, taking the pails.

'Gee, Mister,' Tony cried. But the door had closed. Tony

stood there with his mouth open, feeling almost sick at his stomach, still seeing the red-head's warm, magnificent smile. He couldn't understand it. He couldn't understand, if the red-head were like that, why the pony loved to swing its head to him. Then he realized that the big fellow had simply used him, that that was the kind of thing they took for granted in the world he had wanted to grow into when he had glimpsed it from the garage window.

'You big red-headed bum!' he screamed at the closed door. 'You dirty, double-crossing, red-headed cheat!'

A Wedding-Dress

For fifteen years Miss Lena Schwartz had waited for Sam Hilton to get a good job so they could get married. She lived in a quiet boarding-house on Wellesley Street, the only woman among seven men boarders. The landlady, Mrs. Mary McNab, did not want woman boarders; the house might get a bad reputation in the neighbourhood, but Miss Schwartz had been with her a long time. Miss Schwartz was thirty-two, her hair was straight, her nose turned up a little and she was thin.

Sam got a good job in Windsor and she was going there to marry him. She was glad to think that Sam still wanted to marry her, because he was a Catholic and went to church every Sunday. Sam liked her so much he wrote a cramped homely letter four times a week.

When Miss Schwartz knew definitely that she was going to Windsor, she read part of a letter to Mrs. McNab, who was a plump, tidy woman. The men heard about the letter at the table and talked as if Lena were an old maid. 'I guess it will really happen to her all right,' they said, nudging one another. 'The Lord knows she waited long enough.'

Miss Schwartz quit work in the millinery shop one afternoon in the middle of February. She was to travel by night, arrive in Windsor early next morning and marry Sam as soon as possible.

That afternoon the down-town streets were slushy and the snow was thick alongside the curb. Miss Schwartz ate a little lunch at a soda fountain, not much because she was excited. She had to do some shopping, buy some flimsy underclothes and a new dress. The dress was important. She wanted it charming enough to be married in and serviceable for wear on Sundays. Sitting on the counter stool she ate slowly and remembered how she had often thought marrying Sam would be a matter of course. His love-making had become casual and good-natured in the long time; she could grow old with him and be respected by other women. But now she had a funny aching feeling inside. Her arms and legs seemed almost strange to her.

Miss Schwartz crossed the road to one of the department stores and was glad she had on her heavy coat with the wide sleeves that made a warm muff. The snow was melting and the sidewalk steaming near the main entrance. She went light-heartedly through the store, buying a little material for a dress on the third floor, a chemise on the fourth floor and curling-tongs in the basement. She decided to take a look at the dresses.

She took an elevator to the main floor and got on an escalator because she liked gliding up and looking over the squares of counters, the people in the aisles, and over the rows of white electric globes hanging from the ceiling. She intended to pay about twenty-five dollars for a dress. To the left of the escalators the dresses were displayed on circular racks in orderly rows. She walked on the carpeted floor to one of the racks and a salesgirl lagged on her heels. The girl was young and fair-haired and saucy-looking; she made Miss Schwartz uncomfortable.

'I want a nice dress, blue or brown,' she said, 'about twenty-five dollars.'

The salesgirl mechanically lifted a brown dress from the rack. 'This is the right shade for you,' she said. 'Will you try it on?'

Miss Schwartz was disappointed. She had no idea such a plain dress would cost twenty-five dollars. She wanted something to keep alive the tempestuous feeling in her body, something to startle Sam. She had never paid so much for a dress, but Sam liked something fancy. 'I don't think I like these,' she said. 'I wanted something special.'

The salesgirl said sarcastically, 'Maybe you were thinking of a French dress. Some on the rack in the French room are marked down.'

Miss Schwartz moved away automatically. The salesgirl did not bother following her. 'Let the old maid look around,' she said to herself, following with her eyes the tall commonplace woman in the dark coat and the oddly shaped purple hat as she went into the gray French room. Miss Schwartz stood on a blue pattern on the gray carpet and guardedly fingered a dress on the rack, a black canton crêpe dress with a high collar that folded back, forming petals of burnt orange. From the hem to the collar was a row of buttons, the sleeves were long with a narrow orange trimming at the cuff, and there was a wide corded silk girdle. It was marked seventy-five dollars. She liked the feeling it left in the tips of her fingers. She stood alone at the rack, toying with the material, her mind playing with thoughts she guiltily enjoyed. She imagined herself wantonly attractive in the dress, slyly watched by men with bold thoughts as she walked down the street with Sam, who would be nervously excited when he drew her into some corner and put his hands on her shoulders. Her heart began to beat heavily. She wanted to walk out of the room and over to the escalator but could not think clearly. Her fingers were carelessly drawing the dress into her wide coat sleeve, the dress disappearing steadily and finally slipping easily from the hanger, drawn into her wide sleeve.

She left the French room with a guilty feeling of satisfied exhaustion. The escalator carried her down slowly to the main floor. She hugged the parcels and the sleeve containing the dress tight to her breast. On the street-car she started to cry because Sam seemed to have become something remote, drifting away from her. She would have gone back with the dress but did not know how to go about it.

When she got to the boarding-house she went straight upstairs and put on the dress as fast as she could, to feel that it belonged to her. The black dress with the burnt orange petals on the high collar was short and loose on her thin figure.

And then the landlady knocked at the door and said that a tall man downstairs wanted to see her about something important. Mrs. McNab waited for Miss Schwartz to come out of her room.

Miss Schwartz sat on the bed. She felt that if she did not move at once she would not be able to walk downstairs. She walked downstairs in the French dress, Mrs. McNab watching her closely. Miss Schwartz saw a man with a wide heavy face and his coat collar buttoned high on his neck complacently watching her. She felt that she might just as well be walking downstairs in her underclothes; the dress was like something wicked clinging to her legs and her body. 'How do you do,' she said.

'Put on your hat and coat,' he said steadily.

Miss Schwartz, slightly bewildered, turned stupidly and went upstairs. She came down a minute later in her coat and hat and went out with the tall man. Mrs. McNab got red in the face when Miss Schwartz offered no word of explanation.

On the street he took her arm and said, 'You got the dress on and it won't do any good to talk about it. We'll go over to the station.'

'But I have to go to Windsor,' she said, 'I really have to. It will be all right. You see, I am to be married tomorrow. It's important to Sam.'

He would not take her seriously. The street lights made the slippery sidewalks glassy. It was hard to walk evenly.

At the station the sergeant said to the detective, 'She might be a bad egg. She's an old maid and they get very foxy.'

She tried to explain it clearly and was almost garrulous. The sergeant shrugged his shoulders and said the cells would not hurt her for a night. She started to cry. A policeman led her to a small cell with a plain bed.

Miss Schwartz could not think about being in the cell. Her

head, heavy at first, got light and she could not consider the matter. The detective who had arrested her gruffly offered to send a wire to Sam.

The policeman on duty during the night thought she was a stupid silly woman because she kept saying over and over, 'We were going to be married. Sam liked a body to look real nice. He always said so.' The unsatisfied expression in her eyes puzzled the policeman, who said to the sergeant, 'She's a bit of a fool, but I guess she was going to get married all right.'

At half past nine in the morning they took her from the cell to the police car along with a small wiry man who had been quite drunk the night before, a coloured woman who had been keeping a bawdy-house, a dispirited fat man arrested for bigamy, and a Chinaman who had been keeping a betting-house. She sat stiffly, primly, in a corner of the car and could not cry. Snow was falling heavily when the car turned into the city hall courtyard.

Miss Schwartz appeared in the Women's Court before a little Jewish magistrate. Her legs seemed to stiffen and fall away when she saw Sam's closely cropped head and his big lazy body at a long table before the magistrate. A young man was talking rapidly and confidently to him. The magistrate and the Crown attorney were trying to make a joke at each other's expense. The magistrate found the attorney amusing. A court clerk yelled a name, the policeman at the door repeated it and then loudly yelled the name along the hall. The coloured woman who had been keeping the bawdy-house appeared with her lawyer.

Sam moved over to Miss Schwartz. He found it hard not to cry. She knew that a Salvation Army man was talking to a slightly hard-looking woman about her, and she felt strong and resentful. Sam held her hand but said nothing.

The coloured woman went to jail for two months rather than pay a fine of $200.

'Lena Schwartz,' said the clerk. The policeman at the door shouted the name along the hall. The young lawyer who had been talking to Sam told her to stand up while the clerk read the charge. She was scared and her knees were stiff.

'Where is the dress?' asked the magistrate.

A store detective with a heavy moustache explained that she had it on and told how she had been followed and later on arrested. Everybody looked at her, the dress too short and hanging loosely on her thin body, the burnt orange petals creased and twisted. The magistrate said to himself: 'She's an old maid and it doesn't even look nice on her.'

'She was to be married today,' began the young lawyer affably. 'She was to be married in this dress,' he said and good-humouredly explained that yesterday when she stole it she had become temporarily a kleptomaniac. Mr. Hilton had come up from Windsor and was willing to pay for the dress. It was a case for clemency. 'She waited a long time to be married and was not quite sure of herself,' he said seriously.

He told Sam to stand up. Sam haltingly explained that she was a good woman, a very good woman. The Crown attorney seemed to find Miss Schwartz amusing.

The magistrate scratched away with his pen and then said he would remand Miss Schwartz for sentence if Sam still wanted to marry her and would pay for the dress. Sam could hardly say anything. 'She will leave the city with you,' said the magistrate, 'and keep out of the department stores for a year.' He saw Miss Schwartz wrinkling her nose and blinking her eyes and added, 'Now go out and have a quiet wedding.' The magistrate was quite satisfied with himself.

Miss Schwartz, looking a little older than Sam, stood up in her dress that was to make men slyly watch her and straightened the corded silk girdle. It was to be her wedding-dress, all right. Sam gravely took her arm and they went out to be quietly married.

The Little Business Man

That summer when twelve-year-old Luke Baldwin came to live with his Uncle Henry in the house on the stream by the sawmill, he did not forget that he had promised his dying father he would try to learn things from his uncle; so he used to watch him very carefully.

Uncle Henry, who was the manager of the sawmill, was a big, burly man weighing more than two hundred and thirty pounds, and he had a rough-skinned, brick-coloured face. He looked like a powerful man, but his health was not good. He had aches and pains in his back and shoulders which puzzled the doctor. The first thing Luke learned about Uncle Henry was that everybody had great respect for him. The four men he employed in the sawmill were always polite and attentive when he spoke to them. His wife, Luke's Aunt Helen, a kindly, plump, straightforward woman, never argued with him. 'You should try and be like your Uncle Henry,' she would say to Luke. 'He's so wonderfully practical. He takes care of everything in a sensible, easy way.'

Luke used to trail around the sawmill after Uncle Henry not only because he liked the fresh clean smell of the newly cut wood and the big piles of sawdust, but because he was impressed by his uncle's precise, firm tone when he spoke to the men.

Sometimes Uncle Henry would stop and explain to Luke something about a piece of timber. 'Always try and learn the essential facts, son,' he would say. 'If you've got the facts, you know what's useful and what isn't useful, and no one can fool you.'

He showed Luke that nothing of value was ever wasted around the mill. Luke used to listen, and wonder if there was

62

another man in the world who knew so well what was needed and what ought to be thrown away. Uncle Henry had known at once that Luke needed a bicycle to ride to his school, which was two miles away in town, and he bought him a good one. He knew that Luke needed good, serviceable clothes. He also knew exactly how much Aunt Helen needed to run the house, the price of everything, and how much a woman should be paid for doing the family washing. In the evenings Luke used to sit in the living-room watching his uncle making notations in a black notebook which he always carried in his vest pocket, and he knew that he was assessing the value of the smallest transaction that had taken place during the day.

Luke promised himself that when he grew up he, too, would be admired for his good, sound judgement. But, of course, he couldn't always be watching and learning from his Uncle Henry, for too often when he watched him he thought of his own father; then he was lonely. So he began to build up another secret life for himself around the sawmill, and his companion was the eleven-year-old collie, Dan, a dog blind in one eye and with a slight limp in his left hind leg. Dan was a fat, slow-moving old dog. He was very affectionate and his eye was the colour of amber. His fur was amber too. When Luke left for school in the morning, the old dog followed him for half a mile down the road, and when he returned in the afternoon, there was Dan waiting at the gate.

Sometimes they would play around the millpond or by the dam, or go down the stream to the lake. Luke was never lonely when the dog was with him. There was an old rowboat that they used as a pirate ship in the stream, and they would be pirates together, with Luke shouting instructions to Captain Dan and with the dog seeming to understand and wagging his tail enthusiastically. His amber eye was alert, intelligent, and approving. Then they would plunge into the brush on the other side of the stream, pretending they were hunting tigers. Of course, the old dog was no longer much good for hunting; he was too slow and too lazy. Uncle Henry no longer used him for hunting rabbits or anything else.

When they came out of the brush, they would lie together on the cool, grassy bank being affectionate with each other, with Luke talking earnestly, while the collie, as Luke believed, smiled with the good eye. Lying in the grass, Luke would say things to Dan he could not say to his uncle or his aunt. Not that what he said was important; it was just stuff about himself that he might have told to his own father or mother if they had been alive. Then they would go back to the house for dinner, and after dinner Dan would follow him down the road to Mr. Kemp's house, where they would ask old Mr. Kemp if they could go with him to round up his four cows. The old man was always glad to see them. He seemed to like watching Luke and the collie running around the cows, pretending they were riding on a vast range in the foothills of the Rockies.

Uncle Henry no longer paid much attention to the collie, though once when he tripped over him on the veranda, he shook his head and said thoughtfully, 'Poor fellow, he's through. Can't use him for anything. He just eats and sleeps and gets in the way.'

One Sunday during Luke's summer holidays, when they had returned from church and had had their lunch, they all moved out to the veranda where the collie was sleeping. Luke sat down on the steps, his back against the veranda post, Uncle Henry took the rocking-chair, and Aunt Helen stretched herself out in the hammock, sighing contentedly. Then Luke, eyeing the collie, tapped the step with the palm of his hand, giving three little taps like a signal, and the collie, lifting his head, got up stiffly with a slow wagging of the tail as an acknowledgement that the signal had been heard, and began to cross the veranda to Luke. But the dog was sleepy; his bad eye was turned to the rocking-chair; in passing, his left front paw went under the rocker. With a frantic yelp, the dog went bounding down the steps and hobbled around the corner of the house, where he stopped, hearing Luke coming after him. All he needed was the touch of Luke's hand. Then he began to lick the hand methodically, as if apologizing.

'Luke,' Uncle Henry called sharply, 'bring that dog here.'

When Luke led the collie back to the veranda, Uncle

Henry nodded and said, 'Thanks, Luke.' Then he took out a cigar, lit it, put his big hands on his knees, and began to rock in the chair, while he frowned and eyed the dog steadily. Obviously he was making some kind of an important decision about the collie.

'What's the matter, Uncle Henry?' Luke asked nervously.

'That dog can't see any more,' Uncle Henry said.

'Oh, yes, he can,' Luke said quickly. 'His bad eye got turned to the chair, that's all, Uncle Henry.'

'And his teeth are gone, too,' Uncle Henry went on, paying no attention to what Luke said. Turning to the hammock, he called, 'Helen, sit up a minute, will you?'

When she got up and stood beside him, he went on, 'I was thinking about this old dog the other day, Helen. It's not only that he's just about blind, but did you notice that when we drove up after church he didn't even bark?'

'It's a fact, he didn't, Henry.'

'No, not much good even as a watch-dog now.'

'Poor old fellow. It's a pity, isn't it?'

'And no good for hunting either. And he eats a lot, I suppose.'

'About as much as he ever did, Henry.'

'The plain fact is the old dog isn't worth his keep any more. It's time we got rid of him.'

'It's always so hard to know how to get rid of a dog, Henry.'

'I was thinking about it the other day. Some people think it's best to shoot a dog. I haven't had any shells for that shot-gun for over a year. Poisoning is a hard death for a dog. Maybe drowning is the easiest and quickest way. Well, I'll speak to one of the mill hands and have him look after it.'

Crouching on the ground, his arms around the old collie's neck, Luke cried out, 'Uncle Henry, Dan's a wonderful dog! You don't know how wonderful he is!'

'He's just a very old dog, son,' Uncle Henry said calmly. 'The time comes when you have to get rid of any old dog. We've got to be practical about it. I'll get you a pup, son. A smart little dog that'll be worth its keep. A pup that will grow up with you.'

'I don't want a pup!' Luke cried, turning his face away. Circling around him, the dog began to bark, then flick his long pink tongue at the back of Luke's neck.

Aunt Helen, catching her husband's eye, put her finger on her lips, warning him not to go on talking in front of the boy. 'An old dog like that often wanders off into the brush and sort of picks a place to die when the time comes. Isn't that so, Henry?'

'Oh, sure,' he agreed quickly. 'In fact, when Dan didn't show up yesterday, I was sure that was what had happened.' Then he yawned and seemed to forget about the dog.

But Luke was frightened, for he knew what his uncle was like. He knew that if his uncle had decided that the dog was useless and that it was sane and sensible to get rid of it, he would be ashamed of himself if he were diverted by any sentimental considerations. Luke knew in his heart that he couldn't move his uncle. All he could do, he thought, was keep the dog away from his uncle, keep him out of the house, feed him when Uncle Henry wasn't around.

Next day at noontime Luke saw his uncle walking from the mill toward the house with old Sam Carter, a mill hand. Sam Carter was a dull, stooped, slow-witted man of sixty with an iron-gray beard, who was wearing blue overalls and a blue shirt. Watching from the veranda, Luke noticed that his uncle suddenly gave Sam Carter a cigar, which Sam put in his pocket. Luke had never seen his uncle give Sam a cigar or pay much attention to him.

Then, after lunch, Uncle Henry said lazily that he would like Luke to take his bicycle and go into town and get him some cigars.

'I'll take Dan,' Luke said.

'Better not, son,' Uncle Henry said. 'It'll take you all afternoon. I want those cigars. Get going, Luke.'

His uncle's tone was so casual that Luke tried to believe they were not merely getting rid of him. Of course he had to do what he was told. He had never dared to refuse to obey an order from his uncle. But when he had taken his bicycle and had ridden down the path that followed the stream to the town road and had got about a quarter of a mile along the road, he found that all he could think of was his uncle handing old Sam Carter the cigar.

Slowing down, sick with worry now, he got off the bike and stood uncertainly on the sunlit road. Sam Carter was a gruff, aloof old man who would have no feeling for a dog. Then suddenly Luke could go no farther without getting some assurance that the collie would not be harmed while he was away. Across the fields he could see the house.

Leaving the bike in the ditch, he started to cross the field, intending to get close enough to the house so Dan could hear him if he whistled softly. He got about fifty yards away from the house and whistled and waited, but there was no sign of the dog, which might be asleep at the front of the house, he knew, or over at the sawmill. With the saws whining, the dog couldn't hear the soft whistle. For a few minutes Luke couldn't make up his mind what to do, then he decided to go back to the road, get on his bike, and go back the way he had come until he got to the place where the river path joined the road. There he could leave his bike, go up the path, then into the tall grass and get close to the front of the house and the sawmill without being seen.

He had followed the river path for about a hundred yards, and when he came to the place where the river began to bend sharply toward the house his heart fluttered and his legs felt paralysed, for he saw the old rowboat in the one place where the river was deep, and in the rowboat was Sam Carter with the collie.

The bearded man in the blue overalls was smoking his cigar; the dog, with a rope around its neck, sat contentedly beside him, its tongue going out in a friendly lick at the hand holding the rope. It was all like a crazy dream picture to Luke; all wrong because it looked so lazy and friendly, even the curling smoke from Sam Carter's cigar. But as Luke cried out, 'Dan, Dan! Come on, boy!' and the dog jumped at the water, he saw that Sam Carter's left hand was hanging deep in the water, holding a foot of rope with a heavy stone at the end. As Luke cried out wildly, 'Don't! Please don't!' Carter dropped the stone, for the cry came too late; it was blurred by the screech of the big saws at the

mill. But Carter was startled, and he stared stupidly at the
river bank, then he ducked his head and began to row
quickly to the bank.

But Luke was watching the collie take what looked like
a long, shallow dive, except that the hind legs suddenly
kicked up above the surface, then shot down, and while he
watched, Luke sobbed and trembled, for it was as if the
happy secret part of his life around the sawmill was being
torn away from him. But even while he watched, he seemed
to be following a plan without knowing it, for he was already fumbling in his pocket for his jack-knife, jerking the
blade open, pulling off his pants, kicking his shoes off, while
he muttered fiercely and prayed that Sam Carter would get
out of sight.

It hardly took the mill hand a minute to reach the bank
and go slinking furtively around the bend as if he felt that
the boy was following him. But Luke hadn't taken his eyes
off the exact spot in the water where Dan had disappeared.
As soon as the mill hand was out of sight, Luke slid down
the bank and took a leap at the water, the sun glistening on
his slender body, his eyes wild with eagerness as he ran out
to the deep place, then arched his back and dived, swim-
ming under water, his open eyes getting used to the green-
ish-gray haze of the water, the sandy bottom, and the imbedded rocks.

His lungs began to ache, then he saw the shadow of the
collie, floating at the end of the taut rope, rock-held in the
sand. He slashed at the rope with his knife. He couldn't get
much strength in his arm because of the resistance of the
water. He grabbed the rope with his left hand, hacking with
his knife. The collie suddenly drifted up slowly, like a
water-soaked log. Then his own head shot above the surface, and, while he was sucking in the air, he was drawing in
the rope, pulling the collie toward him and treading water.
In a few strokes he was away from the deep place and his
feet touched the bottom.

Hoisting the collie out of the water, he scrambled toward
the bank, lurching and stumbling in fright because the collie
felt like a dead weight.

He went on up the bank and across the path to the tall

grass, where he fell flat, hugging the dog and trying to warm him with his own body. But the collie didn't stir, the good amber eye remained closed. Then suddenly Luke wanted to act like a resourceful, competent man. Getting up on his knees, he stretched the dog out on its belly, drew him between his knees, felt with trembling hands for the soft places on the flanks just above the hip-bones, and rocked back and forth, pressing with all his weight, then relaxing the pressure as he straightened up. He hoped that he was working the dog's lungs like a bellows. He had read that men who had been thought drowned had been saved in this way.

'Come on, Dan. Come on, old boy,' he pleaded softly. As a little water came from the collie's mouth, Luke's heart jumped, and he muttered over and over, 'You can't be dead, Dan! You can't, you can't! I won't let you die, Dan!' He rocked back and forth tirelessly, applying the pressure to the flanks. More water dribbled from the mouth. In the collie's body he felt a faint tremor. 'Oh, gee, Dan, you're alive,' he whispered. 'Come on, boy. Keep it up.'

With a cough the collie suddenly jerked his head back, the amber eye opened, and there they were looking at each other. Then the collie, thrusting his legs out stiffly, tried to hoist himself up, staggered, tried again, then stood there in a stupor. Then he shook himself like any other wet dog, turned his head, eyed Luke, and the red tongue came out in a weak flick at Luke's cheek.

'Lie down, Dan,' Luke said. As the dog lay down beside him, Luke closed his eyes, buried his head in the wet fur, and wondered why all the muscles of his arms and legs began to jerk in a nervous reaction, now that it was all over. 'Stay there, Dan,' he said softly, and he went back to the path, got his clothes, and came back beside Dan and put them on. 'I think we'd better get away from this spot, Dan,' he said. 'Keep down, boy. Come on.' And he crawled on through the tall grass till they were about seventy-five yards from the place where he had undressed. There they lay down together.

In a little while he heard his aunt's voice calling, 'Luke. Oh, Luke! Come here, Luke!'

'Quiet, Dan,' Luke whispered. A few minutes passed, and

then Uncle Henry called, 'Luke, Luke!' and he began to come down the path. They could see him standing there, massive and imposing, his hands on his hips as he looked down the path, then he turned and went back to the house.

As he watched the sunlight shine on the back of his uncle's neck, the exultation Luke had felt at knowing the collie was safe beside him turned to bewildered despair, for he knew that even if he should be forgiven for saving the dog when he saw it drowning, the fact was that his uncle had been thwarted. His mind was made up to get rid of Dan, and in a few days' time, in another way, he would get rid of him, as he got rid of anything around the mill that he believed to be useless or a waste of money.

As he lay back and looked up at the hardly moving clouds, he began to grow frightened. He couldn't go back to the house, nor could he take the collie into the woods and hide him and feed him there unless he tied him up. If he didn't tie him up, Dan would wander back to the house.

'I guess there's just no place to go, Dan,' he whispered sadly. 'Even if we start off along the road, somebody is sure to see us.'

But Dan was watching a butterfly that was circling crazily above them. Raising himself a little, Luke looked through the grass at the corner of the house, then he turned and looked the other way to the wide blue lake. With a sigh he lay down again, and for hours they lay there together, until there was no sound from the saws in the mill and the sun moved low in the western sky.

'Well, we can't stay here any longer, Dan,' he said at last. 'We'll just have to get as far away as we can. Keep down, old boy,' and he began to crawl through the grass, going farther away from the house. When he could no longer be seen, he got up and began to trot across the field toward the gravel road leading to town.

On the road, the collie would turn from time to time as if wondering why Luke shuffled along, dragging his feet wearily, head down. 'I'm stumped, that's all, Dan,' Luke explained. 'I can't seem to think of a place to take you.'

When they were passing the Kemp place, they saw the old man sitting on the veranda, and Luke stopped. All he could think of was that Mr. Kemp had liked them both and it had been a pleasure to help him get the cows in the evening. Dan had always been with them. Staring at the figure of the old man on the veranda, he said in a worried tone, 'I wish I could be sure of him, Dan. I wish he was a dumb, stupid man who wouldn't know or care whether you were worth anything...Well, come on.' He opened the gate bravely, but he felt shy and unimportant.

'Hello, son. What's on your mind?' Mr. Kemp called from the veranda. He was a thin, wiry man in a tan-coloured shirt. He had a gray, untidy moustache, his skin was wrinkled and leathery, but his eyes were always friendly and amused.

'Could I speak to you, Mr. Kemp?' Luke asked when they were close to the veranda.

'Sure. Go ahead.'

'It's about Dan. He's a great dog, but I guess you know that as well as I do. I was wondering if you could keep him here for me.'

'Why should I keep Dan here, son?'

'Well, it's like this,' Luke said, fumbling the words awkwardly: 'My uncle won't let me keep him any more...says he's too old.' His mouth began to tremble, then he blurted out the story.

'I see, I see,' Mr. Kemp said slowly, and he got up and came over to the steps and sat down and began to stroke the collie's head. 'Of course, Dan's an old dog, son,' he said quietly. 'And sooner or later you've got to get rid of an old dog. Your uncle knows that. Maybe it's true that Dan isn't worth his keep.'

'He doesn't eat much, Mr. Kemp. Just one meal a day.'

'I wouldn't want you to think your uncle was cruel and unfeeling, Luke,' Mr. Kemp went on. 'He's a fine man... maybe just a little bit too practical and straightforward.'

'I guess that's right,' Luke agreed, but he was really waiting and trusting the expression in the old man's eyes.

'Maybe you should make him a practical proposition.'

'I – I don't know what you mean.'

'Well, I sort of like the way you get the cows for me in the evenings,' Mr. Kemp said, smiling to himself. 'In fact,

I don't think you need me to go along with you at all. Now, supposing I gave you seventy-five cents a week. Would you get the cows for me every night?'

'Sure I would, Mr. Kemp. I like doing it, anyway.'

'All right, son. It's a deal. Now I'll tell you what to do. You go back to your uncle, and before he has a chance to open up on you, you say right out that you've come to him with a business proposition. Say it like a man, just like that. Offer to pay him the seventy-five cents a week for the dog's keep.'

'But my uncle doesn't need seventy-five cents, Mr. Kemp,' Luke said uneasily.

'Of course not,' Mr. Kemp agreed. 'It's the principle of the thing. Be confident. Remember that he's got nothing against the dog. Go to it, son. Let me know how you do,' he added, with an amused smile. 'If you know your uncle at all, I think it'll work.'

'I'll try it, Mr. Kemp,' Luke said. 'Thanks very much.' But he didn't have any confidence, for even though he knew that Mr. Kemp was a wise old man who would not deceive him, he couldn't believe that seventy-five cents a week would stop his uncle, who was an important man. 'Come on, Dan,' he called, and he went slowly and apprehensively back to the house.

When they were going up the path, his aunt cried from the open window, 'Henry, Henry, in heaven's name, it's Luke with the dog!'

Ten paces from the veranda, Luke stopped and waited nervously for his uncle to come out. Uncle Henry came out in a rush, but when he saw the collie and Luke standing there, he stopped stiffly, turned pale, and his mouth hung open loosely.

'Luke,' he whispered, 'that dog had a stone around his neck.'

'I fished him out of the stream,' Luke said uneasily.

'Oh. Oh, I see,' Uncle Henry said, and gradually the colour came back to his face. 'You fished him out, eh?' he asked, still looking at the dog uneasily. 'Well, you shouldn't have done that. I told Sam Carter to get rid of the dog, you know.'

'Just a minute, Uncle Henry,' Luke said, trying not to falter. He gained confidence as Aunt Helen came out and stood beside her husband, for her eyes seemed to be gentle, and he went on bravely, 'I want to make you a practical proposition, Uncle Henry.'

'A what?' Uncle Henry asked, still feeling insecure, and wishing the boy and the dog weren't confronting him.

'A practical proposition,' Luke blurted out quickly. 'I know Dan isn't worth his keep to you. I guess he isn't worth anything to anybody but me. So I'll pay you seventy-five cents a week for his keep.'

'What's this?' Uncle Henry asked, looking bewildered. 'Where would you get seventy-five cents a week, Luke?'

'I'm going to get the cows every night for Mr. Kemp.'

'Oh, for heaven's sake, Henry,' Aunt Helen pleaded, looking distressed, 'let him keep the dog!' and she fled into the house.

'None of that kind of talk!' Uncle Henry called after her. 'We've got to be sensible about this!' But he was shaken himself, and overwhelmed with a distress that destroyed all his confidence. As he sat down slowly in the rocking-chair and stroked the side of his big face, he wanted to say weakly, 'All right, keep the dog,' but he was ashamed of being so weak and sentimental. He stubbornly refused to yield to this emotion; he was trying desperately to turn his emotion into a bit of good, useful common sense, so he could justify his distress. So he rocked and pondered. At last he smiled, 'You're a smart little shaver, Luke,' he said slowly. 'Imagine you working it out like this. I'm tempted to accept your proposition.'

'Gee, thanks, Uncle Henry.'

'I'm accepting it because I think you'll learn something out of this,' he went on ponderously.

'Yes, Uncle Henry.'

'You'll learn that useless luxuries cost the smartest of men hard-earned money.'

'I don't mind.'

'Well, it's a thing you'll have to learn some time. I think you'll learn, too, because you certainly seem to have a practical streak in you. It's a streak I like to see in a boy.

O.K., son,' he said, and he smiled with relief and went into the house.

Turning to Dan, Luke whispered softly, 'Well, what do you know about that?'

As he sat down on the step with the collie beside him and listened to Uncle Henry talking to his wife, he began to glow with exultation. Then gradually his exultation began to change to a vast wonder that Mr. Kemp should have had such a perfect understanding of Uncle Henry. He began to dream of some day being as wise as old Mr. Kemp and knowing exactly how to handle people. It was possible, too, that he had already learned some of the things about his uncle that his father had wanted him to learn.

Putting his head down on the dog's neck, he vowed to himself fervently that he would always have some money on hand, no matter what became of him, so that he would be able to protect all that was truly valuable from the practical people in the world.

Father and Son

The old stone farmhouse stood out sharp and clear against the dark hill in the moonlight. He walked up the path a little, then realized that he was walking right into the flood of light from the window. This scared him and he stopped. 'Why did I feel that I had to come?' he thought. 'After waiting four years why do I come now? What am I doing here?' And he looked all around the little valley, at the huge old barn shadowing all the hill and at the little garden beside the house. He heard the old car that had picked him up going rumbling back through the ruts on the road. There was a heavy mist in the valley. The soft Pennsylvanian hills rose up clear above the floating mist and were rounded against the sky.

He was so afraid of his own uneasiness and the valley's silence that he darted forward right through the shaft of window light and rapped firmly on the door. When the door was opened Mona was there with her hand still on the knob and her little body leaning forward, and while all the light was falling on his bewildered, shy face he could do nothing but stare at her and wait. 'Oh, it's you Greg. We were expecting you some time soon,' she said. 'We heard the car coming up and going away and wondered who it was.'

She could not help looking for a long time at Greg Henderson, wondering what had happened in his life to drive him back here after four years. He was hesitating awkwardly there at the door, tall and dark, in his fine expensive city clothes, but really much older, and the light was all on his worried face that looked scared and ashamed: it was puzzling to Mona to see him so reticent and lonely looking, because she knew he had always been full of eagerness, giving all of himself first to one thing and then to another, full of love, and then getting hurt, and then hard and unyielding and never consenting to go anyone else's way. As he blinked his eyes in the light he looked humble. He had none of the fine plausible flow of easy words he had had in the old days. He said, halting, 'I was walking up from the station. They picked me up on the road,' and then he followed her into the big lamplit room with the great open hearth, and for the first time he was able to look at her. Her body was enveloped in a large white apron. Her long black hair fell soft and thick around her oval face, and she was looking at him steadily with her peaceful dark eyes in a way that made him more uneasy than ever. 'I got your letter, Greg, and so you must have got mine.'

'Maybe I oughtn't to have come at all,' he said.

'Why shouldn't you come, if you wanted to?' she asked candidly.

There was the sound of someone moving in the kitchen. A short, broad-shouldered, bony-faced young man with thick light hair appeared holding a pail in his hand. He was wearing a short leather jacket, as if he had just expected to go out, and he stood there, grinning a little at Mona and eyeing Greg with a frank curiosity as if he had heard all about him without ever having seen him.

'You've heard me speak of Greg Henderson, Frank,' Mona said.

'Hello, Mr. Henderson,' Frank said with a kind of good-humoured warmth. There was a broad comprehending smile on his strong face, as he put out his hand and said, 'Are you hungry, old man? Not at all? You'll be staying the night with us anyway, won't you?'

'I hadn't thought about it. Are you sure you have room?'

'We're awfully proud of our guest room,' Mona said. 'Show Greg our guest room, Frank.'

In the young man in the leather jacket there was now the good-natured condescension of a proprietor who realizes that his good nature is gratuitous and not at all necessary. With his laconic, straightforward manner he seemed to be saying to Greg, 'You see, I let you come into my house. I even welcome you. I even smile and shake hands heartily with you because I want you to be comfortable, because what you think is so very important is no longer important at all.' He was saying this with his frank easy smile and his steady shrewd eyes. He was very poor here in the country but very happy. He was a social revolutionary, and by making frequent trips into the city in his old car he tried to participate in many of his party's activities. His strong faith had made Mona happy, too, and the both of them were standing there with such assurance, smiling softly and patiently at Greg as though he were just a child.

'Stay the night,' Mona said.

'Maybe I'd better stay the night.'

'Come on upstairs, old man, and I'll show you we've got a room for you,' Frank said.

'Little Mike is asleep, but maybe we could take a peek at him when you're ready,' Mona said.

Greg followed Frank up the narrow twisting staircase that was built in the thick wall of the old farmhouse, and into a little room with a window, a low-beamed ceiling and a narrow bed. 'You'll be comfortable for the night,' Frank said. 'Feel at home while you're here. We want you to feel at home. Mona has told me all about you.' He was speaking in an easy, jolly, friendly way, but the composure that was in his voice made Greg feel his own utter unimportance.

Greg was an opinionated, arrogant man with a natural fierceness in his nature, and he could not help saying, 'Did she tell you about me?' but then in a panic, without waiting for an answer, he went right on saying, 'This is a fine place in the country. A man ought to have such a place. The country is very beautiful but a little melancholy. I felt it in me walking on the road, maybe it was just the darkness and the softness of the hills,' and he kept on talking like this till they started to go downstairs again.

'I was just going down the road a piece to get the milk,' Frank explained. 'Maybe you'll be wanting to take a peek at Mike with Mona.' Picking up the can that he had brought from the kitchen, he went out brusquely, leaving Mona and Greg standing there, listening first to his footfalls and then to the sound of his whistling as he went down the road.

Then Mona smiled in a sympathetic, agreeable way as she said, 'You can come and see Mike if you want to.' And Greg followed her meekly, going upstairs again and tiptoeing into another little room and standing beside her, bending over a cot. There was enough early moonlight flooding the room to show the soft lines of the sleeping boy's face. Mona and Greg bent down together over the bed and Greg began to feel a strange excitement, then a vast uneasiness like a rising and falling of life within him, as he tried to make out the shape of his own boy's head. It was for this that he had come, after a few years of forgetting and then a short month of restless wondering, and now, bending over the bed and feeling the mother so quiet beside him, he had a wild hope that the great, heavy beating of his own heart might sound so loud in the room it would wake up the boy.

But Mona, with her finger to her lips, was beckoning him, and he tiptoed out behind her and followed her downstairs.

While he walked up and down the room, not daring to look at Mona or speak to her, he felt how undisturbed and peaceful she was as she sat in the old rocking-chair. Mona had always been so tender with him when there had been any suffering in him, and yet now when he was most wretched and deeply suffering, she waited, quiet, still, without any emotion. In her peacefulness he could feel how unimportant he had become, he could almost hear her husband saying to her many times, 'A no-account lawyer, a little bourgeois thinking his little middle-class emotions and his sentimentality can hold you and crucify you forever. That's all over with and it's no longer important that he once loved you and left you. The poor fool.' Greg felt himself hating the brusque confident man in the leather jacket who had gone whistling along the road. Turning, he began to stare at Mona, staring at her white, round, soft face, and then, moving slow, he went over to her and put out his hand and whispered, 'Mona, it's unnatural for you to be so calm with me now,' and he put out his hand to touch her.

Her hands had been quiet in her lap and her face had been full of soft contentment, but when he came toward her, reaching out to touch her with his hand, her face took on a wretched fearful look that destroyed swiftly all the calmness and beauty her new faith had given her. She looked now like she had looked the last times he had seen her and she was saying, frightened, 'Don't come near me, don't touch me.'

'I won't, Mona. Such a feeling isn't really in me and you must forgive me. It's just meanness I was feeling because you were so peaceful and content and I wanted to disturb you,' and he really was ashamed because he knew, too, that it was out of his hatred of her husband's confidence that he was trying to disturb her and trying to assert his own strength. 'The boy is feeling fine, isn't he?'

'His health has been good. In the morning you can talk to him and play with him.'

'I can have him for hours?'

'As long as you wish.'

Then Frank came in with the milk and took off his leather jacket and the three of them sat down to talk for a while. They asked Greg about the city. They were living here in the country, but they longed for any bit of news about the city. Their talk grew quite animated. Gradually, Frank began to talk about social problems with some enthusiasm because it was the subject that had most power over all his thoughts, and he talked at Greg, knowing he had another point of view, and his voice rose and he waved his hand,

and then his voice softened and he was patient with Greg as though he were an old enfeebled man who had been a slave all his life. Greg hated every word he said. But when he interrupted him there was a sharp hostile silence between them. In these moments of silence they looked at each other strangely, they realized they were there together, they felt the country silence outside, and they did not like it. Greg wanted Frank to go on talking. He glanced at Mona and felt how full she was of her husband's faith.

Then Mona said, 'Maybe Greg is tired, Frank, after walking most of the way to the station. Maybe he wants to go to bed.'

'I'm sorry, old man,' Frank said considerately. 'Don't let us keep you up. We go to bed early around here, anyway. Are you sure there's nothing we can do for you?'

'Nothing at all,' Greg said, and after saying good night to them he went up to the bedroom. But he was so wide awake he could hardly keep still. He stood at the window looking out over the little valley lit by the moonlight. He heard the trickling of water in the nearly dried-up creek, but every other part of the night was dreadfully still. And he was thinking that everything that had been tragic or had hurt deeply in Mona's life had been smoothed out here in the quietness of this mist-laden valley; and he was thinking, too, 'She never looked as lovely when she loved me as she did sitting there in the chair tonight. The tortured look that came into her face belonged to our time together.' It was terrible to feel that once there had been such hot strong passion in both of them and now he was here, welcomed calmly by her, as though he were a visitor or a stranger who was utterly unimportant in her life. He wanted to cry out in a loud voice and break the night's calmness, but he threw himself on the bed and sighed and rubbed his head in the pillow and groaned within him, feeling it a terrible thing that all the ecstasy, all the joy of loving that used to be between them was gone, didn't live at all tonight. Then he heard them coming up to bed. He heard them undressing. They must have lain down together, for soon he heard them whispering peacefully. The whispering between them had a fine evenness, her whispering and murmur blending and made one with the low murmur of his voice. 'There's nothing I've held on to. I possess no part of anything that's here,' Greg thought. 'I don't touch their life at all,' and he felt humility and even a little peacefulness in himself.

In the morning he went downstairs with a humble eagerness to see his son. It was like feeling that something mysterious but very gratifying was about to happen. He was shy and smiling when he said good morning to Mona and Frank.

'Mike is in the kitchen finishing his breakfast,' Mona said.

'Can I go in?'

'Come on along,' she said, and they went together into the kitchen where a dark-haired, round-faced little boy was eating a piece of toast very seriously. His eyes were large and brown and soft like his mother's. He was so sturdy, handsome, and rosy-cheeked that Greg felt a marvellous delight in just looking at him and he said suddenly, 'Hello, Mike.'

The boy looked at him gravely and then said without smiling, 'Are you my uncle?'

'A kind of an uncle,' Greg said awkwardly.

'Mother said my uncle might come and see me today. Aren't you really my uncle?'

'Sure, I'm your Uncle Greg.' Greg looked at Mona and they both smiled to each other, then they began to laugh easily. 'Will you go for a walk with your uncle while Daddy and I drive into town, darling?' Mona asked.

'All right,' the boy said laconically, and he went on eating his toast.

So later on, in a straightforward simple way, Mona and Frank got ready to go to town in order that Greg might be alone for a few hours with the boy. He stood at the door watching them get into the old battered automobile. It was a fine, clear spring day. The car was on the other side of the little garden near the barn and beside a pile of red shale. The ground on that side of the house was covered with this powdered red shale. When the car started, Greg and the boy standing beside him waved their hands.

Speaking soft and coaxing, Greg said to Mike, 'Will we

go for a walk down the road, maybe all the way down the road to the river? Is it too far?'

'I've often walked that far with my father in the spring when he went fishing. I can walk twice that far. I can walk three times that far.'

As soon as they started to walk the little boy put up his hand and took Greg's hand firmly in his. This simple gesture moved Greg more than anything that had happened since he had come. He stared down at the boy's neck as they walked hand in hand along the red clay road, waiting for something mysterious to happen between them.

'Where are you from, Mister?' Mike asked.

'I'm from New York.'

'I guess it's too far away to walk there today, eh?'

'Much too far. It's miles away.'

'Are there a lot of little kids there?'

'The streets are full of little kids shouting and playing.'

'Do you know them? I'd like to see some kids. It's nice here, I like it here, but there are hardly any kids to play with,' he said gravely. Then he hesitated, looked up at Greg, wondering if he could be confided in completely. 'Would you let me come and see you in New York some time, Mister?' he asked.

Greg let his hand fall with a light gentleness on the boy's shoulder, caressing the shoulder timidly. 'I certainly will,' he said. But Mike shook his shoulder free of the hand, not that he was offended, but he was simply asserting that he was a boy and not to be petted. Greg loved his unspoiled childish directness. He longed to sit down with him and explain that they belonged to each other, or do some significant thing that would bring a swift light of recognition into the boy's eyes.

Mike was saying, 'Do you see that broken fence along there?'

'I see it.'

'Would you bet me an ice-cream cone I can't jump over it?'

'Sure I will. Do you want a cone, Mike?'

'Well, when we get this far on the road my father always

bets me an ice-cream cone I can't jump that fence.'

'Go ahead then.'

The little boy went leaping forward with short strong steps and took a broad jump over the broken scantling that was only a foot off the ground, and he landed on his knees on the long thick grass by the roadside and rolled over on his back, laughing. Greg ran after him and stood beside him, watching him rolling around while he shouted, 'Ho, ho, ho, ho, I fooled you. You've got to buy me a cone now.' Bending down over him, Greg grabbed him and lifted him high in the air, holding him tight while he squirmed with helpless laughter. When Mike was all out of breath, Greg put him down on the ground again.

When they came to the little bridge over the creek and were standing a moment watching the skeeters on the surface of the shallow water, Greg turned his head, looking far down between the hills, and he was surprised to see how the valley opened up from this point with the hills and the red barns with the hex signs over the doors and the dilapidated farmhouses flowing wide away into the immense valley of the Delaware that was full of noonday light; and down there the great river shone silver white on the green flat land, and farther beyond the river was cultivated land and maybe city land all rolled into soft blue hills, rising there grandly with the colour of a new, unknown country that was suddenly touched by the same sunlight that was overhead. Greg kept looking away off there with a leaping excitement. He had promised Mona that he would not tell Mike that Frank was not his father, but he could not stop thinking, 'Why can't I take him away with me now? Why shouldn't I do it?' Without answering, he gripped the boy's hand tight and began to walk faster, still looking ahead far down the valley.

'Isn't it a fine sight over there on a clear day, Mike?'

'That's nothing,' Mike said. 'From the top of our hill on a clear day you can almost see the ocean.'

'The ocean. There's no ocean there to see.'

'My father said one day if you could only see far enough you'd see an ocean, and that's the furthest of all away.'

'Think of all the towns you'd look over, Mike,' Greg said,

and they kept on walking fast, going straight ahead. But at
the little store where the roads crossed in what was called
the village, they stopped to buy ice-cream and an orange
drink for Mike. Behind the counter was a lean, slow-moving
man with a completely disinterested expression on his face,
who said with surprising amiability, 'You've got Molsens'
kid along with you, eh?' and he made a very comical face
at Mike, who was eating the ice-cream greedily.

Then they went on again, going farther down the road,
going toward the river and away from the hills, with Greg
always holding the boy's hand tight and making him trot beside him. They were off the red clay road and down on the
flat land where the road was gray and dusty when Mike said,
'I'm tired, Mister. Can't we stop a minute?'

'Are you very tired, Mike?'

'I want to sit down,' he said.

So they sat down by the ditch a few feet from the road in
long thick grass and weeds covered with gray dust, and they
didn't say anything, nor were they shy, but Mike merely
began to cross his legs at the ankles the way Greg had
crossed his. Then Greg, watching the boy, leaned all his
weight back on his hands, and Mike did that too, smiling
quickly. And after they had looked at each other a while,
Greg leaned forward and linked his hands around his knees,
whistling between his teeth and pretending to look seriously
across the fields; and soon he heard a thin whistle coming
from Mike, and glancing out of the corner of his eye, he saw
him, too, gravely staring at the fields. This moment became
the most beautiful moment that Greg could remember in his
life. As they sat there in the strong sun with the dust from
an automobile blowing over them, he began to think, "Maybe when he grows up he'll have many little gestures just like
mine. Maybe he'll hold his head on one side the way I do,
or his voice will sound like mine.' But while he was clinging
to this fine moment and feeling real joy in these thoughts,
he became aware that Mike, bit by bit, was snuggling closer
to him, and when he looked down at him he saw that his
eyes were slowly closing. He did not know why he was so
fearful of having him fall asleep. He dared not let him fall
asleep. 'Maybe you'd like to go back to the store, Mike, and

get another ice-cream cone,' he said quickly. They got up and they went back along the road, and Mike was walking with the solemn, expressionless face of a tired little boy.

After Mike had had another cone and another orange drink they both sat down together on the edge of the store veranda. Mike said suddenly, 'I wish mamma would come,' and he kept looking down the road toward the highway. He could not stop his head from drooping and bobbing up and down. It was past his lunch-time. As they sat close together, raising their heads together whenever a farmer or a few city people there for the summer came into the store, Greg was wondering how it was that Mona could be happy with Mike here in these hills. 'Don't you get tired of this little place, Mike?' he asked. Mike heard him but did not answer; he was doing nothing but opening his eyes extraordinarily wide and then letting them close slowly. 'I'll pick him up and carry him to the station,' Greg thought. 'Why should I leave him here in this melancholy place to grow up with the wild notions of that arrogant man?' And while he was planning and pondering he felt the boy's head heavy against him. Mike was in a sound sleep. For a long time Greg stared at the boy's closed eyes and at the long lashes touching the cheeks, and then he thought with utter misery, 'He was sitting there thinking and talking of Mona. I've no right whatever to take him away from her. I'm nothing to him really.' In a kind of panic he picked Mike up and began to hurry back into the hills, saying angrily, 'Why does Mona stay away like this and not care what happens to him?' He hurried on, going back to the house, clutching the sleeping boy and feeling more and more wretched.

He was almost in sight of the farmhouse before he heard the honking of a horn behind him. When he stepped off the road and looked back he saw the Molsens' old car swaying in the ruts. Mona was leaning out, waving her hand cheerfully.

Full of resentment, Greg said, 'He's sound asleep. What do you think of that?' and he stared at her as if she ought to give an account of herself to him. But she only said, 'The poor little boy,' without noticing Greg at all. And Frank, who had nodded with the old, good-natured tolerance, simply put out his arms for Mike, lifted him into the car and put him on Mona's knee. Without moving, Greg stood on the road, flustered, knowing only that he had not wanted Frank to take the boy from him in that way, and then he realized that they were wondering why he did not get into the car. So he sat in the back seat, leaning forward, with his head only a foot from Mike's, listening to Mona clucking sounds all over his head with her lips: and yet he was utterly detached from them. They did not even ask him where he had been with Mike, for it did not occur to them that anything important could have happened. So he said awkwardly, 'I must leave at once. I ought to have left an hour ago.'

'Why didn't you say you had to go? We're so sorry,' Mona said.

'It's all right. Everything's all right,' Greg said.

'Frank will drive you to the station whenever you're ready,' she said.

When they got to the house Greg got out of the car first, and he said eagerly, 'Let me carry him, Mona.'

'No. I'll carry him. You'll wake him,' she whispered.

'Wouldn't it be all right . . .' He intended to say, 'Wouldn't it be all right to wake him just to say good-bye?' but he fumbled, from wanting it so much, and he said instead, ' – all right just to carry him to the house?'

'Sh, sh, sh,' Mona said. Mike's head was moving on her shoulder and he was wetting his red lips with the tip of his tongue. This was while they were going toward the house. So Greg kept watching Mike eagerly, hardly knowing what to hope for, but anxious for something that would destroy the desolation within him. Once he even coughed, just at the door, and cleared his throat noisily, but there was nothing more for him than that one restless move of Mike's head.

And when Greg was ready to leave, he stood at the door with Mona. He wanted to go, to hurry, but he felt such emptiness in going. He wanted to shake hands heartily with Mona, to look at her directly, but his words came slow and groping, 'Good-bye, Mona. You were good to let me come.'

'Good-bye, Greg,' she said, smiling and calm. 'You come any time you want to come.'

'I will,' he said, trying hard to conceal the dragging emptiness inside him. There was one awkward moment, then he turned and was walking to the automobile; and then he heard Mona speaking in her mother voice, 'Did we wake you up, Mike? You still look half asleep.' Looking back, Greg saw Mike pushing past his mother and standing in front of her, and he was staring after him.

'Where are you going, Mister?' Mike called.

'Back to the city, Mike.'

'Good-bye, Mister,' Mike called, and he went running toward Greg. Grinning broadly, Greg bent down and caught him in his arms and lifted him high over his shoulders, shaking him and making him laugh again before putting him down. Then he kissed him with a quick eagerness and went on to the car, where Frank was waiting and watching. But before Greg could get into the car, Mike ran up to him again, only this time he stopped short a few feet away, with a puzzled, shy, wondering look on his face, feeling that someone he liked a lot and had felt very close to immediately was leaving him for some reason he did not understand.

But this look on Mike's face brought a surge of joy to Greg, and he, too, looked back a long time, half smiling, wanting so much to believe that the look on the boy's face came from the same kind of feeling that had been in his own heart when he had felt compelled to return to him. This one look, just making them both feel there might have been much love between them, was something like what he had waited for when he had watched Mike sleeping last night.

So Greg was smiling when he did finally get into the car. He waved cheerfully at Mona. He sat down beside Frank and looked at him in a direct friendly way. He almost wished Frank could forgive him for being a professional man who had done well in the last two years. But he couldn't help saying almost triumphantly as the car started, 'You certainly have to admit he's a fine boy.'

Amuck in the Bush

Gus Rapp, who worked in Howard's lumber-yard near the Spruceport dock on Georgian Bay, lived with his old man in a rough-cast cottage two doors along the road from the boss's house. The road faced the yard and the bay. He had worked in the lumber-yard as a labourer for five years, loafing a lot when the sun was hot. The boss didn't fire him because he looked after his old man. Gus didn't like the boss, Sid Walton, but liked watching Mrs. Walton, who often brought her husband a jug of iced tea on a hot day.

One day Gus was unloading planks from a box-car on the siding at the board platform near the general office. The sun was hot on the platform and burned through the boots of the men piling lumber.

The lumber-yard was on an inlet at the southern pier below the shipyard and the old tinned and weathered brown grain elevator. The inlet's water-line at the lumber-yard had gone back fifty feet, and smooth flat rock and small rocks baked in the sun. Piles of lumber with sloping tops were back a ways from the shore-line. The low brick buildings of the milling plant were at the foot of the pier. On the water side of the plant sawdust was heaped up and packed down. Farther back from the lumber-yard the long road, curving down from the station, followed the shore-line south beyond the town and the wooded picnic park, farther along skirting the bush at Little River, all the way to the rifle-ranges.

Gus Rapp, sweating a lot and chewing his moustache, could stand in the box-car door, looking up the street to the station and over the town to the blue mountains, where a red sun always set brilliantly.

Gus was working in the box-car, kneeling on the lumber close to the roof. The box-car had a stuffy smell of damp fresh wood. He was on his knees swinging the eight-by-two planks loose, shoving them down to the door where they slid into the hands and close to the hips of two men, who trudged across the platform, piling the planks on two sawhorses. By craning his neck to one side Gus could see through the door the wide-brimmed straw hat, the strong neck, and the thick shoulders of Sid Walton, who kept telling the men to show a little life. Gus didn't feel much like working. The planks slid down slowly. He wanted to lie flat on his belly and look out through a wide crack in the car to the milling plant, where little kids in bathing-suits were jumping down from the roof into the sawdust.

Walton yelled to get to work. Gus swore to himself. It was hot and he was sleepy and it would have been fine to sit with his back against the side of the car. Walton yelled and Gus yelled back. Sid told Gus to trade places with one of the men. Gus made sure where Walton stood on the platform and swung a plank loose, sliding it far down, swinging it in a wide curve. A man yelled and Walton ducked. Gus stood sullenly in the box-car door, his brown arm wiping his brown face, his hair and forehead damp. He jumped down to the platform.

'You damn big hunkie,' Walton yelled, running at Gus. He picked up an axe handle and whacked him hard three times across the back. Gus went down on his knees and hollered but got up kicking out. He tried to pick up a plank but the men grabbed him. They held him and he yelled, 'You big son of a bitch.' Sid was bigger than Gus and stood there laughing, legs wide, his big hands on his hips. Gus's back hurt him very much and he rubbed his shoulder.

The boss said seriously, 'All right, Rapp, you can clear out for good.'

Gus picked up his coat and cursed some more on the way over to the time office. He left the yard and went down past the station, cutting across the tracks north of the water-tower, intending to drink squirrel whiskey in Luke Horton's flour and feed store at the end of Main Street. His brown sweater was tucked in at his belt, he carried his coat, and his overalls were rolled four inches above his heavy boots.

He was alone with Luke in the room back of the store that smelt of dog biscuits and chicken feed. Gus sat at the small table feeling good, on the whiskey. Luke sat opposite, kidding him, nodding his bald head sympathetically and stroking his hairy arms.

'I can kick hell out of Walton,' Gus said finally.

'Sure you can, he's not so much.'

'Well, stick around, I'm going to.'

'Sid'll be up at the park at the ball game tonight,' Luke said.

'Damn the ball game.'

'Don't you want to show him up? Don't you want to have a go at him?'

'I'll get him alone when he won't know what hit him.'

'Mrs. Walton'll be there too, Gus.'

'I'd as leave have a go at her, eh, Luke? What do you say, Luke?'

Gus drank the whiskey out of a big cup and his long moustache got wet. He left Horton's place sucking his moustache. He hurried back past the lumber-yard to his house near Walton's place on the road by the bay. It hurt his head thinking how much he hated Walton. Let him put his hand on a gun and he'd maybe go down to the yard. He wasn't drunk, just feeling pretty good.

He went in the house and came out of the back door with the gun. Standing on the porch, he looked over into Walton's place. He didn't hurry back to the yard as he thought he would. He stood on the porch watching Mrs. Walton's big hips and firm back. She didn't speak to Gus because Sid had been having trouble with him, but wondered why he wasn't working. She and her six-year-old Anna were going berry-picking. He saw Mrs. Walton take a blue sweater coat from a nail in the porch and Anna brought a pail and two wooden boxes from the wood-shed.

Gus went around his side entrance to watch Mrs. Walton going back down the road with the girl. He hardly thought about going back to the lumber-yard. He sat on the front steps for twenty minutes, his head in his hands, spitting at a bug crawling on the picket walk and thinking about grabbing and hiding the kid that always became Mrs. Walton when he thought about it very much. 'That'll make Walton sweat all right,' he thought, and got up quickly, happy to go swinging along the road beyond the town to the berry-patch in the bush. He thought about stealing the kid but liked following Mrs. Walton. She had full red lips and a lot of black hair bunched over her ears.

Mrs. Walton passed out of sight behind a bunch of girls in automobiles on the road near the wooded picnic park. He hurried. In sight of the line of spruce trees back from the bay, he saw Mrs. Walton help the kid across the plank over the shallow Little River and follow the path into the bush.

She kept to the path and he followed through the trees, getting excited gradually. He didn't think much about the kid but felt he would take her away all right.

It was shady yet warm in the bush. The afternoon sun was strong. Brownish-green leaves were beginning to fall from the trees on the path. The berry-patch was at the southwest fringe of the bush. Mrs. Walton walked slowly with a strong stride, her wide-brimmed hat flapping regularly. It was warm in the bush and small noises sounded loud but it was cooling to look back through the trees to the blue water-line of the bay. Anna sometimes left her mother and played among the trees, hiding behind a big rock, calling to her mother that she couldn't find her. Many huge rounded rocks were in the bush. Gus followed carefully.

The trees thinned out at the fringe of the bush and the berry-patch. No one else was berry-picking. Mrs. Walton quickly started to work. The berries were black and heavy and fell with a soft little thud in the bottom of the pail. Gus, his side straight against a tree, watched her working, filling the small box, then dumping it into the pail close to her right leg. He watched until the pail was nearly three-quarters full. The little girl at the bush to the left was filling her box slowly and eating the berries. Gus dropped his coat and stepped from behind a tree, leaning his weight back off his step on the twigs. He thought he wanted to grab the kid, but sneaked up behind Mrs. Walton, her shoulder dipping up and down with the picking. He was behind her flinging his arms around her waist, pulling back heavily. The berries sprayed from the box.

'You got to let me have the kid,' he said.

She squealed, frightened at first, but seeing and knowing him, she got mad. 'Let me go, Gus Rapp, you big fool. Just you wait,' she said.

Gus said nothing and stopped thinking. He tried to trip and throw her down but she dropped to her knees, gripping hard at his belt and yelling to the girl to run. He banged her on the mouth and leaned forward and down heavily on her shoulders. The kid got as far as a big rock and stood screeching at him.

'You damn kid, shut up,' he yelled.

The woman kicked and scratched so he flopped down, smothering her, jerking her hands from his belt, getting her between his legs. She yelled, 'Anna, Anna,' but one big hand was on her throat, squeezing. Her clothes ripped and she rolled, but he held, hard pressing, bending her stiff back until the kid ran up and got hold of his ankle just above the thick boot, pulling; his arm swung free and caught the kid by the throat, slamming her down hard, choking her. He tugged and the woman's sweater came away. Twisting around and holding her arm, he grunted, 'You got to lie there,' three times. His legs were thick and heavy and she got weaker. His arms were hard and heavy but she bit deep into his forearm and he hollered, 'God damn it,' gouging her with his knees. He could hardly hold on and couldn't do anything. She was a big strong woman and the kid was yelling. Snarling, he jerked loose, spinning around and pulling at his gun. He felt crazy and didn't know why he was doing it. In at her he jumped shooting, three shots; and one grazed her forehead, gashing her cheek, and one went into a log. Then he ran at the kid to stop her yelling, taking her by the neck. Mrs. Walton said not very loud. 'Don't kill my little girl,' so he shot at the woman to kill, but missed. The kid got up and started to run. Gus took a jump at the woman, knocking her over easily, but didn't know what he wanted. He couldn't help thinking what his boss, Sid Walton, would do about it. Mrs. Walton got up slowly. He was scared, and

said, 'You better lie there.' Her skirt was torn and blood
was on her leg. He wanted to run away. She zigzagged
through the trees after her girl, pushing the hair out of her
eyes and crying softly as she ran. Gus hesitated, watching
her, then ran the other way, through the bush and away from
the town.

He ran and stumbled through the bush, quite sober and
scared, his foot pounding heavily as he banged into little
trees, his shaky legs hardly knowing where to go. He wanted
to get through the bush to the bay and along the road to
the rifle-ranges where he could maybe swipe a boat. After
running until he was tired, he stopped suddenly and thought
it was no use trying. He looked around the bush and down
to the bay. Between him and the lake-shore road was a line
of trees, branches and tops covered with thick old vines that
kids used for tree tag. He climbed a tree to the vines, his
feet slashing through green shoots, but the thick, springy
wood held him. He twined the vines round his legs, resting
most of his weight on a branch near the top. The branch
swayed and he sweated and cursed and shivered, waiting
for the dark. He looked through the leaves up the road and
away over the town at the orange sky on the blue mountains, and at the still waters of the bay and the fading skyline.

It got dark and no one came near the tree. He felt better
but very stiff and still shaky. It would fool everybody to go
back to the town, he muttered. He slid down the vines and
started running, his feet thudding steadily, his breath
whistling.

Where the road went back from the shore-line he left it,
going down by the waterworks and back of Harvey's fishing-
station. The big shadow of the wooded picnic park was
ahead and he was glad thick clouds were over the moon.
The lumber-yard was the best place to go because they'd
think it a silly place to look. The street lights seemed bright
and gave him a funny feeling over the stomach. Maybe
he should have gone looking for a box-car down at the
station, but he ran on to the lumber-yard. There was no
moon and he was sure the lumber was piled too high. He
went through the lumber-yard and over to the elevator.
The *Mississippi*, with a cargo of grain, was docked. He

crawled along the pier but boards were rotten farther out and missing in places. The moon came out and the lapping water underneath the pier scared him so much he lay flat on his belly, breathing drunkenly, trying to pray. 'Holy Mary, Holy Mary, Holy Mary, you can do it. I used to go to church, I used to go with the old lady.' A light was lit on the *Mississippi* and then two more. A pain was in his side but he went slinking back along the pier and out again to the lake-shore road. It was a shame having to pass his own house, and he thought of the old man sleeping in there.

Gus was surprised to feel hungry. He went along the side entrance of a house with a big veranda and crept into the garden where he pulled carrots and onions, stuffing them into his pockets. The back door opened and in the light he hugged the ground and shivered and puked and lay very still. But the door closed.

He took the road again, running along trying to eat the carrot, and puffing hard. The carrot had a bad taste. He wanted to get around the town and up to the hills. A night-bird screeched and his teeth chattered so much he had to drop the carrot. He slowed to a walk.

At a bend in the road near Bell's grocery-store he saw a shadow humped at the foot of a lamp-post and the hump became a man getting up from the gutter. Two other men came at him and Gus took three jumps forward. 'Oh, I thought you was a bear,' he said. He didn't have a chance to run. One of the men was Walton with his big hands, and John Woods, the constable, and Joel Hurst, the teamster. Gus whined out loud, 'Have pity on me.' They grabbed hold of him and Woods got ready to slug him, but he slumped loosely in their arms. He said hoarsely, 'I don't want to die, Mr. Walton. Please, Mr. Walton, for Christ sake.' Sid put his hand over Gus's mouth and squeezed until he spluttered and shut up. 'Truss the skunk up, boys,' he said. They bound his hands and put three ropes around his waist and shoulders, the ropes five feet long, a man at the end of each rope. They twisted the ropes around Gus and the lamp-post while Joel Hurst went in the grocery-store to phone for the police car. Gus couldn't cry, he was so scared of Walton. There was a gray streak of light in the sky across the bay.

The Bells and their four kids came out half dressed, forming a circle around Gus. Lights appeared in the windows of other houses. People were hearing that Gus was caught. Leaning his weight forward on the ropes, he stared hard at the bat that swooped and darted around the light overhead. And the police car came along deliberately and they had no trouble with Gus, and the car turned around and as Gus got in, the kids yelled and threw pebbles and sticks at him.

A Sick Call

Sometimes Father Macdowell mumbled out loud and took a deep wheezy breath as he walked up and down the room and read his office. He was a huge old priest, white-headed except for a shiny baby-pink bald spot on the top of his head, and he was a bit deaf in one ear. His florid face had many fine red interlacing vein lines. For hours he had been hearing confessions and he was tired, for he always had to hear more confessions than any other priest at the cathedral; young girls who were in trouble, and wild but at times repentant young men, always wanted to tell their confessions to Father Macdowell, because nothing seemed to shock or excite him, or make him really angry, and he was even tender with those who thought they were most guilty.

While he was mumbling and reading and trying to keep his glasses on his nose, the house girl knocked on the door and said, 'There's a young lady here to see, father. I think it's about a sick call.'

'Did she ask for me especially?' he said in a deep but slightly cracked voice.

'Indeed she did, father. She wanted Father Macdowell and nobody else.'

So he went out to the waiting-room, where a girl about

thirty years of age, with fine brown eyes, fine cheek-bones, and rather square shoulders, was sitting daubing her eyes with a handkerchief. She was wearing a dark coat with a gray wolf collar. 'Good evening, father,' she said. 'My sister is sick. I wanted you to come and see her. We think she's dying.'

'Be easy, child; what's the matter with her? Speak louder. I can hardly hear you.'

'My sister's had pneumonia. The doctor's coming back to to see her in an hour. I wanted you to anoint her, father.'

'I see, I see. But she's not lost yet. I'll not give her extreme unction now. That may not be necessary. I'll go with you and hear her confession.'

'Father, I ought to let you know, maybe. Her husband won't want to let you see her. He's not a Catholic, and my sister hasn't been to church in a long time.'

'Oh, don't mind that. He'll let me see her,' Father Macdowell said, and he left the room to put on his hat and coat.

When he returned, the girl explained that her name was Jane Stanhope, and her sister lived only a few blocks away. 'We'll walk and you tell me about your sister,' he said. He put his black hat square on the top of his head, and pieces of white hair stuck out awkwardly at the sides. They went to the avenue together.

The night was mild and clear. Miss Stanhope began to walk slowly, because Father Macdowell's rolling gait didn't get him along the street very quickly. He walked as if his feet hurt him, though he wore a pair of large, soft, specially constructed shapeless shoes. 'Now, my child, you go ahead and tell me about your sister,' he said, breathing with difficulty, yet giving the impression that nothing could have happened to the sister which would make him feel indignant.

There wasn't much to say, Miss Stanhope replied. Her sister had married John Williams two years ago, and he was a good, hard-working fellow, only he was very bigoted and hated all church people. 'My family wouldn't have anything to do with Elsa after she married him, though I kept going to see her,' she said. She was talking in a loud voice to Father Macdowell so that he could hear her.

'Is she happy with her husband?'

'She's been very happy, father. I must say that.'

'Where is he now?'

'He was sitting beside her bed. I ran out because I thought he was going to cry. He said if I brought a priest near the place he'd break the priest's head.'

'My goodness. Never mind, though. Does your sister want to see me?'

'She asked me to go and get a priest, but she doesn't want John to know she did it.'

Turning into a side street, they stopped at the first apartment house, and the old priest followed Miss Stanhope up the stairs. His breath came with great difficulty. 'Oh dear, I'm not getting any younger, not one day younger. It's a caution how a man's legs go back on him,' he said. As Miss Stanhope rapped on the door, she looked pleadingly at the old priest, trying to ask him not to be offended at anything that might happen, but he was smiling and looking huge in the narrow hallway. He wiped his head with his handkerchief.

The door was opened by a young man in a white shirt with no collar, with a head of thick, black, wavy hair. At first he looked dazed, then his eyes got bright with excitement when he saw the priest, as though he were glad to see someone he could destroy with pent-up energy. 'What do you mean, Jane?' he said. 'I told you not to bring a priest around here. My wife doesn't want to see a priest.'

'What's that you're saying, young man?'

'No one wants you here.'

'Speak up. Don't be afraid. I'm a bit hard of hearing,' Father Macdowell smiled rosily. John Williams was confused by the unexpected deafness in the priest, but he stood there, blocking the door with sullen resolution as if waiting for the priest to try to launch a curse at him.

'Speak to him, father,' Miss Stanhope said, but the priest didn't seem to hear her; he was still smiling as he pushed past the young man, saying, 'I'll go in and sit down, if you don't mind, son. I'm here on God's errand, but I don't mind saying I'm all out of breath from climbing those stairs.'

John was dreadfully uneasy to see he had been brushed

aside, and he followed the priest into the apartment and said loudly, 'I don't want you here.'

Father Macdowell said, 'Eh, eh?' Then he smiled sadly. 'Don't be angry with me, son,' he said. 'I'm too old to try and be fierce and threatening.' Looking around, he said, 'Where's your wife?' and he started to walk along the hall, looking for the bedroom.

John followed him and took hold of his arm. 'There's no sense in your wasting your time talking to my wife, do you hear?' he said angrily.

Miss Stanhope called out suddenly, 'Don't be rude, John.'

'It's he that's being rude. You mind your business,' John said.

'For the love of God let me sit down a moment with her, anyway. I'm tired,' the priest said.

'What do you want to say to her? Say it to me, why don't you?'

Then they both heard someone moan softly in the adjoining room, as if the sick woman had heard them. Father Macdowell, forgetting that the young man had hold of his arm, said, 'I'll go in and see her for a moment, if you don't mind,' and he began to open the door.

'You're not going to be alone with her, that's all,' John said, following him into the bedroom.

Lying on the bed was a white-faced, fair girl, whose skin was so delicate that her cheek-bones stood out sharply. She was feverish, but her eyes rolled toward the door, and she watched them coming in. Father Macdowell took off his coat, and as he mumbled to himself he looked around the room, at the mauve-silk bed-light and the light wall-paper with the tiny birds in flight. It looked like a little girl's room. 'Good evening, father,' Mrs. Williams whispered. She looked scared. She didn't glance at her husband. The notion of dying had made her afraid. She loved her husband and wanted to die loving him, but she was afraid, and she looked up at the priest.

'You're going to get well, child,' Father Macdowell said, smiling and patting her hand gently.

John, who was standing stiffly by the door, suddenly

moved around the big priest, and he bent down over the bed and took his wife's hand and began to caress her forehead.

'Now, if you don't mind, my son, I'll hear your wife's confession,' the priest said.

'No, you won't,' John said abruptly. 'Her people didn't want her and they left us together, and they're not going to separate us now. She's satisfied with me.' He kept looking down at her face as if he could not bear to turn away.

Father Macdowell nodded his head up and down and sighed. 'Poor boy,' he said. 'God bless you.' Then he looked at Mrş. Williams, who had closed her eyes, and he saw a faint tear on her cheek. 'Be sensible, my boy,' he said. 'You'll have to let me hear your wife's confession. Leave us alone a while.'

'I'm going to stay right here,' John said, and he sat down on the end of the bed. He was working himself up and staring savagely at the priest. All of a sudden he noticed the tears on his wife's cheeks, and he muttered as though bewildered, 'What's the matter, Elsa? What's the matter, darling? Are we bothering you? Just open your eyes and we'll get out of the room and leave you alone till the doctor comes.' Then he turned and said to the priest, 'I'm not going to leave you here with her, can't you see that? Why don't you go?'

'I could revile you, my son. I could threaten you; but I ask you, for the peace of your wife's soul, leave us alone.' Father Macdowell spoke with patient tenderness. He looked very big and solid and immovable as he stood by the bed. 'I liked your face as soon as I saw you,' he said to John. 'You're a good fellow.'

John still held his wife's wrist, but he rubbed one hand through his thick hair and said angrily, 'You don't get the point, sir. My wife and I were always left alone, and we merely want to be left alone now. Nothing is going to separate us. She's been content with me. I'm sorry, sir; you'll have to speak to her with me here, or you'll have to go.'

'No; you'll have to go for a while,' the priest said, patiently.

Then Mrs. Williams moved her head on the pillow and said jerkily, 'Pray for me, father.'

So the old priest knelt down by the bed, and with a sweet unruffled expression on his florid face he began to pray. At times his breath came with a whistling noise as though a rumbling were inside him, and at other times he sighed and was full of sorrow. He was praying that young Mrs. Williams might get better, and while he prayed he knew that her husband was more afraid of losing her to the Church than losing her to death.

All the time Father Macdowell was on his knees, with his heavy prayer book in his two hands, John kept staring at him. John couldn't understand the old priest's patience and tolerance. He wanted to quarrel with him, but he kept on watching the light from overhead shining on the one baby-pink bald spot on the smooth, white head, and at last he burst out, 'You don't understand, sir! We've been very happy together. Neither you nor her people came near her when she was in good health, so why should you bother her now? I don't want anything to separate us now; neither does she. She came with me. You see you'd be separating us, don't you?' He was trying to talk like a reasonable man who had no prejudices.

Father Macdowell got up clumsily. His knees hurt him, for the floor was hard. He said to Mrs. Williams in quite a loud voice, 'Did you really intend to give up everything for this young fellow?' and he bent down close to her so he could hear.

'Yes, father,' she whispered.

'In Heaven's name, child, you couldn't have known what you were doing.'

'We loved each other, father. We've been very happy.'

'All right. Supposing you were. What now? What about all eternity, child?'

'Oh, father, I'm very sick and I'm afraid.' She looked up to try to show him how scared she was, and how much she wanted him to give her peace.

He sighed and seemed distressed, and at last he said to John, 'Were you married in the church?'

'No, we weren't. Look here, we're talking pretty loud and it upsets her.'

'Ah, it's a crime that I'm hard of hearing, I know. Never

mind, I'll go.' Picking up his coat, he put it over his arm;
then he sighed as if he were very tired, and he said, 'I wonder
if you'd just fetch me a glass of water. I'd thank you for it.'

John hesitated, glacing at the tired old priest, who looked
so pink and white and almost cherubic in his utter lack of
guile.

'What's the matter?' Father Macdowell said.

John was ashamed of himself for appearing so sullen, so
he said hastily, 'Nothing's the matter. Just a moment. I won't
be a moment.' He hurried out of the room.

The old priest looked down at the floor and shook his
head; and then, sighing and feeling uneasy, he bent over
Mrs. Williams, with his good ear down to her, and he said,
'I'll just ask you a few questions in a hurry, my child. You
answer them quickly and I'll give you absolution.' He made
the sign of the cross over her and asked if she repented for
having strayed from the Church, and if she had often been
angry, and whether she had always been faithful, and if she
had ever lied or stolen – all so casually and quickly as if it
hadn't occurred to him that such a young woman could have
serious sins. In the same breath he muttered, 'Say a good act
of contrition to yourself and that will be all, my dear.' He
had hardly taken a minute.

When John returned to the room with the glass of water
in his hand, he saw the old priest making the sign of the
cross. Father Macdowell went on praying without even looking up at John. When he had finished, he turned and said,
'Oh, there you are. Thanks for the water. I needed it. Well,
my boy, I'm sorry if I worried you.'

John hardly said anything. He looked at his wife, who had
closed her eyes, and he sat down on the end of the bed. He
was too disappointed to speak.

Father Macdowell, who was expecting trouble, said
'Don't be harsh, lad.'

'I'm not harsh,' he said mildly, looking up at the priest.
'But you weren't quite fair. And it's as though she turned
away from me at the last moment. I didn't think she needed
you.'

'God bless you, bless the both of you. She'll get better,'

Father Macdowell said. But he felt ill at ease as he put on his coat, and he couldn't look directly at John.

Going along the hall, he spoke to Miss Stanhope, who wanted to apologize for her brother-in-law's attitude. 'I'm sorry if it was unpleasant for you, father,' she said.

'It wasn't unpleasant,' he said. 'I was glad to meet John. He's a fine fellow. It's a great pity he isn't a Catholic. I don't know as I played fair with him.'

As he went down the stairs, puffing and sighing, he pondered the question of whether he had played fair with the young man. But by the time he reached the street he was rejoicing amiably to think he had so successfully ministered to one who had strayed from the faith and had called out to him at the last moment. Walking along with the rolling motion as if his feet hurt him, he muttered, 'Of course they were happy as they were . . . in a worldly way. I wonder if I did come between them?'

He shuffled along, feeling very tired, but he couldn't help thinking, 'What beauty there was to his staunch love for her!' Then he added quickly, 'But it was just a pagan beauty, of course.'

As he began to wonder about the nature of this beauty, for some reason he felt inexpressibly sad.

A Cocky Young Man

The grape-vines, miles and miles of grape-vines all through that section of the country, had delighted him. Trees, orchards in patterns along radial lines. He had expected peach trees but so many grape-vines made him enthusiastic. An extraordinary section of the country, he said.

He hadn't talked so much since coming to the city and getting a job on the *Morning Empire*. He was on the lakeboat coming back from Niagara. Patterson, a reporter on the same paper, and his girl, sitting on a deck bench, had seen him leaning over the rail enjoying the sunset on the water. He had moved over near Patterson, taking off his large black fedora, and said, 'Hello, there.' He didn't sit down at once.

'Oh, hello, Hendricks,' Patterson said, frowning slightly. Patterson really didn't know him and wasn't friendly. Patterson had come into the city room one noontime last week when Hendricks, stepping out of the phone booth, saw him, and asked if he'd mind taking a story about a fire, he was awfully busy. Patterson took the story because he hadn't made up his mind about Hendricks's shiny fair hair combed back, his rosy pink cheeks, and little moustache. He had been sure Hendricks was of some importance. Afterwards he discovered Hendricks had started working that morning and was indignant to think he had taken the story.

Hendricks smiled at Patterson's girl and sat down on the bench beside her. Patterson shrugged his shoulders, staring moodily down at the water, making it clear to Hendricks he didn't enjoy his company. Hendricks grinned, understanding perfectly he wasn't wanted. He sat on the bench talking about the grape country, amusing Patterson's girl. He told her about wines and cooking and finally annoyed Patterson

102

by saying, 'What do you do about salads, old man?'

'Kind of clever, isn't he?' Patterson said to his girl.

'Oh, but he has such nice hair,' she said, laughing.

'No, I'm perfectly serious,' he insisted. 'There are no decent salads in the country.'

Patterson who wasn't impressed, tried hard to insult him, so he would move away. It was getting dark on the water and he wanted to move over close to his girl. He did put his arm around her shoulder. Hendricks also put his arm around her shoulder. Polite, but very determined, Patterson removed Hendricks's arm. The girl was amused. A cool breeze came from the water. Hendricks got up quickly and took off his light coat, throwing it around the girl's shoulders. Patterson thanked him gruffly and Hendricks sat on the bench an hour longer.

When the boat docked, he took the girl's hand and said, 'I must cook you a meal some day.'

'Of course,' she said laughing, 'Whereabouts?'

'At the King Edward,' he said, 'the chef is my friend.'

'Go right ahead, enjoy yourself,' Patterson said sarcastically.

In the editorial room next day Hendricks was friendly to Patterson and showed him some paperback French novels he had just bought, but Patterson still regarded him suspiciously. He was no more successful with other men on the staff. They called him 'The Duke', and were polite, only because it was uncertain what he might say if snubbed openly. Mr. H. C. Bronson, the assistant city editor, hesitated to bother him with obituaries in the early morning and said, 'How do you do,' nicely, when Hendricks came in and hung up his large black hat and thick knobby cane. In a week's time Mr. Bronson got used to Hendricks and gave him small assignments along with good ones.

The men saw there was something about Hendricks that worried Bronson and liked him for it. When Bronson, who had short fat legs, hurried down the office and put his hand on Hendricks's shoulder and said confidentially, 'Slide along on the street-car and get a picture of Mrs. Gorman, who died at the age of eighty-four, before you go on your assignment,' Hendricks said, 'I'm very sorry, I'm frightfully busy.' He didn't argue. He didn't even smile. He snubbed Bronson. The expression on his pink-and-white face completely discouraged Bronson, who quickly took the hand off his shoulder. Hendricks didn't go and get pictures, and Bronson didn't tell on him either, or put his hand on his shoulder again. No one understood why Bronson didn't tell on Hendricks, he had told so many stories to Bassler, the editor, about most men on the staff, and it was funny the way he was afraid of Hendricks.

The staff got accustomed to him gradually. In the mornings he sat at the long desk, waiting for the assignment book to come out, on fairly friendly terms with Charlie Lang, who wrote special stories mainly, and whom he had invited up to his room for target practice. Charlie Lang told everybody Hendricks actually had two pistols in his room, and the landlady, with whom he seemed to have a complete understanding, allowed him to practise in her cellar. Lang spent an evening in the cellar shooting poorly at a thick block of wood. Hendricks thanked him profusely, and Lang was embarrassed, for he had been decidely interested; not that he was becoming enthusiastic about Hendricks – he simply looked thoughtful, or had nothing to say when one of the boys said, 'Ho, ho, here comes the duke.'

In early August Hendricks was rarely seen around the office. He didn't talk much or ask fellows where they were eating. No one knew how he was amusing himself and no one asked him, but when he was to share an assignment the other man always seemed surprised to see him actually turn up. Hendricks told Patterson the job was getting uninteresting. That afternoon he went into Mr. Bassler's office and had a long talk. Bassler came out of the office, his arm around Hendricks's back. No one in the office at the time was much surprised to see Bassler's arm around Hendricks, for Hendricks from the first had created the impression that it ought to be so. It would have been different if Bronson had had his arm around him. Hendricks wouldn't stand for that. Bassler was nodding his small round head, his hand tapping Hendricks's shoulder. Hendricks had got himself a special assignment.

Those were the days of prohibition and a sensational

article appeared in the *Morning Empire* at the end of the week, a three-column investigation by an *Empire* reporter who found the most druggists downtown were selling whiskey over the counter. Everybody knew who had written it, though the article was competent. They called Hendricks a sneaking little rotter for writing the story. Mr. Bassler, standing at the office door, said loudly, 'You're the first man I've been able to get in three years, Hendricks, to dig into that story. My best men have come back empty-handed.'

Bronson, who carefully interpreted Bassler's moods, treated Hendricks respectfully, never bothering him in the morning. Hendricks often went into Bassler's office and twice was seen leaving the office of R. S. Smythe, the managing editor. Long stories were in the paper, further investigations by the same reporter, going from hotel to speakeasy, getting samples of beer mysteriously and sending them to the government analyst. Most hotel men were deliberately breaking the law. Pictures of either the government analyst, a bottle of beer or the long rubber tube the reporter had used to draw the beer from bottles, were in the papers every day.

All of it made Hendricks happy. He was also very unpopular, but came into the office when he felt like it, and rarely noticed Bronson. Often he sat near the front window looking down at the traffic moving on the street, tapping his teeth with a long yellow copy pencil. He was the only man on the staff who wasted spare time in the office, and felt secure. He made another effort to be friendly with Patterson, trying to loan him books and starting a literary conversation, but Patterson absolutely refused to take him seriously, telling him almost to his face that he was a faker. Hendricks, who appreciated that he was being insulted, only irritated Patterson further by making him think he ought to know better than to be insulting.

But he couldn't go for weeks discovering hotels that were selling over-strength beer. It had to end somewhere, so the editorial writers called official attention to the astonishing conditions in the city and Hendricks was taken off the assignment. He got a five-dollar increase.

He created an impression in the office that since there was no special work, it was necessary he be left alone and not annoyed with scalping, telephone work, and night assignments. He looked bored when in the office and now carefully avoided coming back after finishing an assignment.

He said to Patterson at noontime, 'Come on out and have a bite to eat with me.'

'I don't want to eat with you,' Patterson said rudely.

'Then come on up to my room and have some gin.'

'Not today, thanks.'

'Oh well, come on along, what's the difference?'

Patterson continued to refuse awkwardly but Hendricks wouldn't be snubbed and was so polite Patterson shrugged his shoulders and agreed to go with him. Going down in the elevator, Patterson noticed that the operator spoke respectfully to Hendricks, saying the missus had asked him to give her regards. They walked along the street, and Patterson wondered why Hendricks had been friendly with the elevator man.

'Do you know the elevator man?' Patterson said.

'He asked me out to see them last Sunday.'

'You're the first guy that's happened to.'

'So he said. They're nice people, and I'll go again but I wish they weren't so respectful.'

His room was tidy. On the walls were some photographs of paintings by Indian artists in California. Patterson looked at the paintings and Hendricks obligingly explained that some of those Indians were fine poets, and one of their best painters was going blind. He talked about Indian rugs while he opened the drawer and took out a bottle of gin. Patterson was sitting on the edge of the bed. Hendricks gave him a glass, and half filled it, then he said, 'Talking about liquor, how did you like my booze stories? Weren't they fine?'

'Sure, I'll tell you what I thought of them.'

'Why waste time? Have a drink first. They were wonderful. They were just what Bassler wanted.'

'What are you getting at?'

'You'd keep a thing to yourself, wouldn't you? Here, fill up the glass.'

'Sure I can – whoa, that'll do.'

'They were some stories.'

'They were worse than that.'

'They were the easiest stories a man ever wrote.'

'Say, boy, what are you driving at?'

'Well, I faked most of them right here in this room, see.'

'I'll be damned. I might have known it, you're such a queer egg.'

'Not at all, old man. When I first suggested it to Bassler he told me what he had been trying to get for years. He told me everything he had ever thought about it, so I simply confirmed his opinions.'

The story affected Patterson the way the target practice had affected Lang, and he laughed, thinking of Bassler. Most fellows talked and whispered about Bassler and Bronson, but Hendricks, without ever discussing them, understood them perfectly.

The last two weeks in August were unpleasant for Hendricks. He did routine work, law courts, churches and schools, city hall, and was unpopular on the beats because he was a snob and had no respect for officials who gave out news. Three times he was scooped and received notes from Mr. Bassler. The notes were gentle and persuasive at first, then they became nasty and suggestive. Hendricks, reading a note standing near the city desk, wasn't much concerned and tearing it up, threw it in the basket. The way he tossed the pieces in the basket offended Mr. Bronson.

Hendricks became more popular when it was apparent that Bassler lost interest in him, though no one was really cordial to him. Bronson, who saw that Hendricks had become unimportant to Bassler, treated him abruptly, finding fault with his work, and keeping him busy early in the morning. Lang said to Patterson that Hendricks had become simply a cocky young man, and there was no room for cocky young men on the *Empire*. Hendricks looked bored. The weather was hot, he wore the big black fedora, and his hair was combed perfectly, but he was bored.

On week-ends he went out of town or took boat trips across the lake. He heard that Charlie Lang was going to Montreal for a week-end, so he took the address, promising to see him there, and actually turned up, and got Charlie very drunk. Then he took him to a hotel and ordered an elaborate dinner, very gratified because he was to have an audience. Three waiters brought mixing bowls to the table, and Hendricks was happy, and finally persuaded the chef to allow him to go into the kitchen. Telling about it, Charlie Lang regretted he had been a little drunk, he would have appreciated it so much more.

Late in August the Rotarians held their international convention in the city. Thousands of Rotarians from all over the world on the streets, in the hotels, the shows, and in the evenings, out at the convention hall in Exhibition Park. The papers gave a full page to the convention every day, though it hadn't much news value. In the afternoons Lang and Patterson were out at the Exhibition, and all night they worked on human-interest stories.

Hendricks called at the Exhibition press room one hot afternoon and said to Patterson, 'Bassler sent me out here.'

'What on earth for?' Patterson said, not in good humour. He had been working all night and Hendricks's hat irritated him. Hendricks didn't create a good impression in the press room.

'Oh, there's a fat lady coming out here, Lena the champion fat lady, or something like that. Bassler wants me to interview her,' he said.

Patterson was irritated because the convention was nearly finished, and few good human-interest stories left, and all afternoon he had been walking in the hot sun, talking to stray Rotarians, hoping to pick up something, and of course Bassler had to send out a man like Hendricks to spoil the fat lady story.

'She ought to be over in the flower building in half an hour,' he said, turning away, and going out of the door. Hendricks hurried after him, tapping his heel with the heavy cane.

'Just a minute, Pat,' he said.

'I'm in a hurry.'

'But it's really too hot, don't you think?'

'Of course, it's too hot.'

'See here, Pat, you know this place better than I do. Where is a good tree?'

They found a tree near the lake. Hendricks took off his

coat and made a pillow. He lay down, putting the cane carefully alongside his leg. He tilted the black hat over his eyes.

'What about the fat lady?' Patterson said.

'Let her go to hell,' Hendricks said.

Patterson didn't see him again till two o'clock in the morning. All the Rotarians had come out to the Exhibition grounds for the banquet, cars were jammed on the road along the waterfront, and Patterson and Lang were very busy. They saw Hendricks at two o'clock in the morning in the *Empire* office. He was bringing in a fake interview with the fat lady, who had avoided him, he said. Lang, who was in good humour because the convention was over, said the three of them should go across to Bowles's for a cup of coffee. They drank coffee in Bowles's and smoked cigarettes till Hendricks said, 'I thought I'd tell you fellows I was quitting the job.'

'When?' Patterson asked.

'Oh, in about three weeks.'

He understood that Bassler was letting him out anyway, so he had decided to quit. Three months was a long time in one place. He had written his resignation to take effect in three weeks, and Bassler couldn't decently fire him in the meantime.

'I heard the little beast Bronson talking to Bassler,' he explained. In any event he had intended to go west. There was a shortage of farm labourers. Lang was sympathetic. They talked about the West, and harvesting. Hendricks told them his uncle had a coffee plantation in Brazil, where he had been most of last year. He had intended to go on down to the Argentine, but had had to change his plans. He talked sincerely and more rapidly than usual.

'It all helps, all sort of fits in,' he said.

'There's no doubt, it's great experience,' Patterson said.

'Yes, it is, and say, have you fellows ever read *Anna Karenina*?' He began to talk about the book and Tolstoi, fingering the brim of his hat. *Anna Karenina* was the most wonderful book in the world, he said. He wanted to write one book. He didn't want to be an author, just write one book something like *Anna Karenina*.

'So I know what I want to do,' he said mildly. 'And there's nothing to worry about.'

'But what do you know about harvesting?'

'Not a damned thing.'

At eight o'clock one evening Patterson and his girl went down to the station to say good-bye to Hendricks. The waiting-room and the station platform were crowded with harvesters, old men, students, bums, huskies, looking for work. They carried heavy bags and bundles. Patterson and his girl walked along the station platform, looking for Hendricks on the harvesters' special. The train was crowded, harvesters singing sentimental songs, playing mouth-organs and ukuleles, groups having a good time, ready for the long trip.

Patterson saw him leaning out of the window. His suit was pressed carefully and he had on the big hat. He was keeping time to a song, his arm out of the window, banging the thick cane against the side of the car. His cheeks looked shiny and pink. He waved his hat at Patterson's girl.

'Oh, what a shame,' he said, grinning.

'What's the matter?' she asked.

'I never got a chance to mix a salad for you. What a shame.'

Patterson, who seemed suddenly to have become fond of Hendricks, asked him quietly if he was sure he ought to go harvesting, the work was so heavy.

'If I don't like it, I don't necessarily have to keep at it,' he said smiling. 'But the transportation is much cheaper this way, though, don't you think so?'

When the train moved out, he was leaning far out of the window, waving the big hat, and smiling politely.

Getting On in the World

That night in the tavern of the Clairmont Hotel, Henry
Forbes was working away at his piano and there was the
usual good crowd of brokers and politicians and sporting
men sitting around drinking with their well-dressed women.
A tall, good-natured boy in the bond business, and his girl,
had just come up to the little green piano, and Henry had
let them amuse themselves playing a few tunes, and then he
had sat down himself again and had run his hand the length
of the keyboard. When he looked up there was this girl
leaning on the piano and beaming at him.

She was about eighteen and tall and wearing one of those
sheer black dresses and a little black hat with a veil, and
when she moved around to speak to him he saw that she had
the swellest legs and an eager, straightforward manner.

'I'm Tommy Gorman's sister,' she said.

'Why, say . . . you're . . .'

'Sure. I'm Jean,' she said.

'Where did you come from?'

'Back home in Buffalo,' she said. 'Tommy told me to be
sure and look you up first thing.'

Tommy Gorman had been his chum; he used to come into
the tavern almost every night to see him before he got con-
sumption and had to go home. So it did not seem so surprising to see his sister standing there instead. He got her a
chair and let her sit beside him. And in no time he saw that
Tommy must have made him out to be a pretty glamorous
figure. She understood that he knew everybody in town, that
big sporting men like Jake Solloway often gave him tips on
the horses, and that a man like Eddie Convey, who just
about ran the city hall and was one of the hotel owners, too,

called him by his first name. In fact, Tommy had even told her that the job playing the piano wasn't much, but that bumping into so many big people every night he was apt to make a connection at any time and get a political job, or something in a stockbroker's office.

The funny part of it was she seemed to have joined herself to him at once; her eyes were glowing, and as he watched her swinging her head around looking at the important clients, he simply couldn't bear to tell her that the management had decided that the piano wouldn't be necessary any more and that he mightn't be there more than two weeks.

So he sat there pointing out people she might have read about in the newspapers. It all came out glibly, as if each one of them was an old friend, yet he actually felt lonely each time he named somebody. 'That's Thompson over there with the horn-rimmed glasses. He's the mayor's secretary,' he said. 'That's Bill. Bill Henry over there. You know, the producer. Swell guy, Bill.' And then he rose up in his chair. 'Say, look, there's Eddie Convey,' he said. As he pointed he got excited, for the big, fresh-faced, hawk-nosed Irishman with the protruding blue eyes and the big belly had seen him pointing. He was grinning. And then he raised his right hand a little.

'Is he a friend of yours?' Jean asked.

'Sure he is. Didn't you see for yourself?' he said. But his heart was leaping. It was the first time Eddie Convey had ever gone out of his way to notice him. Then the world his job might lead to seemed to open up and he started chattering breathlessly about Convey, thinking all the time, beneath his chatter, that if he could go to Convey and get one little word from him, and if something bigger couldn't be found for him he at least could keep his job.

He became so voluble and excited that he didn't notice how delighted she was with him till it was time to take her home. She was living uptown in a rooming-house where there were a lot of theatrical people. When they were sitting on the stone step a minute before she went in she told him that she had enough money saved up to last her about a month. She wanted to get a job modelling in a department store. Then he put his arm around her and there was a soft glowing wonder in her face.

'It seems like I've known you for years,' she said.

'I guess that's because we both know Tommy.'

'Oh, no,' she said. Then she let him kiss her hard. And as she ran into the house she called that she'd be around to the tavern again.

It was as if she had been dreaming about him without even having seen him. She had come running to him with her arms wide open. 'I guess she's about the softest touch that's come my way,' he thought, going down the street. But it looked too easy. It didn't require any ambition, and he was a little ashamed of the sudden, weakening tenderness he felt for her.

She kept coming around every night after that and sat there while he played the piano and sometimes sang a song. When he was through for the night, it didn't matter to her whether they went any place in particular, so he would take her home. Then they got into the habit of going to his room for a while. As he watched her fussing around, straightening the room up or maybe making a cup of coffee, he often felt like asking her what made her think she could come bouncing into town and fit into his life. But when she was listening eagerly, and kept sucking in her lower lip and smiling slowly, he felt indulgent with her. He felt she wanted to hang around because she was impressed with him.

It was the same when she was sitting around with him in the tavern. She used to show such enthusiasm that it became embarrassing. You like a girl with you to look like some of the smart blondes who came into the place and have that lazy, half-mocking aloofness that you have to try desperately to break through. With Jean laughing and talking a lot and showing all her straightforward warm eagerness people used to turn and look at her as if they'd like to reach out their hands and touch her. It made Henry feel that the pair of them looked like a couple of kids on a merry-go-round. Anyway, all that excitement of hers seemed to be only something that went with the job, so in the last couple of nights, with the job fading, he hardly spoke to her and got a little savage pleasure out of seeing how disappointed she was.

She didn't know what was bothering him till Thursday night. A crowd from the theatre had come in, and Henry was feeling blue. Then he saw Eddie Convey and two middle-aged men who looked like brokers sitting at a table in the corner. When Convey seemed to smile at him, he thought bitterly that when he lost his job people like Convey wouldn't even know him on the street. Convey was still smiling, and then he actually beckoned.

'Gees, is he calling me?' he whispered.

'Who?' Jean asked.

'The big guy, Convey,' he whispered. So he wouldn't make a fool of himself he waited till Convey called a second time. Then he got up nervously and went over to him. 'Yes, Mr. Convey,' he said.

'Sit down, son,' Convey said. His arrogant face was full of expansive indulgence as he looked at Henry and asked, 'How are you doing around here?'

'Things don't exactly look good,' he said. 'Maybe I won't be around here much longer.'

'Oh, stop worrying, son. Maybe we'll be able to fix you up.'

'Gee, thanks, Mr. Convey.' It was all so sudden and exciting that Henry kept on bobbing his head, 'Yes, Mr. Convey.'

'How about the kid over there,' Convey said, nodding toward Jean. 'Isn't it a little lonely for her sitting around?'

'Well, she seems to like it, Mr. Convey.'

'She's a nice-looking kid. Sort of fresh and – well . . . uh, fresh, that's it.' They both turned and looked over at Jean, who was watching them, her face excited and wondering.

'Maybe she'd like to go to a party at my place,' Convey said.

'I'll ask her, Mr. Convey.'

'Why don't you tell her to come along, see. You know, the Plaza, in about an hour. I'll be looking for her.'

'Sure, Mr. Convey,' he said. He was astonished that

Convey wanted him to do something for him. 'It's a pleasure,' he wanted to say. But for some reason it didn't come out.

'Okay,' Convey said, and turned away, and Henry went back to his chair at the piano.

'What are you so excited about?' Jean asked him.

His eyes were shining as he looked at her little black hat and the way she held her head to one side as if she had just heard something exhilarating. He was trying to see what it was in her that had suddenly joined him to Convey. 'Can you beat it!' he blurted out. 'He wants you to go up to a party at his place.'

'Me?'

'Yeah, you.'

'What about you?'

'He knows I've got to stick around here, and, besides, there may be a lot of important people around there, and there's always room at Convey's parties for a couple of more girls.'

'I'd rather stay here with you,' she said.

Then they stopped whispering because Convey was going out, the light catching his bald spot.

'You got to do things like that,' Henry coaxed her. 'Why, there isn't a girl around here who wouldn't give her front teeth to be asked up to his place.'

She let him go on telling her how important Convey was and when he had finished, she asked, 'Why do I have to? Why can't we just go over to your place?'

'I didn't tell you. I didn't want you to know, but it looks like I'm through around here. Unless Convey or somebody like that steps in I'm washed up,' he said. He took another ten minutes telling her all the things Convey could do for people.

'All right,' she said. 'If you think we have to.' But she seemed to be deeply troubled. She waited while he went over to the head waiter and told him he'd be gone for an hour, and then they went out and got a cab. On the way up to Convey's place she kept quiet, with the same troubled look on her face. When they got to the apartment house, and they were standing on the pavement, she turned to him. 'Oh, Henry, I don't want to go up there.'

'It's just a little thing. It's just a party,' he said.

'All right. If you say so, okay,' she said. Then she suddenly threw her arms around him. It was a little crazy because he found himself hugging her tight too. 'I love you,' she said. 'I knew I was going to love you when I came.' Her cheek, brushing against his, felt wet. Then she broke away.

As he watched her running in past the doorman that embarrassing tenderness he had felt on other nights touched him again, only it didn't flow softly by him this time. It came like a swift stab.

In the tavern he sat looking at the piano, and his heart began to ache, and he turned around and looked at all the well-fed men and their women and he heard their deep-toned voices and their lazy laughter and he suddenly felt corrupt. Never in his life had he had such a feeling. He kept listening and looking into these familiar faces and he began to hate them as if they were to blame for blinding him to what was so beautiful and willing in Jean. He couldn't sit there. He got his hat and went out and started to walk up to Convey's.

Over and over he told himself he would go right up to Convey's door and ask for her. But when he got to the apartment house and was looking up at the patches of light, he felt timid. It made it worse that he didn't even know which window, which room was Convey's. She seemed lost to him. So he walked up and down past the doorman, telling himself she would soon come running out and throw her arms around him when she found him waiting.

It got very late. Hardly anyone came from the entrance. The doorman quit for the night. Henry ran out of cigarettes, but he was scared to leave the entrance. Then the two broker friends of Convey's came out, with two loud-talking girls, and they called a cab and all got in and went away. 'She's staying. She's letting him keep her up there. I'd like to beat her. What does she think she is?' he thought. He was so sore at her that he exhausted himself, and then felt weak and wanted to sit down.

When he saw her coming out, it was nearly four o'clock in the morning. He had walked about ten paces away, and turned, and there she was on the pavement, looking back at the building.

'Jean,' he called, and he rushed at her. When she turned, and he saw that she didn't look a bit worried, but blooming, lazy, and proud, he wanted to grab her and shake her.

'I've been here for hours,' he said. 'What were you doing up there? Everybody else has gone home.'

'Have they?' she said.

'So you stayed up there with him!' he shouted. 'Just like a tramp.'

She swung her hand and smacked him on the face. Then she took a step back, appraising him contemptuously. She suddenly laughed. 'On your way. Get back to your piano,' she said.

'All right, all right, you wait, I'll show you,' he muttered. 'I'll show everybody.' He stood watching her go down the street with a slow, self-satisfied sway of her body.

The Rejected One

Karl was bringing her along the street early one winter evening. He was taking her to meet his people for the first time. As they walked in step with her elbow snug against his side, she was silent, as though feeling his uneasiness and sharing his thoughts. Karl kept on glancing intently at her smooth powdered face, at her fine massive shoulders, and at the thick blonde hair on her neck. He was wishing she had on a dark dress that might have looked more quietly elegant than this flowing green one. Even her hair, maybe, was too long and yellow, and her wide-brimmed black hat drooping low over her face gave her a startling full red mouth. He was trying to remember how she had looked that first time he had seen her, before he had grown to love her, but he could not remember, and as she turned and smiled at him, he seemed to feel all the warmth and roundness of her moving close to him.

'Remember that Mother's an invalid,' he said cautiously. 'She does funny things sometimes.'

'I'll remember,' she said timidly. Then she began to look puzzled, as if his seriousness had begun to frighten her.

'Anyway, you'll like my brother,' he said reassuringly. 'I feel sure of that.'

When they went into the house, Mamie hung back a little behind Karl so that Karl's brother and his young wife could not quite see her as they came out of the sitting-room to the hall. Karl's brother was tall and slender, and had big deep-set brown eyes that kept shifting around restlessly. Karl went up to him, took his arm affectionately, and said, 'This is Mamie, John. I know you'll like her. And you, too, Helen.'

Then they all turned and looked at Mamie, who had been trying to keep close to Karl, but was now alone. She seemed to feel that his brother and his wife were looking at her more shrewdly than Karl had ever done. She swung her head to one side with awkward shyness. The young wife, tall and slim, with a little head and a dainty face, and girlish in her simple gray dress, glanced swiftly at her husband and her face grew troubled, but she said graciously, 'Won't you come in and sit down?' and she led the way into the sitting-room.

Mamie then seemed to find the words she had prepared so carefully. 'Gee, I'm mighty glad to see you, John,' she said. 'And you, too, Mrs. Henderson. I feel like we were old friends almost.' There was so much warmth in the way she put out her large hands that Mrs. Henderson smiled good-naturedly. 'Karl has talked to us, too,' she said. 'Shall we go and meet Karl's mother?'

At the other end of the long room, a white-haired old lady was sitting in an invalid's chair. She was dozing, with her head drooping forward, but when they all came toward her she opened her eyes, which were blue and soft, and so much like Karl's. 'I'd like you to meet a young lady, Mother,' Karl said.

'Who is it, Karl?'

'It's Mamie. I'm awfully fond of her, Mother.'

'Tell her to come here and let me see her.'

Karl was proud of the way Mamie stepped across the room to meet his mother: she seemed to walk across the carpet like a lovely mannequin, with a mysterious smile on her face as though she had been practising for this moment for a long time. She had never looked so elegant as she did now to Karl, so he couldn't understand why his brother turned his head away and would not look at her, or why Helen began to bite her lip and look angry.

'What's the matter, John?' he whispered.

'Nothing. Nothing at all. What do you mean, Karl?'

Mamie was saying sweetly, 'Good evening, Mrs. Henderson. Karl has often talked about you to me, so of course I've been most anxious to meet you,' but she spoke with an almost mechanical sedateness. Then she suddenly smiled and said simply, 'What I mean, I guess, is that you're Karl's mother and that's enough for me,' and she grinned broadly. For a long time old Mrs. Henderson stared at her, and then her thin lips began to tremble. Then she said bluntly like one wise woman speaking to another and sure that she will be understood, 'Karl is just a boy. I suppose you know he's just a boy. . . . Sit down, though, and have them get you a cup of coffee. Please don't pay any attention to me. I'm very tired.' The old lady took a deep breath, closed her eyes, and would not open them again.

Mamie seemed too bewildered to move: something seemed to be holding her to the spot in spite of her resentment, while her face reddened. But she started to laugh and said, 'For the love of Mike, why are we all acting so stiff?' And yet she moved over closer to Karl with a kind of independent swagger. The way old Mrs. Henderson had closed her eyes made them all feel uneasy. Young Mrs. Henderson was instantly anxious to be hospitable and friendly to Mamie. But Karl noticed that his brother was still glancing furtively at her in the way men turn on the street to watch a flashy woman who has just passed by, and he did not know whether to like this or not. 'Let's sit down,' he said, 'and I'll tell you a story I heard today.'

With a fine flow of words and many easy gestures, he told one of his favourite jokes, and for the first time they heard Mamie's loud, deep, husky laughter.

'Shall I tell one now, Karl?' she said.

'Go ahead, Mamie.'

'I'd better make sure it's not the one about the travelling salesman and the farmer's daughter, eh?' she said, wrinkling the skin around her eyes slyly. But she told no story. She began to talk quite wildly, as if she had to keep on chattering or grow desperate, and all the while Karl was trying to motion to her to be quiet. When she did see him staring at her, she grew sullen and did not know what to say. For some reason that he could not figure out, Karl was ashamed. He felt Mamie's fumbling uneasiness there with his people and he remembered how proud she had been the first time she had taken him to her home. He remembered how her father, a big, rough, tousle-headed, genial man, had jumped up hastily and put down his glasses and his paper and how he had talked to him warmly and with such respect.

'I'll go and get the coffee,' young Mrs. Henderson was saying. When she had gone half-way across the room, she stopped, turned, and looked back, looking really at Karl, whom she liked and admired so much because he had such a fine instinct for pleasing people with his impulsive ways, and in this one glance backward trying to figure out what he could see in a buxom, gaudy-looking girl like Mamie. She called out, 'Do you want to help me, John?' and she waited so that her husband dared not refuse to follow her.

As soon as they left, Karl said irritably to Mamie, 'I never heard you talking so much. What's the matter?'

'I don't know. I just feel crazy.'

'What's the matter, Mamie? Don't you think they're nice?'

'Sure I think they're nice. They're fine people, but I just feel crazy. Maybe it's the way they look at me. I don't know what I'm saying.'

When John returned, he was smiling and trying to be very gay. And yet as he walked up and down making many gracious little remarks, he was obviously thinking of the conversation he had had with his wife. He was very fond of his young brother. Every time he passed him, walking up and down, he began to look at him more sympathetically. He never stopped talking to Mamie, but he was talking more quietly and easily now, and sometimes gently as if he knew all about her. The peaceful tone of his brother's voice suddenly filled Karl with hope, and he became so eager to ask him if he liked Mamie that he said, 'Why don't you go and help Helen with the coffee, Mamie?'

'All right,' Mamie said reluctantly. But she got up very slowly. She walked across the room with her head down, as if she could not bear to go into the kitchen and be alone with young Mrs. Henderson. Turning once, she looked back, almost pleading with Karl.

Karl said quickly to his brother, 'How do you like her, John?'

'I like her all right,' John said cautiously. But he would not look directly at his brother. Then he said mildly, 'Do you think you're in love with her, Karl?'

'I think I am, John.'

'Where did you meet her?'

'At Coney Island with a fellow from the office.'

'I suppose you know all about her.'

'All there is to know, John.'

'I don't know what to say, Karl. She looks like a . . . She looks like a rather easy-going girl.' John was hating himself for speaking this way about his brother's girl, but he was very fond of Karl and he felt he had to speak. 'Like a . . . Maybe I mean not like a girl for you.'

'You may have noticed the unimportant things,' Karl said. Then his face looked tense and he said suddenly, 'I'm going to marry her.'

'Don't do it, Karl. It'll finish you before you start. You'll have to go her way the rest of your life. You'll see later on. Please don't.'

Then Mamie and Helen returned with the coffee. But it was impossible now to make an easy conversation. Maybe it was because the mother, solemn, aloof, and forbidding, was dozing there in her chair and they were suddenly aware of her. They looked at each other and spoke and the sentences trailed away. Mamie had become suddenly quiet; a few fumbling words came to her, then she was still. She had begun to feel very strongly that they were reticent because they had such love for Karl, and she was trying to put it against her own love, and it gave her a wondering, shy, and lonely look. She sat very straight in her bright-green dress, with a cup of coffee in her hand and the light shining on her massive shoulders and fair hair under her big hat. Her mouth looked wide, red, and barbaric. Karl noticed the simple candour in her eyes as she looked around fearfully, and with this stillness that was in her now she looked as he had so often seen her look when he had loved her most. He felt excited. He kept glancing restlessly at his brother, wondering why he, too, did not notice Mamie now.

Then Mamie said hesitantly, 'I think we'd better go now.'

'Maybe we'd better,' Karl said.

'You say good-bye to your mother for me,' she said to John.

At the door, they all shook hands. 'Well, I wanted to meet you all and I met you,' Mamie said. 'Good night.'

'Good night. Good night, Karl,' they said.

Outside Karl and Mamie were silent. They walked in step. It was fine and clear out on the street. Karl was thinking, 'Why didn't they look at Mamie when she was sitting there at the end? They would have seen what she's really like.' He felt angry. 'That was the only time they had a chance to see what she was really like.' He went on thinking how splendid she had looked sitting there, how she had suddenly been changed and had begun to look like such a fine person. 'Gee, you'd think they would have noticed it,' he thought.

He heard Mamie asking quietly, 'What do you think they thought of me?'

'I don't know yet,' he said casually. But then he could not stop remembering how his brother had said so earnestly, 'Please don't do it,' and the voice almost coaxing, the voice gentle and full of love. 'She looks like a . . .' He heard the voice still trying to finish the sentence. Now there was not fear but dreadful uneasiness and then heavy deadness within him.

'What do you think of Helen?' he asked.

'I didn't like her,' Mamie said, 'she's a little snip.'

'She was nice to you.'

'She was nice to me just as if I was her idea of a fallen woman.' Then she added in a rage, 'I'd like to wring her neck.'

'Maybe she didn't like you either,' he said angrily.

'I don't want her to.'

'She's nicer than anyone you'll ever meet,' he said sharply.

This sharp hostility, rising so quickly, startled them, but they welcomed it with eagerness. They wanted to hurt each other savagely, so they could pull against whatever was holding them together. They kept on hurting each other till she said quickly, 'I'll not walk along here feeling you hate me. Don't come home with me. I'll go alone,' and she pushed him away from her and hurried across the road.

'Let her go if she feels that way,' Karl thought. So he stood and watched her cross the street, watched the swaying of her hips, her legs moving, and the blonde hair at her neck. He almost felt the firmness and warmth and roundness of her passing away from him.

Then he darted after her and called out, 'Mamie!'

'Go away!' she called as she turned. Her face showed all that was breaking inside her. Her face, bewildered and desolate, showed how well she knew they had rejected her.

He watched her fading out of sight while he remembered all the happiness he had expected to have with her. He started to follow her slowly, feeling sure he was doing something irrevocable that could not be undone. But he only knew that he dared not let her out of sight.

An Escapade

Snow fell softly and the sidewalks were wet but Mrs. Rose Carey had on her galoshes and enjoyed feeling thick snow crunching underfoot. She walked slowly, big flakes falling on her lamb coat and clinging to hair over her ears, the lazily falling snow giving her, in her thick warm coat, a fine feeling of self-indulgence. She stood on the corner of Bloor and Yonge, an impressive build of a woman, tall, stout, good-looking for forty-two, and watched the traffic-signal.

Few people were on this corner at half past eight, Sunday evening. A policeman, leaning against a big plate-glass window, idly watched her cross the road and look up the street to the clock on the firehall and down the street at the theatre lights, where Reverend John Simpson held Sunday service. She had kept herself late deliberately, intending to enter the theatre quietly and unnoticed, and sit in a back seat, ready to leave as soon as the service was over. She walked with dignity, bothered by her own shyness, and thinking of her husband asking if Father Conley was speaking tonight in the Cathedral. She didn't want to think of Father Conley, or at least she didn't want to compare him with Mr. Simpson, who was simply interesting because all her bridge friends were talking about him. It was altogether different about Father Conley.

She was under the theatre lights, turning in, and someone said to her: 'This way, lady. Step this way, right along now.'

She stopped abruptly, nervously watching the little man with the long nose and green sweater, pacing up and down in front of the entrance, waving his hands. He saw her hesitating and came close to her. He had on a funny flat black hat, and walked with his toes turned way out. 'Step

124

lively, lady,' he muttered, wagging his head at her.

She was scared of him and would have turned away but a man got out of a car at the curb and smiled at her. 'Don't be afraid of Dick,' he said. The man had on a christie and had gray h r a tie-pin in a wide black tie. He was going into the theatre, but had noticed her embarrassment.

'Run along, Dick,' he said to the silly fellow, and turning to Mrs. Carey, he explained. 'He's absolutely harmless. They call him Crazy Dick.'

'Thank you very much,' Mrs. Carey said.

'I hope he didn't keep you from going in,' he said, taking off his hat. His hair was quite thick and he had a generous smile.

'I didn't know him, that was all,' she said, feeling foolish as he opened the door for her. She heard Crazy Dick talking rapidly, then the door closed.

The minister was moving on the stage and talking quietly. She knew it was the minister because she had seen his picture in the papers and recognized the Prince Albert coat and the four-in-hand tie with the collar open at the throat. She took three steps down the aisle, fearfully aware that many people were looking at her, and sat down, four rows from the back. Only once before had she been in a strange church, when a friend of her husband had got married, and it hadn't seemed like church. She unbuttoned her coat carefully, leaving a green and black scarf lying across her full breasts, and relaxed in the seat, getting her big body comfortable. Someone sat down beside her. The man with the gray hair and red face was sitting down beside her. She was annoyed because she knew she was too definitely aware of him sitting beside her. The minister walked the length of the platform, his voice pleasant and soothing, one of the city's most interesting ministers, and she tried to follow the flow of words but was too restless. She had come in too late, that was the trouble. So she tried concentrating, closing her eyes, but at once thought of a trivial and amusing argument she had had with her husband, and three or four words she might have used effectively. The minister was giving an idea of an after life and some words seemed beautiful, but she was disappointed because it was not what she had expected, and she had never intended to take his religious notions seriously.

The seat was becoming uncomfortable, and she stretched a little, crossing her legs at the ankles. The minister had a lovely voice, but so far wasn't a bit sensational, and she might just as well have gone to the Cathedral. She felt slightly ashamed, and out of place in the theatre.

The man on her right was sniffling. Puzzled, she watched him out of the corner of her eye, as he gently rubbed his eyes with a large white handkerchief. The handkerchief was fresh and the creases firm. One plump hand held four corners, making a pad, and he dabbed his eyes, watching the minister intently.

Mrs. Carey was anxious not to appear ill-bred, but a respectable man, moved by the minister's words, or an old thought, was sitting beside her, crying. She tried to adjust her thoughts so the man's misery would belong to a pattern of a Sunday service in a theatre, and did not glance at him again till she realized that his elbow was on the arm of her seat, supporting his chin, while he blinked his eyes and slowly moved his head. He was feeling so bad she was uncomfortable, but thought that he looked gentlemanly, even though feeling so miserable. He was probably a nice man, and she was sorry for him.

She expected him to get up and go out. Other people were noticing him. A fat woman, in the seat ahead, craned her neck so much Mrs. Carey wanted to slap her. The man put the handkerchief over his face and didn't lift his head. The minister was talking rapidly, but Mrs. Carey suddenly felt absolutely alone in the theatre, rows of heads simply sloped down to the orchestra. Impulsively she touched the man's arm, leaning toward him, whispering, 'I'm awfully sorry for you, sir.'

She patted his arm a second time, and he looked at her helplessly, and went to speak, but merely shook his head and patted the back of her hand.

'I'm sorry,' she repeated gently.

'Thank you very much,' he said sincerely.

'I hope it's all right now,' she whispered.

He spoke quietly and slowly: 'Something the minister said reminded me of my brother who died last week. My younger brother.'

People in the row ahead were turning angrily, annoyed by

Mrs. Carey. She became embarrassed, and leaned back in her seat, very dignified and looked directly ahead till aware that the man was holding her hand. Startled, she twitched it nervously, but he didn't notice. His eyes were still moist. His thoughts seemed so far away. She reflected it could do no harm to let him hold her hand a moment, if it helped him.

She listened to the minister but didn't understand a word he was saying, and glanced curiously at the gray-haired man, who didn't look at her but still held her hand. He was good-looking, and a feeling she had not had for years was inside her, her hand had suddenly become so sensitive. She closed her eyes. Then the minister stopped speaking and she opened them, knowing the congregation was ready to sing a hymn. She looked directly at him. He had put away the handkerchief and now was smiling sadly. Uneasily, she avoided his eyes, firmly removing her hand, as she stood up to sing the last hymn. Her cheeks were warm. She tried to stop thinking altogether. It was necessary to leave at once only she had to squeeze by his knees to reach the aisle.

She buttoned her coat while they were singing, ready to slip past him. She was surprised when he stepped out to the aisle, allowing her to pass, but didn't look at him. Erect and dignified, she walked slowly up the aisle, her eyes on the door.

Then she heard steps behind her and knew definitely he was following. An usher held open the door and she smiled awkwardly. The usher smiled. Outside, she took a few quick steps, then stood still, bewildered, expecting Crazy Dick to be on the street. She thought of the green sweater and funny flat hat, then looked back hurriedly. Through the doorway she saw him smiling at the usher and putting on his hat, the tie-pin shining in the light. Sinking her chin into her high fur collar she walked rapidly down the street, looking only at the ground immediately ahead of her. It was snowing harder, driving along on a wind.

When she got to a car stop she looked back and saw the gray-haired man standing on the sidewalk in front of the theatre doors. A street-car was coming. She was sure he took a few steps toward her, but she got on the car.

The conductor said, 'Fares please,' but hardly glancing at him, she shook wet snow from her coat, and sat down, taking three deep breaths, while her cheeks tingled. She felt tired suddenly, and her heart was thumping unevenly.

She got off the car at Shuter Street. She didn't want to go straight home, and was determined to visit the Cathedral.

On the side streets snow was thick. Men from some of the rooming-houses were shovelling it from the sidewalks, the shovels scraping on concrete. She lifted her eyes occasionally to the illuminated cross on the Cathedral spire.

One light was over the church door. The congregation had come out half an hour ago, and she felt lonely walking in the dark toward the single light.

Inside the Cathedral she knelt down half-way up the centre aisle, her eyes on the altar lights. She closed her eyes to pray, and remembered midnight mass in the Cathedral, the Archbishop with his mitre and staff, and the choir of boys' voices. A vestry door opened, a priest passed in the shadow beside the altar, took a book from a pew, and went out. She closed her eyes again and said many prayers, repeating her favourite ones over and over, but often she thought of her husband at home. She prayed hard so she could go home and not be bothered by anything that had happened in the theatre. She prayed for half an hour, feeling better gradually, till she hardly remembered the man in the theatre, and fairly satisfied, she got up and left the Cathedral.

Now That April's Here

As soon as they got the money they bought two large black hats and left America to live permanently in Paris. They were bored in their native city in the Middle West and convinced that the American continent had nothing to offer them. Charles Milford, who was four years older than Johnny Hill, had a large round head that ought to have belonged to a Presbyterian minister. Johnny had a rather chinless faun's head. When they walked down the street the heads together seemed more interesting. They came to Paris in the late autumn.

They got on very quickly in Montparnasse. In the afternoons they wandered around the streets, looking in art gallery windows at the prints of the delicate clever unsubstantial line work of Foujita. Pressing his nose against the window Johnny said, 'Quite a sound technique, don't you think, Charles?'

'Oh sound, quite sound.'

They never went to the Louvre or the museum in the Luxembourg Gardens, thinking it would be in the fashion of tourists, when they intended really to settle in Paris. In the evenings they sat together at a table on the terrace of the café, and clients, noticing them, began thinking of them as 'the two boys'. One night, Fanny Lee, a blonde, fat American girl who had been an entertainer at Zelli's until she lost her shape, but not her hilarity, stepped over to the boys' table and yelled, 'Oh, gee, look what I've found.' They were discovered. Fanny, liking them for their quiet, well-mannered behaviour, insisted on introducing them to everybody at the bar. They bowed together at the same angle, smiling so cheerfully, so obviously willing to be obliging, that Fanny

was anxious to have them follow her from one bar to another, hoping they would pay for her drinks.

They felt much better after the evening with Fanny.
Johnny, the younger one, who had a small income of $100
a month, was supporting Charles, who, he was sure, would
one day become a famous writer. Johnny did not take his
own talent very seriously; he had been writing his memoirs
of their adventures since they were fifteen, after reading
George Moore's *Confessions of A Young Man*. George
Moore's book had been mainly responsible for their visit to
Paris. Johnny's memoirs, written in a snobbishly aristocratic
manner, had been brought up to the present and now he was
waiting for something to happen to them. They were much
happier the day they got a cheaper room on Boulevard
Arago near the tennis court.

They were happy at the cafés in the evenings but liked
best being at home together in their own studio, five minutes
away from the cafés. They lay awake in bed together a long
time talking about everything that happened during the day,
consoling each other by saying the weather would be finer
later on and anyway they could always look forward to the
spring days next April. Fanny Lee, who really like them,
was extraordinarily friendly and only cost them nine or ten
drinks an evening. They lay awake in bed talking about her,
sometimes laughing so hard the bed springs squeaked.
Charles, his large round head buried in the pillow, snickered
gleefully listening to Johnny making fun of Fanny Lee.

Soon they knew everybody in the Quarter, though no one
knew either of them very intimately. People sitting at the
café in the evening when the lights were on, saw them crossing the road together under the street lamp, their bodies
leaning forward at the same angle, and walking on tiptoe. No
one knew where they were going. Really they weren't going
anywhere in particular. They had been sitting at the café,
nibbling pieces of sugar they had dipped in coffee, till Johnny
said, 'We're being seen here too much, don't you think,
Charles?' And Charles said, 'I think we ought to be seen at
all the bars. We ought to go more often to the new bar.' So
they had paid for their coffee and walked over to a side-street
bar panelled in the old English style, with a good-natured

English bartender, and sat together at a table listening to the careless talk of five customers at the bar, occasionally snickering out loud when a sentence overheard seemed incredibly funny. Stan Mason, an ingenuous heavy drinker, who had cultivated a very worldly feeling sitting at the same bars every night, explaining the depth of his sophistication to the same people, saw the boys holding their heads together and yelled, 'What are you two little goats snickering at?' The boys stood up, bowing to him so politely and seriously he was ashamed of himself and asked them to have a drink with him. The rest of the evening they laughed so charmingly at his jokes he was fully convinced they were the brightest youngsters who had come to the Quarter in years. He asked the boys if they liked Paris, and smiling at each other and raising their glasses together they said that architecturally it was a great improvement over America. They had never been in New York or any other large American city but had no use for American buildings. There was no purpose in arguing directly with them. Charles would simply have raised his eyebrows and glanced slyly at Johnny, who would have snickered with his fingers over his mouth. Mason, who was irritated, and anxious to make an explanation, began talking slowly about the early block-like houses of the Taos Indians and the geometrical block style of the New York skyscrapers. For ten minutes he talked steadily about the Indians and a development of the American spirit. The boys listened politely, never moving their heads at all. Watching them, while he talked, Mason began to feel uncomfortable. He began to feel that anything he had to say was utterly unimportant because the two boys were listening to him so politely. But he finished strongly and said, 'What do you think?'

'Do you really believe all that's important?' Charles said.

'I don't know, maybe it's not.'

'Well, as long as you don't think it important,' Johnny said.

At home the boys sat on the edge of the bed, talking about Stan Mason and snickered so long they were up half the night.

They had their first minor disagreement in the Quarter

one evening in November with Milton Simpson, a prosperous, bright and effeminate young American business man who was living in Paris because he felt vaguely that the best approach to life was through all the arts together. He was secretly trying to write, paint and compose pieces for the piano. The boys were at a small bar with a floor for dancing and an American jazz artist at the piano, and Simpson and his wife came in. Passing, Simpson brushed against Charles, who, without any provocation at all, suddenly pushed him away. Simpson pushed too and they stood there pushing each other. Simpson began waving his arms in circles, and the man at the piano threw his arms around Charles, dragging him away. Neither one of them could have hurt each other seriously and everybody in the room was laughing at them. Finally Simpson sat down and Charles, standing alone, began to tremble so much he had to put his head down on the table and cry. His shoulders were moving jerkily. Then everybody in the room was sorry for Charles. Johnny, putting his arm around him, led him outside. Simpson, whose thin straight lips were moving nervously, was so impressed by Charles's tears, that he and his wife followed them outside and over to the corner café where they insisted on sitting down with them at one of the brown oblong tables inside. Simpson bought the boys a brandy and his wife, who was interested in the new psychology, began to talk eagerly with Charles, evidently expecting some kind of an emotional revelation. The boys finished their brandies and Simpson quickly ordered another for them. For an hour the boys drank brandies and listened patiently and seriously to Simpson, who was talking ecstatically because he thought they were sensitive, sympathetic boys. They only smiled at him when he excitedly called them 'sensitive organisms'. Charles, listening wide-eyed, was nervously scratching his cheek with the nail of his right forefinger till the flesh was torn and raw.

Afterwards, undressing slowly at home, Johnny said, 'Simpson is such a bore, don't you think so, Charles?'

'I know, but the brandies were very good.' They never mentioned the fight at the bar.

'It was so funny when you looked at him with that blue-eyed Danish stare of yours,' Johnny said, chuckling.

'People think I expect them to do tricks like little animals when I look at them like that,' Charles explained.

Naked, they sat on the edge of the bed, laughing at Simpson's eagerness to buy them brandies, and they made so many witty sallies they tired themselves out and fell asleep.

For two weeks they weren't seen around the cafés. Charles was writing another book and Johnny was typing it for him. It was a literary two weeks for both of them. They talked about all the modern authors and Johnny suggested that not one of them since Henry James had half Charles's perception or subtle delicacy. Actually Charles did write creditably enough and everything he did had three or four good paragraphs in it. The winter was coming on and when this literary work was finished they wanted to go south.

No one ever knew how they got the money to go to the Riviera for the winter. No one knew how they were able to drink so much when they had only Johnny's hundred dollars a month. At Nice, where Stan Mason was living, they were very cheerful and Mason, admiring their optimism because he thought they had no money, let them have a room in his apartment. They lived with him till the evening he put his ear against the thin wall and heard them snickering, sitting on the edge of the bed. They were talking about him and having a good laugh. Stan Mason was hurt because he had thought them bright boys and really liked them. He merely suggested next morning that they would have to move since he needed the room.

The boys were mainly happy in Nice because they were looking forward to returning to Paris in April. The leaves would be on all the trees and people would be sitting outside on the terraces at the cafés. Everybody they met in Nice told them how beautiful it was in Paris in the early spring, so they counted upon having the happiest time they had ever had together. When they did leave Nice they owed many thousand francs for an hotel bill, payment of which they had avoided by tossing their bags out of the window at two o'clock in the morning. They even had a little extra money at the time, almost twenty dollars they had received from an elderly English gentleman, who had suggested, after talking to them all one morning, he would pay well to see the boys make a 'tableau' for him. The old fellow was enthusiastic about the 'tableau' and the boys had something to amuse them for almost two weeks.

They returned to Paris the first week in April. Now that April was here they had expected to have so much fun, but the weather was disagreeable and cold. This year the leaves were hardly on the trees and there was always rain in the dull skies. They assured each other that the dull days could not last because it was April and Paris was the loveliest city in the world in the early spring.

Johnny's father had been writing many irritable letters from England, where he was for a few months, and the boys decided it was an opportune time for Johnny to go and see him for a week. When he returned they would be together for the good days at the end of the month.

People were not very interested in Charles while Johnny was away. They liked him better when he was with Johnny. All week he walked around on tiptoe or sat alone at a corner table in the café. The two boys together seemed well mannered and bright, but Charles, alone, looked rather insignificant. Without thinking much about it he knew the feeling people had for him and avoided company, waiting impatiently for the days to pass, worrying about Johnny. He said to Stan Mason late one night, 'I hope Johnny has enough sense not to pick up with a girl over in England.'

'Why worry? Do it yourself now.'

'Oh I do, too, only I don't take them as seriously as Johnny does. Not that I mind Johnny having a girl,' he said, 'only I don't want him to have a complicated affair with one.'

The night Johnny returned to Paris they went around to all the bars and people, smiling, said, 'There go the two boys.' They were happy, nervously happy, and Charles was scratching his cheek with his nail. Later on they wanted to be entirely alone and left the café district and the crowds to walk down the narrow side streets to the Seine while Johnny, chuckling, related the disagreeable circumstances of his visit to his father. His father had contended that he was a wastrel who ought to be earning his own living, and Johnny had jeeringly pointed out that the old man had inherited his money without having to work for it. They were angry with each other, and the father had slapped Johnny, who retaliated by poking him in the jaw. That was the most amusing part of the story the boys talked about, walking along the left bank of the Seine opposite the Louvre. Casually Johnny told about a few affairs he had with cheap women in London, and Charles understood that these affairs had not touched him at all. It was a warm clean evening, the beginning of the real spring days in April, and the boys were happy walking by the river in the moonlight, the polished water surface reflecting the red and white lights on the bridges.

Near the end of the month Constance Foy, whom the boys had known at Nice, came to Paris, and they asked her to live with them. She was a simple-minded fat-faced girl with a boy's body and short hair dyed red, who had hardly a franc left and was eager to live with anybody who would keep her. For a week the three of them were happy in the big studio. The boys were proud of their girl and took her around to all the bars, buying drinks for her, actually managing to do it on the hundred dollars a month. In the nighttime they were impartial and fair about Constance, who appeared to have all her enthusiasm for the one who, at the moment, was making love to her. But she said to Stan Mason one evening, 'I don't know whether or not I ought to be there messing up that relationship.'

'Aren't the three of you having a good time?'

'Good enough, but funny things are happening.'

The boys were satisfied till Charles began to feel that Johnny was making love to Constance too seriously. It was disappointing, for he had never objected to having her in the studio, and now Johnny was so obvious in his appreciation of her. Charles, having this feeling, was now unable to touch her at all, and resented Johnny's unabated eagerness for her. It was all the same to Constance.

Before the end of the month the two boys were hardly speaking to each other, though always together at the cafés in the evening. It was too bad, for the days were bright and clear, the best of the April weather, and Paris was gay and lively. The boys were sad and hurt and sorry but determined to be fair with each other. The evening they were at the

English bar, sitting at one of the table beer barrels, Charles had a hard time preventing himself crying. He was very much in love with Johnny and felt him slipping away. Johnny, his fingers over his mouth, sometimes shook his head but didn't know what to say.

Finally they left the bar to walk home. They were going down the short, quiet street leading to the Boulevard.

'What are you going to do about Constance?' Charles said.

'If it's all the same to you I'll have her to myself.'

'But what are you going to do with her?'

'I don't know.'

'You'd let a little tart like that smash things,' Charles said, shaking his hand at Johnny.

'Don't you dare call her a tart.'

'Please, Johnny, don't strike at me.'

But Johnny who was nearly crying with rage swung his palm at Charles, hitting him across the face. Stan Mason had just turned the corner at the Boulevard, coming up to the bar to have a drink, and saw the two of them standing there.

'What's wrong?' he said.

'I begged him, I implored him not to hit me,' Charles said.

'Oh, I hit him, I hit him, I hit him, what'll I do?' Johnny said, tears running down his cheeks.

They stood there crying and shaking their heads, but would not go home together. Finally Charles consented to go with Stan to his hotel and Johnny went home to Constance.

Charles stayed with Mason all week. He would not eat at all and didn't care what he was drinking. The night Mason told him Johnny was going back to America, taking Constance with him, he shook his head helplessly and said, 'How could he hit me, how could he hit me, and he knew I loved him so much.'

'But what are you going to do?'

'I don't know.'

'How are you going to live?'

'I'll make enough to have a drink occasionally.'

At the time, he was having a glass of Scotch, his arm trembling so weakly he could hardly lift the glass.

The day Johnny left Paris it rained and it was cold again, sitting at the café in the evening. There had been only one really good week in April. The boys always used to sit at the cafés without their hats on, their hair brushed nicely. This evening Charles had to go home and get his overcoat and the big black hat he had bought in America. Sitting alone at his table in the cool evening, his overcoat wrapped around him, and the black hat on, he did not look the same at all. It was the first time he had worn the hat in France.

Very Special Shoes

All winter eleven-year-old Mary Johnson had been dreaming of a pair of red leather shoes she had seen in a shoe-store window on the avenue one afternoon when she was out with her mother doing the shopping. Every Saturday she had been given twenty-five cents for doing the housework all by herself and the day had come at last when it added up to six dollars, the price of the shoes. Moving around the house very quietly so she would not wake her mother who seemed to need a lot of sleep these days, Mary finished up the last of the dusting and hurried to the window and looked out: on such a day she had been afraid it might rain but the street was bright in the afternoon sunlight. Then she went quickly into the bedroom where her mother slept, with one light cover thrown half over her. 'Mother, wake up,' she whispered excitedly.

Mrs. Johnson, a handsome woman of fifty with a plump figure and a high colour in her cheeks, was lying on her left side with her right arm hanging loosely over the side of the bed: her mouth was open a little, but she was breathing so softly Mary could hardly hear her. Every day now she seemed to need more sleep, a fact which worried Mary's older sisters, Barbara and Helen, and was the subject of their long whispering conversations in their bedroom at night. It seemed to trouble Mr. Johnson too, for he started taking long walks by himself and he came home with his breath smelling of whiskey. But to Mary her mother looked as lovely and as healthy as ever. 'Mother,' she called again. She reached over and gave her shoulder a little shake, and then watched her mother's face eagerly when she opened her eyes to see if she had remembered about the shoes.

When her mother, still half asleep, only murmured, 'Bring me my purse, Mary, and we'll have our little treat,' Mary was not disappointed. She gleefully kept her secret. She took the dime her mother gave her and went up to the store to get the two ice-cream cones, just as she did on other days, only it seemed that she could already see herself coming down the street in the red leather shoes: she seemed to pass herself on the street, wearing the outfit she had planned to wear with the shoes, a red hat and a blue dress. By the time she got back to the house she had eaten most of her own cone. It was always like that. But then she sat down at the end of the kitchen table to enjoy herself watching her mother eat her share of the ice-cream. It was like watching a big eager girl. Mrs. Johnson sat down, spread her legs, and sighed with pleasure and licked the ice-cream softly and smiled with satisfaction and her mouth looked beautiful. And then when she was finished and was wiping her fingers with her apron Mary blurted out, 'Are we going to get my shoes now, Mother?'

'Shoes. What shoes?' Mrs. Johnson asked.

'The red leather shoes I've been saving for,' Mary said, looking puzzled. 'The ones we saw in the window that we talked about.'

'Oh. Oh, I see,' Mrs. Johnson said slowly as if she hadn't thought of those particular shoes since that day months ago. 'Why, Mary, have you been thinking of those shoes all this time?' And then as Mary only kept looking up at her she went on fretfully, 'Why, I told you at the time, child, that your father was in debt and we couldn't afford such shoes.'

'I've got the six dollars saved, haven't I? Today.'

'Well, your father . . .'

'It's my six dollars, isn't it?'

'Mary, darling, listen. Those shoes are far too old for a little girl like you.'

'I'm twelve next month. You know I am.'

'Shoes like that are no good for running around, Mary. A pair of good serviceable shoes is what you need, Mary.'

'I can wear them on Sunday, can't I?'

'Look, Mary,' her mother tried to reason with her, 'I know I said I'd get you a pair of shoes. But a good pair of shoes. Proper shoes. Your father is going to have a lot more expense soon. Why, he'd drop dead if he found I'd paid six dollars for a pair of red leather shoes for you.'

'You promised I could save the money,' Mary whispered. And then when she saw that worried, unyielding expression on her mother's face she knew she was not going to get the shoes; she turned away and ran into the bedroom and threw herself on the bed and pulled the pillow over her face and started to cry. Never in her life had she wanted anything as much as she wanted the red shoes. When she heard the sound of her mother moving pots and pans in the kitchen she felt that she had been cheated deliberately.

It began to get dark and she was still crying, and then she heard her mother's slow step coming toward the bedroom. 'Mary, listen to me,' she said, her voice almost rough as she reached down and shook Mary. 'Get up and wipe your face, do you hear?' She had her own hat and coat on. 'We're going to get those shoes right now,' she said.

'You said I couldn't get them,' Mary said.

'Don't argue with me,' her mother said. She sounded blunt and grim and somehow far away from Mary. 'I want you to get them. I say you're going to. Come on.'

Mary got up and wiped her face, and on the way up to the store her mother's grim, silent determination made her feel lonely and guilty. They bought a pair of red leather shoes. As Mary walked up and down in them on the store carpet her mother watched her, unsmiling and resolute. Coming back home Mary longed for her mother to speak to her, but Mrs. Johnson, holding Mary's hand tight, walked along, looking straight ahead.

'Now if only your father doesn't make a fuss,' Mrs. Johnson said when they were standing together in the hall, listening. From the living-room came the sound of a rustled newspaper. Mr. Johnson, who worked in a publishing house, was home. In the last few months Mary had grown afraid of her father: she did not understand why he had become so moody and short-tempered. As her mother, standing there, hesitated nervously, Mary began to get scared. 'Go on into the bedroom,' Mrs. Johnson whispered to her. She followed Mary and had her sit down on the bed and she knelt down and put the red shoes on Mary's feet. It was a strangely solemn, secret little ceremony. Mrs. Johnson's breathing was heavy and laboured as she straightened up. 'Now don't you come in until I call you,' she warned Mary.

But Mary tiptoed into the kitchen and her heart was pounding as she tried to listen. For a while she heard only the sound of her mother's quiet voice, and then suddenly her father cried angrily, 'Are you serious? Money for luxuries at a time like this!' His voice became explosive. 'Are we going crazy? You'll take them back, do you hear?' But her mother's voice flowed on, the one quiet voice, slow and even. Then there was a long and strange silence. 'Mary, come here,' her father suddenly called.

'Come on and show your father your shoes, Mary,' her mother urged her.

The new shoes squeaked as Mary went into the living-room and they felt like heavy weights that might prevent her from fleeing from her father's wrath. Her father was sitting at the little table by the light and Mary watched his face desperately to see if the big vein at the side of his head had started to swell. As he turned slowly to her and fumbled with his glasses a wild hope shone in Mary's scared brown eyes.

Her father did not seem to be looking at her shoes. With a kind of pain in his eyes he was looking steadily at her as if he had never really been aware of her before. 'They're fine shoes, aren't they?' he asked.

'Can I keep them? Can I really?' Mary asked breathlessly.

'Why, sure you can,' he said quietly.

Shouting with joy Mary skipped out of the room and along the hall, for she had heard her sisters come in. 'Look, Barbara, look, Helen,' she cried. Her two older sisters, who were stenographers, and a bit prim, were slightly scanda-

lized. 'Why, they're far too old for you,' Barbara said. 'Get
out, get out,' Mary laughed. 'Mother knows better than you
do.' Then she went out to the kitchen to help her mother
with the dinner and watch her face steadily with a kind of
rapt wonder, as if she was trying to understand the strange
power her mother possessed that could make an angry man
like her father suddenly gentle and quiet.

Mary intended to wear the shoes to church that Sunday,
but it rained, so she put them back in the box and decided
to wait a week. But in the middle of the week her father told
her that her mother was going to the hospital for an
operation.

'Is it for the pains in her legs?' Mary asked.

'Well, you see, Mary, if everything comes off all right,'
her father answered, 'she may not have any pains at all.'

It was to be an operation for cancer, and the doctor said
the operation was successful. But Mrs. Johnson died under
the anaesthetic. The two older sisters and Mr. Johnson kept
repeating dumbly to the doctor, 'But she looked all right. She
looked fine.' Then they all went home. They seemed to hud-
dle first in one room then in another. They took turns trying
to comfort Mary, but no one could console her.

In the preparations for the funeral they were all busy for
a while because the older sisters were arranging for everyone to have the proper clothes for mourning. The new blue
dress that Helen, the fair-haired one, had bought only a
few weeks ago, was sent to the cleaners to be dyed black,
and of course Mary had to have a black dress and black
stockings too. On the night when they were arranging these
things Mary suddenly blurted out, 'I'm going to wear my
red shoes.'

'Have some sense, Mary. That would be terrible,' Helen
said.

'You can't wear red shoes,' Barbara said crossly.

'Yes, I can,' Mary said stubbornly. 'Mother wanted me to
wear them. I know she did. I know why she bought them.'
She was confronting them all with her fists clenched
desperately.

'For heaven's sake, tell her she can't do a thing like that,'
Helen said irritably to Mr. Johnson. Yet he only shook his

head, looking at Mary with that same gentle, puzzled expression he had had on his face the night his wife had talked to him about the shoes. 'I kind of think Mary's right,' he began, rubbing his hand slowly over his face.

'Red shoes. Good Lord, it would be terrible,' said Helen, now outraged.

'You'd think we'd all want to be proper,' Barbara agreed.

'Proper. It would be simply terrible, I tell you. It would look as if we had no respect.'

'Well, I guess that's right. All the relatives will be here,' Mr. Johnson agreed reluctantly. Then he turned hopefully to Mary. 'Look, Mary,' he began. 'If you get the shoes dyed you can wear them to the funeral and then you'll be able to wear them to school every day too. How about it?'

But it had frightened Mary to think that anyone might say she hadn't shown the proper respect for her mother. She got the red shoes and handed them to her father that he might take them up to the shoemaker. As her father took the box from her, he fumbled with a few apologetic words. 'It's just what people might say. Do you see, Mary?' he asked.

When the shoes, now dyed black, were returned to Mary the next day she put them on slowly, and then she put her feet together and looked at the shoes a long time. They were no longer the beautiful red shoes, and yet as she stared at them, solemn-faced, she suddenly felt a strange kind of secret joy, a feeling of certainty that her mother had got the shoes so that she might understand at this time that she still had her special blessing and protection.

At the funeral the shoes hurt Mary's feet for they were new and hadn't been worn. Yet she was fiercely glad that she had them on. After that she wore them every day. Of course now that they were black they were not noticed by other children. But she was very careful with them. Every night she polished them up and looked at them and was touched again by that secret joy. She wanted them to last a long time.

Their Mother's Purse

Joe went around to see his mother and father, and while he was talking with them and wondering if he could ask for the loan of a dollar, his sister Mary, who was dressed to go out for the evening, came into the room and said, 'Can you let me have fifty cents tonight, Mother?'

She was borrowing money all the time now, and there was no excuse for her, because she was a stenographer and made pretty good pay. It was not the same with her as it was with their older brother, Stephen, who had three children, and could hardly live on his salary.

'If you could possibly spare it, I'd take a dollar,' Mary was saying in her low and pleasant voice as she pulled on her gloves. Her easy smile, her assurance that she would not be refused, made Joe feel resentful. He knew that if he had asked for money, he would have shown that he was uneasy and a little ashamed, and that his father would have put down his paper and stared at him and his mother would have sighed and looked dreadfully worried, as though he were the worst kind of spendthrift.

Getting up to find her purse, their mother said, 'I don't mind lending it to you, Mary, though I can't figure out what you do with your money.'

'I don't seem to be doing anything with it I didn't use to do,' Mary said.

'And I seem to do nothing these days but hand out money to the lot of you. I can't think how you'll get along when I'm dead.'

'I don't know what you'd all do if it weren't for your mother's purse,' their father said, but when he spoke he nodded his head at Joe, because he would rather make it appear that he was angry with Joe than risk offending Mary by speaking directly to her.

'If anybody wants money, they'll have to find my purse for me,' the mother said. 'Try and find it, Mary, and bring it to me.'

Joe had always thought of Mary as his young sister, but the inscrutable expression he saw on her face as she moved around the room picking up newspapers and looking on chairs made him realize how much more self-reliant, how much apart from them, she had grown in the last few years. He saw that she had become a handsome woman. In her tailored suit and felt hat, she looked almost beautiful, and he was suddenly glad she was his sister.

By this time his mother had got up and was trying to remember where she had put the purse when she came in from the store. In the way of a big woman, she moved around slowly, with a far-away expression in her eyes. The purse was a large, black, flat leather purse, but there never had been a time when his mother had been able to get up and know exactly where her purse was, though she used to pretend she was going directly to the spot where she had placed it.

Now she had got to the point where her eyes were anxious as she tried to remember. Her husband, making loud clucking noises with his tongue, took off his glasses and said solemnly, 'I warn you, Mrs. McArthur, you'll lose that purse some day, and then there'll be trouble and you'll be satisfied.'

She looked at him impatiently, as she had hunted in all the likely corners and cupboards. 'See if you can find my purse, will you, son?' she begged Joe, and he got up and began to help, as he used to do when he was a little boy.

Because he remembered that his mother sometimes used to put her purse under the pillow on her bed, he went to look in the bedroom. When he got to the door, which was half closed, and looked in, he saw Mary standing in front of the dresser with her mother's purse in her hands. He saw at once that she had just taken out a bill and was slipping it into her own purse – he even saw that it was a two-dollar bill. He ducked back into the hall before she could catch sight of him. He felt helpless and knew only that he couldn't bear that she should see him.

Mary, coming out of the bedroom, called, 'I found it. Here it is, Mother.'

'Where did you find it, darling?'

'Under your pillow.'

'Ah, that's right. Now I remember,' she said, and looked at her husband triumphantly, for she never failed to enjoy finding the purse just when it seemed to be lost forever.

As Mary handed the purse to her mother, she was smiling, cool, and unperturbed, yet Joe knew she had put the two dollars into her own purse. It seemed terrible that she was able to smile and hide her thoughts like that when they had all been so close together for so many years.

'I never have the slightest fear that it's really lost,' the mother said, beaming. Then they watched her, as they had watched her for years after she had found her purse; she was counting the little roll of bills. Her hand went up to her mouth, she looked thoughtful, she looked down into the depths of the purse again, and they waited almost eagerly, as if expecting her to cry out suddenly that the money was not all there. Then, sighing, she took out fifty cents, handed it to Mary, and it was over, and they never knew what she thought.

'Good night, Mother. Good night, Dad,' Mary said.

'Good night, and don't be late. I worry when you're late.'

'So long, Joe.'

'Just a minute,' Joe called, and he followed Mary out to the hall. The groping, wondering expression on his mother's face as she counted her money had made him feel savage.

He grabbed Mary by the arm just as she was opening the door. 'Wait a minute,' he whispered.

'What's the matter, Joe? You're hurting my arm.'

'Give that bill back to them. I saw you take it.'

'Joe, I needed it.' She grew terribly ashamed and couldn't look at him. 'I wouldn't take it if I didn't need it pretty bad,' she whispered.

They could hear their father making some provoking remark, and they could hear the easy, triumphant answer of their mother. Without looking up, Mary began to cry a little; then she raised her head and begged in a frightened whisper, 'Don't tell them, Joe. Please don't tell them.'

'If you needed the money, why didn't you ask them for it?'

'I've been asking for a little nearly every day.'

'You only look after yourself, and you get plenty for that.'

'Joe, let me keep it. Don't tell them, Joe.'

Her hand tightened on his arm as she pleaded with him. Her face was now close against his, but he was so disgusted with her he tried to push her away. When she saw that he was treating her as though she were a cheap crook, she looked helpless and whispered, 'I've got to do something. I've been sending money to Paul Farrel.'

'Where is he?'

'He's gone to a sanitarium, and he had no money,' she said.

In the moment while they stared at each other, he was thinking of the few times she had brought Paul Farrel to their place, and of the one night when they had found out that his lung was bad. They had made her promise not to see him any more, thinking it was a good thing to do before she went any further with him.

'You promised them you'd forget about him,' he said.

'I married him before he went away,' she said. 'It takes a lot to look after him. I try to keep enough out of my pay every week to pay for my lunches and my board here, but I never seem to have enough left for Paul, and then I don't know what to do.'

'You're crazy. He'll die on your hands,' he whispered. 'Or you'll have to go on keeping him.'

'He'll get better,' she said. 'He'll be back in maybe a year.' There was such an ardent fierceness in her words, and her eyes shone with such eagerness, that he didn't know what to say to her. With a shy, timid smile, she said, 'Don't tell them, Joe.'

'O.K.,' he said, and he watched her open the door and go out.

He went back to the living-room, where his mother was

saying grandly to his father, 'Now you'll have to wait till next year to cry blue ruin.'

His father grinned and ducked his head behind his paper. 'Don't worry. There'll soon be a next time,' he said.

'What did you want to say to Mary?' his mother asked.

'I just wanted to know if she was going my way, and she wasn't,' Joe said.

And when Joe heard their familiar voices and remembered Mary's frightened, eager face, he knew he would keep his promise and say nothing to them. He was thinking how far apart he had grown from them; they knew very little about Mary, but he never told them anything about himself, either. Only his father and mother had kept on going the one way. They alone were still close together.

The Blue Kimono

It was hardly more than dawn when George woke up so suddenly. He lay wide awake listening to a heavy truck moving slowly on the street below; he heard one truck-driver shout angrily to another; he heard a hundred small street sounds multiplying and rolling with the motion of the city awakening.

For many mornings in the last six months George had lain awake waiting to hear all the noises of people preparing to go to work, the noises of doors slamming, of women taking in the milk, of cars starting, and sometimes, later on in the morning, he had wondered where all these people went when they hurried out briskly with so much assurance.

Each morning he awakened a little earlier and was wide awake at once. But this time he was more restless than ever and he thought with despair, 'We're unlucky, that's it. We've never had any luck since we've come here. There's something you can't put your hands on working to destroy us. Everything goes steadily against us from bad to worse. We'll never have any luck. I can feel it. We'll starve before I get a job.'

Then he realized that his wife, Marthe, was no longer in the bed beside him. He looked around the room that seemed so much larger and so much emptier in that light and he thought, 'What's the matter with Marthe? Is it getting that she can't sleep?' Sitting up, he peered uneasily into the room's dark corners. There was a light coming from the kitchenette. As he got out of bed slowly, with his thick hair standing up straight all over his head, and reached for his slippers and dressing-gown, the notion that something mysterious and inexorable was working to destroy them was so strong in him that he suddenly wanted to stand in front of his wife and shout in anger, 'What can I do? You tell me something to do. What's the use of me going out to the streets today. I'm going to sit down here and wait, day after day.' That time when they had first got married and were secure now seemed such a little far-away forgotten time.

In his eagerness to make his wife feel the bad luck he felt within him, he went striding across the room, his old, shapeless slippers flapping on the floor, his dressing-gown only half pulled on, looking in that dim light like someone huge, reckless, and full of sudden savage impulse, who wanted to pound a table and shout. 'Marthe, Marthe,' he called, 'what's the matter with you? Why are you up at this time?'

She came into the room carrying their two-year-old boy. 'There's nothing the matter with me,' she said. 'I got up when I heard Walter crying.' She was a small, slim, dark woman with black hair hanging on her shoulders, a thin eager face, and large soft eyes, and as she walked over to the window with the boy she swayed her body as though she were humming to him. The light from the window was now a little stronger. She sat there in her old blue kimono holding the boy tight and feeling his head with her hand.

'What's the matter with him?' George said.

'I don't know. I heard him whimpering, so I got up. His head felt so hot.'

'Is there anything I can do?' he said.

'I don't think so.'

She seemed so puzzled, so worried and aloof from even the deepest bitterness within him, that George felt impatient, as if it were her fault that the child was sick. For a while he watched her rocking back and forth, making always the same faint humming sound, with the stronger light showing the deep frown on her face, and he couldn't seem to think of the child at all. He wanted to speak with sympathy, but he burst out, 'I had to get up because I couldn't go on with my own thoughts. We're unlucky, Marthe. We haven't had a day's luck since we've come to this city. How much longer can this go on before they throw us out on the street? I tell you we never should have come here.'

She looked up at him indignantly. He couldn't see the fierceness in her face because her head was against the window light. Twice he walked the length of the room, then he stood beside her, looking down at the street. There was now traffic and an increasing steady hum of motion. He felt chilled and his fingers grasped at the collar of his dressing-gown, pulling it across his chest. 'It's cold here, and you can imagine what it'll be like in winter,' he said. And when Marthe again did not answer, he said sullenly, 'You wanted us to come here. You wanted us to give up what we had and come to a bigger city where there were bigger things ahead. Where we might amount to something because of my fine education and your charming manner. You thought we didn't have enough ambition, didn't you?'

'Why talk about it now, George?'

'I want you to see what's happened to us.'

'Say I'm responsible. Say anything you wish.'

'All right. I'll tell you what I feel in my bones. Luck is against us. Something far stronger than our two lives is working against us. I was thinking about it when I woke up. I must have been thinking about it all through my sleep.'

'We've been unlucky, but we've often had a good time, haven't we?' she said.

'Tell me honestly, have we had a day's luck since we got married?' he said brutally.

'I don't know,' she said with her head down. Then she looked up suddenly, almost pleading, but afraid to speak.

The little boy started to whimper and then sat up straight, pushing away the blanket his mother tried to keep around him. When she insisted on covering him, he began to fight and she had a hard time holding him till suddenly he was limp in her arms, looking around the darkened room with the bright wonder that comes in a child's fevered eyes.

George watched Marthe trying to soothe the child. The morning light began to fall on her face, making it seem a little leaner, a little narrower and so dreadfully worried. A few years ago everybody used to speak about her extraordinary smile, about the way the lines around her mouth were shaped for laughter, and they used to say, too, that she had a mysterious, tapering, Florentine face. Once a man had said to George, 'I remember clearly the first time I met your wife. I said to myself, "Who is the lady with that marvellous smile?" '

George was now looking at this face as though it belonged to a stranger. He could think of nothing but the shape of it. There were so many angles in that light; it seemed so narrow. 'I used to think it was beautiful. It doesn't look beautiful. Would anybody say it was beautiful?' he thought, and yet these thoughts had nothing to do with his love for her.

In some intuitive way she knew that he was no longer thinking of his bad luck, but was thinking of her, so she said patiently, 'Walter seems to have quite a fever, George.' Then he stopped walking and touched Walter's head, which was very hot.

'Here, let me hold him a while and you get something,' he said. 'Get him some aspirin.'

'I'll put it in orange juice, if he'll take it,' she said.

'For God's sake, turn on the light, Marthe,' he called. 'This ghastly light is getting on my nerves.'

He tried talking to his son while Marthe was away. 'Hello, Walter, old boy, what's the matter with you? Look at me, big boy, say something bright to your old man.' But the little boy shook his head violently, stared vacantly at the wall a moment, and then tried to bury his face in his father's shoulder. So George, looking disconsolately around the cold room, felt that it was more barren than ever.

Marthe returned with the orange juice and the aspirin. They both began to coax Walter to take it. They pretended to be drinking it themselves, made ecstatic noises with their tongues as though it were delicious and kept it up till the boy cried, 'Orange, orange, me too,' with an unnatural animation. His eyes were brilliant. Then he swayed as if his spine were made of putty and fell back in his mother's arms.

'We'd better get a doctor in a hurry, George,' Marthe said. 'Do you think it's that bad?'

'Look at him,' she said, laying him on the bed. 'I'm sure he's very sick. You don't want to lose him, do you?' and she stared at Walter, who had closed his eyes and was sleeping.

As Marthe in her fear kept looking up at George, she was fingering her old blue kimono, drawing it tighter around her to keep her warm. The kimono had been of a Japanese pattern adorned with clusters of brilliant flowers sewn in silk. George had given it to her at the time of their marriage; now he stared at it, torn as it was at the arms, with pieces of old padding hanging out at the hem, with the light-coloured lining showing through in many places, and he remembered how, when the kimono was new, Marthe used to make the dark hair across her forehead into bangs, fold her arms across her breasts, with her wrists and hands concealed in the sleeve folds, and go around the room in the bright kimono, taking short, prancing steps, pretending she was a Japanese girl.

The kimono now was ragged and gone; it was gone, he thought, like so many bright dreams and aspirations they had once had in the beginning, like so many fine resolutions he had sworn to accomplish, like so many plans they had made and hopes they had cherished.

'Marthe, in God's name,' he said suddenly, 'the very first money we get, even if we just have enough to put a little down, you'll have to get a decent dressing-gown. Do you hear?'

She was startled. Looking up at him in bewilderment, she swallowed hard, then turned her eyes down again.

'It's terrible to have to look at you in that thing,' he muttered.

After he had spoken in this way he was ashamed, and he was able to see for the first time the wild terrified look on her face as she bent over Walter.

'Why do you look like that?' he asked. 'Hasn't he just got a little fever?'

'Did you see the way he held the glass when he took the orange juice?'

'No. I didn't notice.'

'His hand trembled. Earlier, when I first went to him, and gave him a drink I noticed the strange trembling in his hand.'

'What does it mean?' he said, awed by the fearful way she was whispering.

'His body seemed limp and he could not sit up either. Last night I was reading about such symptoms in the medical column in the paper. Symptoms like that with a fever are symptoms of infantile paralysis.'

'Where's the paper?'

'Over there on the table.'

George sat down and began to read the bit of newspaper medical advice very calmly; over and over he read it, very calmly. Marthe had described the symptoms accurately; but in a stupid way he could not get used to the notion that his son might have such a dreadful disease. So he remained there calmly for a long time.

And then he suddenly realized how they had been dogged by bad luck; he realized how surely everything they loved was being destroyed day by day and he jumped up and cried out, 'We'll have to get a doctor.' And as if he realized to the full what was inevitably impending, he cried out, 'You're right, Marthe, he'll die. That child will die. It's the luck that's following us. Then it's over. Everything's over. I tell you I'll curse the day I ever saw the light of the world. I'll curse the day we ever met and ever married. I'll smash everything I can put my hands on in this world.'

'George, don't go on like that. You'll bring something dreadful down on us,' she whispered in terror.

'What else can happen? What else can happen to us worse than this?'

'Nothing, nothing, but please don't go on saying it, George.'

Then they both bent down over Walter and they took turns putting their hands on his head. 'What doctor will come to us at this house when we have no money?' he kept muttering. 'We'll have to take him to a hospital.' They remained kneeling together, silent for a long time, almost afraid to speak.

Marthe said suddenly, 'Feel, feel his head. Isn't it a little cooler?'

'What could that be?'

'It might be the aspirin working on him.'

So they watched, breathing steadily together while the child's head gradually got cooler. Their breathing and their silence seemed to waken the child, for he opened his eyes and stared at them vaguely. 'He must be feeling better,' George said. 'See the way he's looking at us.'

'His head does feel a lot cooler.'

'What could have been the matter with him, Marthe?'

'It might have been a chill. Oh, I hope it was only a chill.'

'Look at him, if you please. Watch me make the rascal laugh.'

With desperate eagerness George rushed over to the table, tore off a sheet of newspaper, folded it into a thin strip about eight inches long and twisted it like a cord. Then he knelt down in front of Walter and cried, 'See, see,' and thrust the twisted paper under his own nose and held it with his upper lip while he wiggled it up and down. He screwed up his eyes diabolically. He pressed his face close against the boy's.

Laughing, Walter put out his hand. 'Let me,' he said. So George tried to hold the paper moustache against Walter's lip. But that was no good. Walter pushed the paper away and said, 'You, you.'

'I think his head is cool now,' Marthe said. 'Maybe he'll be all right.'

She got up and walked away from the bed, over to the window with her head down. Standing up, George went to follow her, but his son shouted tyrannically so he had to kneel down and hold the paper moustache under his nose and say, 'Look here, look, Walter.'

Marthe was trying to smile as she watched them. She took

one deep breath after another, as though she would never succeed in filling her lungs with air. But even while she stood there, she grew troubled. She hesitated, she lowered her head and wanted to say, 'One of us will find work of some kind, George,' but she was afraid.

'I'll get dressed now,' she said quietly, and turned to take off her kimono.

As she took off the kimono and was holding it on her arm, her face grew full of deep concern. She held the kimono up so the light shone on the gay silken flowers. Sitting down in the chair, she spread the faded silk on her knee and looked across the room at her sewing basket which was on the dresser by the mirror. She fumbled patiently with the lining, patting the places that were torn; and suddenly she was sure she could draw the torn parts together and make it look bright and new.

'I think I can fix it up so it'll look fine, George,' she said.

'Eh,' he said. 'What are you bothering with that for?' Then he ducked down to the floor again and wiggled his paper moustache fiercely at the child.

The Shining Red Apple

It was the look of longing on the boy's face that made Joe Cosentino, dealer in fruits and vegetables, notice him. Joe was sitting on his high stool at the end of the counter where he sat every afternoon looking out of the window at the bunches of bananas and the cauliflowers and the tomatoes and apples piled outside on the street stand, and he was watching to see that the kids on the way home from school didn't touch any of the fruit.

This skinny little boy, who was wearing a red sweater and blue overalls, stood near the end of the fruit stand where there was a pyramid of big red apples. With his hands linked loosely together in front of him, and his head, with the straight, untidy brown hair that hung almost down to his blue eyes, cocked over to one side, he stood looking with longing at the apples. If he moved a little to the right, he would be out of sight of the window, but even so if he reached his hand out to take an apple, Joe, sitting at the end of the counter and watching, would surely see the hand. The sleeves of Joe's khaki shirt were rolled up, and as he sat on his stool he folded his hairy forearms across his deep chest. There wasn't much business, there seemed to be a little less every day, and sitting there week after week, he grew a little fatter and a little slower and ever so much more meditative. The store was untidy, and the fruit and the vegetables no longer had the cool, fresh appearance they had in the stores of merchants who were prosperous.

If the kid, standing outside, had been a big, resolute-looking boy, Joe would have been alert and suspicious, but as it was, it was amusing to sit there and pretend he could feel the kid's longing for the apple growing stronger. As though making the first move in a game, Joe leaned forward suddenly, and the boy, lowering his head, shuffled a few feet away. Then Joe, whistling thinly, as if he hadn't noticed anything, got up and went out, took out his handkerchief, and started to polish a few of the apples on the pile. They were big, juicy-looking apples, a little over-ripe and going soft. He polished them till they gleamed and glistened in the sun. Then he said to the kid, 'Fine day, eh, son?'

'Yeah,' the kid said timidly.

'You live around here?'

'No.'

'New around here, eh?' Joe said.

The kid, nodding his head shyly, didn't offer to tell where he lived, so Joe, chuckling to himself, and feeling powerful because he knew so surely just what would happen, went back to the store and sat down on the stool.

At first the little kid, holding his hands behind his back now, shuffled away out of sight, but Joe knew he would go no farther than the end of the stand; he knew the kid would be there looking up and down the street furtively, stretching his hand out a little, then withdrawing it in fear before he touched an apple, and always staring, wanting the apple more and more.

Joe got up and yawned lazily, wetting his lips and rubbing his hand across them, and then he deliberately turned his back to the window. But at the moment when he was sure the kid would make up his mind and shoot out his hand, he swung around, and he was delighted to see how the child's hand, empty and faltering, was pulled back. 'Ah, it goes just like a clock. I know just what he'll do,' Joe thought. 'He wants it, but he doesn't know how to take it because he's scared. Soon he wants it so much he'll have to take it. Then I catch him. That's the way it goes,' and he grinned.

But in a little while Joe began to feel that maybe he was making it far too hard for the kid, as though the apples were something precious and untouchable. So, doing a thing he hardly ever did, he went out onto the street, and, paying no attention to the kid, who had jumped away nervously, he mopped his shining forehead and wiped his red mouth and lazily picked up one of the apples from the top of the pile, as though all such luxuries of the world were within his reach. He munched it slowly with great relish, spitting out bits of red skin, and gnawing it down to the core. The kid must have been very hungry, for his mouth dropped open helplessly, and his blue eyes were innocent and hopeless.

After tossing the core in a wide arc far out on the street, where it lay in the sunlight and was attacked by two big flies, Joe started back into the store thinking, 'Now for sure he'll grab one. He won't wait now. He can't.' Yet to tantalize him, he didn't go right into the store; he turned at the door, looked up at the sky, as though expecting it to rain suddenly.

The frightened kid had really been ready to take an apple then. He had been so ready that he couldn't turn his head away, even though he knew Joe was watching him, for the apple seemed to belong to him now that he had made up his mind to take it and it was so close to him.

While Joe was grinning and feeling pleased with his cunning, his wife came in from the room at the back of the store. She was a black-haired woman, wide-hipped and slow-moving now, with tired brown eyes. When she stood beside her husband with her hands on her hips, she looked determined and sensible. 'The baby's sleeping now, I think, Joe. It's been pretty bad the way she's been going on.'

'That's good,' Joe said.

'She feels a lot better today.'

'She's all right.'

'I feel pretty tired. I think I'll lie down,' she said, but she walked over to the window and looked out at the street.

Then she said sharply, 'There's a kid out there near the apples. One's gone from the top.'

'I sold it,' Joe lied.

'Watch the kid,' she said.

'O.K.,' Joe said, and she went back to the bedroom.

Eagerly Joe looked again for the kid, who stood rooted there in spite of the hostile glance of the woman. 'I guess he doesn't know how to do it,' Joe thought. Yet the look of helpless longing was becoming so strong in the kid's face, so bold and unashamed, that it bothered Joe and made him irritable. He wanted to quarrel openly with the boy. 'Look at the face on you. Look out, kid, you'll start and cry in a minute,' he said to himself. 'So you think you can have everything you want, do you?' The agony of wanting was so plain in the boy's face that Joe was indignant. 'Who does the kid think he is?' he muttered.

In the room back of the store there was a faint whimpering and the sound of a baby stirring. 'Look at that, son,' Joe said to himself, as though still lecturing the kid. 'It's a nice baby, but it's not a boy. See what I mean? If you go round with that look on your face when you want things and can't get them, people'll only laugh at you.' As he spoke Joe grew restless and unhappy, and he looked helplessly around the untidy store, as if looking upon his own fate.

The kid on the sidewalk, who had shuffled away till he was out of sight, came edging back slowly. And Joe, getting excited, whispered, 'Why doesn't he take it when he wants it so much? I couldn't catch him if he took it and ran,' and he got up to be near the corner of the window, where he could see the boy's hand if it came reaching out. 'Now. Right now,' he muttered, really hoping it would happen.

Then he thought. 'What's the matter with him?' for the

kid was walking away, brushing by the fruit stand. One of his hands was swinging loose at his side. Then Joe realized that that swinging hand was to knock an apple off the pile and send it rolling along the sidewalk, and he got up eagerly and leaned forward with his head close to the window.

The kid, looking up warily, saw Joe's face and he grew frightened. His own face was full of terror. Ducking, he ran.

'Hey!' Joe yelled, running out to the sidewalk.

In a wild way the kid looked around, but he kept on running, his legs in the blue overalls pumping up and down.

Grabbing an apple and yelling, 'Hey, hey, kid, you can have it!' Joe followed a few steps, but the kid wouldn't look back.

Joe stood on the sidewalk, an awful eagerness growing in him as he stared at the shiny red apple and wondered what would happen to the kid he was sure he would never see again.

Guilty Woman

Mary Slater was a slim-bodied, dark-haired, nervous girl, with big brown eyes, who dressed very plainly because she felt that the men in the neighbourhood were no longer interested in her.

She was accustomed to doing the housework for her father, talking in the afternoon with the women on the street who had been married a long time, and waiting on her young sister, Peg, and on Peg's sweetheart, Stevenson, whenever he came to the house. He came almost every night to the old house on Grove Street and sat in the front room with the plump, fair-haired, rosy-cheeked Peg; and Mary passed back and forth from the front room to the kitchen carrying coffee and sandwiches. Most of the evening Mary remained in the kitchen, talking with her father, a quick-tempered, devout, hard-working man in the trucking business. It never occurred to Mary that Stevenson ever noticed her at all.

For months Stevenson had thought of Mary just as Peg's older sister, till one night when he glanced at her timidly with his soft blue eyes. Sometimes, after that, he was embarrassed by her presence when he wanted to be alone with Peg, so she went back to the kitchen.

When Mary was carrying a tray with coffee and sandwiches one night, Peg left the room for a moment. Stevenson and Mary were alone. As she passed him he reached out and took hold of her hand while he looked at her helplessly. He wanted to say something quickly: instead, he looked down at her slender white hand, coarsened a bit from doing nearly all the housework, raised his eyes fearfully, then dropped her hand abruptly as if he had become suddenly bewildered. When Peg returned, he was silent and almost afraid. He seemed to have been thinking about Mary for so long that it had been necessary finally to reach out his hand and touch her.

All that night the warmth of his hand was on Mary's hand and she could not sleep. The simple peacefulness of her life had been upset: she wondered if she ought to tell her sister. As she lay awake, she felt like crying because it seemed that her faith in people had been disturbed, and then she thought gropingly that if the strong feeling had been in Stevenson for a long time, everything was spoilt for her sister anyway.

She was upset all next morning, especially whenever she looked at her plump, self-reliant sister, who was mending a dress on the sewing-machine. Mary felt like a very guilty woman.

On Friday night Mary's father was jovial with Stevenson. Mouse-like and timid now, Mary stood by the door and listened as her father asked Stevenson if he would mind his taking Peg to visit his brother in the country on his half-holiday the next day. Stevenson said no.

Slater went back to the kitchen, and Peg followed him. Quite loudly, Stevenson congratulated Mary on the lemonade, and then whispered uneasily, 'Tomorrow evening. I'll come here.'

Mary hurried out to the kitchen and sat down with her elbows on the table. Then she sat up very straight in the chair, listening for every small sound from the other room. Her body was so erect and her heart beating so heavily, she was sure her father would notice her. When she heard Peg's light, careless laughter, she felt dreadfully ashamed, and full of love for her young sister.

Before Peg could speak to her, Mary went upstairs to bed to try to sleep so she would not have to feel her sister in the bed beside her. But as she buried her thin face in the pillow, she couldn't help thinking with fierce eagerness that made her tingle, that she really had a lover.

Next afternoon she stood on the stoop watching her father and Peg going along the street together, and all she thought was that her father was getting older; he was leaning forward, his hat on the back of his head.

The afternoon passed slowly. In the early evening, just before it got dark, she dressed carefully and went over to the avenue to do the shopping for Sunday, a rather graceful, slender, timid woman, with moistened lips and alert eyes, wearing a light print dress.

On the way home a neighbour, Mrs. Johnston, asked her to sit down for a while, and Mary was glad because she felt now that she had an excuse for not going home till late. Mrs. Johnston rocked back and forth and wondered why Mary was answering her so jerkily. In the dark she couldn't see the warm flush on Mary's face. Mary was feeling a strange new tenderness for Stevenson and an intimation of a curious happiness. She left Mrs. Johnston and walked home.

She had decided, as a compromise, that she would be in the house, but wouldn't answer the door, if Stevenson should come.

She went up to her own room and lay down with the light lit, and once she muttered, 'I'd love him, far more than Peg would, and if he really and truly loves me, that's the main thing.' When she heard someone knocking on the front door she closed her eyes and did not move. She heard the door open and someone moving downstairs. From the hall Stevenson called softly, 'Mary, Mary, where are you?'

'You'd better go,' she said weakly.

But he came and stood by her door, blinking his blue eyes in the light. He was excited and a little bewildered as he fumbled for words. Mary sat on the edge of her bed, staring at him with her dark, earnest eyes.

When he saw that she was really glad to see him he sat down beside her and said, 'Nobody saw me come in. I had to come. I just kept on looking at you. I didn't know what to do about it. I don't know what we can do.' But she shook her head as if she didn't want him to talk at all.

'I'm glad you came,' she said simply. 'Don't worry about it.'

Then he put his arms around her, and as she stroked his fair hair with her long slender hand, it seemed to her that she would never again have as much delight and contentment as she had at that moment, running her fingers through his damp, curly hair. Like a boy he held his head down to her breast.

She was kissing him for the first time when she heard an automobile stopping outside. She didn't pay much attention till she heard laughter, and Peg's voice, and then her father's voice calling, 'Good night, Mr. Redmond, thanks for the ride. We got home in no time at all.'

Abruptly, Mary said to Stevenson, who was shaking his head awkwardly, 'Please go.' But he was staring helplessly, with a frightened expression on his face. With her fingers on her lips she was hoping he would not go. But she said, 'Hurry, hurry.'

'What will I do?' he asked.

'I don't know,' she said, hearing her father's footsteps in the hall.

As her father began to come upstairs young Stevenson listened, then went to the window; the roof of the back porch was only a few feet away below. He opened the window and said desperately, his eyes wide, 'Please don't tell him. You won't tell, will you?'

'No, I won't,' she said.

Her father, calling, 'Who's there, Mary?' came into the room just as he heard Stevenson dropping to the porch roof, sliding on the shingles, and running.

Slater's face was red and swollen with anger. 'Who was

it?' he said, moving closer to her. 'Will you tell me? I heard a man talking. Will you tell me?'

'No,' she said, feeling like a completely abandoned woman.

Her father swung his palm at her face. Screaming, as he hit her, she darted past him to run downstairs. He followed and at the bottom step caught hold of her dress. She slipped, and lay still.

Her father was mumbling, 'You, you, you, and in my house. So that's what's been going on, eh?'

He was so angry, he didn't know what to do. Grabbing an umbrella from the hall rack, he began to beat her. He hit her on the back and the hips. She crawled along the hall, without even crying out. He hit her again as she pushed open the back door and reached the steps. She tripped and sprawled on the cement.

Gasping for breath, Slater looked down at her, then looked at the umbrella and tossed it away awkwardly.

'I never knew she was that kind of a woman,' he muttered.

Peg, who came out crying quietly, said, 'Please, Papa, don't touch her any more, take her in.'

Slater stared down at Mary. He lifted her and carried her upstairs and left her in her own room.

She lay alone in the darkness, moaning softly, for her hip was badly hurt. She heard Peg come into the room and sit down.

'You must have been crazy,' Peg said, stroking her sister's head, 'I can't imagine who it was.'

'I was crazy, I guess, but don't ask me who it was, Peg.'

In the morning, when Mary woke up, she heard her father and her sister going out to church. She knew that Peg was to meet Stevenson at church.

'He may tell them that he really loves me,' she whispered. She could hardly move her hip.

But when they came home from church and she heard Peg laughing and talking cheerfully, she knew that Stevenson hadn't mentioned her at all. She wondered why he was so sure she wouldn't tell, and then she felt sorry for him, for he seemed so young, and he didn't know how to have her when he really wanted her. As she began to think of the few moments she had had with him, his smooth face and his damp curly hair pressed down against her breast, she said softly, 'Maybe he didn't know the way it was with me,' and part of a world that nobody else could ever touch seemed to belong to her alone.

The Faithful Wife

Until a week before Christmas George worked in the station restaurant at the lunch counter. The last week was extraordinarily cold, then the sun shone strongly for a few days, though it was always cold again in the evenings. There were three other men working at the counter. For years they must have had a poor reputation. Women, unless they were careless and easy-going, never started a conversation with them when having a light lunch at noontime. The girls at the station always avoided the red-capped porters and the counter-men.

George, who was working there till he got enough money to go back home for a week and then start late in the year at college, was a young fellow with fine hair retreating far back on his forehead and rather bad upper teeth, but he was very polite and generous. Steve, the plump Italian with the waxed black moustaches, who had charge of the restaurant, was very fond of George.

Many people passed the restaurant window on the way to the platform and the trains. The four men, watching them frequently, got to know some of them. Girls, brightly dressed and highly powdered, loitered in front of the open door, smiling at George, who saw them so often he knew their first names. At noontime, other girls, with a few minutes to spare before going back to work, used to walk up and down the tiled tunnel to the waiting-room, loafing the time away, but they never even glanced in at the counter-men. It was cold outside, the streets were slippery, and it was warm in the station, that was all. George got to know most of these girls too, and talked about them with the other fellows.

George watched carefully one girl every day at noon hour. The other men had also noticed her, and two or three times she came in for a cup of coffee, but she was so gentle, and aloofly pleasant, and so unobtrusively beyond them, they were afraid to try and amuse her with easy cheerful talk. George wished earnestly that she had never seen him there in the restaurant behind the counter, even though he knew she had never noticed him at all. Her cheeks were usually rosy from the cold wind outside. When she went out of the door to walk up and down for a few minutes, an agreeable expression on her face, she never once looked back at the restaurant. George, following her with his eye while pouring coffee slowly, did not expect her to look back. She was about twenty-eight, pretty, rather shy, and dressed plainly and poorly in a thin blue-cloth coat without any fur on it. Most girls managed to have a piece of fur of some kind on their coats.

With little to do in the middle of the afternoon, George used to think of her because of seeing her every day and looking at her face in profile when she passed the window. Then, on the day she had on the light-fawn felt hat, she smiled politely at him, when having a cup of coffee, and as long as possible he remained opposite her, cleaning the counter with a damp cloth.

The last night he worked at the station he went out at about half past eight in the evening, for he had an hour to himself, and then worked on till ten o'clock. In the morning he was going home, so he walked out of the station and down the side street to the docks, and was having only pleasant thoughts, passing the warehouses, looking out over the dark cold lake and liking the tang of the wind on his face. Christmas was only a week away. The snow was falling lazily and melting slowly when it hit the sidewalk. He was glad he was through with the job at the restaurant.

An hour later, back at the restaurant, Steve said, 'A dame

just phoned you, George, and left her number.'

'Do you know who she was?'

'No, you got too many girls, George. Don't you know the number?'

'I never saw it before.'

He called the number and did not recognize the voice that answered him. A woman was asking him pleasantly enough if he remembered her. He said he did not. She said she had had a cup of coffee that afternoon at noontime, and added that she had worn a blue coat and a tan-coloured felt hat, and even though she had not spoken to him, she thought he would remember her.

'Good Lord,' he said.

She wanted to know if he would come and see her at half past ten that evening. Timidly he said he would, and hardly heard her giving the address. Steve and the other boys started to kid him brightly, but he was too astonished, wondering how she had found out his name, to bother with them. The boys, saying good-bye to him later, winked and elbowed him in the ribs, urging him to celebrate on his last night in the city. Steve, who was very fond of him, shook his head sadly and pulled the ends of his moustaches down into his lips.

The address the girl had given him was only eight blocks away, so he walked, holding his hands clenched tightly in his pockets, for he was cold from nervousness. He was watching the automobile headlights shining on slippery spots on the sidewalk. The house, opposite a public-school ground on a side street, was a large old rooming-house. A light was in a window on the second storey over the door. Ringing the bell he didn't really expect anyone to answer, and was surprised when the girl herself opened the door.

'Good evening,' he said shyly.

'Oh, come upstairs,' she said smiling and practical.

In the front room he took off his overcoat and hat and sat down slowly, noticing, out of the corner of his eye, that she was even slimmer, and had nice fair hair and lovely eyes. But she was moving very nervously. He had intended to ask at once how she found out his name, but forgot about it as soon as she sat down opposite him on a camp bed and smiled shyly. She had on a red woollen sweater, fitting her tightly at the waist. Twice he shook his head, unable to get used to having her there opposite him, nervous and expectant. The trouble was she had always seemed so aloof.

'You're not very friendly,' she said awkwardly.

'Oh yes I am. Indeed I am.'

'Why don't you come over here and sit beside me?'

Slowly he sat down beside her on the camp bed, smiling stupidly. He was even slow to see that she was waiting for him to put his arms around her. Ashamed of himself, he finally kissed her eagerly and she held on to him tightly. Her heart was thumping underneath the red woollen sweater. She just kept on holding him, almost savagely, closing her eyes slowly and breathing deeply every time he kissed her. She was so delighted and satisfied to hold him in her arms that she did not bother talking at all. Finally he became very eager and she got up suddenly, walking up and down the room, looking occasionally at the cheap alarm clock on a bureau. The room was clean but poorly furnished.

'What's the matter?' he said irritably.

'My girl friend, the one I room with, will be home in twenty minutes.'

'Come here anyway.'

'Please sit down, please do,' she said.

Slowly he sat down beside her. When he kissed her she did not object but her lips were dry, her shoulders were trembling, and she kept on watching the clock. Though she was holding his wrist so tightly her nails dug into the skin, he knew she would be glad when he had to go. He kissed her again and she drew her left hand slowly over her lips.

'You really must be out of here before Irene comes home,' she said.

'But I've only kissed and hugged you and you're wonderful.' He noticed the red ring mark on her finger. 'Are you sure you're not waiting for your husband to come home?' he said a bit irritably.

Frowning, looking away vaguely, she said, 'Why do you have to say that?'

'There's a ring mark on your finger.'

'I can't help it,' she said, and began to cry quietly. 'Yes, oh yes, I'm waiting for my husband to come home. He'll be here at Christmas.'

'It's too bad. Can't we do something about it?'

'I tell you I love my husband. I do, I really do, and I'm faithful to him too.'

'Maybe I'd better go,' he said uncomfortably, feeling ridiculous.

'Eh, what's that? My husband, he's at a sanitarium. He got his spine hurt in the war, then he got tuberculosis. He's pretty bad. They've got to carry him around. We want to love each other every time we meet, but we can't.'

'That's tough, poor kid, and I suppose you've got to pay for him.'

'Yes.'

'Do you have many fellows?'

'No, I don't want to have any.'

'Do they come here to see you?'

'No. No, I don't know what got into me. I liked you, and felt a little crazy.'

'I'll slide along then. What's your first name?'

'Lola. You'd better go now.'

'Couldn't I see you again?' he said suddenly.

'No, you're going away tomorrow,' she said, smiling confidently.

'So you've got it all figured out. Supposing I don't go?'

'Please, you must.'

Her arms were trembling when she held his overcoat. She wanted him to go before Irene came home. 'You didn't give me much time,' he said flatly.

'No. Irene comes in at this time. You're a lovely boy. Kiss me.'

'You had that figured out too.'

'Just kiss and hold me once more, George.' She held on to him as if she did not expect to be embraced again for a long time, and he said, 'I think I'll stay in the city a while longer.'

'It's too bad, but you've got to go. We can't see each other again.'

In the poorly lighted hall she looked lovely. Her cheeks were flushed, and though still eager, she was quite satisfied with the whole affair. Everything had gone perfectly for her.

As he went out of the door and down the walk to the street he remembered that he hadn't asked how she had found out his name. Snow was falling lightly and there were hardly any footprints on the sidewalk. All he could think of was that he ought to go back to the restaurant, and ask Steve for his job again. Steve was fond of him. But he knew he could not spoil it for her. 'She had it all figured out,' he muttered, turning up his coat collar.

Ancient Lineage

The young man from the Historical Club with a green magazine under his arm got off the train at Clintonville. It was getting dark but the station lights were not lit. He hurried along the platform and jumped down on the sloping cinder path to the sidewalk.

Trees were on the lawns alongside the walk, branches drooping low, leaves scraping occasionally against the young man's straw hat. He saw a cluster of lights, bluish-white in the dusk across a river, many lights for a small town. He crossed the lift-lock bridge and turned on to the main street. A hotel was at the corner.

At the desk a bald-headed man in a blue shirt, the sleeves rolled up, looked critically at the young man while he registered. 'All right, Mr. Flaherty,' he said, inspecting the signature carefully.

'Do you know many people around here?' Mr. Flaherty asked.

'Just about everybody.'

'The Rowers?'

'The old lady?'

'Yeah, an old lady.'

'Sure, Mrs. Anna Rower. Around the corner to the left,

then turn to the right out the first street, the house opposite the Presbyterian church on the hill.'

'An old family,' suggested the young man.

'An old-timer all right.' The hotel man made it clear by a twitching of his lips that he was a part of the new town, canal, water power, and factories.

Mr. Flaherty sauntered out and turned to the left. It was dark and the street had the silence of small towns in the evening. Turning a corner he heard girls giggling in a doorway. He looked at the church on the hill, the steeple dark against the sky. He had forgotten whether the man had said beside the church or across the road, but could not make up his mind to ask the fellow who was watering the wide church lawn. No lights in the shuttered windows of the rough-cast house beside the church. He came down the hill and had to yell three times at the man because the water swished strongly against the grass.

'All right, thanks. Right across the road,' Mr. Flaherty repeated.

Tall trees screened the square brick house. Looking along the hall to a lighted room, Mr. Flaherty saw an old lady standing at a sideboard. 'She's in all right,' he thought, rapping on the screen door. A large woman of about forty, dressed in blue skirt and blue waist, came down the stairs. She did not open the screen door.

'Could I speak to Mrs. Anna Rower?'

'I'm Miss Hilda Rower.'

'I'm from the University Historical Club.'

'What did you want to see Mother for?'

Mr. Flaherty did not like talking through the screen door. 'I wanted to talk to her,' he said firmly.

'Well, maybe you'd better come in.'

He stood in the hall while the large woman lit the gas in the front room. The gas flared up, popped, showing fat hips and heavy lines on her face. Mr. Flaherty, disappointed, watched her swaying down the hall to get her mother. He carefully inspected the front room, the framed photographs of dead Conservative politicians, the group of military men hanging over the old-fashioned piano, the faded greenish wallpaper and the settee in the corner.

An old woman with a knot of white hair and good eyes came into the room, walking erectly. 'This is the young man who wanted to see you, Mother,' Miss Hilda Rower said. They all sat down. Mr. Flaherty explained he wanted to get some information concerning the Rower genealogical tree for the next meeting of his society. The Rowers, he knew, were a pioneer family in the district, and descended from William the Conqueror, he had heard.

The old lady laughed thinly, swaying from side to side. 'It's true enough, but I don't know who told you. My father was Daniel Rower, who came to Ontario from Cornwall in 1830.'

Miss Hilda Rower interrupted. 'Wait, Mother, you may not want to tell about it.' Brusque and businesslike, she turned to the young man. 'You want to see the family tree, I suppose.'

'Oh, yes.'

'My father was a military settler here,' the old lady said.

'I don't know but what we might be able to give you some notes,' Miss Hilda spoke generously.

'Thanks awfully, if you will.'

'Of course you're prepared to pay something if you're going to print it,' she added, smugly adjusting her big body in the chair.

Mr. Flaherty got red in the face; of course he understood, but to tell the truth he had merely wanted to chat with Mrs. Rower. Now he knew definitely he did not like the heavy nose and unsentimental assertiveness of the lower lip of this big woman with the wide shoulders. He couldn't stop looking at her thick ankles. Rocking back and forth in the chair she was primly conscious of lineal superiority; a proud unmarried woman, surely she could handle a young man, half-closing her eyes, a young man from the University indeed. 'I don't want to talk to her about the University,' he thought.

Old Mrs. Rower went into the next room and returned with a framed genealogical tree of the house of Rower. She handed it graciously to Mr. Flaherty, who read, 'The descent of the family of Rower, from William the Conqueror, from Malcolm 1st, and from the Capets, Kings of France.' It bore the *imprimatur* of the College of Arms, 1838.

'It's wonderful to think you have this,' Mr. Flaherty said, smiling at Miss Hilda, who watched him suspiciously.

'A brother of mine had it all looked up,' old Mrs. Rower said.

'You don't want to write about that,' Miss Hilda said, crossing her ankles. The ankles looked much thicker crossed. 'You just want to have a talk with Mother.'

'That's it,' Mr. Flaherty smiled agreeably.

'We may write it up ourselves some day.' Her heavy chin dipped down and rose again.

'Sure, why not?'

'But there's no harm in you talking to Mother if you want to, I guess.'

'You could write a good story about that tree,' Mr. Flaherty said, feeling his way.

'We may do it some day but it'll take time,' she smiled complacently at her mother, who mildly agreed.

Mr. Flaherty talked pleasantly to this woman, who was so determined he would not learn anything about the family tree without paying for it. He tried talking about the city, then tactfully asked old Mrs. Rower what she remembered of the Clintonville of seventy years ago. The old lady talked willingly, excited a little. She went into the next room to get a book of clippings. 'My father, Captain Rower, got a grant of land from the Crown and cleared it,' she said, talking over her shoulder. 'A little way up the Trent River. Clintonville was a small military settlement then . . .'

'Oh, Mother, he doesn't want to know all about that,' Miss Hilda said impatiently.

'It's very interesting indeed.'

The old woman said nervously, 'My dear, what difference does it make?' You wrote it all up for the evening at the church.'

'So I did too,' she hesitated, thinking the young man ought to see how well it was written. 'I have an extra copy.' She looked at him thoughtfully. He smiled. She got up and went upstairs.

The young man talked very rapidly to the old lady and took many notes.

Miss Rower returned. 'Would you like to see it?' She

handed Mr. Flaherty a small gray booklet. Looking quickly through it, he saw it contained valuable information about the district.

'The writing is simply splendid. You must have done a lot of work on it.'

'I worked hard on it,' she said, pleased and more willing to talk.

'Is this an extra copy?'

'Yes, it's an extra copy.'

'I suppose I might keep it,' he said diffidently.

She looked at him steadily. 'Well . . . I'll have to charge you twenty-five cents.'

'Sure, sure, of course, that's fine.' He blushed.

'Just what it costs to get them out,' the old lady explained apologetically.

'Can you change a dollar?' He fumbled in his pocket, pulling the dollar out slowly.

They could not change it but Miss Rower would be pleased to go down to the corner grocery store. Mr. Flaherty protested. No trouble, he would go. She insisted on asking the next-door neighbour to change it. She went across the room, the dollar in hand.

Mr. Flaherty chatted with the nice old lady and carefully examined the family tree, and wrote quickly in a small book till the screen door banged, the curtains parted, and Miss Hilda Rower came into the room. He wanted to smirk, watching her walking heavily, so conscious of her ancient lineage, a virginal mincing sway to her large hips, seventy-five cents' change held loosely in drooping fingers.

'Thank you,' he said, pocketing the change, pretending his work was over. Sitting back in the chair he praised the way Miss Rower had written the history of the neighbourhood and suggested she might write a splendid story of the family tree, if she had the material, of course.

'I've got the material, all right,' she said, trying to get comfortable again. How would Mr. Flaherty arrange it and where should she try to sell it? The old lady was dozing in the rocking chair. Miss Rower began to talk rather nervously about her material. She talked of the last title in the family and the Sir Richard who had been at the court of Queen Elizabeth.

Mr. Flaherty chimed in gaily, 'I suppose you know the O'Flahertys were kings in Ireland, eh?'

She said vaguely, 'I daresay, I daresay,' conscious only of an interruption to the flow of her thoughts. She went on talking with hurried eagerness, all the fine talk about her ancestors bringing her peculiar satisfaction. A soft light came into her eyes and her lips were moist.

Mr. Flaherty started to rub his cheek, and looked at her big legs, and felt restive, and then embarrassed, watching her closely, her firm lower lip hanging loosely. She was talking slowly, lazily, relaxing in her chair, a warm fluid oozing through her veins, exhausting but satisfying her.

He was uncomfortable. She was liking it too much. He did not know what to do. There was something immodest about it. She was close to forty, her big body relaxed in the chair. He looked at his watch and suggested he would be going. She stretched her legs graciously, pouting, inviting him to stay a while longer, but he was standing up, tucking his magazine under his arm. The old lady was still dozing. 'I'm so comfortable,' Miss Rower said, 'I hate to move.'

The mother woke up and shook hands with Mr. Flaherty. Miss Rower got up to say good-bye charmingly.

Half-way down the path Mr. Flaherty turned. She was standing in the doorway, partly shadowed by the tall trees, bright moonlight filtering through leaves touching soft lines on her face and dark hair.

He went down the hill to the hotel unconsciously walking with a careless stride, wondering at the change that had come over the heavy, strong woman. He thought of taking a walk along the river in the moonlight, the river on which old Captain Rower had drilled troops on the ice in the winter of 1837 to fight the rebels. Then he thought of having a western sandwich in the café across the road from the hotel. That big woman in her own way had been hot stuff.

In the hotel he asked to be called so he could get the first train to the city. For a long time he lay awake in the fresh, cool bed, the figure of the woman whose ancient lineage had taken the place of a lover in her life, drifting into his thoughts and becoming important while he watched on the wall the pale moonlight that had softened the lines of her face, and wondered if it was still shining on her bed, and on her throat, and on her contented, lazily relaxed body.

Let Me Promise You

Alice kept on returning to the window. Standing with her short straight nose pressed against the window pane, she watched the rain falling and the sidewalk shining under the street light. In her black crêpe dress with the big white nun-like collar and with her black hair drawn back tight from her narrow nervous face she looked almost boldly handsome.

Earlier in the evening it had started to snow, then it had begun to drizzle and now the rain was like a sharp sleet. As Alice stood at the window, she began to wish that the ground had been covered with an unbroken layer of fine thin snow, a white sheet that would remain undisturbed till Georgie came with his single line of footprints marking a path up to her door. Though her eyes remained wide open, she began to dream of a bitterly cold dry evening, of Georgie with a red scarf and a tingling face bursting in on her, grinning, his arms wide open. But the wind drove the sleet steadily against the pane. Sighing, she thought, 'He won't come in such weather. But he would if it weren't for the weather. I can't really expect him tonight.' So she walked away from the window and sat down.

Then her heart began to thump so slowly and heavily inside her she could hardly move, for someone was knocking. Opening the door in a rush, she cried, 'Georgie, you dear boy, I'm so glad you came,' and she put out her hands to help him off with his dripping coat. In the light belted coat he looked very tall and he had a smooth round face that would never look old. The wind and the rain had left his face wet and glowing, but he was pouting because he was uncomfortable in his damp clothes. As he pushed his fair wavy hair back from his eyes, he said, 'This isn't exactly a night for visiting.' He sat down, still a bit embarrassed by her enthusiasm, and he looked around the room as if he thought now that he had made a mistake in coming and didn't expect to be very comfortable. 'It's rotten out on a night like this when it can't make up its mind to snow or rain. Maybe you didn't think I'd come.'

'I wanted you to come, and because I wanted it, I thought you would, I guess,' she said candidly. So many days seemed to have passed since she had been alone with Georgie that now she wanted to take his head in her hands and kiss him. But she felt too shy. A year ago, she knew, he would have been waiting anxiously for her to kiss him.

'Alice,' he said suddenly.

'What's bothering you, Georgie, frowning like that?'

'What did you want me for? You said you wanted to speak about something in particular.'

'Such curiosity. You'll just sit there unable to rest till you find out, I suppose,' she said. She knew he was ill at ease, but she wanted to pretend to herself that he was just impatient and curious. So her pale handsome face was animated by a warm secret delight as she went across the room to a chest of drawers and took out a long cardboard box which she handed to him after making a low girlish curtsy. 'I hope you like it . . . darling,' she said shyly.

'What's this? What's the idea?' Georgie said as he undid the box and pulled out the tissue paper. When he saw that she was giving something to him, he became embarrassed and almost too upset to speak, and then, because he did not want to hurt her, he tried to be full of enthusiasm, 'Lord, look at it,' he said. 'White, turtle-necked sweater. If I wore that I'd look like a movie actor in his spare time. Should I put it on now, Al?' Grinning at her, he took off his coat and pulled the white sweater over his shirt. 'Do I look good? How about a mirror, Al?'

Alice held the mirror in front of him, watching him with

the same gentle expression of devotion all the time, and feeling within her a contentment she had hardly dared to hope for. The high-necked sweater made his fair head look like a faun's head.

'It's pretty swell, Al,' he said, but now that he couldn't go on pleasing her with enthusiasm, his embarrassment increased. 'You shouldn't be giving me this, Al,' he said. 'I didn't figure on anything like this when you phoned me and said you wanted to see me.'

'Today is your birthday, isn't it, Georgie?'

'Imagine you remembering that. You shouldn't be bothering with birthday presents for me now.'

'I thought you'd like the sweater,' she said. 'I saw it this afternoon. I knew it would look good on you.'

'But why give me anything, Al?' he said, feeling his awkwardness increasing.

'Supposing I want to?'

'You shouldn't waste your money on me.'

'Supposing I have something else, too,' she said teasing him.

'What's the idea, Al?'

'I saw something else, something you used to want an awful lot. Do you remember? Try and guess.'

'I can't imagine,' he said, but his face got red and he smiled awkwardly at being forced in this way to remember a time which only made him feel uncomfortable now when he recalled it.

Laughing huskily and showing her small even teeth because she was glad to be able to hold out something before him and tease him as she used to do, she moved lazily over to the chest of drawers, and this time took out a small leather watch case. 'Here you are,' she said.

'What is it, let me see,' he said, for he couldn't help being curious. He got up. But when he held the watch in his hand, he had to shake his head to conceal his satisfaction. 'It's funny the way you knew I always wanted something like that, Al,' he said. All his life he had wanted an expensive wrist-watch like this one, but had never expected to be able to buy it, and he was so pleased now that he smiled serenely.

But after a moment he put the watch irresolutely on the table, and was too embarrassed to speak. Walking the length of the room he began to whistle. As she watched him halt by the window, Alice knew he was uneasy. 'You're a great girl, Al,' he was saying. 'I don't know anybody like you.' After pausing, he added, 'Is it never going to stop raining? I've got to be on my way.'

'You're not going now, George, are you?'

'Yes, I promised to see a fellow. He'll be waiting.'

'George, don't go. Please don't,' she said, and she clench-ed the wet sleeve of the coat he had lifted from the chair. He was really ashamed to be going, especially if he picked up the watch from the table, but he felt if he stayed it would be like beginning everything all over again. He didn't know what to do about the watch, so he put out his hand hesitantly, knowing she was watching him and picked it up.

'So you're just coming here like this and then going?' she said.

'I've got to.'

'Have you got another girl?'

'No. I don't want another girl.'

'Yet you won't stay a little while with me?'

'That's over, Al. I don't know what's the matter with you. You phoned and wanted me to drop in for a moment.'

'It wasn't hard to see that you liked looking at the watch more than at me,' she said moodily.

'Here, if you don't want me to take the watch, all right,' he said, and with relief, he put it back on the table, and smiled.

For a moment she stared at the case, almost blinded by her disappointment, and hating his smile of relief, and then she cried out, 'You're just trying to humiliate me. Take it out of my sight.' She swung the back of her hand across the table, knocked the case to the floor and the watch against the wall where the glass broke, and trying not to cry, she clenched her fists and glared at him.

But he didn't even look at her. With his mouth drooping open, he looked longingly at the watch, for he realized how much he wanted it now that he saw it smashed on the floor. He had always wanted such a watch. As he looked up at her, his blue eyes were innocent with the sincerity of his full dis-appointment. 'Gee, Al,' was all he said.

The anger began to go out of her, and she felt how great

was his disappointment. She felt helpless. 'I shouldn't have done that, Georgie,' she said.

'It was a crazy thing to do. It was such a beauty,' he said. 'Why did you do it?'

'I don't know,' she said. She knelt down and started to cry. 'Maybe it's not broken much,' she faltered, moving around on her knees and picking up the pieces of glass carefully. In her hand she held the pieces but her eyes were blinking so that she could not see them. 'It was a crazy thing to do,' she was thinking. 'It helps nothing. It can't help bring him back to me. Why does he stand there like that? Why doesn't he move?' At last she looked up at him and saw his round smooth chin above the white neck of the sweater, and her dark eyes were shining with tears, for it seemed, as he watched her without speaking or moving, that everything ought to have turned out differently. They both looked at the broken pieces of glass she held in her hand in such abject despair, and for that moment while they looked, they began to share a common, bitter disappointment which made Georgie gravely silent and drew him close to her. 'Never mind, Al,' he said with awkward tenderness. 'Please get up.'

'No. Go away. Leave me alone.'

'You've got to get up from there. I can't stand here like this with you there.'

'Oh, why don't you go. I know I'm mean and jealous. I wish someone would shake me and hurt me. I'm a little cat.'

'No, you're not, Al. Who'd want to shake you? Please get up,' he said, putting his hand on her shoulder.

'Say you'll stay, Georgie,' she said, holding on to his hand. 'It's so warm here. It's miserable outside. Just listen to the wind. Do you hear it? I'll get you something to eat. You don't want to go, do you?'

'It's no worse than when I came,' he said, but his sudden tenderness for her was making him uneasy. He had known Al so well for a long time, she had been one of his girls, one he could feel sure of and leave at any time, but now he felt that he had never looked right at her and seen her before. He did not know her. The warmth of her love began to awe him. Her dark head, her pale oval face seemed so close to him that he might have put out his hand timidly and touched her and felt her whole ardent being under the cloth of her dress, but the sharp tremor inside him made him catch his breath, and destroyed all his old confidence. Faltering, he said, 'Gee, Al, I never got you right. Not in this way. I don't want to go. Look how I want to stay.'

'Georgie, listen to me,' she said eagerly. 'I'll get that watch for you. Or I'll get a new one. I'll save up for it. Or I'll get you anything else you say.'

'Don't think about it,' he said, shamefaced. 'I feel just like a bum.'

'But I want so much to do it, and you can look forward to it. We both can look forward. Please let me promise it to you.'

She was still crouched on the carpet. He glanced at her handsome dark face above the white nun-like collar and at her soft pleading eyes. 'You look lovely right now, Al,' he said. 'You look like a wild thing. Honest to God you do.'

Touched by happiness, she smiled. Then with all her heart she began to yearn for something more to give him. If there were only more things she had and could give, she thought; if she could only give everything in the world and leave herself nothing.

Soldier Harmon

There were twelve pool-tables in the club, a shaded pyramid of white light over each one of the tables, and the corners of the room were shadowed. On a bench at the wall four fellows in peak caps and one in a hard hat were watching a game and spitting alternately at a spittoon near an end of the table. It was ten minutes to seven, Saturday evening.

They were watching Joe Harmon, a big man with a slow grin and a dark smudge under his left eye, and his manager, Doc Barnes, a small, neat man with shiny black hair. Doc Barnes, concentrating, looked carefully at three balls on the table, then looked at them from another angle, and finally, with his hip on the end of the table, leaned over the green baize.

'All right, one foot on the floor,' Joe said.

'It's there; keep your shirt on,' the Doc said, feinting with his cue.

'On the floor, Doc.'

'I got it on the floor, I tellya.'

'Yea, if your leg was three inches longer, Doc.'

The Doc was sore but before he could reply, someone yelled and shoes scraped on the floor near the door, and he sat on the table, his mouth open. Joe turned. The young men on the bench got up and moved over to the door. The club bouncer had grabbed a wide-shouldered man in a tight overcoat. 'Throw him out!' someone yelled. The bouncer, pressing his head against the man's chest, tried to swing him off his feet toward the open door. A fat man in his shirt-sleeves was holding the door open. The wide-shouldered man, breaking away, pulled off his overcoat quickly, swinging it at arm's length, and draped it over the bouncer's head and, laughing, jabbed at the head under the coat while everybody laughed with him.

Joe Harmon watched it, one hand on his hip. In his other hand he held the cue, the handle-butt on the floor. Clearing his throat loudly, he aimed at the spittoon. He let the cue drop against the table, then he took two slow steps toward the crowd, his heavy red face wrinkling at the mouth and under the eyes, and lines on his forehead. Doc Barnes, jumping down from the table suddenly, grabbed Joe's arm.

'Lay off, Joe,' he said, coaxingly.

'Sit down, Doc.'

'Don't get in it, Joe. Come on; get out of here,' and he jerked Joe around. 'You big sap,' he said. 'What do you want mixing up in that stuff? Come on, you thickhead.' He grabbed Joe's vest from a peg on the wall, then held his coat for him and his overcoat, trying to keep him from looking at the fight near the door.

They went down the back stairs and out of the lane to the street. Snow had gone from the streets by the middle of March, though ice was close to the curb. They went into the Chink's at the corner. The Doc ordered two hot roast-beef sandwiches, pumpkin pie, and coffee, and, leaning back in the chair, watched Joe, who had his elbows on the hard white table, a stubborn expression on his face.

'It simply don't do, Joe,' he said.

'No.'

'Absolutely no. Who the hell's going to pay to see you fight if they just have to hang around a pool-room and get it for nothing? It's not business. Don't give your stuff away.'

Joe grinned. 'A guy's got to have a little fun now and again. That stuff up in the club there's real. The other ain't. The other's just motions.'

'Not when you're right, Joe. Not on your life, old boy, when you're ready to let them have it,' and he reached over and slapped Joe on the back. The Chink brought the hot roast-beef sandwiches with lots of gravy.

'We could have been up there for half an hour yet,' Joe said, sticking his fork in the sandwich, 'though I guess it's time to eat anyhow.'

'What do you care? Go on and see Molly.'

'Maybe I might as well,' Joe said. He ate the sandwich rapidly.

After leaving the Chink's, Joe went eight blocks east to Leslie Street to see Molly Turner. He had been going with Molly for four years and would have married her, but was uncertain of himself since taking up boxing professionally. She was so eager for him to work hard at training he often imagined he really liked it, though he had explained to her he got tired of sparring and road-work and even watching bouts, because he was interested only in the big moment in a fight and everything led up to it.

Her apartment was a two minutes' walk from the car stop and he went in without knocking. She was sitting in a rocking-chair near a floor-lamp, reading a paper, and eating chocolates. The box was on the arm of the rocking-chair. Joe saw the chocolates and looked at the box deliberately, but didn't actually suggest having one because he didn't want to argue for five minutes about training, before eating it. The chocolate wasn't worth it. She had on a black skirt and a neat gray sweater. He kissed her, looked thoughtful, then kissed her again.

'You're a little early, eh, Joe?'

'Maybe a little, but the earlier the better; we won't have to line up for the show.'

He watched her putting on her coat, and pale-blue hat, having only pleasant thoughts, and wondering why he had expected some kind of an argument.

She asked questions about Doc Barnes. He answered agreeably, so she kept on asking questions till he said, irritated: 'Molly, you know how this bothers me.' She was sullen, and in the show looked directly at the picture, pulling away her hand whenever his fingers groped for it, though sometimes she let him hold it just long enough to realize he had it.

They didn't quarrel openly, and for the rest of the evening talked politely, but when he had left her he felt unhappy. He lived with his father and mother. When he opened the door, his bull pup, coming clumsily along the hall, jumped at him. And he tapped it lightly on the skull and slapped its back, going on through to the kitchen with the pup still biting at his heels and ankles. His mother and father were in bed. Sitting at the end of the table, he bit his nails and worried about Molly. Then he pushed the chair back from the table and faced the dog that jumped eagerly while he swept the legs from under it, rolling it on the floor. Molly wanted to talk about big purses, opportunities, contenders, and hard work. Her ambition bothered him, since he was making good money fighting preliminary bouts at the Coliseum and main bouts at the Standard Theatre. He was Soldier Harmon, a favourite, a reliable fighter. The engagements at the Coliseum were more profitable, but he preferred the Standard where the crowd, friendly and close to the ring, appreciated his style. They cheered every time he climbed through the ropes. He was earning a living and was satisfied. Molly was not satisfied. Doc Barnes wasn't satisfied. His father and mother weren't satisfied. He got up, gave the dog something to eat, put it in the cellar, and went to bed.

In the morning he put a chain on the dog and walked as far as the church with his mother. Every Sunday morning he and the dog walked to church with his mother. At the church he left her and stood on the curb, urging the dog to become playful, while kids going into church looked at him respectfully, noticing the dark smudge under his left eye, and older fellows said distinctly: 'There's Soldier Harmon.' Many men had seen his picture in the paper. He stood near the curb, dressed smartly, a handkerchief tucked carelessly in his breast-pocket. He snapped his fingers at the dog but it wasn't feeling playful.

On Sunday evening he walked with Molly in University Park, and though it was chilly, and frost still in the ground, they sat down in the shadow of a University building. Carefully avoiding asking any questions that would irritate him. She sat close to him on the bench, a plump and pretty little girl in a dark-blue overcoat. Sitting there he was so pleased and good-natured, and she was so intensely interested in his work, he seemed to be asking himself questions. He kissed her and told her he was matched with Harry Greb, the middle-weight champion, in September, out at the Coliseum. She was enthusiastic, but it was too cold to be sitting on a park bench, her nose was red, her feet were cold. So they got up, both shivering, to look for a café where they could get coffee.

He remembered that Sunday evening, because he had felt like definitely suggesting they get married, but was glad he had hesitated, for in the hot summer months, every time he saw her she seemed to be looking at him critically, ready to ask about training and road-work. At times he wished she didn't know so much about fighting. She was working at a notion-counter in Woolworth's and in the afternoons he used to go in and see her.

One afternoon, leaning against her counter, he said: 'I think I'll get a real job, Molly.'

'My heavens, man, what do you mean?' she said.

'I'm getting tired of doing nothing.'

'Nothing!'

'Sure; I don't think much of work-outs and sparring and all that stuff.'

Her boss came along the aisle and Joe left. He walked all the way home. He had intended to tell her how eager he was to get a job and just fight when he felt like it. She wouldn't listen seriously. He had had an argument with Doc, who was trying to teach him foot-work, and he said to Barnes: 'Look here, Doc, I'm a fighter, not a boxer; I don't ever want to be a boxer.' The Doc had told him he had a thick head, that was the trouble. For the first time he had been disgusted with Barnes, and the idea of being a professional boxer. He understood finally that he was a business investment for Barnes.

In August he fought twice at the Standard Theatre and wasn't interested in his opponents. He defeated Indian Sam Burns because the Indian was afraid of him, and the other man fouled him. Joe told his father he was losing interest in his work; too many things were getting on his nerves. His father suggested that he get married and settle down, and Joe felt unhappy.

'I think maybe Molly's a little too much for me,' he said.

Alone in his own room he felt sorry for Molly and disappointed in himself. He had been going with her four years and knew he ought to marry her. He liked her, but felt it would be unfair to marry her, knowing he would only disappoint her. She was a business woman, and a lovely girl, but very determined.

For two weeks he trained seriously for his fight with Harry Greb. Greb was a smaller man than the Soldier, though always impressive against a slow, awkward man. The crowd enjoyed watching his arms moving like a windmill while he pounded a slow man. Joe was eager to meet him because he thought he might knock him out. Only very good men beat Greb.

After training an hour at the Adonis in the evening, Joe took the street-car to Molly's house and together they went out to Sunnyside, the amusement park on the lake-front. They had two hot dogs and stood on the board walk listening to the orthophonic victrola. Joe wanted to buy some French-fried potatoes, a few glasses of pineapple juice, and some toasted waffles, but Molly insisted it would be hard on his wind. They argued. She was considerate, understanding but firm. She reminded him how important it was for them that he should knock out Greb. When he stood in front of the waffle-stand, arguing, she took him by the arm and they walked out of the park, along to the road that leads into High Park, a natural park with hills, a pond, many bridle-paths through trees, and benches in unexpected places.

They sat down on a bench in a hollow between low hills. There was a moon. Molly looked pretty, her clothes seemed to fit her, and she was neater than when he had met her four years ago. He was silent a long time, knowing she was feeling irritable. To get her feeling good, he began to talk about big purses he would get, if he knocked out Greb.

'What do you think of that?' he said.

'You know what I think.'

'Yeah?'

'Sure; I suppose we'll get married at once and take a trip,' she said.

'Sure we would, Molly.'

'Yes, we would.' She looked very sad. He felt uncomfortable. It was a time to suggest getting married at once, but he could only stretch his legs, feeling unhappy. Then he felt that he owed a great deal to her, a sincere feeling, and his thick fingers were running through her hair, but he couldn't bring himself to speak. Her silence embarrassed him as he watched automobile headlights on the road that dipped out of sight.

She got up and said angrily: 'You're an old slow-poke, Joe; that's all there is to it.'

They walked back the way they had come.

When he left her, later on in the evening, he kissed her roughly, but within himself he was unsatisfied because he couldn't think of a satisfactory solution. Instead of going home he went into a soda fountain and had two chocolate sodas, sitting on the high stool his elbows on the counter, trying to feel good. He wanted to marry her. Sooner or later he would marry her, and then she'd see that he got many bouts and good purses. He decided to tell her that he had no use for boxing-matches, and would rather have a job, getting into a fight occasionally. He rarely got the right feeling out of one of the boxing-matches.

On Saturday night Harry Greb beat Soldier Harmon out at the Coliseum. The Soldier fought with such distinction his name was in all the papers. He knocked Greb out in the third round but the bell saved him. His seconds worked over him so he could stall through the fourth round and then he punched Joe so often he got tired. The Soldier's face was badly marked, but on Sunday morning he walked with his mother to church.

Molly couldn't understand why Joe was so pleased with himself.

'I hit him dead on, didn't I?' he said.

'That's not the point.'

'He was really out, wasn't he?'

'But if you could have finished him.'

'It was wonderful, really wonderful,' he said.

The third round was the only part of the fight he seemed to remember distinctly. Many people talked to him about it, Doc Barnes, his father and mother, sporting writers, and he reminded them of the third round, grinning happily. Doc Barnes was so impressed by Joe's durability he consented to a bout with Tommy Goldie, a big, Negro heavy-weight, a graceful boxer, whom he had carefully avoided because of his speed.

Joe shook hands with Barnes when he heard of the match with Goldie. He was interested in meeting the Negro, not because of local rivalry, although Goldie had been jeering at him for months, but he had watched him working out at one of the gyms, a big lean body working smoothly, and he had been aware of a nervous eagerness, the old feeling that came to him when watching a man he wanted to knock out. He rarely saw a man who was to be his opponent until they met in the ring. He liked the surprise and satisfaction of looking across the ring and seeing someone who excited him. Some of them were disappointing. He knew instinctively that Goldie would be satisfactory.

Two weeks before the fight he quarrelled with Molly. She had become nervous and irritable. In a temper she had used some words that had surprised him. When his father and mother stubbornly insisted that he was being unfair to the girl, he tried to make it clear for everybody concerned, explaining carefully his feeling that marriage with Molly would mean a long, tiresome effort to become a champion, till he had lost all interest in fighting. They were sitting in the kitchen. His father had his feet up on the stove.

'You're lazy, Joe; mighty damned lazy,' his father said.

'You're all wrong, Pa; I'll get a job tomorrow, but that won't please anybody.'

'But good Lord, Joe, what about the big money?'

'It just don't appeal to me. I want to fight when I feel like it,' Joe said. 'And I can't do it and get married.'

Three days before the fight with Goldie he developed an unusual interest in road-work, jogging along five or six miles a day. Doc Barnes, becoming enthusiastic and eager to encourage the Soldier, talked about the absolute necessity of strong legs and good wind, and offered to accompany him. But Joe went alone, leaving the Adonis at two o'clock in the afternoon, running unevenly with a clumsy, jerky stride. He had never done much road-work. He jogged up Broadview Avenue, slowing to a walk occasionally, his eyes always on the ground. The steady pounding of his feet as he ran helped him to think clearly, and he had long imaginary conversations with Molly. Outside the city limits there were more trees and open fields. He lay down on the bank at the roadside, his hands behind his head, his eyes closed. He wondered if Molly would be at the fight.

He felt strong and very confident the night of the fight. He was sitting in the dressing-room talking to Doc Barnes, waiting for the last of the preliminaries to finish, and the Doc, wearing a new silk shirt, was leaning against a table, giving him advice. Barnes always gave him advice before a fight, though he knew it didn't help him. The Soldier was more interested in his bull pup which he was holding on the table, regarding it critically. Many thoughts had been bothering him all day but now he was worried because it looked as if the pup's legs weren't going to bow sufficiently to give him a really ferocious appearance. He grabbed the legs at the joints, hunching up the shoulders. He pulled down the lower lip, showing strong teeth. The dog liked it and looked splendid as long as he could hold the position. Doc Barnes went on talking. The Soldier studied the dog carefully. They could hear the crowd shouting.

Doc Barnes stepped out of the room. He came back quickly and said: 'All set, Joe.'

'Yep.'

'How you feelin'?'

'Fine as silk, Doc.'

The Soldier wrapped his green dressing-gown tightly around his waist and they walked down the aisle to the ring. A crowd of nearly eight thousand was in the Coliseum, an arena with tiers of seats around a level tan-bark surface sometimes used for horse-shows. The ringside seats were on the tan-bark. Before the Soldier reached the ring Goldie climbed through the ropes, both hands held high over his head. The crowd cheered. The cheering was louder when the Soldier skipped lightly along the ropes. Then the crowd laughed and kidded him.

When they were being introduced, he glared at Goldie. He waved his hand three times at someone calling to him, but concentrated on Goldie's black body, glistening under the arc-lights.

The crowd yelled at the sound of the bell and Joe walked slowly from his corner, stared intently at Goldie's chin. He crouched, his head forward, most of the weight on his right foot, his right hand held steadily at his hip. He rocked gently back and forward on the balls of his feet. Goldie danced in, hitting him twice with his left, once on the side of the head, once on the chin. Joe grinned. He stood up straight and grinned. He hadn't touched the smooth brown body that slid by him. He settled back to the crouch, sticking his chin out farther while he pawed with his left hand. Then he laughed and the crowd yelled and Goldie got sore, smashing him over the eye with his right hand. Joe shook his head. Blood was in his eye. He swung his right hand for the first time but didn't really expect to land, or get the old feeling, the emotional release. It would come later, everything working up to that point, the inner excitement growing but not yet strong enough. The brown body, glistening with sweat, swung in close, and the Soldier flailed it with his left hand. Goldie hit him six times in the body, twice just over the solar plexus, and he felt sick. The crowd laughed.

'Oh, you Soldier.'

'Take aim, Joe.'

The Soldier half turned his back on Goldie and stuck out his tongue at the crowd. Catcalls didn't bother him; they warmed him up. Goldie, slightly puzzled, stared at him suspiciously. The bell ended the round. Joe skipped lightly to his corner.

He sat on the stool, his gloves on his knees, listening to Doc Barnes talking excitedly. He stared at the arc-lights, blinking his eyes, then at the small yellow lights over the crowd. He wondered if Molly were out there under the small yellow lights, and his mental picture of her seemed indistinct. The thought of her was utterly unimportant at the moment. He couldn't be bothered thinking of her.

In the second round his weight held Goldie on the ropes, but Goldie swung back on the rebound before the Soldier could adjust himself at the new angle, and swung both hands to the head, jarring, jolting, till the crowd yelled for a knockout. The thud and slap-thud jarred the Soldier, his knees sagged; and dazed, he stood up straight, dropping his guard,

and despising the crowd and Goldie's smart work. He
swayed, shook his head, and crouched, rocking gently on his
feet, his big body tense as Goldie, grinning, jabbed prettily.
The Soldier got it on the chin but swung his right hand from
his hip. He felt the impact stiffening his arm, his heart
pounding, his breath held in, the emotion quickly carried to
a peak, then slowly subsiding as Goldie toppled, his head
banging against the canvas, his right leg twitching, trembling.

The Soldier waved to the crowd. He ran to his corner. The
crowd kept on roaring as he tried to climb through the ropes
and his seconds pushed him back. The referee had counted
six when Goldie rolled over and got up on one knee. The
Soldier saw Goldie trying to balance himself on the one
knee. Slightly bewildered he watched him, then rushed
across the ring and pushed aside the referee, eager to hit
Goldie. The time-keeper stopped counting. The referee held
on to Joe, trying to push him away. Joe could think only of
Goldie attempting to get up after he had landed satisfac-
torily and knocked him down.

Goldie was on the floor for thirty seconds but the Soldier
should have retired to his corner, and there had been no
count after six. Goldie got up, staggering clumsily, groping
away from the Soldier. The crowd was booing and whistling.
A hard hat fell in the ring, then a great many hard hats. Joe
did not go after Goldie. He grinned weakly. He wasn't
anxious to hit him again. There could be nothing further in
it for him. Goldie leaned against the ropes and watched the
Soldier, then advanced determinedly. The Soldier crouched
mechanically and stuck out his left hand. He puckered his
forehead and with his right glove tried to block Goldie's
left swing and counter with his left, but had no further
energy. He was just making motions. Goldie came in, the
glove came dully against the Soldier's chin and he fell on
the ropes. The glove came again and Joe fell over the ropes
onto the knees of reporters. He rolled onto the tan-bark.
The crowd howled.

They carried the Soldier into his dressing-room. He was
heavy in their arms and aware, very casually, of Doc Barnes
swearing rapidly.

Barnes drove him home in his car. Joe sat beside Barnes

and rubbed his hand over his chin. He hadn't shaved his chin for five days. Barnes turned corners recklessly, infringing upon traffic laws. Each time they turned a corner Joe knew how the Doc felt about it. Twice he opened his mouth to speak and said finally, 'I'm sorry, Doc, but I guess, I'm through.'

'Oh, you're all right,' Doc said generously.

'No, I'm through.'

'Hell, man, you can still earn a living at it.'

'No, there's absolutely nothing in it for me.'

'Well, you'll have to do something.'

'I know it.'

The Doc was driving more carefully. A few drops of rain hit the wind-shield. The Soldier went on rubbing his chin. He had a thought of the fight and tried to forget the aching disappointment that was heavy inside him.

'Oh, it's not so bad,' he said.

'How you figurin'?'

'I'll get a job.'

'Yeah.'

'Yeah, I've thought about getting a steady job before, Doc.'

'I know.'

'And if I get a job I'll get married, and that's that, and it's all settled.'

'She wanted you to go across big, didn't she?'

'I know, but mostly she wants to get married.'

The Doc, driving with one hand, put a cigarette in his mouth. 'Well, it's your funeral,' he said.

'I know it, Doc, but I want to get it settled. See? And tonight sorta fixes it up for me with her. She won't have no ambitions for me now, see?'

The Young Priest

Father Vincent Sullivan was only one of three curates at the Cathedral but he had been there long enough to understand that some men and women of the parish deserved to be cultivated more intimately than others. He had some social talent, too. At the seminary, four years ago, he had been lazy, good-natured, and very fond of telling long funny stories, and then laughing easily, showing his white teeth. He had full red lips and straight black hair. But as soon as he was ordained he became solemn, yet energetic. He never told stories. He tried to believe that he had some of the sanctity that a young priest ought to have. At his first mass, in the ordination sermon, an old priest had shouted eloquently that a very young priest was greater and holier and more worthy of respect than anyone else on earth. Father Vincent Sullivan, hearing this, couldn't believe it entirely, but it gave him courage even if it did make him more solemn and serious.

But he still had his red lips and his black hair and his clear skin and a charming, lazy, drawling voice, which was very pleasant when he was actually trying to interest someone. Since he had so much zeal and could be so charming he was a good man to send calling upon the men and women of the parish, seeking donations for various parish activities. The really important people in the congregation like Mrs. Gibbons, whom he bowed to every Sunday after eleven o'clock mass, he hardly ever met socially; they were visited usually by the priest, who sometimes even had a Sunday dinner with them or a game of cards in the evening.

Father Sullivan had a sincere admiration for Mrs. Gibbons. Her donations were frequent and generous. She went regularly to communion, always made a novena to the little flower, St. Teresa. And sometimes in the summer evenings, when he was passing down the aisle from the vestry and it was almost dark in the Cathedral, he saw this good woman saying a few prayers before the altar of the Virgin. Of course he hardly glanced at her as he passed down the aisle, his face grave and expressionless, but he thought about her when he was at the door of the church and wished that she would stop and talk to him, if he stayed there, when she passed out. She was the kind of a woman, he thought, that all priests of the parish ought to know more intimately. So he did happen to be near the door when she passed and bowed gravely, but she went by him and down to the street hardly more than nodding. She was a large, plump, well-kept woman walking erectly and slowly to the street. Her clothes were elegant. Her skin had been pink and fine. It was very satisfactory to think that such a well-groomed, dignified, and competent woman should appreciate the necessity of strict religious practice in her daily life. If he had been older and had wanted to speak to her he could readily have found some excuse, but he was young and fully aware of his own particular dignity. Honestly, he would rather have been the youngest priest at the Cathedral at this time than be a bishop or a cardinal. It was not only that he always remembered the words of the old priest who had preached his ordination sermon, but he realized that he sometimes trembled with delight at his constant opportunity to walk upon the altar, and when hearing confessions he was scrupulous, intensely interested, and never bored by even the most tiresome old woman with idiotic notions of small sins. It exalted him further, even if it also made him a little sad to see that older priests were more mechanical about their duties, and when he once mentioned to Father Jimmerson about it, the oldest priest at the Cathedral, the old man had smiled and sighed and said it was the inevitable lot of them all, and that the most beautiful days of his life had been when he was young and had known the ecstasy of being hesitant, timid, and full of zeal. Of course, he added, older priests were just as confident in their faith, and just as determined to be good, but they could not have the eagerness of the very young men.

One evening at about nine o'clock when Father Sullivan

was sitting in the library reading a magazine, the house-keeper came into the room and said that someone, phoning from Mrs. Gibbons' house, wanted to speak to a priest.

'Was any priest in particular asked for?' Father Sullivan said.

'No. The woman – I don't know who she was – simply said she wanted to speak to a priest.'

'Then I'll speak to her, of course,' Father Sullivan said, putting aside his magazine and walking to the telephone. He was delighted at the opportunity of having a conversation with Mrs. Gibbons. He picked up the receiver and said 'Hello'.

A woman's voice, brusque, practical, said, 'Who's that?'

'Father Sullivan,' he said encouragingly.

'Well, I'm Mrs. Gibbons' sister-in-law, and I'm at her house now. Things have come to a pretty pass around here. If you've got any influence, you ought to use it. Just at present Mrs. Gibbons is broken up thinking she's going to die and she's been howling for a priest. There's really nothing wrong with her, but if you've got any influence you ought to use it on her. She's a terrible woman. Come over and talk to her.'

'Are you sure?' he said a bit timidly.

'Sure of what?'

'Sure that you're not mistaken about Mrs. Gibbons.'

'Indeed, I'm not. Are you coming?'

'Oh yes, at once,' he said.

He put on his hat and mechanically looked at himself in the hall mirror. Then he glanced at his hands, which were perfectly manicured and clean. His collar was spotless. The blood showed through his clear skin and his lips were very red.

As he walked along the street he was a little nervous because the woman had sounded so abrupt, and he was wondering uneasily if Mrs. Gibbons really was a terrible woman. There had been some rumours of a certain laxity in her life since her husband had either disappeared or deliberately gone away some time ago, but the parish pastor had shrugged his shoulders and spoken of scandalmongers. Insinuations against the good name of Mrs. Gibbons, who, they knew, was one of the finest women of the parish, were in a measure an insinuation against the Church. Father Sullivan had decided some time ago that Mrs. Gibbons was really a splendid woman and a credit to any community.

It was a short walk from the Cathedral to Mrs. Gibbons' home. A light was in the hall. A light was in the front room upstairs. Father Sullivan paused at the street light a moment, looking up at the house, and then walked quickly up to the door, feeling clean, aloof, dignified, and impressive, and at the same time vaguely eager.

He rang the bell. The door was opened wide by a woman, slim, brightly dressed, florid-faced, and with her hair dyed red, who stepped back and looked at him critically.

'I'm Father Sullivan,' he said apologetically but seriously.

'Oh, yes, I see.'

'I believe Mrs. Gibbons wanted to see me.'

'Well, I don't know whether she knows you or not,' the woman added a bit doubtfully. 'I'm her sister-in-law. I'm the one that phoned you.'

'I'll see her,' he said with a kind of grave finality as he stepped into the house. He felt cool, dignified and important.

'I mean that I was going to talk to you first,' the red-headed woman said. 'She's a Tartar, you know – only it just happened that she feels broken up now about something, and it's time for someone to give her a talking to.'

'I'll talk to her,' he said. Really he didn't know what he was expected to say.

The slim woman walked ahead upstairs and Father Sullivan followed. The door of the front room was open and the slim woman stood looking into the room. The light shone on her red hair. Father Sullivan was close behind and followed her into the room. Mrs. Gibbons was lying on a divan, a purple kimono thrown loosely around her. One of her plump arms was revealed as she held her head up, resting on her elbow. Her plump body was hardly concealed under the kimono. She looked depressed and unhappy as though she had been crying. When she saw Father Sullivan she didn't even open her mouth, just shrugged her shoulders and held the same dejected expression. The red-headed slim woman stared at her alertly and then glanced at Father

Sullivan, who was bending forward trying to attract Mrs. Gibbons' attention while he got ready to speak in his slow, drawling, and pleasing voice. But then he noticed a beer bottle on the table close to the divan. Mrs. Gibbons was now looking at him curiously, and then she smiled slowly. 'Can't ask you to have a drink, father,' she said. She was obviously thinking what a nice young fellow he was. Then she started to laugh a little, her whole body shaking.

'I thought you wanted to talk to him, Jessie,' the other woman said.

'Oh, I don't think I do.'

'But you said you wanted to.'

'Oh, father won't mind; will you, father?'

'Go on, talk to her, father,' the red-headed woman said impatiently. 'I've had a row with her and I've been trying to tell her what a trollop she is. She's low, if anyone ever was. Now tell it to her.'

If Mrs. Gibbons had started talking to him Father Sullivan might not have been embarrassed, but as he looked at her waiting, and saw her stretched out so sloppily and noticed again the beer bottle on the table, he felt he was going to hear something that would disgrace her and the parish forever. She kept on looking at him, her underlip hanging a little, her eyes old and wise. The red-headed woman was standing there, one hand on her hip, her mouth drooping cynically at the corners. They were both waiting for him to say something. In the darkness of the confessional it would have been different, but now Father Sullivan felt his face flushing, for he couldn't help thinking of Mrs. Gibbons as one of the finest women of the parish, and there she was stretched out like a loose old woman. He tried to hold his full, red, lower lip with his white teeth. He felt humiliated and ashamed and they were both watching him. His nervous embarrassment began to hurt and bewilder him.

'If I can be of any assistance –' he muttered, feeling almost ready to cry.

They didn't speak to him, just kept on looking at him steadily and he had a sudden nervous feeling that the red-headed woman might go out and leave him alone with Mrs. Gibbons.

Some words did actually come into his head, but Mrs. Gibbons, sitting up suddenly, stared at him and said flatly: 'Oh, he's too young. How do you expect me to talk to him?' Then she lay down again and looked away into the corner of the room.

The sister-in-law took hold of Father Sullivan firmly by the arm and led him out to the hall. 'She's right about that,' she said. 'I thought so from the start.'

'There are some things that are hard to talk about, I know,' he said, flustered and ashamed. 'If in her life...I mean I have the greatest faith in Mrs. Gibbons,' he said desperately. 'Please let me go back and talk to her.'

'No, I sized up the situation and know that once she got talking to you she'd pull the wool over your eyes.'

'I was just about to say to her –' Father Sullivan said, following her downstairs, and still trembling a little. 'I know she's a good woman.'

'No, you're too young for such a job. And she hasn't the morals of a tomcat.'

'I ought to be able to do something.'

'Oh no, never mind, thanks. She's got over the notion she's going to die. I could tell that when she shrugged her shoulders.'

'But please explain what she wanted to say to me,' he said. 'I respect Mrs. Gibbons,' he added helplessly.

'It's no use – you're too young a man,' the woman said abruptly. 'You wouldn't be able to do anything with her anyway.'

'I'm sorry,' he said. 'I'm awfully sorry,' he kept on saying. She had hold of his arm and was actually opening the front door. 'Thanks for coming, anyway,' she said. 'We've been rowing all afternoon and I told her plenty and I wanted someone else she respected to take a hand in it.'

'I'm sorry,' he said. 'Was she feeling badly?'

'Pretty badly. I came around here, as I do about once a month, to give her a piece of my mind, but she was all broken up. Something got into her.'

'Something must have happened, because she's a fine woman. I know that.'

'You do, eh? Her daughter Marion has gone away with

her young man Peter. They must have had an awful row here earlier in the evening.'

'I didn't know the daughter very well,' the priest said.

'No? Well, it looks to me as if old Jess wanted to know Peter too well. That was the trouble. When I came around here she was lying down half dressed looking at herself in a hand mirror. What's the matter with her? She's got to grow old some time. Thanks, though, for coming. Good night.'

'Good night. I'm sorry I couldn't help her.'

As he walked down the street he had a feeling that the woman might take him by the arm and lead him down to the corner.

It was a mild warm night. He was walking very slowly. The Cathedral spire stuck up in the night sky above all the houses in the block. He was still breathing irregularly and feeling that he had been close to something immensely ugly and evil that had nearly overwhelmed him. He shook his head a little because he still wanted to go on thinking that Mrs. Gibbons was one of the finest women in the parish, for his notion of what was good in the life in the parish seemed to depend upon such a belief. And as he walked slowly he felt, with a kind of desperate clarity, that really he had been always unimportant in the life around the Cathedral. He was still ashamed and had no joy at all now in being a young priest.

Day by Day

Late afternoon sunlight just tipped the end of the bench in Bryant Park where pretty young Mrs. Winslow was resting a moment before walking home. For hours she had wandered through the department stores, looking in all the shop windows, and had finally begun to feel a quiet contentment in her heart. Every afternoon when she went out, she tried to look gay, attractive, and carefree. Now, glancing idly at an old man who bobbed his head jerkily as he passed by, she hoped she would never lose this contentment. Only a few slight changes in her life, she felt, would make her happy forever.

She sat absolutely still on the bench and the sunlight no longer shone directly on the park. The sun was dipping out of sight behind the office buildings. Two well-dressed young men who were crossing by the bench turned their heads so they could see her, and one whispered something to the other and she knew they had looked at her with earnest admiration. Mrs. Winslow became so delighted with her own peace of mind that she began to long for the few small things that ought to go with it. All of a sudden she felt like saying a prayer, but then her heart became so humble in its eagerness that she could say nothing. Her silence and her wish really became more eloquent than any prayer she could make. Timidly at first, as though it were hard to get it clear, she began to ask God to make her husband content, without any suspicion of her. She asked that she might never be permitted to do anything that might make John think he was losing her. If they could only go on living together as they had done two years ago, when they first got married, she would be satisfied. She was not complaining that their plans had failed, that bad fortune was always with them, or that her husband went from one job to another and the work was always less suited to him. 'What is there about me that makes him feel so uneasy?' she asked. 'If I say I'm going shopping he seems suspicious, and if I dress up and put on rouge it makes him jealous. I'd stay at home all the time and wouldn't mind looking dowdy if I thought it would make him happy.' Then she said, in her quiet little prayer: 'Just let us go on loving each other as we used to before we were married.'

She leaned back on the bench, full of rich inner consolation. It was so nice to sit on the bench and close her eyes and pretend it was the time three years ago when she and John were going dancing, first driving out to a wayside inn that served a famous chicken dinner. There had been three such fine full years before they had got married; just closing her eyes, she could see the way he used to grin and wave his hand high over his head when he came to the door to see her. She sat there with her hands in her lap, having this very satisfactory dream, without noticing that it had become twilight and many people were passing. At last she looked up at the pale lights in the office buildings around the park, sighed deeply, and then, as though awakening, said: 'Oh, my goodness, what time is it?' She got up and started to hurry home.

Traffic was heavy on the streets; everybody was hurrying; but for a moment she stood on the pavement, a tall, inexpensively dressed but distinguished-looking girl whose thoughts were still so pleasing to her that she looked really radiant. She wished she were home so she could share her happiness; then she thought: 'What's got into me? John will be home waiting. I ought to be ashamed of myself.' She lived only a few blocks from the corner and she had a childish hope that somehow she might get home before her husband. When she got to the apartment, she was out of breath.

As soon as she opened the door, she heard John moving in the kitchen, moving from the cupboard to the table putting down plates for the dinner that had not been prepared. He was a tall, thin young man with short-cropped, fair, curling hair, a lean boyish face, a small, fair moustache, and worried blue eyes. He was wearing a white shirt frayed at the sleeves and old gray, unpressed trousers. For the past two months, he had had a job, a temporary one he hoped, collecting instalments for a radio house, and his thin face looked tired. When his wife saw him, she suddenly felt ashamed of her sleek hair and red lips, and more ashamed of being late. 'John, darling, sit down,' she said, hurrying to put an apron around her. 'I was out shopping and I'm late. I'm awfully sorry.' But she couldn't quite take the expression of warm, secret contentment off her face.

'You'd think you'd get tired being out all the time,' he grumbled as he sat down, crossed his long legs, and began to watch her. She looked so flushed and out of breath and so neat and pretty. She was still glowing from hurrying and from the animation of her thoughts. He frowned and said: 'You were shopping, eh, Madge?'

'Not really,' she laughed. 'I didn't bring anything home.'

'You're dressed up every afternoon as if you'd been some place.'

'There's no harm in window-shopping if I don't spend anything, is there?' she said quickly.

'Go ahead. Remind me that you ought to have something to spend.'

'I'd never mention it.'

'No, but you think it. You're so self-consciously patient about it. God knows, if I thought you were more contented, I might do better.'

She was so surprised, she felt like crying.

'Please don't say I'm not contented, John, please don't.'

But as she watched him cross his legs awkwardly, shift his body around on the chair, and then let his hands drop between his knees, she knew he hadn't said yet what was in his mind, and what had been agitating him while he waited for her to come home. Like a sullen boy, he suddenly blurted out: 'What kept you so late, Madge? Where were you?'

'I was just around the stores,' she began, smiling. She paused and thought of telling how she sat down on the bench and thought of him, then she suddenly realized he would not believe her, so she added lamely: 'I thought I'd walk home, but it took quite a long time.' She actually felt her face flushing.

'Madge,' he said, watching her closely, 'you're lying. I know. Good God, you're lying.' He jumped up, walked over to her, put his hands on her shoulders, and said: 'What were you looking so excited about when you first came in? I noticed it.'

'There was nothing; I was out of breath from hurrying,' she said.

He began to clutch her shoulders as if desperately aware that he could not hold her, as if he felt that she belonged completely to the life they had lived before they were married. 'You might as well tell me what you did. I know you've been lying,' he said. 'You're lying, lying.' His big hand was trembling as he took hold of her wrist, and she cried out: 'Oh, don't hurt me, John. Don't hurt me.'

'Admit you're lying.'

'I was lying, John; but not really.'

'I've known it all along. Why don't you get out?'

'Let go my wrist. I've always loved you, John, I was just sitting on a bench in the park. I forgot all about the time. I got thinking and I sort of prayed everything would get better for both of us, and I sat there forgetting it was late. Can't you see I'm telling the truth?'

Dazed from his anger, he began to walk up and down the room. He muttered: 'Sitting around on a bench having pipe dreams. You refuse to try and get used to things. You ought to have something to keep you home. You ought to have about six children. Anyway, I'm tired of it. It's beginning to get on my nerves.'

Without looking at her, as if he were a bit ashamed, he snatched up his coat and took his great, long strides out the room. She heard him slamming the door.

Rubbing her wrist, she sat down to wait for him. She felt he would return when he was tired out from walking and be sorry he had hurt her. Tears were in her eyes as she looked around the mean little kitchen. She had such a strange feeling of guilt. White-faced and still, she tried to ask herself what it was that was slowly driving them apart day by day.

Lunch Counter

Ever since he had been a kid Fred Sloane had wanted to be a cook, not just a cook in a beanery but a man who might some day be called an important chef. For two years he had done the cooking for the O'Neils, who owned a small quick-lunch.

Mrs. O'Neil, who sometimes helped him in the kitchen, was a heavy, hard-working woman with gray hair, a very clean, sober, earnest woman, always a little afraid of her husband, whom she obeyed from a strong sense of religious duty. Mrs. O'Neil thought Fred boyish but inclined to be profligate and easy-going, a young fellow who grinned too knowingly and was apt to laugh recklessly when she seriously tried to advise him about a more earnest way of living. She was a good woman herself and because of her strong convictions would not do any work in the restaurant kitchen on Sundays. Fred liked her because she was so kind and motherly, and he was sorry for her when her husband openly quarrelled with her. One morning when she had been very tired and had remained in bed late, her husband told Fred that she was a lazy good-for-nothing slut.

But Fred liked Jerry O'Neil, too, mainly because he was so jovial and so childishly eager to ask questions about low joints in the city. Jerry was a huge man, a few inches over six feet, big-framed, red-faced, a bit bald. He kidded all the customers at the counter, and to strangers he winked and whispered hoarsely: 'You see that fellow with the cap at the end of the counter? He's sore at me because his wife's in love with me. Heh, heh.' The man wearing the cap, a steady customer, laughed heartily. Everybody laughed. Jerry shook his head repeatedly as if to apologize for having so much good humour.

When they were not busy in the restaurant and Mrs. O'Neil was upstairs, Jerry talked through the wicket to Fred, who was in the kitchen. Invariably they talked about girls, Jerry had been married a long time, and though Mrs. O'Neil thought him a wild roustabout, he was far too steady and respectable to be unfaithful to her. He just enjoyed telling Fred many pointless jokes and laughing till his face was the colour of a sliced beet; and because he was so eager for information, Fred used to tell him ridiculous stories about women.

A niece of Mrs. O'Neil's, very young and clean and pretty, came to stay with them one night, and wanted to see them cooking in the kitchen. It was necessary for Mrs. O'Neil to help Fred during the seven-o'clock rush hour before she could have her own evening meal upstairs, and the niece was amusing herself looking around the kitchen while waiting for her aunt. Jerry O'Neil was on the other side of the wicket waiting on two customers. When Fred saw the girl, Marion, standing beside him, he smiled and adroitly flipped an omelette in the small pan. Marion was only fifteen years old but well developed, dark-haired, eager, and round-eyed. She smiled her warm admiration to Fred. Though slender, she was built firmly and gracefully, the sweater she wore fitting her tightly. Her skirt was too short; it was the right length for a girl her age, but in a longer skirt she would have looked like a full-grown woman. She was enjoying Fred's self-assurance and the way he flipped an omelette in the small pan. Fred was glad to have her standing beside him, watching him, and out of the corner of his eye noted her eager admiration. More dexterously than ever he tried to manipulate his pans, for he wanted her to see that he was far more capable a cook than one would expect to find in such a small restaurant, and he tried to intimate by his movements that he had all the assurance of a first-class chef. Jerry O'Neil, pressing his wide face to the wicket, called in another order. Fred, who was enjoying himself immensely, rubbed his hands together just to show off and appear more professional. So far he hadn't spoken to the girl. Suddenly he said: 'Would you like to try and flip an omelette?'

'Show me. I don't think I could do it right,' she said.

'It comes easy, just like this.'

The omelette, browned on one side, turned in the air and flopped down to the pan, sizzling freshly as the blue flames licked the edge. Though he could hardly help laughing out loud, Fred smiled only slightly. Marion smiled brightly every time he smiled, and thought him unusually interesting. 'Another thing,' he said. 'You ought to learn how to break an egg properly. Just tap it smartly once on the edge of the pan.' After he had prepared another omelette she took hold of the handle of the pan. She was just a kid, he thought, and went on talking importantly. She seemed timid about flipping the omelette, so he, too, held the handle, his hand partly covering hers, and when the omelette was done on one side, he said, 'Ready,' and jerked the pan upward.

The girl, her cheeks flushed from the heat of the kitchen, laughed happily. 'That was swell,' she said. 'I can do it myself now.'

'Sure. You just need confidence. Cooking eggs is like boiling water. Anybody can do it.'

And as he stood there, his hands on his hips, grinning and good-humoured, he noticed Mrs. O'Neil, who was cutting bread at the other end of the table. 'If you want to get your dinner, I can look after the place now,' he said.

She said sharply: 'You aren't so willing other nights.'

At first he was surprised, and then so angry he hated the heavy, thin-lipped woman. By her sharp reply she was intimating that he merely wanted to be alone with her niece, that she understood his feeling when he took hold of Marion's hand to help her flip the omelette. And so she remained there, big and old and heavy and alert. He was especially hurt because he had been only trying to show off with the girl and had not thought of her as a woman at all: she was just someone who admired his work, a young girl who seemed to like him and smiled warmly and frankly when he grinned at her.

So he went on working steadily while Marion stood beside him. Finally Mrs. O'Neil left the kitchen. At the door she turned and said briefly: 'Come right upstairs, Marion.'

Fred was so angry at Mrs. O'Neil that he could not be

bothered with Marion, who was walking around the kitchen examining the pots and the mixing bowls and asking questions which he answered shortly. 'Mrs. O'Neil is a fool,' he thought. But she was such a respectable woman herself that he could not remain angry at her, even though he thought her a silly woman. Marion was standing beside him and he was telling her how to make a special sandwich. Gradually he became more enthusiastic, and looking around for something that might interest her, he showed her all the mixing bowls.

Jerry O'Neil passed through the kitchen on his way upstairs. 'Keep an eye on the place,' he said to Fred. While the O'Neils were eating Fred had to wait on any customers that might come in and look after the kitchen, too.

Fred went on talking with Marion for a few minutes till O'Neil called suddenly from the top of the stairs: 'Fred, come here.'

Fred opened the door and looked up the stairs. Jerry O'Neil muttered down to him: 'Look here, what are you keeping the girl down there for?' His big face was red in the light and he was very angry. He had never seemed so serious. 'Cut it out,' he said. 'Cut it out.' And he added: 'Tell her to come up and have dinner.'

Breathing heavily, Fred returned to the kitchen. His hands were trembling a little. Marion was waiting for him, her hands linked behind her back, eyeing him candidly. 'They're sure I'm after the kid. It's the one thing the O'Neils ever agreed about,' he thought.

'Your uncle wants you to go upstairs,' he said.

'All right, he ought to call me,' she said smiling. 'Are you through showing me things?'

'I am.'

Reluctantly she moved toward the door. On the way she had to pass the scales they used for weighing supplies. Stopping, she at once insisted Fred show her how to operate the scales, and then asked if he could guess her weight within three pounds.

The O'Neils had spoiled the simple pleasure he had been having with the girl, and looking at her now, he thought he ought to do something about it. For the first time he thought nervously of putting his arms around her and kissing her. So when she was standing on the scales he placed his two hands on her waist, the edge of his palms pressing down on the curve of her slender hips, and for no reason she put her small warm hands on his as they both bent forward to read the scales. On the nape of her neck he saw the fine thin hair, and when she straightened up, suddenly her back was arched and slender. 'You're a lovely little thing,' he said, almost shyly.

'I like you too, Fred,' she said. By the way her hands were resting on his he knew he could put his arms around her and kiss her. And while he was having these thoughts and feeling a new, nervous love for the young girl as her hands held his, he heard Mrs. O'Neil coming slowly downstairs. 'Marion,' she called, and then, 'Fred.'

As she went out of the kitchen Marion called, 'So long, Fred,' and smiled over her shoulder.

'So long, kid.'

Mrs. O'Neil waited till Marion had gone upstairs, then she said to Fred: 'Jerry is sore at you. He's so mad he's ready to eat you alive.'

'What for?'

'You know.' She was cross and irritable.

'Then tell him to come right down here and tell it to me,' he called after her as she climbed the stairs.

He sat on an upturned box waiting for O'Neil to come down, and knew he would not come. No one was in the restaurant; he waited, listening. He heard them talking upstairs. He would never see the girl again, he thought, and trying to remain cool he wondered why such honest, sober people as the O'Neils suddenly repelled him. Angrily he stood up, hating Mrs. O'Neil and her way of living. He hated Jerry O'Neil intensely because he had called his wife an old slut. He hated them both because they were old, and alert, and sly, and sure of what to expect from him.

Two Fishermen

The only reporter on the town paper, the *Examiner,* was
Michael Foster, a tall, long-legged, eager young fellow, who
wanted to go to the city some day and work on an important
newspaper.

The morning he went into Bagley's Hotel, he wasn't at all
sure of himself. He went over to the desk and whispered to
the proprietor, Ted Bagley, 'Did he come here, Mr. Bagley?'

Bagley said slowly, 'Two men came here from this morning's train. They're registered.' He put his spatulate forefinger on the open book and said, 'Two men. One of them's
a drummer. This one here, T. Woodley. I know because he
was through this way last year and just a minute ago he
walked across the road to Molson's hardware store. The
other one ... here's his name, K. Smith.'

'Who's K. Smith?' Michael asked.

'I don't know. A mild, harmless-looking little guy.'

'Did he look like the hangman, Mr. Bagley?'

'I couldn't say that, seeing as I never saw one. He was
awfully polite and asked where he could get a boat so he
could go fishing on the lake this evening, so I said likely
down at Smollet's place by the power-house.'

'Well, thanks. I guess if he was the hangman, he'd go
over to the jail first,' Michael said.

He went along the street, past the Baptist church to the
old jail with the high brick fence around it. Two tall maple
trees, with branches drooping low over the sidewalk, shaded
one of the walls from the morning sunlight. Last night, behind those walls, three carpenters, working by lamplight,
had nailed the timbers for the scaffold. In the morning,
young Thomas Delaney, who had grown up in the town,

was being hanged: he had killed old Mathew Rhinehart whom he had caught molesting his wife when she had been berry-picking in the hills behind the town. There had been a struggle and Thomas Delaney had taken a bad beating before he had killed Rhinehart. Last night a crowd had gathered on the sidewalk by the lamp-post, and while moths and smaller insects swarmed around the high blue carbon light, the crowd had thrown sticks and bottles and small stones at the out-of-town workmen in the jail yard. Billy Hilton, the town constable, had stood under the light with his head down, pretending not to notice anything. Thomas Delaney was only three years older than Michael Foster.

Michael went straight to the jail office, where Henry Steadman, the sheriff, a squat, heavy man, was sitting on the desk idly wetting his long moustaches with his tongue. 'Hello, Michael, what do you want?' he asked.

'Hello, Mr. Steadman, the *Examiner* would like to know if the hangman arrived yet.'

'Why ask me?'

'I thought he'd come here to test the gallows. Won't he?'

'My, you're a smart young fellow, Michael, thinking of that.'

'Is he in there now, Mr. Steadman?'

'Don't ask me. I'm saying nothing. Say, Michael, do you think there's going to be trouble? You ought to know. Does anybody seem sore at me? I can't do nothing. You can see that.'

'I don't think anybody blames you, Mr. Steadman. Look here, can't I see the hangman? Is his name K. Smith?'

'What does it matter to you, Michael? Be a sport, go on away and don't bother us any more.'

All right, Mr. Steadman,' Michael said very competently, 'just leave it to me.'

Early that evening, when the sun was setting, Michael Foster walked south of the town on the dusty road leading to the power-house and Smollet's fishing pier. He knew that if Mr. K. Smith wanted to get a boat he would go down to the pier. Fine powdered road dust whitened Michael's shoes. Ahead of him he saw the power-plant, square and low, and the smooth lake water. Behind him the sun was hanging over the blue hills beyond the town and shining brilliantly on square patches of farm land. The air around the power-house smelt of steam.

Out of the jutting, tumbledown pier of rock and logs, Michael saw a little fellow without a hat, sitting down with his knees hunched up to his chin, a very small man with little gray baby curls on the back of his neck, who stared steadily far out over the water. In his hand he was holding a stick with a heavy fishing-line twined around it and a gleaming copper spoon bait, the hooks brightened with bits of feathers such as they used in the neighbourhood when trolling for lake trout. Apprehensively Michael walked out over the rocks toward the stranger and called, 'Were you thinking of going fishing, mister?' Standing up, the man smiled. He had a large head, tapering down to a small chin, a birdlike neck and a very wistful smile. Puckering his mouth up, he said shyly to Michael, 'Did you intend to go fishing?'

'That's what I came down here for. I was going to get a boat back at the boat-house there. How would you like if we went together?'

'I'd like it first rate,' the shy little man said eagerly. 'We could take turns rowing. Does that appeal to you?'

'Fine. Fine. You wait here and I'll go back to Smollet's place and ask for a row-boat and I'll row around here and get you.'

'Thanks. Thanks very much,' the mild little man said as he began to untie his line. He seemed very enthusiastic.

When Michael brought the boat around to the end of the old pier and invited the stranger to make himself comfortable so he could handle the line, the stranger protested comically that he ought to be allowed to row.

Pulling strongly at the oars, Michael was soon out in the deep water and the little man was letting his line out slowly. In one furtive glance, he had noticed that the man's hair, gray at the temples, was inclined to curl to his ears. The line was out full length. It was twisted around the little man's forefinger, which he let drag in the water. And then Michael looked full at him and smiled because he thought he seemed so meek and quizzical. 'He's a nice little guy,' Michael assured himself and he said, 'I work on the town paper, the *Examiner*.'

'Is it a good paper? Do you like the work?'

'Yes. But it's nothing like a first-class city paper and I don't expect to be working on it long. I want to get a reporter's job on a city paper. My name's Michael Foster.'

'Mine's Smith. Just call me Smitty.'

'I was wondering if you'd been over to the jail yet.'

Up to this time the little man had been smiling with the charming ease of a small boy who finds himself free, but now he became furtive and disappointed. Hesitating, he said, 'Yes, I was over there first thing this morning.'

'Oh, I just knew you'd go there,' Michael said. They were a bit afraid of each other. By this time they were far out on the water which had a mill-pond smoothness. The town seemed to get smaller, with white houses in rows and streets forming geometric patterns, just as the blue hills behind the town seemed to get larger at sundown.

Finally Michael said, 'Do you know this Thomas Delaney that's dying in the morning?' He knew his voice was slow and resentful.

'No. I don't know anything about him. I never read about them. Aren't there any fish at all in this old lake? I'd like to catch some fish,' he said rapidly. 'I told my wife I'd bring her home some fish.' Glancing at Michael, he was appealing, without speaking, that they should do nothing to spoil an evening's fishing.

The little man began to talk eagerly about fishing as he pulled out a small flask from his hip pocket. 'Scotch,' he said, chuckling with delight. 'Here, take a swig.' Michael drank from the flask and passed it back. Tilting his head back and saying, 'Here's to you, Michael,' the little man took a long pull at the flask. 'The only time I take a drink,' he said still chuckling, 'is when I go on a fishing trip by myself. I usually go by myself,' he added apologetically as if he wanted the young fellow to see how much he appreciated his company.

They had gone far out on the water but they had caught nothing. It began to get dark. 'No fish tonight, I guess, Smitty,' Michael said.

'It's a crying shame,' Smitty said. 'I looked forward to coming up here when I found out the place was on the lake. I wanted to get some fishing in. I promised my wife I'd bring

her back some fish. She'd often like to go fishing with me,
but of course, she can't because she can't travel around from
place to place like I do. Whenever I get a call to go some
place, I always look at the map to see if it's by a lake or on
a river, then I take my lines and hooks along.'

'If you took another job, you and your wife could probably go fishing together,' Michael suggested.

'I don't know about that. We sometimes go fishing together anyway.' He looked away, waiting for Michael to be
repelled and insist that he ought to give up the job. And he
wasn't ashamed as he looked down at the water, but he
knew that Michael thought he ought to be ashamed. 'Somebody's got to do my job. There's got to be a hangman,' he
said.

'I just meant that if it was such disagreeable work,
Smitty.'

The little man did not answer for a long time. Michael
rowed steadily with sweeping, tireless strokes. Huddled at
the end of the boat, Smitty suddenly looked up with a kind
of melancholy hopelessness and said mildly, 'The job hasn't
been so disagreeable.'

'Good God, man, you don't mean you like it?'

'Oh, no,' he said, to be obliging, as if he knew what
Michael expected him to say. 'I mean you get used to it,
that's all.' But he looked down again at the water, knowing
he ought to be ashamed of himself.

'Have you got any children?'

'I sure have. Five. The oldest boy is fourteen. It's funny,
but they're all a lot bigger and taller than I am. Isn't that
funny?'

They started a conversation about fishing rivers that ran
into the lake farther north. They felt friendly again. The
little man, who had an extraordinary gift for story-telling,
made many quaint faces, puckered up his lips, screwed up
his eyes and moved around restlessly as if he wanted to get
up in the boat and stride around for the sake of more
expression. Again he brought out the whiskey flask and
Michael stopped rowing. Grinning, they toasted each other
and said together, 'Happy days.' The boat remained motionless on the placid water. Far out, the sun's last rays gleamed

on the water-line. And then it got dark and they could only see the town lights. It was time to turn around and pull for the shore. The little man tried to take the oars from Michael, who shook his head resolutely and insisted that he would prefer to have his friend catch a fish on the way back to the shore.

'It's too late now, and we may have scared all the fish away,' Smitty laughed happily. 'But we're having a grand time, aren't we?'

When they reached the old pier by the power-house, it was full night and they hadn't caught a single fish. As the boat bumped against the rocks Michael said, 'You can get out here. I'll take the boat around to Smollet's.'

'Won't you be coming my way?'

'Not just now. I'll probably talk with Smollet a while.'

The little man got out of the boat and stood on the pier looking down at Michael. 'I was thinking dawn would be the best time to catch some fish,' he said. 'At about five o'clock. I'll have an hour and a half to spare anyway. How would you like that?' He was speaking with so much eagerness that Michael found himself saying, 'I could try. But if I'm not here at dawn, you go on without me.'

'All right. I'll walk back to the hotel now.'

'Good night, Smitty.'

'Good night, Michael. We had a fine neighbourly time, didn't we?'

As Michael rowed the boat around to the boat-house, he hoped that Smitty wouldn't realize he didn't want to be seen walking back to town with him. And later, when he was going slowly along the dusty road in the dark and hearing all the crickets chirping in the ditches, he couldn't figure out why he felt so ashamed of himself.

At seven o'clock next morning Thomas Delaney was hanged in the town jail yard. There was hardly a breeze on that leaden gray morning and there were no small whitecaps out over the lake. It would have been a fine morning for fishing. Michael went down to the jail, for he thought it his duty as a newspaperman to have all the facts, but he was afraid he might get sick. He hardly spoke to all the men and women who were crowded under the maple trees by the jail wall. Everybody he knew was staring at the wall and muttering angrily. Two of Thomas Delaney's brothers, big, strapping fellows with bearded faces, were there on the sidewalk. Three automobiles were at the front of the jail.

Michael, the town newspaperman, was admitted into the courtyard by old Willie Mathews, one of the guards, who said that two newspapermen from the city were at the gallows on the other side of the building. 'I guess you can go around there, too, if you want to,' Mathews said, as he sat down slowly on the step. White-faced, and afraid, Michael sat down on the step with Mathews and they waited and said nothing.

At last the old fellow said, 'Those people outside there are pretty sore, ain't they?'

'They're pretty sullen, all right. I saw two of Delaney's brothers there.'

'I wish they'd go,' Mathews said. 'I don't want to see anything. I didn't even look at Delaney. I don't want to hear anything. I'm sick.' He put his head back against the wall and closed his eyes.

The old fellow and Michael sat close together till a small procession came around the corner from the other side of the yard. First came Mr. Steadman, the sheriff, with his head down as though he were crying, then Dr. Parker, the physician, then two hard-looking young newspapermen from the city, walking with their hats on the backs of their heads, and behind them came the little hangman, erect, stepping out with military precision and carrying himself with a strange cocky dignity. He was dressed in a long black cutaway coat with gray striped trousers, a gates-ajar collar and a narrow red tie, as if he alone felt the formal importance of the occasion. He walked with brusque precision till he saw Michael, who was standing up, staring at him with his mouth open.

The little hangman grinned and as soon as the procession reached the doorstep, he shook hands with Michael. They were all looking at Michael. As though his work were over now, the hangman said eagerly to Michael, 'I thought I'd see you here. You didn't get down to the pier at dawn?'

'No. I couldn't make it.'

'That was tough, Michael. I looked for you,' he said. 'But never mind. I've got something for you.' As they all went into the jail, Dr. Parker glanced angrily at Michael, then turned his back on him. In the office, where the doctor prepared to sign a certificate, Smitty was bending down over his fishing-basket which was in the corner. Then he pulled out two good-sized salmon-bellied trout, folded in a newspaper, and said, 'I was saving these for you, Michael. I got four in an hour's fishing.' Then he said, 'I'll talk about that later, if you'll wait. We'll be busy here, and I've got to change my clothes.'

Michael went out to the street with Dr. Parker and the two city newspapermen. Under his arm he was carrying the fish, folded in the newspaper. Outside, at the jail door, Michael thought that the doctor and the two newspapermen were standing a little apart from him. Then the small crowd, with their clothes all dust-soiled from the road, surged forward, and the doctor said to them, 'You might as well go home, boys. It's all over.'

'Where's old Steadman?' somebody demanded.

'We'll wait for the hangman,' somebody else shouted.

The doctor walked away by himself. For a while Michael stood beside the two city newspapermen, and tried to look as nonchalant as they were looking, but he lost confidence in them when he smelled whiskey. They only talked to each other. Then they mingled with the crowd, and Michael stood alone. At last he could stand there no longer looking at all those people he knew so well, so he, too, moved out and joined the crowd.

When the sheriff came out with the hangman and two of the guards, they got half-way down to one of the automobiles before someone threw an old boot. Steadman ducked into one of the cars, as the boot hit him on the shoulder, and the two guards followed him. The hangman, dismayed, stood alone on the sidewalk. Those in the car must have thought at first that the hangman was with them for the car suddenly shot forward, leaving him alone on the sidewalk. The crowd threw small rocks and sticks, hooting at him as the automobile backed up slowly towards him. One small stone hit him on the head. Blood trickled from

the side of his head as he looked around helplessly at all
the angry people. He had the same expression on his face,
Michael thought, as he had had last night when he had
seemed ashamed and had looked down steadily at the water.
Only now, he looked around wildly, looking for someone to
help him as the crowd kept pelting him. Farther and farther
Michael backed into the crowd and all the time he felt
dreadfully ashamed as though he were betraying Smitty, who
last night had had such a good neighbourly time with him.
'It's different now, it's different,' he kept thinking, as he held
the fish in the newspaper tight under his arm. Smitty started
to run toward the automobile, but James Mortimer, a big
fisherman, shot out his foot and tripped him and sent him
sprawling on his face.

Mortimer, the big fisherman, looking for something to
throw, said to Michael, 'Sock him, sock him.'

Michael shook his head and felt sick.

'What's the matter with you, Michael?'

'Nothing. I got nothing against him.'

The big fisherman started pounding his fists up and down
in the air. 'He just doesn't mean anything to me at all,'
Michael said quickly. The fisherman, bending down, kicked
a small rock loose from the road bed and heaved it at the
hangman. Then he said, 'What are you holding there,
Michael, what's under your arm? Fish. Pitch them at him.
Here, give them to me.' Still in a fury, he snatched the fish,
and threw them one at a time at the little man just as he was
getting up from the road. The fish fell in the thick dust in
front of him, sending up a little cloud. Smitty seemed to
stare at the fish with his mouth hanging open, then he didn't
even look at the crowd. That expression on Smitty's face as
he saw the fish on the road made Michael hot with shame
and he tried to get out of the crowd.

Smitty had his hands over his head, to shield his face as
the crowd pelted him, yelling, 'Sock the little rat. Throw the
runt in the lake.' The sheriff pulled him into the automobile.
The car shot forward in a cloud of dust.

A Regret for Youth

The first time Mrs. Jerry Austin's husband went away she cried a good deal and wrote a long letter home, but in two months' time he came back. They had a big dinner and agreed never to quarrel again and he promised not to feel restless any more. The second time he left her she didn't even bother looking for a job. She told the landlady, Mrs. Oddy, that Mr. Austin had gone travelling and was doing well. Mrs. Oddy, who had red hair, a toothy accent and a loud voice, said that whenever Mr. Oddy did any travelling she liked to keep him company, but after all, it was none of her business.

Mrs. Austin had paid a month's rent in advance so she was friendly with Mrs. Oddy, who occasionally invited her to go motoring. Mr. and Mrs. Oddy sat in the front seat and Mrs. Austin sat in the back seat. She liked watching the hairline clipped high on the back of Mr. Oddy's thick neck and the bone protruding at the base of Mrs. Oddy's neck. Mr. Oddy was in the Civil Service, a good job, but his wife got twice as much money from her three rooming-houses. Mr. Oddy always drove the car as fast as possible along the smooth Lakeshore Drive and Mrs. Oddy made a long conversation over her shoulder about a trip to Europe she had planned for next year.

In the long summer evenings Mrs. Austin was sometimes lonesome. She sat on the front step till dusk talking to Mrs. Oddy, then she went upstairs to her kitchen to sit down at the window and look out through the leaves on the tree across the street to the well-kept school ground, the shadowed building and the few stars coming out over the roof of the school. Four fellows standing underneath a lamp-post at the corner were trying to make a harmony with their voices, but only one fellow had a good voice, the others were timid. She listened eagerly, leaning out of the window, hoping they would follow through with the next piece instead of laughing out loud in the middle of it. She heard a loud laugh, the fellows moved farther down the street singing softly, lazily, and disappointed, she pulled down the blind and turned on the light.

She heard the Oddys talking downstairs, Mrs. Oddy's voice loud and sharp because her husband was a little deaf. She talked to everybody as though they were a little deaf. That was mainly the trouble with Mrs. Oddy. Mrs. Austin got out her ironing-board, adjusting the electric plug in the wall. She patted the board two or three times, hesitating indifferently till she decided she didn't feel like ironing at the moment, so she went into her bedroom and looked at herself in the big mirror hanging on the wall, a large expensive mirror her mother had given her. Mrs. Austin patted her hair, the knot at the back of the neck, and the wave at the side. She had fine, fair hair. Her nose wasn't a good nose and she was too plump for her height. She was only thirty but looked at least five years older, and wore a strong corset. Her legs were short and plump but shaped nicely at the ankles. She wanted to get thin but couldn't diet for more than five days at a time. The small scales she had once bought to measure calories were being used as an ornament on the mantel.

She combed her hair carelessly, staring idly in the mirror, not concentrating on the image but simply passing time, pleasant thoughts in her head. In the next room she heard a noise and knew the young man, Mr. Jarvis, would be going out soon. She hoped he would speak to her as he passed the open door and maybe ask her to go for a walk. Before Jerry went away she had thought of Mr. Jarvis only occasionally, after a quarrel usually, and had been unhappy when she found herself thinking too often of him. Now that Jerry had left her she enjoyed having long imaginary conversations with the young man and was glad her ankles were slender and she wore the heavy corset all day to give a youthful appearance. She was at least eight years older than he, and really didn't know him very well but liked his small hands, and his slim body, and was sure he had a good education, and would probably wear spats in the winter. Once she had given him a cup of tea and another time had made his bed. She liked making his bed. Vaguely she thought of Jerry, missing him merely because she was used to him. A picture of him walking in the door didn't excite her at all.

She knotted her hair again and returned to the ironing-board. Mr. Jarvis, going along the hall, passed the open door and called, 'How's the little lady tonight?'

'Fine and dandy,' she said.

He passed quickly and she caught only a glimpse of him, but his shoes were shiny and his suit well pressed. She thought of going downstairs and suggesting to Mrs. Oddy that they ask the young man to go motoring with them some night, but realized that Mr. Oddy, who didn't like Jarvis, would say something unpleasant. Oddy had often said the young fellow was too deep for him and he wouldn't be surprised to hear anything about him.

At the end of the month Mrs. Austin had a hard time paying the rent. The landlady suggested Jerry was indeed a peculiar travelling man, and the suggestion irritated Mrs. Austin, so she took twenty-one dollars out of the bank and for three dollars sold a small bookcase to a second-hand dealer who called at the house once a week for rags, bones, and bottles. At four o'clock in the afternoon, Mrs. Oddy, not quite so friendly now, came upstairs to examine critically Mrs. Austin's furniture. She offered to buy the mirror because it was an awkward size and not much use to anybody. Mrs. Austin said her husband might object. Mrs. Oddy eagerly disagreed for she had been waiting a long time to talk plainly about Mr. Austin. She talked rapidly, waving her arms jerkily till Mrs. Austin said, 'For heaven's sake, Mrs. Oddy, you'll have a haemorrhage if you don't watch out.'

But afterward she cried, eager to leave the city and go home, but was ashamed to tell the folks Jerry had left her again. Besides it wasn't unlikely Jerry would be back soon. Stretched out on the bed, she dabbed her nose with a handkerchief and was glad she had at least been dignified with Mrs. Oddy, practically insisting the woman mind her own business. She got up and looked out of the window at the clean streets in the sunlight. She decided to go out for a walk; many people passing on the street would be company for her.

She took off her house-dress and before putting on her blue serge suit with the coat that was a little tight, she stood in front of the mirror, patting her sides and hips critically, dissatisfied with her stays that were losing firmness. She needed another corset, she thought. She had only a few dollars in the bank, and little food in the house, but was worried mainly about having a good strong corset. She nodded vigorously at her image in the mirror, many angry words that she might have used to Mrs. Oddy coming into her head.

It was a hot day, there was bright sunlight and men were carrying their coats. She walked all the way downtown. In one of the department stores she bought a corset and arranged to have it sent up C.O.D. It took a long time to get the corset and it was five o'clock before she started to walk home. At her own corner she saw Mr. Jarvis getting off the car. He raised his hat, slowing down so that they could walk home together. She talked eagerly about Mrs. Oddy and about being a little lonesome. He sympathized with her, saying that such a charming little lady should never be lonesome. He had many splendid words he could use carelessly. Nearly all the words pleased her and made her feel happy. He was carrying a yellow slicker though it didn't look like rain, carrying it neatly hooked under his arm close to his hip. She liked his clean fedora at a jaunty angle on his head and was sorry his mouth turned down a little at the corners.

Opposite the Women's Christian Temperance Union they turned the corner. Some boys were playing catch on the road and over in the school-yard girls were playing indoor baseball.

'I don't think I'll go right up,' she said. 'I think I'll sit on the steps a while and watch the kids play indoor.'

'Want some company?' He grinned at her.

'Oh, I nearly always like company.'

They sat on the stone alongside the steps. Mr. Jarvis went on talking, enjoying his own jokes and Mrs. Austin's laughter. For a while she tried watching the girls playing indoor, her eyes following white and red blouses and light and dark skirts on the green grass across the road, and she listened to high-pitched shouting, but losing interest in the game, she wondered how she could keep him talking.

She saw Mr. Oddy turn the corner, a paper under his arm. He came along the street, a big man. He turned up the walk. He nodded curtly and went in the house.

'That guy's an egg,' Mr. Jarvis said.

'A what?'

'An egg, boiled a little too long. See what I mean?'

'I don't like him much myself.'

Mr. Jarvis, getting up, held open the door, and followed her upstairs where he smiled good-naturedly and said good evening. Three minutes later she heard him going downstairs again.

She took off her hat and coat and smiled at herself in the mirror. She fingered her hair. For the first time in months she looked closely at her hair and was glad it was so nice. Unfortunately she had had on her hat when she met Mr. Jarvis but she smiled and knew she wouldn't feel lonesome for some time. She moved around the room, glancing occasionally in the looking-glass to catch glimpses of herself moving, pretending she was not alone. She ate some supper and found herself comparing Mr. Jarvis with Jerry. She didn't think of Jerry as her husband, simply a man she had known a long time before he had gone away.

Three days after the walk along the street with Mr. Jarvis she wrote home to tell her mother Jerry had gone away again. Her mother said in a long letter that Jerry was a good-for-nothing who would never amount to a hill of beans in this world, and enclosed was the railroad fare home, if she wanted to come. There was some gossip in the letter about people she had known, two or three girls she had known at school had got married and had babies. Thinking of these girls with their babies made her feel bad, and she was sorry it was all in the letter. Rather than go home and meet these people she would try and get a job in one of the department stores. She put the money for the railroad fare in the bank.

She went downtown next day but it was hard to get a job

because of summer holidays and slack time in all the big stores. In the evening she took stock of her furniture, wondering what she could sell to the second-hand dealer, and finally selected two chairs. She put the chairs in a corner, and standing a few feet away, her hands on her hips, made up her mind to pay rent by the week from now on. Mrs. Oddy rapped on the door and merely wanted to know how Mrs. Austin was getting on with the rent money.

'At the end of the month I'll start paying by the week,' Mrs. Austin said.

'Oh, that's up to you, of course.'

'Yes, it's up to me.'

'Are you sure you can get it? Of course it's none of my business.'

'Oh, I'll get it all right.'

Mrs. Oddy looked around the room and saw the chairs in the corner. Not sure of herself, she said, 'Maybe you'll need to be selling something soon.'

'Just a thing or two. I don't know what's the matter with Jerry, he should be back any day now.' She knew she didn't want Jerry to come back.

'Well, if you're selling stuff, I'll always take that mirror for a fair price.'

'Oh, no thanks.'

'It's not such a bad looking-glass. How much do you want for it?'

'I really wouldn't sell it.'

'No?'

'Really no.'

Mrs. Oddy, sucking her lips, said mildly, 'You're becoming a laughing-stock, Mrs. Austin. The girls across the hall say you're a bit cuckoo, you and the mirror, I mean.'

'Well, I certainly like the nerve of those hussies.'

'Oh, I don't know, they say you're looking for a husband in the mirror. Clever, eh?'

'Very, very clever.'

'I thought so myself.'

The girls across the hall had peeked and seen her combing her hair a few times, Mrs. Oddy explained. And the hard time she had hooking her stays amused the two girls across the hall. Mrs. Austin, listening politely, became indignant. Mrs. Austin had intended to speak fiercely but simply said, 'The mirror is company for me in a way.'

Mrs. Oddy laughed good-humouredly as if the whole matter had become a fine joke. 'We do have some queer people around here, quaint, I mean. You and the uppish Mr. Jarvis. We'll find out a thing or two about him yet and out he'll go.'

Mr. Jarvis had been two days late paying his room rent, she explained. Mrs. Austin knew that the landlady would not go near the young man's room to clean it or make the bed till she felt he had fully realized the extent of her displeasure.

'What's the matter with him?' she asked.

'Ask me now. There's something fishy.'

'How do you mean, Mrs. Oddy?'

'For one thing, where does he work?'

'I don't know. Do you?'

'Nor no one else. He doesn't work, that's the point, and he's so superior.'

'I don't think so.'

'And so much above anyone else around here, a mighty suspicious character, I tell you.'

'That's silly, very silly, Mrs. Oddy.'

Mrs. Oddy went out. When the door was closed Mrs. Austin started to laugh at her, a suspicious woman, a ridiculous woman with a long tongue and a loud voice, but thinking suddenly of the girls across the hall she felt unhappy. Two waitresses from the Golden Rod found her so amusing, commonplace girls with two old-country lovers who always called at the same time, big men with huge hands who took off their coats as soon as they got into the house and sat around in their vests. She had never seen Mr. Jarvis without his coat on. Then she thought Mr. Jarvis would go away and there were many things she wanted to say to him. There would be no time to talk to him. She encouraged herself to think he was anxious to have a conversation with her. Before going to bed that evening she combed her hair, smiling at herself in the mirror, wondering if she would be able to find the right words to interest him so she could tell him how much she liked him and would be happy if she could please him. For the first time she looked carefully at the mirror, the handsome oak frame, the wide bevel. She laughed out loud, thinking of Mrs. Oddy and the girls across the hall.

A week later Mrs. Oddy told her that Mr. Jarvis was again late with his rent and that they had come to a definite conclusion about him, and Mr. Oddy was going to give him so many hours to get out. Mr. Oddy had two minds to go over to a police station and see if the young man had a record.

Mrs. Austin waited for Mr. Jarvis to come home at five-thirty that evening. She imagined herself talking to him till she had convinced him she really loved him and they would be happy together in another city after she divorced Jerry. She was excited, feeling timidly that there was an understanding between them so she could talk freely.

He came upstairs at about half past five. Mrs. Austin sitting in the rocking-chair, heard Mrs. Oddy follow him upstairs. Then Mr. Oddy called from downstairs and came up slowly.

Mrs. Austin opened her door. Mrs. Oddy was saying, 'My husband has something to say to you, young man.'

'That's unusual,' Mr. Jarvis said.

'I've got nothing much to say,' Mr. Oddy said. 'You'd better clear out, that's all. This ain't a charity circus.'

'No.'

'No. You heard me.'

'All right, any old time, and would you mind telling me what's eating you?'

'You got two hours to get out,' Oddy said. 'I know all about you, I had you looked up.'

'You're a stupid man, Mr. Oddy.'

'Don't worry about that,' Oddy said.

'You're a great ox, Mr. Oddy.'

Mrs. Austin, stepping out in the hall, looked coldly at Mrs. Oddy and put her hands on her hips.

'You just can't help being ridiculous, Mrs. Oddy,' she said.

'Well, I like your nerve, Mrs. Austin,' the landlady said.

Mr. Jarvis was surprised. He opened his mouth and closed it abruptly. Mrs. Oddy talked rapidly, her voice getting louder. 'An abandoned woman like you,' she said. 'We've too many people like you and this fresh Aleck around here.

The house'll get a bad name.' She slapped the palms of her hands together, grinning maliciously when Mrs. Austin said she would certainly leave the house next day.

Alone in her room, Mrs. Austin sat down to write home, a poor letter with many blots because she was excited and felt she wouldn't really go home at all. She lay awake in bed wondering if she would be able to talk to Mr. Jarvis before he went away.

At noontime the next day he rapped at her door. He smiled and said he heard her say she was going home this afternoon and he would like to escort her to the station. He was polite and good-humoured. The train didn't go till four, she said. He offered to come at three. When he had gone she hurriedly looked at herself in the mirror but felt self-conscious.

She phoned an express company and arranged to have her furniture shipped home. She worked hard for an hour packing and cleaning. She dressed slowly and carefully as if it were absolutely necessary she present a youthful appearance. She took many deep breaths, puffing and tiring herself while she tried to hook her corset. She put on the blue serge suit and wore a small green felt hat fitting her head snugly.

At three o'clock he called. She smiled prettily while she daubed some powder on her nose, and she hurried around the room, fussing, and getting herself excited. He said not to hurry, they had lots of time to walk to the station. They walked along the street, talking agreeably, a stout little woman with a green felt hat, and a short blue coat a little tight around the waist, trying not to feel much older than the neatly dressed fellow. She let herself think they were going away together. She didn't think he would actually get on the train but it seemed as if he ought to. They talked about the Oddys. He said he would have a new job next week. When she could see the clock on the station tower she was uneasy because she couldn't bring the conversation to a point where she could explain her feeling for him.

'I'm glad I met you at the Oddys', anyway,' she said.

'Well, it was a relief to meet you,' he said sincerely. He added that very few women knew how to mind their own business.

In the station she bought her ticket, fumbling in her purse

for coins. She felt that something was slipping away from her. 'He ought to speak to me,' she said to herself, fiercely, then felt foolish for thinking it.

'It's funny the Oddys had something against both of us,' she said, having them become one in opposition to the Oddys. He laughed boyishly and helped her on the train.

'What did they have against you?' he said.

'They thought I was seeing things in a looking-glass. How about you?'

'I was holding something back, something up my sleeve, I guess.'

'Funny the way they linked us up together,' she said shyly.

'Yeah.'

'Don't you think it was funny?'

'Yeah, you bet. The old dame was seeing things, not you.'

She stood on the last step, looking down at him and smiling awkwardly. She got confused when the train moved. 'You're a good sport,' he said. 'I got an aunt just like you.'

He waved cheerfully. 'Good luck, Mrs. Austin.'

'Good luck,' she repeated vaguely.

'Good-bye.'

'Good-bye.'

Mr. and Mrs. Fairbanks

In the afternoon sunlight, young Mrs. Fairbanks and her husband were walking in the park. They had been married just a year. She was a small girl with fair bobbed hair, wearing a little tilted felt hat, who walked with a short light step. Her thin, boyish husband looked very tall beside her. They were walking close together as if sharing a secret that made them silent and a little afraid, but gradually an expression of uneasy discontent settled on Mrs. Fairbanks' plump smooth face. Sometimes she glanced up at her husband, not knowing whether to be upset or pleased by his eagerness. He looked as if he wanted to go striding forward in the sunlight with a wide grin on his face.

'I don't know why you seem so glad. Weren't you happy as we were before?' she asked suddenly.

'Sure we were happy, and everything is still working along splendidly,' he said.

'In a way it would have been nice if everything could have remained as it was,' she said. 'I don't want to grow old.'

'Why should you grow old?' he said, bending down confidentially as if she were a little girl and didn't quite know what she wanted. 'You just wait a while. You just wait till you get used to the idea, then you'll see what I mean.'

'Tell me why you feel so good.'

'I don't know why. It just makes me feel more expansive, more abundant, a kind of full and overflowing feeling,' he said, grinning.

'That's very nice of you,' she said, teasing him. 'You don't have to put up with anything, though. You won't have to look like me.'

'You just ought to see how you look, Helen,' he said ear-

227

nestly. 'Your face is soft and plump and kind of all glowing, and your neck and shoulders are rounder and fuller than they ever were. You look lovely, Helen.'

'But I'm scared, Bill.'

'Why should you be scared? It's happening all the time, isn't it? It happens to nearly all women.'

'I know. But I'm such a little coward, really I am. I can never stand anything. I'll be terribly scared,' she said, hanging on to his arm tightly. And there was really a fear in her, a deep uneasiness mixed with wonder at what was taking place within her. She glanced up at the side of Bill's long face and smiled, for he couldn't conceal his ridiculous pride in himself. 'I don't feel sure about anything,' she thought to herself. 'We hadn't counted on this at all. Everything will change now. The things we used to look forward to are already passing away.' For a few moments she walked along holding her husband's arm with her eyes closed, and she knew his arm was squeezing her wrist as if he never wanted her to get away from him. Opening her eyes, she looked around the park in the strong sunlight and smiled up innocently at her husband. They smiled at each other, went walking along the dry path, and Mrs. Fairbanks wondered if anyone passing would see her as Bill had seen her, glowing with contentment.

They were passing a bench by the walk where an old man with a short, red face, as if the blood had all gone to his head, was sitting. One half of the bench was shaded by his tired body. His hat was off and the sun was shining on straggly wisps of gray hair at his temples. One of his shoes was laced up with a piece of string. He was slouched back on the bench with his eyes closed, looking like a beggar who was too weary to beg even with his eyes. The moment Mrs. Fairbanks looked at him she forgot her own mild discontent. She stopped on the path, wanting to give something to the tired shabby man.

'I'm going to give him something,' she said, looking up eagerly at her husband.

'Go ahead,' he said. 'Only you can't give to all the bums.'

'He looks so tired with his eyes closed and the sun shining,' she said. Smiling, she fumbled in her purse, feeling sure

Bill wanted her to do anything that would make her happy. From her purse she took twenty-five cents and stepped over to the bench, saying to the man, 'Please, here you are.' She was smiling broadly, quite pleased with herself. Lifting his head quickly, the man opened his eyes and saw she was holding out her hand to him. He had pale blue watery eyes with red rims, and when he saw she was offering him money, he did not smile nor even open his mouth, he just turned his eyes up and looked at her steadily with simple dignity and then turned away.

'Oh, I'm so sorry,' she said, drawing her hand back hastily.

But the old man merely nodded his head as she stepped back to her husband, took hold of his arm, and tried to walk him away rapidly.

'I feel terrible, something terrible,' she said to Bill. A warm flush of colour came into her face, and her head began to feel hot from embarrassment. 'The poor fellow, he wasn't a beggar at all and I was insulting him like a clumsy stupid woman.' Mrs. Fairbanks felt completely humiliated, but her pride, too, was hurt and soon she began to resent this humiliation which was becoming like a heavy weight of dejection inside her. She dared not look round. 'It was a crazy thing to do,' she said. 'I feel terrible and I guess he feels terrible, too.'

'It was an embarrassing situation all right,' Bill said.

'He feels bad enough as it is and I probably made him feel worse,' she said. 'I felt like running away.'

'There's no use feeling that way, dear. He's probably just an old fellow out of work, or maybe even he does work. You can't tell. It's all right. He ought to be grateful.'

'If he was out of work it would make him feel more resentful.'

'Forget about it, dear. There are plenty of men out of work these days and if you offer a bum a dime and he won't take it, well, lots will, so he's got no reason to be snooty.'

'He wasn't a bum and it was a quarter, not a dime, that I offered him,' she said shortly.

'Don't argue, just stop worrying.'

'I'm not arguing. But I do wish you wouldn't seem so insensitive.'

'I just don't want you worrying, pet. We've got to look after you now.'

'Can't I sympathize with him? Can't I regret that he's sitting there looking so hopeless? Doesn't it make any impression on you at all?'

'Sure it does. But day after day you see a lot of guys like that and you get used to them.'

'There's a ruthless streak in you, I guess, Bill. You haven't got much feeling. That's what I was saying to you a while ago when we first came into the park and you were strutting along beside me and not worrying about me at all. You were grinning and thinking of yourself,' she said excitedly. 'You thought it made a man feel expansive. Thinking of yourself and not wondering at all what I'd have to put up with.'

He tried to plead with her, coaxing her with soft words, but she pushed his arm away and walked on alone, a sullen frown remaining on her face. And for no reason, she began to think that the afternoon sunlight was hot and withering, drying up the little bit of freshness there was in the park. Now she had none of the contentment she had had half an hour ago, instead there was fear in her, not fear of physical pain, but a deeper fear that there would be only poverty and ugliness in their life in the city.

Around the park were the great upright surfaces of the skyscrapers with windows glistening in the afternoon sunlight. When they had got married they had both intended to go on working, she thought. Bill had been studying law, but he had decided they would have to wait too long to get married if he went on with it, so he had quit and got a job in an office. That night, not much more than a year ago, when they had decided to marry, he had said, 'With the two of us working we'll get along in fine style,' and they had both started to laugh, feeling strong and eager. Now she would have to stop working. She began to think of the cold expression that had come into the red-rimmed eyes of the old fellow when he looked up at her. He was old and near the end, all the suffering that had been in his life was there to see on the bench: she and Bill were young, she thought. But they were poor. They would be poor. Suddenly she said, 'I don't want to have a baby.'

'Still being afraid, I suppose,' he said irritably.

'Yes, I'm afraid. Why shouldn't I be? And why should you understand?'

'Please, pet, don't get excited. I'm very, very sorry if I irritated you. See how sorry I am? I just didn't want you to go on having unpleasant thoughts because they're not good for the baby.'

'I tell you I won't have a baby. We'll do something. Besides we're too poor, and it would just mean a lot of misery and maybe more children afterward. We can't afford it. It would make me so old.'

'But it's making you look lovelier than ever now.'

'I never, never want to grow old. I'll not do anything to make me old.'

'Well, I'm trying not to appear important,' he said mildly, 'but you're being very unreasonable, dear.' Then he stopped and shrugged his shoulders. She saw that his eyes were full of angry resentment, as if she were rejecting him and he felt savage. She was glad to see him feeling like this and wanted to hurt him more. 'If you want to talk so haughtily about what we ought to do in this world,' she said, 'why don't you see to it that we have more money? I've never worried you very much, though I've had to slave harder than ever since we got married.'

'You knew all about that when you married me,' he said. 'Listen to you. You worked a long time before you married me and you didn't save a nickel, either.'

'I want to go home,' she snapped at him.

'That suits me,' he said.

'We'll go back then.'

They turned, walked back the way they had come, walking now a little more rapidly, as if anxious to get somewhere in a hurry. The sun was not shining so strongly on the path. Looking dogged and resentful, they kept a step away from each other, so their elbows would not touch. Mrs. Fairbanks was taking deep breaths. All the eagerness to quarrel had gone out of her, but she wanted to get home and throw herself on the bed and cry. With his great long legs Bill was covering the ground far too quickly for her and she was getting all out of breath, but she dared not beg him to go slower. His mouth was set firmly, a pouting, stubborn mouth that looked so much nicer when he smiled.

Soon they were passing again the bench where the old man was sitting, and Mrs. Fairbanks, hurrying and looking down at the ground, hoped they would not be noticed. And when they had passed, and she felt secure, she couldn't help looking back timidly like a little girl. The man on the bench, who had seemed so sad, was looking after them, and suddenly he smiled at her, smiling gently as if he had noticed in the first place that they had been happy and now were like two lovers who had quarrelled. So she smiled at him timidly, and then quite warmly, feeling full of humility.

As she walked on, still thinking of the man on the bench, she felt more and more peaceful. She put out her hand and took hold of her husband's arm and he slowed down at once, thinking she was trying to get her breath. She was feeling glad and almost humble, as they walked along slowly, while gradually she accepted all the strange reverence for her that had been in her husband all day. They went walking along slowly and peacefully, and soon she was wondering if people could notice that she felt all soft and glowing.

The Cheat's Remorse

Phil was sipping a cup of coffee in Stewart's one night, sitting at the table near the radiator so that the snow would melt off his shoes and dry, when he saw a prosperous-looking hairy, blue-jowled man at the next table pushing a corned-beef sandwich on rye bread away from him slowly as if the sight of it made him sick. By the way the man sighed as he concentrated on the untouched sandwich anyone could see he was pretty drunk. He was clutching his food check firmly in his left hand as he used the other to tug and fumble at a roll of bills in his pocket. He was trying to get hold of himself, he was trying to get ready to walk up to the cashier in a straight line without stumbling, pay his check with dignity, and get into a taxi and home before he fell asleep.

The roll of bills that hung in the man's hand underneath the table as he leaned his weight forward staring at the cashier started Phil thinking how much he needed a dollar. He had been across the country and back on a bus, he was broke, his shirts were in a hand laundry on Twenty-sixth Street, and a man he had phoned yesterday, a man he had gone to school with, and who worked in a publisher's office now, had told him to come around and see him and he might be able to get him a few weeks' work in the shipping-room. But they wouldn't let him have the shirts at the laundry unless he paid for them. And he couldn't bear to see a man he had grown up with who was making a lot of money unless he had at least a clean shirt on.

As he leaned forward eagerly watching the man's thick fingers thumbing the roll of bills stiffly, trying to detach a bill while he concentrated on the goal which was the cashier's desk, the thing that Phil had hardly been daring to hope for happened: a bill was thumbed loosely from the roll, the fat fingers clutched at it, missed it, and it fluttered in a little curve under the table and fell in the black smudge on the floor from the man's wet rubbers.

With a dreamy grin Phil kept looking beyond the man's head, beyond all the tables as if he were sniffing the rich odours from the food counter. But his heart gave a couple of jerks. And he had such a marvellously bright picture of himself going into the laundry in the morning and getting the shirts and putting on the light-blue one with the fine white stripe that he had paid seven dollars for a year ago in Philadelphia.

But the drunk, having noticed him, was shaking his head at him. He was staring at Phil's battered felt hat and his old belted coat and his mussy shirt. He didn't like what he saw. It didn't help to make him feel secure and in full possession of himself. The dreamy look on Phil's face disgusted him.

'Hey, dreamy,' he said, 'what's eating you?'

'Me?'

'Yeah, you, dreamy.'

'I wasn't looking at you. I'm making up my mind what I want.'

'Excuse me, dreamy. Maybe you're right. I've been

making mistakes all evening and I don't want to make any more,' he said.

While he smiled very humbly at Phil a girl in a beige-coloured coat spotted with raindrops and snow, a girl with untidy fair hair that needed curling at the ends, and with good legs and a pale face, came over and sat down at his table. An unpunched food check was in her hand. She put her elbows on the table and looked around as if she were waiting for someone. The dollar bill on the floor was about two feet away from her foot.

The drunk rose from the table with considerable dignity and began to glide across the floor toward the cashier, his check held out with dreadful earnestness, his roll of bills tight in the other hand now. And when he had gone about twenty feet Phil glanced at the girl, their eyes met in a wary appraisal of each other, they looked steadily at each other, neither one moving, her eyes were blue and unwavering, and then, in spite of herself her glance shifted to the floor before she had time to move.

Phil got scared and lurched at the bill, one knee on the floor as he grabbed it, but she knew just where the bill was and her foot swung out and her toe held it down with all her weight, absolutely unyielding as he tugged at it, and he knew there was no chance of his getting even a piece of it unless he tore it. While he kept holding the edge of the bill he stared helpless at her worn shoe that was wet, and then he looked at her ankle and at the run in her stocking that went half-way up the calf of her leg. He knew she was bending down. Her face was close to his.

'I guess it's a saw-off,' he said, looking up.

'Looks like it,' she said, her toe still on the bill, her face tense with eagerness.

'Maybe you want to run after him with it?'

'That wasn't in my mind,' she said. She smiled a little in a bright, hard, unyielding way.

If she had taken her toe off the bill while they talked he mightn't have done the thing he did, but she made him feel she was only waiting for him to straighten up and be friendly to draw the bill closer to her; and the expectation of having the dollar and getting the shirt had given him quite a lift too, so he said, shrugging good-humouredly, 'What do you think we should do?'

'What do you think yourself?'

'Tell you what I'll do,' he said. 'Figuring maybe we both saw it at the same time and that we both need it, how about if I toss you for it?'

She hesitated and said, 'Seems fair enough. Go ahead.'

They both smiled as he took a nickel from his vest pocket, and when she smiled like that he saw that she was quite young, there was a little bruise under her eye as though someone had hit her, but her face seemed to open out to him in spite of the pallor, the bruise and her untidy hair, and it was full of a sudden, wild breathless eagerness. 'Heads I win, tails you win,' he said, getting ready to toss the coin.

'Let it land on the table and don't touch it and let it roll,' she said, nodding her head and leaning forward.

'Watch me, lady,' he said, and he spun the coin beautifully and it rolled in a wide arc on the table around the little stand that held the sugar, mustard, vinegar, and horse-radish sauce. When it stopped spinning they leaned forward so quickly their heads almost bumped.

'Heads, eh? Heads,' she said, but she kept on looking down at it as if she couldn't see it. She was contemplating something, something in her head that was dreadful, a question maybe that found an answer in the coin on the table. Her face was close to his, and there were tears in her eyes, but she turned away and said faintly: 'Okay, pal. It's all yours.' She raised her foot and smiled a little while he bent down and picked up the bill.

'Thanks,' he said. 'Maybe you're lucky in love.'

'Very likely. More power to you,' she said, and she walked away and over to the cashier, where she handed in her unpunched food check.

He watched her raising the collar of her beige coat that was spotted from the rain and snow. A little bit of hair was caught and held outside the collar. While she was speaking to the cashier he was looking at the coin flat in the palm of his hand, looking at it and feeling dreadfully ashamed. He turned it over slowly and it was heads on both sides, the lucky phony coin he had found two years ago. And then he could hardly see the coin in his hand: he could see nothing but the expression on her face as she watched it spinning on the table; he heard her sigh, as if all the hope she had ever had in her life was put on the coin; he remembered how she had stiffened and then smiled: he felt that somehow her whole fate had depended on her having the bill. She had been close to it, just close enough to be tantalized, and then he had cheated her.

She was going out, and he rushed after her, and he saw her standing twenty feet away in the door of a cigar store. It was snowing again. She had walked through the snow; her bare shoes were carrying the snow as she stood there in the wet muddy entrance looking up and down the street. Before he could get near her she put hands deep in her pockets and started to walk away rapidly with her head down.

'Just a minute, lady. Hey, what's the hurry?' he called.

Unsmiling and wondering she turned and waited. 'What's the matter with you?' she said.

'Do me a good turn, will you?'

'Why should I?'

'Why not if it don't hurt?'

'That depends on what it is,' she said.

'Take the buck, will you, that's all,' he said.

She tried to figure him out a moment, then she said: 'What is this, mister? You won it fair and square enough. Okay. Let it go at that.' Her face looked much harder, suddenly much older than it had in the restaurant.

'No, I didn't win it on the level,' he said. 'Here miss, take it, please,' and he reached out and held her arm, but she pulled away from him, frowning. He grew flustered. 'That was a phony coin I tossed, don't you see? I'll show it to you if you want to. You didn't have a chance.'

'Then why the big heart now?' she said.

'I don't know. I was watching you go out and I got a hunch it was worse for you than it was for me. You had a bigger stake in it –' He went on pleading with her earnestly.

Mystified, she said, 'Look here, if you cheated me you cheated me and I might have known it would be phony anyway, but –'

'I thought I needed the buck badly, but I felt lousy watching you go out. I needed to get my laundry tomorrow. I needed a clean shirt. That's what I was thinking watching the guy fingering the roll. And it was tough to see you come in on it. I didn't stop to think. I just went after it.'

She was listening earnestly as if his remorse truly puzzled her, and then she put out her hand and gave him a pat on the arm that made him feel they knew each other well and had been together all evening, and that she was very old and he was just a green kid.

'Listen, you figure a clean shirt'll help you?' she said.

'I figured it would give me a head start, that's all.'

'Maybe it will. Go ahead. Get the shirts.'

'No, please, you take it.'

'A clean shirt won't help me, nor the price of one,' she said harshly. 'So long,' she said, with that bright, unyielding smile.

She walked away resolutely this time, as if she had made some final destructive decision, a decision she had dreaded and that she mightn't have made if he hadn't cheated her and she had got the dollar.

Worried, he went to run after her, but he stopped, startled and shaken, perceiving the truth as she had seen it, that a dollar in the long run was no good to her, that it would need a vast upheaval that shook the earth to really change the structure of her life. Yet she had been willing to stop and help him.

But the clean shirt became an absurd and trivial thing and the dollar felt unclean in his hand. He looked down the street at the tavern light. He had to get rid of the dollar or feel that he'd always see her walking away resolutely with her hands deep in her pockets.

A Girl with Ambition

After leaving public school when she was sixteen Mary Ross
worked for two weeks with a cheap chorus at the old La
Plaza, quitting when her stepmother heard the girls were a
lot of toughs. Mary was a neat clean girl with short fair curls
and blue eyes, looking more than her age because she had
very good legs, and knew it. She got another job as cashier
in the shoe department of Eaton's Store, after a row with
her father and a slap on the ear from her stepmother.

She was marking time in the store, of course, but it was
good fun telling the girls about imaginary offers from big
companies. The older salesgirls sniffed and said her hair was
bleached. The salesmen liked fooling around her cage, telling jokes, but she refused to go out with them; she didn't
believe in running around with fellows working in the same
department. Mary paid her mother six dollars a week for
board and always tried to keep fifty cents out. Mrs. Ross
managed to get the fifty cents, insisting every time that Mary
would come to a bad end.

Mary met Harry Brown when he was pushing a truck on
the second floor of the store, returning goods to the department. Every day he came over from the mail-order building,
stopping longer than necessary in the shoe department,
watching Mary in the cash cage out of the corner of his eye
while he fidgeted in his brown wicker truck. Mary found out
that he went to high school and worked in the store for the
summer holidays. He hardly spoke to her, but once when
passing, he slipped a letter written on wrapping paper under
the cage wire. It was such a nice letter that she wrote a long
one the next morning and dropped it in his truck when he

passed. She liked him because he looked neat and had a serious face and wrote a fine letter with big words that was hard to read.

In the morning and early afternoons they exchanged wise glances that held a secret. She imagined herself talking very earnestly, all about getting on. It was good having someone to talk to like that because the neighbours on her street were always teasing her about going on the stage. If she went to the corner butcher to get a pound of round steak cut thin, he saucily asked how was the village queen and the actorine. The lady next door, who had a loud voice and was on bad terms with Mrs. Ross, often called her a hussy, saying she should be spanked for staying out so late at night, waking decent people when she came in.

Mary liked to think that Harry Brown knew nothing of her home or street, for she looked up to him because he was going to be a lawyer. Harry admired her ambition but was a little shy. He thought she knew too much for him.

In the letters she called herself his sweetheart but never suggested they meet after work. Her manner implied it was unimportant that she was working in the store. Harry, impressed, liked to tell his friends about her, showing off the letters, wanting them to see that a girl who had a lot of experience was in love with him. 'She's got some funny ways but I'll bet no one gets near her,' he often said.

They were together the first time the night she asked him to meet her downtown at 10:30 p.m. He was at the corner early and didn't ask where she had been earlier in the evening. She was ten minutes late. Linking arms they walked east along Queen Street. He was self-conscious. She was trying to be very practical, though pleased to have on her new blue suit with the short stylish coat.

Opposite the Cathedral at the corner of Church Street, she said: 'I don't want you to think I'm like the people you sometimes see me with, will you now?'

'Gee no, I think you away ahead of the girls you eat with at noon hour.'

'And look, I know a lot of boys, but that don't mean nothing. See?'

'Of course, you don't need to fool around with tough guys, Mary. It won't get you anywhere,' he said.

'I can't help knowing them, can I?'

'I guess not.'

'But I want you to know that they haven't got anything on me,' she said, squeezing his arm.

'Why do you bother with them?' he said, as if he knew the fellows she was talking about.

'I go to parties, Harry. You got to do that if you're going to get along. A girl needs a lot of experience.'

They walked up Parliament and turned east, talking confidentially as if many things had to be explained before they could be satisfied with each other. They came to a row of huge sewer pipes along the curb for a hundred yards to the Don River Bridge. The city was repairing the drainage. Red lights were about fifty feet apart on the pipes. Mary got up on the pipes and walked along, supporting herself with a hand on Harry's shoulder, while they talked in a silly way, laughing. A night-watchman came along and yelled at Mary, asking if she wanted to knock the lights over.

'Oh, have an apple,' Mary yelled back at him.

'You better get down,' Harry said, very dignified.

'Aw, let him chase me,' she said. 'I'll bet he's got a wooden leg,' but she jumped down and held on to his arm.

For a time they stood on the bridge, looking beyond the row of short poplars lining the hill in the good district on the other side of the park. Mary asked Harry if he didn't live over there, wanting to know if they could see his house from the bridge. They watched the lights on a street-car moving slowly up the hill. She felt that he was going to kiss her. He was looking down at the slow-moving water wondering if she would like it if he quoted some poetry.

'I think you are swell,' he said finally.

'I'll let you walk home with me,' she said.

'Gee, I wish you didn't want to be an actress,' he said.

They retraced their steps until a few blocks from her home. They stood near the police station in the shadow of the fire hall. He coaxed so she let him walk just one block more. In the light from the corner butcher store keeping open, they talked for a few minutes. He started to kiss her.

'Oh, the butcher will see us,' she said, but didn't care, for Harry was very respectable-looking and she wanted to be kissed. Harry wondered why she wouldn't let him go to the door with her. She left him and walked ahead, turning to see if he was watching her. It was necessary she walk a hundred yards before Harry went away. She turned and walked back home, one of a row of eight dirty frame houses jammed under one long caving roof.

She talked a while with her father, but was really liking the way Harry had kissed her, and talked to her, and the very respectable way he had treated her, all evening. She hoped he wouldn't meet any boys who would say bad things about her.

She might have been happy if Harry had worked on in the store. It was the end of August and his summer holidays were over. The last time he pushed his wicker truck over to the cash cage, she said he was to remember she would always be a sincere friend and would write often. They could have seen each other for he wasn't leaving the city, but they took it for granted they wouldn't.

Every week she wrote to him about offers and rehearsals that would have made a meeting awkward. She liked to think of him not because of being in love but because he seemed so respectable. Thinking of how he liked her made her feel a little better than the girls she knew.

When she quit work to spend a few weeks up at Georgian Bay with a girl friend, Hilda Heustis, who managed to have a good time without working, she forgot about Harry. Hilda had a party in a cottage on the beach and they came home the night after. It was cold and it rained all night. One of Hilda's friends, a fat man with a limp, had chased her around the house and down to the beach, shouting and swearing, and into the bush, limping and groaning. She got back to the house all right. He was drunk. A man in pajamas from the cottage to the right came and thumped on the door, shouting that they were a pack of strumpets, hussies and rotters and if they didn't clear out he would have the police on them before they could say Tom Thumb. He was shivering and looked very wet. Hilda, a little scared, said they ought to clear out next day.

Mary returned to Toronto and her stepmother was waiting, very angry because Mary had left her job. They had a big row. Mary left home, slamming the door. She went two blocks north to live with Hilda.

It was hard to get a job and the landlady was nasty. She tried to get work in a soldiers' company touring the province with a kind of musical comedy called 'Mademoiselle from Courcelette', but the manager, a nice young fellow with tired eyes, said she had the looks but he wanted a dancer. After that Mary and Hilda every night practised a step dance, waiting for the show to return.

Mary's father one night came over to the boarding-house and coaxed her to come back home because she was really all he had in the world, and he didn't want her to turn out to be a good-for-nothing. He rubbed his brown face in her hair. She noticed for the first time that he was getting old and was afraid he was going to cry. She promised to live at home if her stepmother would mind her own business.

Now and then she wrote to Harry just to keep him thinking of her. His letters were sincere and free from slang. Often he wrote, 'What is the use of trying to get on the stage?' She told herself he would be astonished if she were successful, would look up to her. She would show him.

Winter came and she had many inexpensive good times. The gang at the east-end roller-rink knew her and she occasionally got in free. There she met Wilfred Barnes, the son of a grocer four blocks east of the fire hall, who had a good business. Wilfred had a nice manner but she never thought of him in the way she thought of Harry. He got fresh with little encouragement. Sunday afternoons she used to meet him at the rink in Riverdale Park where a bunch of the fellows had a little fun. Several times she saw Harry and a boy friend walking through the park, and leaving her crowd, she would talk to him for a few minutes. He was shy and she was a little ashamed of her crowd that whistled and yelled while she was talking. These chance meetings got to mean a good deal, helping her to think a lot about Harry during the first part of the week.

In the early spring 'Mademoiselle from Courcelette' returned to Toronto. Mary hurried to the man that had been nice to her and demonstrated the dance she had practised all winter. He said she was a good kid and should do well, offering her a try-out at thirty dollars a week. Even her stepmother was pleased because it was a respectable company that a girl didn't need to be ashamed of. Mary celebrated by going to a party with Wilfred and playing strip poker until four a.m. She was getting to like being with Wilfred.

When it was clear she was going on the road with the company, she phoned Harry and asked him to meet her at the roller-rink.

She was late. Harry was trying to roller-skate with another fellow, fair-haired, long-legged, wearing large glasses. They had never roller-skated before but were trying to appear unconcerned and dignified. They looked very funny because everyone else on the floor was free and easy, willing to start a fight. Mary got her skates on but the old music box stopped and the electric sign under it flashed 'Reverse'. The music started again. The skaters turned and went the opposite way. Harry and his friend skated off the floor because they couldn't cut corners with the left foot. Mary followed them to a bench near the soft-drink stand.

'What's your hurry, Harry?' she yelled.

He turned quickly, his skates slipping, and would have fallen, but his friend held his arm.

'Look here, Mary, this is the damnedest place,' he said.

His friend said roguishly, 'Hello, I know you because Harry has told me a lot about you.'

'Oh, well, it's not much of a place but I know the gang,' she said.

'I guess we don't have to stay here,' Harry said.

'I'm not fussy. Let's go for a walk, the three of us,' she said.

Harry was glad his friend was noticing her classy blue coat with the wide sleeves and her light brown fur. Taking off his skates he tore loose a leather layer on the sole of his shoe.

They left the rink and arm-in-arm the three walked up the street. Mary was eager to tell about 'Mademoiselle from Courcelette'. The two boys were impressed and enthusiastic.

'In some ways I don't like to think of you being on the stage, but I'll bet a dollar you get ahead,' said Harry.

'Oh, baby, I'll knock them dead in the hick towns.'

'How do you think she'll do, Chuck?' said Harry.

The boy with glasses could hardly say anything, he was so impressed. 'Gee whiz,' he said.

Mary talked seriously. She had her hand in Harry's coat pocket and kept tapping his fingers. Harry gaily beat time as they walked, flapping the loose shoe leather on the sidewalk. They felt that they should stay together after being away for a long time. When she said that it would be foolish to think she would cut up like some girls in the business did, Harry left it to Chuck if a fellow couldn't tell a mile away that she was a real good kid.

The lighted clock in the tower of the fire hall could be seen when they turned a bend in the street. Then they could make out the hands on the clock. Mary, leaving them, said she had had a swell time, she didn't know just why. Harry jerked her into the shadow of the side door of the police station and kissed her, squeezing her tight. Chuck leaned back against the wall, wondering what to do. An automobile horn hooted. Mary, laughing happily, showed the boys her contract and they shook their heads earnestly. They heard footfalls around the corner. 'Give Chuck a kiss,' said Harry suddenly, generously. The boy with the glasses was so pleased he could hardly kiss her. A policeman appeared at the corner and said, 'All right, Mary, your mother wants you. Beat it.'

Mary said, 'How's your father?' After promising to write Harry she ran up the street.

The boys, pleased with themselves, walked home. 'You want to hang on to her,' Chuck said.

'I wonder why she is always nice to me just when she is going away,' Harry said.

'Would you want her for a girl?'

'I don't know. Wouldn't she be a knock-out at the school dance? The old ladies would throw a fit.'

Mary didn't write to Harry and didn't see him for a long time. After two weeks she was fired from the company. She wasn't a good dancer.

Many people had a good laugh and Mary stopped talking about her ambitions for a while. And though usually careful and fairly strict, she slipped into easy careless ways with Wilfred Barnes. She never thought of him as she thought of Harry, but he won her and became important to her. Harry was like something she used to pray for when a little girl and never really expected to get.

It was awkward when Wilfred got into trouble for tampering with the postal pillars that stood on the street corners. He had discovered a way of getting all the pennies people put in the slots for stamps. The police found a big pile of coppers hidden in his father's stable. The judge sent him to jail for only two months because his parents were very respectable people. He promised to marry Mary when he came out.

One afternoon in the late summer they were married by a Presbyterian minister. Mrs. Barnes made it clear that she didn't think much of the bride. Mr. Barnes said Wilfred would have to go on working in the store. They took three rooms in a big rooming-house on Berkeley Street.

Mary cried a little when she wrote to tell Harry she was married. She had always been too independent to cry in that way. She would be his sincere friend and still intended to be successful on the stage, she said. Harry wrote that he was surprised that she had married a fellow just out of jail even though he seemed to come from respectable people.

In the dancing-pavilion at Scarboro beach, a month later, she talked to Harry for the last time. The meeting was unexpected and she was with three frowsy girls from a circus that was in the east end for a week. Mary had on a long blue knitted cape that the stores were selling cheaply. Harry turned up his nose at the three girls but talked cheerfully to Mary. They danced together. She said that her husband didn't mind her taking another try at the stage and he wondered if he should say that he had been to the circus. Giggling and watching him closely, she said she was working for the week in the circus, for the experience. He gave her to understand that always she would do whatever pleased her, and shouldn't try for a thing that wasn't natural to her. He wasn't enthusiastic when she offered to phone him, just curious about what she might do.

Late in the fall a small part in a local company at the La Plaza for a week was offered to her. She took the job because she detested staying around the house. She wanted Harry to see her really on the stage so she phoned and asked if he would come to the La Plaza on Tuesday night. Good-humouredly, he offered to take her dancing afterward. It was funny, he said laughing, that she should be starting all over again at the La Plaza.

But Harry, sitting solemnly in the theatre, watching the ugly girls in tights on the stage, couldn't pick her out. He wondered what on earth was the matter when he waited at the stage door and she didn't appear. Disgusted, he went home and didn't bother about her because he had a nice girl of his own. She never wrote to tell him what was the matter.

But one warm afternoon in November, Mary took it into her head to sit on the front seat of the rig with Wilfred, delivering groceries. They went east through many streets until they were in the beach district. Wilfred was telling jokes and she was laughing out loud. Once he stopped his wagon, grabbed his basket and went running along a side entrance, yelling 'Grocer'. Mary sat on the wagon seat. Three young fellows and a woman were sitting up on a veranda opposite the wagon. She saw Harry looking at her and vaguely wondered how he got there. She didn't want him to see that she was going to have a baby. Leaning on the veranda rail, he saw that her slimness had passed into the shapelessness of her pregnancy and he knew why she had been kept off the stage that night at the La Plaza. She sat erect and strangely dignified on the seat of the grocery wagon. They didn't speak. She made up her mind to be hard up for someone to talk to before she bothered him again, as if without going any further she wasn't as good as he was. She smiled sweetly at Wilfred when he came running out of the alley and jumped on the seat, shouting 'Gidup' to the horse. They drove on to a customer farther down the street.

Rocking-Chair

All the way home from work that evening Thomas Boultbee thought of Easter Sunday, which was only two days
away, and of his young wife, Elsie, who had died of pneumonia and been buried in the last winter month. As Thomas
Boultbee started to climb the stairs to his apartment he felt
very lonely. His feet felt heavy. By the time he got to the
landing he seemed unreasonably weary and he rested to take
a deep breath. He was a tall, thin young man wearing a
baggy tweed suit. He had a fair curling moustache which he
sometimes touched with the tip of his tongue, and his blue
eyes behind the heavy tortoise-shell glasses were deep-set
and wistful. He had been thinking how all the church bells
would ring on Easter Sunday while the choirs sang of the
Lord who had risen from the dead, and he hoped it would
be a crystal-clear, sunlit day. Last Easter, at a time when
he and Elsie had been married only a few weeks, they had
gone to the church together and he had held her hand tightly
even while they knelt down to pray. Her eyes had been
closed as she knelt beside him and he had kept on looking
at the expression of contentment on her nervous face half-
framed in her bobbed dark hair. 'I guess there's no use
thinking of that,' he said, as he started to climb the stairs
again, yet he went on thinking stubbornly that all over the
country on Sunday there would be a kind of awakening after
the winter, in the city the church choirs would chant that the
dead had returned to life, and for some reason it stirred
him to feel that Elsie was so alive and close to him in his own
thoughts.

In the narrow hall below his own apartment he encountered Hilda Adams, a friend of his wife, who was going out,

dressed in a smart blue suit and a little blue straw hat. She was an assertive, fair-haired, solidly built girl. Since Elsie had died Hilda Adams had taken it for granted with too much confidence that Boultbee wanted her to look after him. In the dimly lit hall, she waited, smiling, leaning back against the wall.

'Hello, Hilda,' he said. 'Have you got your new Easter suit on?'

'I sure have. How do you like it, Tom?' she said turning and pivoting with one foot off the floor.

'It looks good. When I was coming along the street I was thinking that Easter was Elsie's favourite time of the year.'

'I know, Tom, but be a little fairer to yourself,' she said brusquely as she pulled on her black gloves. 'You oughtn't to go around always with a long face like that. It isn't right.' And for no reason than that she had a malicious disposition and was irritated by his persistent devotion to his dead wife, she said, 'Poor little Elsie. I was thinking of her today. She didn't have much of a chance to enjoy anything, did she? There were even little things she missed.'

'What little things?' he said.

'Oh, nothing much,' she said, smoothing her coat at the hips with her gloved hands. 'You know, just a few days before she died the poor soul told me about a rocking-chair she saw downtown and had her heart set on. Fancy that.'

'You must have got her wrong,' he said. 'She didn't really want that chair. We were saving to get along. I was studying engineering at nights and we needed every nickel. But I had planned to get her the chair for her birthday.'

Taking a sly, knowing look at him, Hilda Adams patted him on the shoulder, took a deep, sighing breath and said, 'Cheer up. See you later, bye-bye.'

Thomas Boultbee was such a serious young man that as soon as he was alone in his own room he sat down, took off his glasses and thought of the last time he had been downtown with Elsie and they had seen the wicker rocking-chair in the furniture department. She had hardly mentioned wanting the chair. When passing along the aisle in the department she had felt tired and had sat down in the rocker and smiled up at him. Then she had got up, still smiling, and had patted the chair with her hand. It had never occurred to him that she would come home and tell Miss Adams that she wanted that chair.

That night Boultbee did not sleep well: he had a bad dream, and then he lay awake wondering why Elsie had been afraid to ask him for the chair.

All the next day while at work Boultbee was wishing earnestly that he could find some way to show Elsie that he would not have begrudged her anything in the world. He thought of telling her in a prayer. The more he thought of it the closer she seemed to him and then he decided at noontime when he was out in the crowded streets that he would like to do something more definite than praying. He had just come out of a drugstore after having a sandwich and a cup of coffee and was looking at the noonday crowd passing along the street. A great many of the women were wearing their winter clothes for the last time. On Easter Sunday they would put on their new dresses and if it was a fine clear day they would go for a walk down the avenue, with men carrying canes and wearing spats. Boultbee and his wife had watched the fashion parade last year. It had been like watching people coming to life in new raiment and getting ready for the new season. As he lit a cigarette, he smiled and thought, 'Maybe nothing, or no one, ever dies.'

Then he grinned shyly to himself and said, 'I'd like an awful lot to go and buy that chair and take it home and have it in the room for Easter Sunday.' He wouldn't admit to himself at all that he was trying to prove he had never begrudged anything to Elsie.

On Saturday afternoon Boultbee went downtown to the store and into the furniture department. At first he had the notion that the one wicker chair might be gone, but as he stood in the aisle, looking around at long rows of chairs, he at once saw eight or nine brown wicker ones just like the one Elsie had wanted, plain wicker rockers with a little padding on the seat and on the arms. But when the salesman approached him he felt uneasy and foolish. 'If I want to buy a chair why can't I buy a chair?' he thought stubbornly. His sudden amiable grin startled the salesman who had been too tired to notice him particularly. 'I've had this chair picked out for some time,' Boultbee said as he put his hand in his pocket for the money. Then he surprised himself by adding confidentially, 'I had planned to get this chair for my wife. I don't know why she liked this one particularly.'

'If she liked it then, she'll like it now,' the salesman said with judicial assurance. 'And it'll stand up against a lot of wear, too.'

'Well, that's what you always want in a chair,' Boultbee agreed. 'It isn't so much what a chair looks like as what it'll stand up under,' he added, wanting the fellow to think him a sage and practical man who had bought hundreds of chairs.

On Easter Sunday when he got up he wouldn't admit that he was eager, but he was quite pleased with himself. He didn't wait to dress. He put on his old brown dressing-gown and his bathroom slippers and went into the living-room to look at the rocking-chair. There it was by the table. With a gentle motion he rocked it back and forth a few times, a faint, tender smile at the corners of his mouth because it was so easy to imagine that Elsie was sitting there in her pale-blue printed house-dress. He began to walk up and down, his slippers slapping the floor. Then he went over to the window and looked out: it was just the kind of a Sunday he had wanted it to be, with a cloudless blue sky and streaming sunlight. For a long time he listened to the clanging church bells and watched the people moving down on the sidewalk. 'I ought to let Hilda Adams look at the chair and see if she gets the idea at all,' he said.

He got dressed in a hurry. But when he went downstairs and rapped on Miss Adams's door he felt both shy and awkward, for it occurred to him it would be hard to explain why he bought the chair, if he were asked, especially if she didn't get the idea at once. Her blue eyes snapped wide open when she saw him. She held her pink dressing-gown across her throat. As she began to show that she was pleased at seeing him there, with a kind of boyish expression on his face, he said, 'Say, Hilda, come on upstairs and have a bit of breakfast with me, will you? You know, it's Easter and we'll boil a lot of eggs.'

'That's a fine idea. Just sit down like a good boy,' she said. Miss Adams almost laughed to herself. 'The poor fellow's lonely and can't hold out any longer,' she thought. As she ran in and out of her bedroom, daubing powder on her face and twisting her yellow hair back into a knot, she smiled brightly and gaily at him. She began to hum. And when they went upstairs together to his apartment she had hold of his arm as if they were going off to some quiet place to have tea.

'I bought something yesterday. Maybe it'll surprise you a bit to see it,' he said with a certain diffidence.

'What is it?'

'Just something I thought I ought to have around,' he said.

In his living-room he stood behind her to conceal his embarrassment as she glanced quickly at the chair. She turned and he gave her one wistful smile. Miss Adams seemed to puff out with good humour. 'He's trying to please me by showing me he's not afraid to spend his money now on something he was too tight to give Elsie,' she thought. Flustered with pleasure, she began to giggle. Then she sat down slowly in the chair, relaxed, put her heels together and rocked back and forth. 'You're a dear boy, Tom,' she said. 'You really are a dear boy.'

Running his hand through his mop of hair, he waited for her to participate in his own secret feeling. But she was rocking back and forth, her face creased with little fat smiles, with both her hands on the arms of the chair as if she were solidly established in the room and in his life forever. He felt angry. 'The stupid woman,' he thought. He knew she thought he was trying in some clumsy way to please her. As she rocked back and forth, beaming good nature, she looked so comfortable he felt outraged.

'Please don't sit in that chair,' he said in a mild voice.

'What's the matter with me sitting here, Tom?'

He felt that he was going to appear absurd, so he said, coaxing her, 'I just want you to come over here by the window, that's all.'

'This chair's so comfortable. You come here,' she said coyly.

'Why do you want to stay there?' he said impatiently. 'You can't have your breakfast there, can you?'

Reluctant, she got up, and as she came towards him, humming, she started to sway her hips. But he went right past her to the chair and sat down himself with a stubborn expression on his face while he blinked his eyes and watched her putting her hands on her hips and her head on one side in exasperation. He watched her embarrassment increase. Her face got red. With sober angry faces they kept on staring at each other. 'My, you're rude,' she said at last. 'Such a stupid way to act.'

He took off his glasses and wiped them with his handkerchief because his eyes felt moist. 'I suppose I didn't want anybody to sit in this chair,' he said, trying to make a decent apology. 'It's something I thought Elsie would like, that's all.'

'I see, I see,' Miss Adams said sharply as she tried to prevent herself from going into a jealous rage. 'Of course I see. But I can't help thinking you're a fool,' she said. 'You can't blame me for that. Though I suppose it's more likely you went out and bought the chair for yourself.' Nodding her head up and down in little jerks, she said contemptuously, 'Imagine you going out and buying that chair after refusing it to your poor wife.'

'You don't get the idea at all.' he said.

'Maybe I don't,' she said. 'But I'll be hanged if I stay and have breakfast with anybody as rude as you.' She gave him one bitter glance and walked out of the room.

He put his glasses on and adjusted them on his nose. Then he closed his eyes and with his hands on the arms of the chair he rocked back and forth, back and forth. 'What did I expect anyway?' he thought. He pondered the matter: in the beginning he had been thinking of the church choirs that would sing, 'Christ the Lord has risen today.' He stopped rocking and leaned forward with his eyes open and his hands gripped between his knees. 'But what did I expect the chair to do, did I actually think it would help bring Elsie closer to me?' Then he started to rock again and frowning he wondered why he had bought the chair at all. Outside the last of the church bells were ringing. Closing his eyes, he went rocking, rocking, back and forth.

Ellen

Old Mr. Mason had always longed with a desperate earnestness that his daughter, Ellen, should be happy, and now she was in trouble. She had lived alone with him ever since she had been a little girl. Years ago his wife, after a long time of bickering and secret bitterness over his failure to get along in business, had left him, left him to a long monotony of steady working days and evenings at home, listening to music from the gramophone or waiting for election time so that he could go to the meetings. He had hoped for a bright joyousness in Ellen's life, and whenever he heard her laugh, saw how independently she walked along the street, and felt her cool reticence, he was sure she would be content. Ellen was a small girl with little hands and feet, blue eyes set far apart, and a wide forehead and a face that tapered smoothly to her chin. She had never had much money, even since she had grown up and had a job, but she wore her clothes with such grace that, with her natural assurance, she looked almost elegant.

Before going out in the evenings, whenever she had a new hat or dress and was sure of her beauty, she used to pretend to annoy her father, who was reading his paper, by saying coaxingly, 'Please tell me that I don't look a fright. Could anybody say I looked pretty, Dad?' And she would smile to herself with secret amusement while he was saying, 'You're a beauty, Ellen. Bless my soul, if you're not! When I was a young fellow, I'd twist my neck out of place on the street if a girl like you passed by.' Until she went out the front door he would wait, apparently interested only in the paper; then he would jump up and hurry to the window with his pipe in one hand and the paper under the other arm and watch her hurrying along the street with her short, rapid steps.

From the beginning she had been very much in love with Joe Eaton. Joe was a handsome, good-natured fellow – a big, broad-shouldered young man with a fine head of untidy brown hair who laughed often, was always at ease, and was marvellously gentle with Ellen when he was with her. This gentleness in such a big man used to make Mr. Mason warm with joy, and sometimes when he went to bed after watching Joe and Ellen, it seemed wonderful that Ellen should have the love of a man who had so much tenderness for her. Joe Eaton hadn't much money but he wanted to be an architect and he loved the work, and he liked talking about the things he planned to do, especially when he and Ellen had come into the house with the elation of two children after the evening out together. Ellen used to listen to him with a grave wonder, and then, a little later, with laughter in her eyes, she would try to get him to tease her father. Joe could tell stories that would keep them all laughing till two o'clock in the morning, especially if he had brought a bottle or two of red wine. Three times Mr. Mason coaxed Joe to play a game of checkers and then enjoyed giving him a bad beating; Joe was too impulsive to be a success at the game.

Mr. Mason had hoped that Ellen and Joe would get married and have a place of their own, and after a year, perhaps, he hoped they might invite him to go and live with them. But instead of that, Joe stopped coming to the house. 'He's gone. It's over. We won't see him again.' Ellen said. Her solemn face could not conceal her fierce resentment.

She went from day to day with a set little smile on her face, and there was growing in her a strange gravity and stillness that made her father, watching her, ache with disappointment. They used to get up in the morning at the same hour and have breakfast together before going out to work. Her face on these mornings looked pinched and weary, as if she had not slept, and her blue eyes, which at first had shown so easily that she was hurt, now had a dull expression of despair. Yet she walked along the street in the old way, dressed smartly in bright colours, her body erect, and when she came home in the evenings and saw her father looking at her anxiously, she wrinkled the corners of her mouth into a smile and began, 'Do you know, Dad, the most amusing thing happened today...' She would begin to tell some trivial story, but in a few moments she was so grave again that she frightened him.

Mr. Mason began to get so upset that he hardly knew what he was doing. One night he left Ellen sitting by herself in the living-room and went into his bedroom to read himself to sleep. He had put on his night-gown and was standing on the carpet in his bare feet, staring at the reading-light with his evening paper under his arm. The pillows were propped up on the bed, as they were every night, and he patted them with his hand. At last he sighed, half smiled, and dragged himself into bed as if his old body were heavy with disappointment. The reading-light shone on his white head and on the intricate network of veins on his red neck as he lay back with his glasses in his hand. 'There's no use worrying and wondering about these things,' he said to himself, so he set his glasses firmly on his nose and started turning the pages of the paper. But no matter how he stared, or even rubbed his hand over his eyes, he kept on having the same thought. All of a sudden he sat up and felt a surge of anger. The hand holding the paper began to tremble, his face got as red with the sudden rush of blood at the back of his neck, and it looked as if he were going to have one of his rare bursts of bad temper. He felt a hatred of Joe Eaton, a resentment against all the days of the past year. 'This has got to end,' he thought. 'Ellen's not going to worry herself and me into the grave. What's she doing sitting in that room by herself at this hour? I'll tell her to go to bed. I'll put an end to this once and for all.'

He hurried, throwing his old brown dressing-gown around him, feeling strong with independence. With his old slippers slapping on the floor, and his white hair, ruffled by the pillow, sticking out from his head at all angles, he went striding along the hall to the living-room.

The light was out, but from the door he could see Ellen sitting over by the window with her elbows on the sill. First he coughed, then he walked over softly and sat down on a chair beside her. Moonlight was shining on the side of her face, touching her wide forehead where her long hair was pushed back from her temples. He suddenly wanted to touch her cheek and her hair, but he was determined to speak firmly. He did not know how to begin such a conversation. He said very hesitantly, 'Aren't you up late, Ellen?'

'Weren't you able to sleep, Dad?' she said.

'Yes, but I didn't want you sitting in here feeling alone.'

'It isn't late, and I'm all right.'

'The house seemed so quiet,' he said. 'I got thinking you might be feeling lonely. I got thinking of Joe Eaton, too. Are you thinking he might still marry you?'

'He can't marry me. He's not here to marry me. He's gone away to Detroit.' And, still without turning her head to look at him, she said, 'It will get unpleasant for you, Dad. If you don't want me to stay here, I won't. Soon the neighbours will notice me and begin to talk.'

He thought she must hear his heart beating with such slow heaviness that it hurt him, and he said, 'I wasn't thinking anything like that.'

'It doesn't take people long to notice things,' she said.

'Ellen, it's all right. Don't waste yourself on such thoughts. I know you can't be happy, but try not to feel miserable,' he said. His voice faltered, he thought he was going to lose control of himself. Then he said with simple dignity, 'I'll look after you as long as I live, you know. Please don't feel miserable.'

'I don't, Dad,' she said, turning toward him. He saw the soft light on all her face. Her face was so smooth and serene that he was startled. There was a sweet, full contentment in it he had never seen before. The soft light gave her face a glowing happiness.

'Ellen,' he whispered. 'You look happy, child.'

'I'm very happy,' she said.

'Why are you so happy? How can you have such a feeling?'

'I feel very contented now, that's all,' she said simply. 'Tonight everything is so still on the street outside and in the dark here. I was so very happy while Joe was with me,' she whispered. 'It was as though I had never been alive before.

It's so sweetly peaceful tonight, waiting, and feeling so much stirring within me, so lovely and still. '

'What are you waiting for?' he asked.

'It seems now he'll come back again,' she said.

'When, Ellen?'

'I don't know. I just feel that he will.' She smiled patiently, with such a depth of certainty and peace that he dared not speak. For many minutes he sat beside her, stirred and wondering. Deep within him was a pain that seemed to be a part of all the years of his own life, but he could really feel nothing but her contentment now. Nothing that had ever happened to him seemed as important as this secret gladness Ellen was sharing with him.

He got up at last and said quietly, 'I'll go now, Ellen. Good night.'

'Good night, Dad,' she said, and he felt that she was smiling.

Timothy Harshaw's Flute

Although they were both out of work, Timothy Harshaw and his wife were the happiest people in the Barrow Street house. Timothy was a round, smooth-faced, very fair young fellow who never thought of wearing a coat with trousers to match, and yet somehow looked neat and distinguished.

In the evenings, Mr. Weeks, a bank teller who lived in the one-room apartment behind the Harshaws, used to hear Timothy playing on his silver flute. One night, when Mr. Weeks could stand the flute-playing no longer, he rapped on the Harshaws' door and pretended he was making a social call. Mrs. Harshaw opened the door. She was at least thirty-two, but she was so eager, with her short, straight black hair, her high-bridged nose, and her sparkling black eyes that she seemed like a young girl. She nearly always wore a plain gray sweater that made her look slim and attractive. Mr. Weeks was welcomed so enthusiastically by the Harshaws that he began to feel ashamed of his own surliness: they both bowed so politely, and ran to get him a cigarette and something to drink. They explained that Timothy had learned to play the silver flute at the Sorbonne in Paris, where he had had a scholarship.

Louise Harshaw had never been in France she said, but she talked about Paris as if she knew every boulevard, bistro, bal musette, and café, until she was out of breath and ready to laugh at her own eagerness. On this night both the Harshaws seemed to feel really jubilant, as if they had suddenly settled all their important problems. Mr. Weeks couldn't help asking, 'What's making you so happy tonight, Mrs. Harshaw?' and she burst out at once, 'We've just decided we'll never get anywhere in this country. We're going to go away for good and live in Paris; aren't we, Timothy?'

Mr. Weeks looked at Timothy, who was sitting cross-legged and very shining-haired on the bed, still holding his silver flute loosely in his hand. The Harshaws had cut the four posts off their bed so it would look more like a couch. 'That's right, Louise,' Timothy said, his face brightening. 'There's nothing here for us, Weeks. I ought to have seen that long ago. I'll live as a translator in Paris. The main thing, though, is to get there.'

'Are you going right away?'

'Oh, no,' they both said together, 'we're awfully poor now.'

'How are you going to do it, then?'

'We'll both get a job and work,' they said. 'Then we'll save.'

Beginning the next day, the Harshaws went out every morning looking for work. At noontime they used to meet in Childs' and amuse each other mimicking the peculiar mannerisms of everyone they had encountered. Sitting there, amusing each other, they both seemed to have all of the shining enthusiasm that makes every obstacle a stimulation. Timothy was the first to get a job, a position in the advertising and publicity department of a publishing house. The more he talked about it to Louise, the more he felt like celebrating, so he borrowed five dollars from the bank teller, who loaned it with reluctance, though he became more cheerful when Timothy, slapping him on the back, invited him to go with him and help spend it. They went to a delicatessen store to buy some cheese. 'People don't seem to understand that a gentleman ought to know his cheeses every bit as well as his wines,' Timothy explained, and he bought bits of Brie, Camembert, Gorgonzola, Munster, and Gruyère cheeses. He also bought a bottle of red Italian wine. When they got home, Mr. Weeks thought Mrs. Harshaw might resent Timothy's initial extravagance, but instead she moved around eagerly getting plates and glasses as though they were about to start playing a new, delightful game. It occurred to her, too, to phone her friend, Selma Simpson, who did publicity for a small theatrical producer, so they would have more of a party.

That night the Harshaws talked a good deal about France; they wanted to take over the whole European tradition, because Timothy had been so happy at the Sorbonne. Besides, there were the trips you could take outside to places like Chartres: Louise was dying to see the cathedral.

'We'd like to take over the whole blamed tradition, if you see what we mean,' Timothy said, leaning forward.

'It sounds swell. Maybe I'll take a trip like that some day,' Mr. Weeks said, feeling guilty of a sordid materialism because he saved his money so consistently. 'When are you going?'

'In the spring. Everybody goes to Paris in the spring; it's the season. Why don't you come with us?'

'I may at that,' the teller said vaguely, feeling ashamed of himself for lying.

Timothy was making forty dollars a week and they put ten in a bank that had given them a red bank-book. In order that they would not sacrifice money on foolish pleasures, they decided to stay in the house at night and Timothy would teach Louise French. When they began the lessons, Louise learned rapidly, Timothy was full of joy, and they were both so pleased with themselves they thought their friend, Mr.

Weeks, might like to take the lessons, too. At first, Mr. Weeks tried seriously to speak French, but they were both so eager to help him he became self-conscious and made a joke of the whole business.

It was in the second week of November that Timothy lost his job at the publishing house for a reason that perplexed and angered him. As he told it to Louise, walking up and down rubbing his hand through his hair, it seemed ridiculous; he had got into an argument with his boss about theosophy and had suggested that modern Americans might be the ancient Egyptians reincarnated, and the boss, slamming his fists on the desk, had begun to tell Timothy everything that was wrong with him: when he wrote advertising, he couldn't understand he was appealing to the masses; he was always making sly jokes for his own amusement; anyway, he couldn't adapt himself to the routine of the place. And Timothy was fired. 'There was something underhand about it, Louise. We didn't seem to face each other like gentlemen at all.' He kept looking anxiously at his wife.

Louise wanted to cry. Her face was white and pinched, as if once again she had reached out and tried to touch something that had always eluded her. But she said earnestly, 'It's all right, Timothy. You can't destroy your character for such people. I'll get a job and we'll go right on saving.'

There were two difficult weeks when they hardly spent a cent for food, because Louise wouldn't draw money out of the bank. They ate canned food and cereals, and were most hungry when they talked about the good times they would have in Europe in the spring.

Then they had an unbelievable piece of good fortune. They could hardly believe such luck: Louise's friend, Selma, quit her job to get married, and she asked Louise if she would like to take it. Louise wouldn't say anything; she kept swallowing hard till she went around to see the producer with Selma. He was a short Jew who listened respectfully while Selma swore there wasn't a girl like Louise in the whole country; then he smiled benevolently. Louise got the job at thirty-five a week.

For a while the Harshaws were happier than they had been at any time since they were married; they had a splendid goal ahead of them – Europe, with a tradition and environment that would appeal to Timothy – and they had some money in the bank. Louise worked hard, rebuffed her sly, sentimental employer sweetly, and hurried home every night to Timothy, who cooked the dinner for her. He used to stand at the window waiting for her, with one of her aprons around his waist. He had taken a special fancy to cooking.

On toward the end of December, the Harshaws had the calmness and deep inner contentment of people who can see far and clear ahead. They had one hundred and twenty dollars in the bank. They talked of going third-class on the boat. Whenever they talked very long about it in the room, they became silent, almost hushed with expectancy, and then they put on their coats and hats and went out together to walk through the rain without talking at all. Once they went into a church and knelt with their heads down and prayed, and when they had finished praying, they sat there in the pew instead of going out. They sat there, very close together.

And then, without letting Timothy notice it, Louise began to get very tired and nervous. All that Timothy noticed was that she was sometimes short-tempered, and when Selma, who often dropped in on them, came around intending to speak to him about Louise, he was so happy and confident he made Selma feel like an old chaperon who wasn't wanted, so she simply said, 'Keep your eye on Louise, Timothy,' and looked at him searchingly. Timothy smiled, thanked her for her solicitude, and became silent and very worried.

One night when Louise came home from work, she was so tired she couldn't eat. She sat looking at Timothy with a kind of helpless earnestness, and then she almost fainted. When he was rubbing her forehead and her wrists, she told him she was going to have a baby, and she watched him with a dogged eagerness, her whole manner full of apology. At last he took a deep breath, and said, 'Good, good. That gives

a man a sense of completion. Let's hope it's a boy, Louise.'
He became very gay. He played his flute for her. He explained he had bought a neat little machine for rolling his
own cigarettes, and his good humour so pleased her she let
herself whisper, 'Wouldn't it be wonderful if we could have
the baby born in France?'

She worked the rest of the winter, but in March she simply
had to stop. The baby was born early one gray morning in
May. Timothy had got a young obstetrical specialist who
was willing to take the case without having Louise go to a
hospital. It never occurred to Timothy that he would have to
pay him. All that damp spring night the doctor and Timothy
sat in the kitchen waiting. Timothy was polite, but he
looked sick. With a mild graciousness, while the light overhead shone on his fair bright head, he explained about his
course at the Sorbonne, though sometimes he halted and
listened for sounds from the other room. The doctor liked
him and shook his head patiently.

At five o'clock in the morning, the doctor called Timothy
into the other room, and he went in and kissed his wife. For
a moment he was so relieved he could only grin boyishly
without even thinking of the baby. With all the eagerness
gone out of her eyes, Louise, looking waxen-faced and
fragile, smiled at Timothy and said, 'We've got a boy even
if we're not in Paris, Timothy.'

'It's splendid,' he said, beaming with pride and relief and
making her love him. And he bent down and whispered,
'Last time I was in Paris in the spring, it was cold and damp.
The fall is a far better time, dear. Paris'll wait. It'll always be
there for us.'

Then the doctor beckoned to Timothy and they went back
to the kitchen. The doctor said, 'I might as well tell you,
Mr. Harshaw, you'll have to give your wife your undivided
attention for a while. However, I congratulate you.' They
shook hands very solemnly. 'Remember, be cheerful; don't
let this interfere with your wife's plans. Do what you want
to do.'

'We were going to go to Europe. We won't be able to do
that for a while.'

'No. Not for a while, of course.'

'Of course not. Not for months, anyway,' Timothy said. Then they were both silent.

'If I can be of any assistance at all,' the doctor at last said diffidently.

Timothy, reflecting a moment, said eagerly, 'By the way, tell me, do you know a good indoor tennis court? When Mrs. Harshaw gets up, I'd like her to take exercise. We don't want her to lose her shape, you know. She wouldn't want this to make any difference.'

'I'll let you know if I hear of one,' the doctor said, as he picked up his bag to go out. The doctor went outside to the street. The gray, misty morning had become a morning of fine, thin rain. On the street the doctor stopped suddenly, listening. He stood there, looking back at Timothy's place, hearing a bit of faint flute music.

The Red Hat

It was the kind of hat Frances had wanted for months, a plain little red felt hat with the narrow brim tacked back, which would look so smart and simple and expensive. There was really very little to it, it was so plain, but it was the kind of hat that would have made her feel confident of a sleek appearance. She stood on the pavement, her face pressed close against the shop window, a slender, tall, and good-looking girl wearing a reddish woollen dress clinging tightly to her body. On the way home from work, the last three evenings, she had stopped to look at the hat. And when she had got home she had told Mrs. Foley, who lived in the next apartment, how much the little hat appealed to her. In the window were many smart hats, all very expensive. There was only one red felt hat, on a mannequin head with a silver face and very red lips.

Though Frances stood by the window a long time she had no intention of buying the hat, because her husband was out of work and they couldn't afford it; she was waiting for him to get a decent job so that she could buy clothes for herself. Not that she looked shabby, but the fall weather was a little cold, a sharp wind sometimes blowing gustily up the avenue, and in the twilight, on the way home from work with the wind blowing, she knew she ought to be wearing a light coat. In the early afternoon when the sun was shining brightly she looked neat and warm in her woollen dress.

Though she ought to have been on her way home Frances couldn't help standing there, thinking she might look beautiful in this hat, if she went out with Eric, her husband, for the evening. Since he had been so moody and discontented recently she now thought with pleasure of pleasing him by wearing something that would give her a new kind of elegance, of making him feel cheerful and proud of her and glad, after all, that they were married.

But the hat cost fifteen dollars. She had eighteen dollars in her purse, all that was left of her salary after shopping for groceries for the week. It was ridiculous for her to be there looking at the hat, which was obviously too expensive for her, so she smiled and walked away, putting both hands in the small pockets of her dress. She walked slowly, glancing at two women who were standing at the other end of the big window. One of the two women, the younger one, wearing a velvet coat trimmed with squirrel, said to the other: 'Let's go in and try some of them on.'

Hesitating and half turning, Frances thought it would be quite harmless and amusing if she went into the shop and tried on the red hat, just to see if it looked as good on her as it did on the mannequin head. It never occurred to her to buy the hat.

In the shop, she walked on soft, thick, gray carpet to the chair by the window, where she sat alone for a few minutes, waiting for one of the saleswomen to come to her. At one of the mirrors an elderly lady with bleached hair was fussing with many hats and talking jerkily to a deferential and patient saleswoman. Frances, looking at the big dominant woman with the bleached hair and the expensive clothes, felt embarrassed, because she thought it ought to be apparent to everyone in the shop, by the expression on her face, that she had no intention of taking a hat.

A deep-bosomed saleswoman, splendidly corseted, and wearing black silk, smiled at Frances, appraising her carefully. Frances was the kind of customer who might look good in any one of the hats. At the same time, while looking at her, the saleswoman wondered why she wasn't wearing a coat, or at least carrying one, for the evenings were often chilly.

'I wanted to try on the little hat, the red one in the window,' Frances said.

The saleswoman had decided by this time that Frances intended only to amuse herself by trying on hats, so when she took the hat from the window and handed it to Frances she merely smiled politely and watched her adjusting it on her head. Frances tried the hat and patted a strand of fair hair till it curled by the side of the brim. And then, because she was delighted to see that it was as attractive on her as it had been on the mannequin head with the silver face, she smiled happily, noticing in the mirror that her face was the shape of the mannequin face, a little long and narrow, the nose fine and firm, and she took out her lipstick and marked her lips heavily. Looking in the glass again she felt elated and seemed to enjoy a kind of freedom. She felt elegant and a little haughty. Then she saw in the mirror the image of the deep-bosomed and polite saleslady.

'It is nice, isn't it?' Frances said, wishing suddenly that she hadn't come into the store.

'It is wonderfully becoming to you, especially to you.'

And Frances said suddenly: 'I suppose I could change it, if my husband didn't like it?'

'Of course.'

'Then I'll take it.'

Even while paying for the hat and assuring herself that it would be amusing to take it home for the evening, she had a feeling that she ought to have known when she first came into the store that she intended to take the hat home. The saleswoman was smiling warmly. Frances, no longer embarrassed, thought with pleasure of going out with Eric and wearing the hat, without detaching the price tag. In the morning she could return it.

But as she walked out of the store there was a hope 'way down within her that Eric would find her so charming in the red hat he would insist she keep it. She wanted him to be freshly aware of her, to like the hat, to discover its restrained elegance. And when they went out together for the evening they would both share the feeling she had had when first she had looked in the shop window. Frances, carrying the box, hurried, eager to get home. The sharp wind had gone down. When there was no wind on these fall evenings it was not cold, and she would not have to wear a coat with her woollen dress. It was just about dark now and all the lights were lit in the streets.

The stairs in the apartment house were long, and on other evenings very tiring, but tonight she seemed to be breathing lightly as she opened the door. Her husband, Eric, was sitting by the table lamp, reading the paper. A black-haired man with a well-shaped nose, he semed to be utterly without energy, slumped down in the chair. A slight odour of whiskey came from him. For four months he had been out of work and some of the spirit had gone out of him, as if he felt that he could never again have independence, and most of the afternoon he had been standing in the streets by the theatres, talking with actors who were out of work.

'Hello, Eric boy,' she said, kissing him on the head. He hardly looked up.

' 'Lo France,' he said.

'Let's go out and eat tonight,' she said.

'What with?'

'Two bucks, big boy, a couple of dollar dinners.'

So far he had hardly looked at her. She went into the bedroom and took the hat out of the box, adjusting it on her head at the right angle, powdering her nose and smiling cheerfully. Jauntily she walked into the living-room, swinging her hips a little and trying not to smile too openly.

'Take a look at the hat, Eric. How would you like to step out with me?'

Smiling faintly, he said: 'You look snappy, but you can't afford a hat.'

'Never mind that. How do you like it?'

'What's the use if you can't keep it?'

'But hasn't it got class? Did you ever see anything look so good on me?'

'Was it bargain day somewhere?'

'Bargain day! I got it at one of the best shops in town. Fifteen bucks.'

'You'd bother looking at fifteen-dollar hats with me out of work,' he said angrily, getting up and glaring at her morosely.

'I would.'

'Sure. It's your money. You do what you want.'

Frances felt hurt, as if for months there had been a steady pressure on her, and she said stubbornly: 'I paid for it. Of course, I can take it back if you insist.'

'If I insist,' he said, getting up slowly and sneering at her as though he had been hating her for months. 'If I insist. And you know how I feel about the whole business.'

Frances felt hurt and yet strong from indignation, so she shrugged her shoulders. 'I wanted to wear it tonight,' she said.

His face was white, his eyes almost closed. Suddenly he grabbed hold of her by the wrist, twisting it till she sank down on one knee.

'You'll get rid of that hat quickly, or I'll break every bone in your body; then I'll clear out of here for good.'

'Don't, Eric, please don't.'

'You've been keeping me, haven't you?'

'Don't hurt me, Eric.'

'Get your fifteen-dollar hat out of my sight quick. Get rid of it, or I'll get out of here for good.'

'I will, Eric.'

As he let go her wrist he snatched the hat from her head, pulling it, twisting it in his hands, then throwing it on the floor. He kicked it far across the room. 'Get it out of here quick, or we're through,' he said.

All the indignation had gone out of Frances. She was afraid of him; afraid, too, that he would suddenly rush out of the room and never come back, for she knew he had thought of doing it before. Picking up the hat she caressed the soft felt with her fingers, though she could hardly see it with her eyes filled with tears. The felt was creased, the price tag had been torn off, leaving a tiny tear at the back.

Eric, who kept on wetting his lips, was sitting there, watching her.

The hat was torn and she could not take it back. Hurriedly she put it in the box, wrapping the tissue paper around it, and then she went along the hall to Mrs. Foley's apartment.

Mrs. Foley, a smiling, fat woman with a round, cheerful face, opened the door. She saw Frances was agitated and felt sorry for her. 'Frances, dear, what's the matter with you?'

'You remember the hat I was telling you about? Here it is. It doesn't look good on me. I was disappointed and pulled it off my head and there's a tiny tear in it. Maybe you'd want it.'

Mrs. Foley thought at once that Frances had been quarrelling with her husband. Mrs. Foley held up the hat and looked at it shrewdly. Then she went back into her bedroom and tried it on. The felt was good, and though it had been creased, it was quite smooth now. 'Of course, I never pay more than five dollars for a hat,' she said. The little felt hat did not look good on her round head and face. She was sure that Frances was trying to sell the hat cheaply just to irritate her husband.

'I hate to offer you five dollars for it, Frances, but ...'

'All right. Give me five dollars.'

As Mrs. Foley took the five dollars from her purse, Frances said suddenly: 'Listen, dear, if I want it back next week you sell it to me for five, will you?'

'Sure I will, kid.'

Frances hurried back to her own apartment. Though she knew Eric could not have gone out while she was standing in the hall, she kept on saying to herself: 'Please, Heaven, please don't let me do anything to make him leave me while he's feeling this way.'

Eric, with his arms folded across his chest, was looking out of the window.

Frances put the five dollars Mrs. Foley had given her, and the three dollars left over from her salary, on the small table by Eric's chair. 'I sold it to Mrs. Foley,' she said.

'Thanks,' he said, without looking at her.

'Eric, I'm absolutely satisfied,' she said, softly and sincerely.

'All right, I'm sorry,' he said briefly.

'I mean I don't know what makes you think I'm not satisfied – that's all,' she said.

Sitting beside him she put her elbow on her knee and thought of the felt hat on Mrs. Foley's head: it did not look good on her; her face was not at all the shape of the long silver face of the mannequin head. And as Frances thought of the way the hat had looked on the mannequin head in the window she hoped vaguely that something would turn up so that she could get it back from Mrs. Foley by the end of the week. And just thinking of it, sitting there, she felt an eagerness and a faint elation; it was a plain little red hat, the kind of hat she had wanted for months, elegant and expensive, a plain felt hat, but so very distinctive.

An Old Quarrel

Mrs. Massey, a stout, kindly woman of sixty, full of energy for her age, and red-faced and healthy except for an occasional pain in her left leg which she watched very carefully, had come from Chicago to see her son who was a doctor. The doctor's family made a great fuss over her, and she felt in such good humour that she said suddenly one night: 'I declare, I'll go and see Mary Woolens. I wonder what's happened to her? Find out where she lives for me.'

She had grown up with Mary Woolens. Thirty years ago they had quarrelled, she had married and gone West, and they had not seen each other since.

So the next afternoon Mrs. Massey was back in her old neighbourhood on the avenue at the corner of Christopher Street, staring around longingly for some familiar sight that might recall an incident in her childhood. Looking carefully to the right and left, she had darted forward across the street with a determined look on her face, for traffic now made her nervous, and had arrived on the other side breathless with relief.

She walked slowly along the street, taking one deep breath after another, and leaning forward to lift some of the weight off her feet. Her face was screwed up as she peered at the numbers on the houses, and as she stopped to put on her glasses she was smiling eagerly like a woman who nurses a secret.

If she had closed her eyes and stood there, she could have remembered vividly almost every word of her quarrel with Mary Woolens. Mary had been a foolish, rather homely girl who found herself in love with a deceitful man who kept on promising to marry her while he borrowed her money. Then Mary had borrowed a hundred dollars from her, and it turned out that she had given it to the fellow, who had gone away, and of course Mary was not able to pay the money back. There had been so much bitterness. She had wanted to have the man arrested. For a while Mary and she seemed to hate each other, then their friendship was over.

Now, walking along the street, Mrs. Massey was full of shame to think there had been a quarrel about money. It seemed now that they both had been mean and spiteful, and she couldn't bear to think Mary might not know that she had forgiven her long ago. 'This must be the place here,' she said, looking up at a brownstone house. For a moment she felt awkward and still a bit ashamed, then she went up the steps, feeling like a self-possessed, well-dressed woman in good circumstances.

It was a clean-looking house with a little sign advertising small apartments and a few rooms for rent. As Mrs. Massey rang the bell in the hall, she peered up the stairs, waiting, and then saw a woman in a plain dark blue dress and with astonishingly white hair coming toward her. This woman, who had a pair of earnest blue eyes and a mild, peaceful expression, asked politely, 'Were you wanting to see somebody?'

'I was wanting to see Miss Woolens,' Mrs. Massey said.

Then she said, 'Goodness, you're Mary. Mary, don't you really know me?'

'I can't quite see you in that light. If you'd turn your head to the side. There now, well. Elsie Wiggins! It can't be Elsie Wiggins. I mean Elsie Massey.'

The little white-haired woman was so startled that her hands, held up to her lips, began to shake. Then she was so pleased she could not move. 'I never thought of such a thing in my life,' she said. She was very flustered, so she cried out suddenly, 'Oh, I'm so glad to see you; come in, please come in, Elsie,' and she went hurrying along the hall to a room at the back of the house, while Mrs. Massey, following more slowly, smiled to herself with deep enjoyment.

And even when they were sitting in the big carpeted room with the old-fashioned couch and arm-chairs, she knew that Mary was still looking at her as though she were a splendid creature from a strange world. Mrs. Massey smiled with indulgent good humour. But Mary had no composure at all. 'I just don't know what to say to you, Elsie. I'm so delighted to see you.' Then darting up like a small bird, she said, 'I'll put on the kettle and we'll have a cup of tea.'

While she waited, Mrs. Massey felt a twinge of uneasiness, wondering how she would mention that she had long ago forgiven Mary, for she was sure that was what was making the poor woman so flustered, even though, so far, she was pretending there had never been bitterness between them. With a pot of tea on a tray, and beaming with childish warmth, Mary returned, saying, 'I was just trying to count up the years since we last saw each other.'

'It must be thirty years. Fancy that,' Mrs. Massey said.

'But I've heard about you, Elsie. I once met a woman who had lived in Chicago, and she told me that you had a son who was a doctor, and I read about some wonderful operation he performed in one of the hospitals here. It was in all the papers. You must be awfully proud, Elsie. Who does he look like?'

'They always said he looked like his father.'

'Maybe so. But of course I always think of him as Elsie's boy.'

'Has your health been good, Mary?'

'I've nothing to complain about. I don't look strong, do I? But outside of a pain in my head that the doctor says might be caused by an old tooth, I'm in good health. You look fine, though.'

'Well, I am, and I'm not. I've a pain in the leg and sometimes a swelling here, just at the ankle, that may be from my heart. Never mind. Have the years been good to you, Mary? What's happened?'

'Why, nothing. Nothing at all, I suppose,' Mary said, looking around the room as though puzzled. As she smiled, she looked sweet and frail. 'I look after the house here. I learned to save my money,' she said. All of a sudden she added, 'Tell me all about your son, the doctor,' and she leaned forward, as though seeking a confirmation of many things she might have dreamed. 'I ought to pour the tea now,' she said, 'but you go right on talking. I'll hear everything you say.'

Mrs. Massey began to talk quietly with a subdued pride about her son, and sometimes she looked up at Mary, who was pouring the tea with a thin trembling hand. The flush of excitement was still on Mary's face. Her chest looked almost hollow. She was a woman who, of course, had worked hard for years, every day wearing clothes that looked the same, seeing that her house was cleaned in the morning, going to the same stores every afternoon, and getting much pleasure out of a bit of lively gossip with a neighbour on the street.

'I need more hot water,' she said now, and hurried to the kitchen with short steps, and then, when she returned, she stood there with a cup in her hand, lost in her thoughts. 'Goodness,' she said. 'There are so many things to say I don't know what I'm doing.'

Mrs. Massey continued to talk with gentle tolerance, remembering that her own life had been rich and fruitful, and having pity for Mary, who had remained alone. But when a bit of sunlight from the window shone on Mary's white head and thin face as she sat there with a teacup in her hand, her face held so much sweetness and gentleness that Mrs. Massey was puzzled, for Mary had been a rather homely girl.

'It upset me terribly to stand on the corner and feel so strange,' Mrs. Massey was saying.

'Elsie, heavens above! I didn't ask about Will, your husband.'

'Will? Why, Will's been dead for five years, Mary.'

'Dead. Think of that. I hardly knew him. It seems like yesterday.'

'We were married twenty-five years.'

'You used to love him very much, didn't you, Elsie? I remember that. He was a good-living man, wasn't he?'

'He was a good man,' Mrs. Massey said vaguely, and they both sat there, silent now, having their own thoughts.

Mary Woolens, the small white-haired one, was leaning forward eagerly, but Mrs. Massey, stout and red-faced, sighed, thinking of the long, steady years of married life; and though there had been children and some bright moments and some hopes fulfilled, she was strangely discontented now, troubled by a longing for something she could not see or understand.

Perhaps it was Mary's eagerness that was stirring her, but she aroused herself by thinking, 'Has she forgotten I once told her I hated her? Won't she mention it at all?' And since she had been the one who had held the old grievance, she felt resentful, for the old mean quarrel had bothered her a long time, had filled her with shame so that she had been eager to forgive Mary; and now Mary seemed to have forgotten it.

She looked full into Mary's face, and then couldn't help wondering what was making her smile so happily. 'What are you thinking of, Mary?' she asked.

'Do you remember how we grew up around here, and were little bits of kids together?'

'I sort of half remember.'

'Do you remember when we were such little things, we used to sit together on the steps and you used to tell me all kinds of fairy stories, making them up. I'll bet you can't remember.'

'I do remember,' Mrs. Massey said, leaning forward eagerly. 'There was another girl used to sit with us sometimes. Bertha, Bertha – oh, dear, now, what was it?'

'Bertha Madison. We wore big hair ribbons. I can remember some of the fairy stories now. The night I read about your son being the fine surgeon and performing that wonderful operation, I lay awake in bed thinking about you, and I remembered the stories. It used to seem so wonderful that you could make up such fine stories as you went along, and it seemed just right, when I thought about it, that your boy should be doing the things he was. I remember there was one story you kept carrying on, and like a whole lot of bright patches it was.'

'I remember,' Mrs. Massey said, holding on to her animation.

Mary looked up suddenly. Her face was flushed, her blue eyes were brilliant. She was looking up with a kind of desperate eagerness. With a rapt interest and mysterious delight, Mrs. Massey was leaning forward, her heavy face holding a little smile that kept her lips parted. They were both filled with delight, leaning close to each other, almost breathing together, while they were silent. Then, without any warning, Mary began to cry, shaking her head hopelessly from side to side, and dabbing at her eyes with a small handkerchief.

'Mary dear, Mary! What is the matter? Why are you crying?'

'I don't know,' Mary said.

'You shouldn't go on like that, then,' Mrs. Massey said, fretfully. But she, too, felt her eyes moistening. 'Oh, dear, oh, dear, Mary,' she said, rocking from side to side, 'oh, dear, oh, dear.' She tried bravely to smile, but it no longer seemed important that they had once quarrelled bitterly, or that her life had been full and Mary's quite barren – just that once they had been young together. A great deal of time had passed, and now they were both old.

The Runaway

In the lumber-yard by the lake there was an old brick building two storeys high and all around the foundations were heaped great piles of soft sawdust, softer than the thick moss in the woods. There were many of these golden mounds of dust covering that part of the yard right down to the blue lake. That afternoon all the fellows followed Michael up the ladder to the roof of the old building and they sat with their legs hanging over the edge looking out at the whitecaps on the water. Michael was younger than some of them but he was much bigger, his legs were long, his huge hands dangled awkwardly at his sides and his thick black hair curled up all over his head. 'I'll stump you all to jump down,' he said suddenly, and without thinking about it, he shoved himself off the roof and fell on the sawdust where he lay rolling around and laughing.

'You're all stumped,' he shouted. 'You're all yellow,' he said, coaxing them to follow him. Still laughing, he watched them looking down from the roof, white-faced and hesitant, and then one by one they jumped and got up grinning with relief.

In the hot afternoon sunlight they all lay on the sawdust pile telling jokes till at last one of the fellows said, 'Come on up on the old roof again and jump down.' There wasn't much enthusiasm among them, but they all went up to the roof again and began to jump off in a determined, desperate way till only Michael was left and the others were all down below grinning up at him and calling, 'Come on, Mike. What's the matter with you?' Michael longed to jump down there and be with them, but he remained on the edge of the roof, wetting his lips, with a silly grin on his face, wondering why it

had not seemed such a long drop the first time. For a while
they thought he was only kidding them, then they saw him
clenching his fists. He was trying to count to ten and then
jump, and when that failed, he tried to take a long breath
and close his eyes.

In a while the fellows began to jeer at him; they were
tired of waiting and it was getting on to dinner-time. 'Come
on, you're yellow, do you think we're going to sit here all
night?' they began to shout, and when he did not move they
began to get up and walk away, still jeering. 'Who did this in
the first place? What's the matter with you guys?' he
shouted.

But for a long time he remained on the edge of the roof,
staring unhappily and steadily at the ground. He remained
all alone for nearly an hour while the sun like a great orange
ball getting bigger and bigger rolled slowly over the gray line
beyond the lake. His clothes were wet from nervous sweating. At last he closed his eyes, slipped off the roof, fell
heavily on the pile of sawdust and lay there a long time.
There were no sounds in the yard, the workmen had gone
home. As he lay there he wondered why he had been unable
to move; and then he got up slowly and walked home feeling
deeply ashamed and wanting to avoid everybody.

He was so late for dinner that his stepmother said to him
sarcastically, 'You're big enough by this time surely to be
able to get home in time for dinner. But if you won't come
home, you'd better try staying in tonight.' She was a well-
built woman with a fair, soft skin and a little touch of gray
in her hair and an eternally patient smile on her face. She
was speaking now with a restrained, passionless severity, but
Michael, with his dark face gloomy and sullen, hardly heard
her; he was still seeing the row of grinning faces down below
on the sawdust pile and hearing them jeer at him.

As he ate his cold dinner he was rolling his brown eyes
fiercely and sometimes shaking his big black head. His
father, who was sitting in the arm-chair by the window, a
huge man with his hair nearly all gone so that his smooth
wide forehead rose in a beautiful shining dome, kept looking
at him steadily. When Michael had finished eating and had
gone out to the veranda, his father followed, sat down beside
him, lit his pipe and said gently, 'What's bothering you, son?'

'Nothing, Dad. There's nothing bothering me,' Michael said, but he kept on staring out at the gray dust drifting off the road.

His father kept coaxing and whispering in a voice that was amazingly soft for such a big man. As he talked, his long fingers played with the heavy gold watch fob on his vest. He was talking about nothing in particular and yet by the tone of his voice he was expressing a marvellous deep friendliness that somehow seemed to become a part of the twilight and then of the darkness. And Michael began to like the sound of his father's voice, and soon he blurted out, 'I guess by this time all the guys around here are saying I'm yellow. I'd like to be a thousand miles away.' He told how he could not force himself to jump off the roof the second time. But his father lay back in the arm-chair laughing in that hearty, rolling, easy way that Michael loved to hear; years ago when Michael had been younger and he was walking along the paths in the evening, he used to try and laugh like his father only his voice was not deep enough and he would grin sheepishly and look up at the trees overhanging the paths as if someone hiding up there had heard him. 'You'll be all right with the bunch, son,' his father was saying. 'I'm betting you'll lick any boy in town that says you're yellow.'

But there was the sound of the screen door opening, and Michael's stepmother said in her mild, firm way, 'If I've rebuked the boy, Henry, as I think he ought to be rebuked, I don't know why you should be humouring him.'

'You surely don't object to me talking to Michael.'

'I simply want you to be reasonable, Henry.'

In his grave, unhurried way Mr. Lount got up and followed his wife into the house and soon Michael could hear them arguing; he could hear his father's firm, patient voice floating clearly out to the street; then his stepmother's voice, mild at first, rising, becoming hysterical till at last she cried out wildly, 'You're setting the boy against me. You don't want him to think of me as his mother. The two of you are against me. I know your nature.'

As he looked up and down the street fearfully, Michael began to make prayers that no one would pass by who would think, 'Mr. and Mrs. Lount are quarrelling again.' Alert, he listened for faint sounds on the cinder path, but he heard only the frogs croaking under the bridge opposite Stevenson's place and the far-away cry of a freight train passing behind the hills. 'Why did Dad have to get married? It used to be swell on the farm,' he thought, remembering how he and his father had gone fishing down at the glen. And then while he listened to the sound of her voice, he kept thinking that his stepmother was a fine woman, only she always made him uneasy because she wanted him to like her, and then when she found out that he couldn't think of her as his mother, she had grown resentful. 'I like her and I like my father. I don't know why they quarrel. They're really such fine people. Maybe it's because Dad shouldn't have sold the farm and moved here. There's nothing for him to do.' Unable to get interested in the town life, his father loafed all day down at the hotel or in Bailey's flour-and-feed store but he was such a fine-looking, dignified, reticent man that the loafers would not accept him as a crony. Inside the house now, Mrs. Lount was crying quietly and saying, 'Henry, we'll kill each other. We seem to bring out all the very worst qualities in each other. I do all I can and yet you both make me feel like an intruder.'

'It's just your imagination, Martha. Now stop worrying.'

'I'm an unhappy woman. But I try to be patient. I try so hard, don't I, Henry?'

'You're very patient, dear, but you shouldn't be so suspicious of everyone and everybody, don't you see?' Mr. Lount was saying in the soothing voice of a man trying to pacify an angry and hysterical wife.

Then Michael heard footsteps on the cinder path, and then he saw two long shadows flung across the road: two women were approaching, and one was a tall, slender girl. When Michael saw this girl, Helen Murray, he tried to duck behind the veranda post, for he had always wanted her for his girl. He had gone to school with her. At night-time he used to lie awake planning remarkable feats that would so impress her she would never want to be far away from him. Now the girl's mother was calling, 'Hello there, Michael,' in a very jolly voice.

'Hello, Mrs. Murray,' he said glumly, for he was sure his father's or his mother's voice would rise again.

'Come on and walk with home with us, Michael,' Helen called. Her voice sounded so soft and her face in the dusk light seemed so round, white and mysteriously far away that Michael began to ache with eagerness. Yet he said hurriedly, 'I can't. I can't tonight,' speaking almost rudely as if he believed they only wanted to tease him.

As they went on along the path and he watched them, he was really longing for that one bright moment when Helen would pass under the high corner light, though he was thinking with bitterness that he could already hear them talking, hear Mrs. Murray saying, 'He's a peculiar boy, but it's not to be wondered at since his father and mother don't get along at all,' and the words were floating up to the verandas of all the houses; inside one of the houses someone had stopped playing a piano, maybe to hear one of the fellows who had been in the lumber-yard that afternoon laughing and telling that young Lount was scared to jump off the roof.

Still watching the corner, Michael suddenly felt that the twisting and pulling in the life in the house was twisting and choking him. 'I'll get out of here. I'll go away,' and he began to think of going to the city. He began to long for freedom in strange places where everything was new and fresh and mysterious. His heart began to beat heavily at the thought of this freedom. In the city he had an uncle Joe who sailed the lake-boats in the summer months and in the winter went all over the south from one race-track to another following the horses. 'I ought to go down to the city tonight and get a job,' he thought: but he did not move; he was still waiting for Helen Murray to pass under the light.

For most of the next day, too, Michael kept to himself. He was uptown once on a message, and he felt like running on the way home. With long sweeping strides he ran steadily on the paths past the shipyard, the church, the railway tracks, his face serious with determination.

But in the late afternoon when he was sitting on the veranda reading, Sammy Schwartz and Ike Hershfield came around to see him. 'Hello Mike, what's new with you?' they said, sitting on the steps very seriously.

'Hello, Sammy, hello, Ike. What's new with you?'

They began to talk to Michael about the coloured family

that had moved into the old roughcast shack down by the tracks. 'The big coon kid thinks he's tough,' Sammy said. 'He offered to beat up any of us so we said he wouldn't have a snowball's chance with you.'

'What did the nigger say?'

'He said he'd pop you one right on the nose if you came over his way.'

'Come on, guys. Let's go over there,' Michael said. 'I'll tear his guts out for you.'

They went out to the street, fell in step very solemnly, and walked over to the field by the tracks without saying a word. When they were about fifty paces away from the shack, Sammy said, 'Wait here. I'll go get the coon,' and he ran on to the unpainted door of the white-washed house calling, 'Oh, Art, oh, Art, come on out.' A big coloured boy with closely cropped hair came out and put his hand up, shading his eyes from the sun. Then he went back into the house and came out again with a big straw hat on his head. He was in his bare feet. The way he came walking across the field with Sammy was always easy to remember because he hung back a little, talking rapidly, shrugging his shoulders and rolling the whites of his eyes. When he came close to Michael he grinned nervously, flashing his teeth, and said, 'What's the matter with you white boys? I don't want to do no fighting.' He looked scared.

'Come on. Get ready. I'm going to do a nice job on you,' Michael said.

The coloured boy took off his big straw hat and with great care laid it on the ground while all the time he was looking mournfully across the field and at his house, hoping maybe that somebody would come out. Then they started to fight, and Michael knocked him down four times, but he, himself, got a black eye and a cut lip. The coloured boy had been so brave and he seemed so alone, licked and lying on the ground, that they sat down around him, praising him, making friends with him and gradually finding out that he was a good ball player, a left-handed pitcher who specialized in a curve ball, and they agreed they could use him, maybe, on the town team.

Lying there in the field, flat on his back, Michael liked it so much that he almost did not want to go away. Art, the coloured boy, was telling how he had always wanted to be a jockey but had got too big; he had a brother who could make the weight. So Michael began to boast about his Uncle Joe who went around to all the tracks in the winter making and losing money at places like Saratoga, Blue Bonnets and Tia Juana. It was a fine, friendly, eager discussion about far-away places.

It was nearly dinner-time when Michael got home; he went in the house sucking his cut lip and hoping his mother would not notice his black eye. But he heard no movement in the house. In the kitchen he saw his stepmother kneeling down in the middle of the floor with her hands clasped and her lips moving.

'What's the matter, Mother?' he asked.

'I'm praying,' she said.

'What for?'

'For your father. Get down and pray with me.'

'I don't want to pray, Mother.'

'You've got to,' she said.

'My lip's all cut. It's bleeding. I can't do it,' he said.

Late afternoon sunshine coming through the kitchen window shone on his stepmother's graying hair, on her soft smooth skin and on the gentle, patient expression that was on her face. At that moment Michael thought that she was desperately uneasy and terribly alone, and he felt sorry for her even while he was rushing out of the back door.

He saw his father walking toward the woodshed, walking slow and upright with his hands held straight at his side and with the same afternoon sunlight shining so brightly on the high dome of his forehead. He went right into the woodshed without looking back. Michael sat down on the steps and waited. He was afraid to follow. Maybe it was because of the way his father was walking with his head held up and his hands straight at his sides. Michael began to make a small desperate prayer that his father should suddenly appear at the woodshed door.

Time dragged slowly. A few doors away Mrs. McCutcheon was feeding her hens who were clucking as she called them. 'I can't sit here till it gets dark,' Michael was thinking, but he was afraid to go into the woodshed and afraid to think of what he feared.

So he waited till he could not keep a picture of the interior of the shed out of his thoughts, a picture that included his father walking in with his hands as though strapped at his sides and his head stiff, like a man they were going to hang.

'What's he doing in there, what's he doing?' Michael said out loud, and he jumped up and rushed to the shed and flung the door wide.

His father was sitting on a pile of wood with his head on his hands and a kind of beaten look on his face. Still scared, Michael called out, 'Dad, Dad,' and then felt such relief he sank down on the pile of wood beside his father and looked up at him.

'What's the matter with you, son?'

'Nothing. I guess I just wondered where you were.'

'What are you upset about?'

'I've been running. I feel all right.'

So they sat there quietly till it seemed time to go into the house. No one said anything. No one noticed Michael's black eye or his cut lip.

Even after they had eaten Michael could not get rid of the fear within him, a fear of something impending. In a way he felt that he ought to do something at once, but he seemed unable to move; it was like sitting on the edge of the roof yesterday, afraid to make the jump. So he went back to the house and sat on the stoop and for a long time looked at the shed till he grew even more uneasy. He heard the angry drilling of a wood-pecker and the quiet rippling of the little water flowing under the street bridge and flowing on down over the rocks into the glen. Heavy clouds were sweeping up from the horizon.

He knew now that he wanted to run away, that he could not stay there any longer, only he couldn't make up his mind to go. Within him was that same breathless feeling he had had when he sat on the roof staring down, trying to move. Now he walked around to the front of the house and kept going along the path as far as Helen Murray's house. After going around to the back door, he stood for a long time staring at the lighted window, hoping to see Helen's shadow or her body moving against the light. He was breathing deeply and smelling the rich heavy odours from the flower garden. With his head thrust forward he whistled softly.

'Is that you Michael?' Helen called from the door.

'Come on out, Helen.'

'What do you want?'

'Come on for a walk, will you?'

For a moment she hesitated at the door, then she came toward him, floating in her white organdie party dress over the grass toward him. She was saying, 'I'm dressed to go out. I can't go with you. I'm going down to the dance hall.'

'Who with?'

'Charlie Delaney.'

'Oh, all right,' he said. 'I just thought you might be doing nothing.' As he walked away he called back to her, 'So long, Helen.'

It was then, on the way back to the house, that he felt he had to go away at once. 'I've got to go. I'll die here. I'll write to Dad from the city.'

No one paid any attention to him when he returned to the house. His father and stepmother were sitting quietly in the living-room reading the paper. In his own room he took a little wooden box from the bottom drawer of his dresser and emptied it of twenty dollars and seventy cents, all that he had saved. He listened solemnly for sounds in the house, then he stuffed a clean shirt into his pocket, a comb and a toothbrush.

Outside he hurried along with his great swinging strides, going past the corner house, on past the long fence and the bridge and the church, and the shipyard, and past the last of the town lights to the highway. He was walking stubbornly with his face looking solemn and dogged. Then he saw the moonlight shining on the hay stacked in the fields, and when he smelled the oats and the richer smell of sweet clover he suddenly felt alive and free.Headlights from cars kept sweeping by and already he was imagining he could see the haze of bright light hanging over the city. His heart began to thump with eagerness. He put out his hand for a lift, feeling full of hope. He looked across the fields at the dark humps, cows standing motionless in the night. Soon someone would stop and pick him up. They would take him among a million new faces, rumbling sounds and strange smells. He got more excited. His Uncle Joe might get him a job on the boats for the rest of the summer; maybe, too, he might be able to move around with him in the winter. Over and over he kept thinking of places with beautiful names, places like Tia Juana, Woodbine, Saratoga and Blue Bonnets.

The Snob

It was at the book counter in the department store that John Harcourt, the student, caught a glimpse of his father. At first he could not be sure in the crowd that pushed along the aisle, but there was something about the colour of the back of the elderly man's neck, something about the faded felt hat, that he knew very well. Harcourt was standing with the girl he loved, buying a book for her. All afternoon he had been talking to her, eagerly, but with an anxious diffidence, as if there still remained in him an innocent wonder that she should be delighted to be with him. From underneath her wide-brimmed straw hat, her face, so fair and beautifully strong with its expression of cool independence, kept turning up to him and sometimes smiled at what he said. That was the way they always talked, never daring to show much full, strong feeling. Harcourt had just bought the book, and had reached into his pocket for the money with a free, ready gesture to make it appear that he was accustomed to buying books for young ladies, when the white-haired man in the faded felt hat, at the other end of the counter, turned half toward him, and Harcourt knew he was standing only a few feet away from his father.

The young man's easy words trailed away and his voice became little more than a whisper, as if he were afraid that everyone in the store might recognize it. There was rising in him a dreadful uneasiness; something very precious that he wanted to hold seemed close to destruction. His father, standing at the end of the bargain counter, was planted squarely on his two feet, turning a book over thoughtfully in his hands. Then he took out his glasses from an old, worn leather case and adjusted them on the end of his nose, looking down over them at the book. His coat was thrown open, two buttons on his vest were undone, his gray hair was too long, and in his rather shabby clothes he looked very much like a working-man, a carpenter perhaps. Such a resentment rose in young Harcourt that he wanted to cry out bitterly, 'Why does he dress as if he never owned a decent suit in his life? He doesn't care what the whole world thinks of him. He never did. I've told him a hundred times he ought to wear his good clothes when he goes out. Mother's told him the same thing. He just laughs. And now Grace may see him. Grace will meet him.'

So young Harcourt stood still, with his head down, feeling that something very painful was impending. Once he looked anxiously at Grace, who had turned to the bargain counter. Among those people drifting aimlessly by with hot red faces, getting in each other's way, using their elbows but keeping their faces detached and wooden, she looked tall and splendidly alone. She was so sure of herself, her relation to the people in the aisles, the clerks behind the counter, the books on the shelves, and everything around her. Still keeping his head down and moving close, he whispered uneasily, 'Let's go and have tea somewhere, Grace.'

'In a minute, dear,' she said.

'Let's go now.'

'In just a minute, dear,' she repeated absently.

'There's not a breath of air in here. Let's go now.'

'What makes you so impatient?'

'There's nothing but old books on that counter.'

'There may be something here I've wanted all my life,' she said, smiling at him brightly and not noticing the uneasiness in his face.

So Harcourt had to move slowly behind her, getting closer to his father all the time. He could feel the space that separ-

ated them narrowing. Once he looked up with a vague, side-
long glance. But his father red-faced and happy, was still
reading the book, only now there was a meditative expression on his face, as if something in the book had stirred him
and he intended to stay there reading for some time.

Old Harcourt had lots of time to amuse himself, because
he was on a pension after working hard all his life. He had
sent John to the university and he was eager to have him dis-
tinguish himself. Every night when John came home,
whether it was early or late, he used to go into his father's
and mother's bedroom and turn on the light and talk to
them about the interesting things that had happened to him
during the day. They listened and shared this new world with
him. They both sat up in their night-clothes and, while his
mother asked all the questions, his father listened attentively
with his head cocked on one side and a smile or a frown on
his face. The memory of all this was in John now, and there
was also a desperate longing and a pain within him growing
harder to bear as he glanced fearfully at his father, but he
thought stubbornly, 'I can't introduce him. It'll be easier for
everybody if he doesn't see us. I'm not ashamed. But it will
be easier. It'll be more sensible. It'll only embarrass him to
see Grace.' By this time he knew he was ashamed, but he
felt that his shame was justified, for Grace's father had the
smooth, confident manner of a man who had lived all his
life among people who were rich and sure of themselves.
Often when he had been in Grace's home talking politely to
her mother, John had kept on thinking of the plainness of
his own home and of his parents' laughing, good-natured
untidiness, and he resolved desperately that he must make
Grace's people admire him.

He looked up cautiously, for they were about eight feet
away from his father, but at that moment his father, too,
looked up and John's glance shifted swiftly far over the aisle,
over the counters, seeing nothing. As his father's blue, calm
eyes stared steadily over the glasses, there was an instant
when their glances might have met. Neither one could have
been certain, yet John, as he turned away and began to talk
to Grace hurriedly, knew surely that his father had seen him.
He knew it by the steady calmness in his father's blue eyes.

John's shame grew, and then humiliation sickened him as he waited and did nothing.

His father turned away, going down the aisle, walking erectly in his shabby clothes, his shoulders very straight, never once looking back. His father would walk slowly along the street, he knew, with that meditative expression deepening and becoming grave.

Young Harcourt stood beside Grace, brushing against her soft shoulder, and made faintly aware again of the delicate scent she used. There, so close beside him, she was holding within her everything he wanted to reach out for, only now he felt a sharp hostility that made him sullen and silent.

'You were right, John,' she was drawling in her soft voice. 'It does get unbearable in here on a hot day. Do let's go now. Have you ever noticed that department stores after a time can make you really hate people?' But she smiled when she spoke, so he might see that she really hated no one.

'You don't like people, do you?' he said sharply.

'People? What people? What do you mean?'

'I mean,' he went on irritably, 'you don't like the kind of people you bump into here, for example.'

'Not especially. Who does? What are you talking about?'

'Anybody could see you don't,' he said recklessly, full of a savage eagerness to hurt her. 'I say you don't like simple, honest people, the kind of people you meet all over the city.' He blurted the words out as if he wanted to shake her, but he was longing to say, 'You wouldn't like my family. Why couldn't I take you home to have dinner with them? You'd turn up your nose at them, because they've no pretensions. As soon as my father saw you, he knew you wouldn't want to meet him. I could tell by the way he turned.'

His father was on his way home now, he knew, and that evening at dinner they would meet. His mother and sister would talk rapidly, but his father would say nothing to him, or to anyone. There would only be Harcourt's memory of the level look in the blue eyes, and the knowledge of his father's pain as he walked away.

Grace watched John's gloomy face as they walked through the store, and she knew he was nursing some private rage, and so her own resentment and exasperation kept growing, and she said crisply, 'You're entitled to your moods on a hot afternoon, I suppose, but if I feel I don't like it here, then I don't like it. You wanted to go yourself. Who likes to spend very much time in a department store on a hot afternoon? I begin to hate every stupid person that bangs into me, everybody near me. What does that make me?'

'It makes you a snob.'

'So I'm a snob now?' she said angrily.

'Certainly you're a snob,' he said. They were at the door and going out to the street. As they walked in the sunlight, in the crowd moving slowly down the street, he was groping for words to describe the secret thoughts he had always had about her. 'I've always known how you'd feel about people I like who didn't fit into your private world,' he said.

'You're a very stupid person,' she said. Her face was flushed now, and it was hard for her to express her indignation, so she stared straight ahead as she walked along.

They had never talked in this way, and now they were both quickly eager to hurt each other. With a flow of words, she started to argue with him, then she checked herself and said calmly, 'Listen, John, I imagine you're tired of my company. There's no sense in having tea together. I think I'd better leave you right here.'

'That's fine,' he said. 'Good afternoon.'

'Good-bye.'

'Good-bye.'

She started to go, she had gone two paces, but he reached out desperately and held her arm, and he was frightened, and pleading, 'Please don't go, Grace.'

All the anger and irritation had left him; there was just a desperate anxiety in his voice as he pleaded, 'Please forgive me. I've no right to talk to you like that. I don't know why I'm so rude or what's the matter. I'm ridiculous. I'm very, very ridiculous. Please, you must forgive me. Don't leave me.'

He had never talked to her so brokenly, and his sincerity, the depth of his feeling, began to stir her. While she listened, feeling all the yearning in him, they seemed to have been brought closer together, by opposing each other, than ever before, and she began to feel almost shy. 'I don't know what's the matter. I suppose we're both irritable. It must be the weather,' she said. 'But I'm not angry, John.'

He nodded his head miserably. He longed to tell her that he was sure she would have been charming to his father, but he had never felt so wretched in his life. He held her arm tight, as if he must hold it or what he wanted most in the world would slip away from him, yet he kept thinking, as he would ever think, of his father walking away quietly with his head never turning.

The Bride

That last night at the hotel, Eleanor, standing in front of the bureau mirror, was smiling at herself with her warm soft eyes as she put on her black hat with the nose veil. She had been married only six days. She was such a gentle, quiet girl, with her small black head, her slender ankles, her dainty hands, and the fine high bridge on her nose, that everybody who knew her thought she ought to have married a doctor or a lawyer with a good practice who could have given her some security.

Eleanor was waiting for her husband to come in and take her out to the theatre. Since she had never worn a veil with a hat before, she kept hurrying seriously from the bureau to the bathroom mirror, peering at herself for a long time and fretting and feeling quite sure that Walter's eyes would light up with helpless admiration as soon as he saw her. 'Then we'll rush out to the show and rush back and get some sleep and get up early in the morning,' she thought. They had come from Middletown. In the morning they were going third-class on the boat to Europe. Everything was taking place so rapidly. They were alone and together, they were actually married, and there was a kind of sweet, uneasy pleasure in letting each small new experience astonish and sweep her from one day into another without letting her stop to grow timid at all. 'I just love this little veil. It's perfect, it's stunning,' she thought.

Walter, coming into the room, called out, 'Are you ready, Eleanor?' As she glanced for the last time at her pretty face in the mirror, she said, 'I'm all ready. I'm waiting and won't keep you a minute,' and she watched with placid assurance for him to take one long, admiring look at her before they hurried out together. He came slowly into the bathroom, looking straight ahead, yet hardly seeing her. There was a dreamy, pleased expression in his eyes. Walter was a lazy-moving young fellow of middle height whose face kept folding in warm smiles. He was carrying a newspaper which he held folded open at a particular page. In a most casual manner, to conceal his own deep satisfaction, he held out the paper and said, 'Look at this, Eleanor. There's a little piece here about my winning the scholarship.'

'Isn't that lovely,' she said. 'Is it a big piece? Let me see.' She pushed her veil back from her eyes.

As he handed her the paper, he seemed rather bored, so she just glanced once at the article to see his name and the space devoted to him and then she smiled up and said, 'That's splendid, isn't it, dear?' Eleanor still thought they were in a hurry to go out and that he wouldn't want her to delay and read the paper. 'I'm ready, darling,' she said, hoping he would notice her little black veil.

But he frowned and there was a sullen expression on his face. His blue eyes got bright with bewildered indignation and he blurted out, 'Do you mean to say you won't take time to read that little bit there?'

'I thought we were in a hurry, that's all,' she said, but she faltered and felt disturbed beyond all reason. 'I mean I thought we could read it when we came home. You told me to be sure and be ready.'

'But imagine your being able to go out without reading it when you know it all means so much to me. Imagine. Just imagine.'

'I'll read it,' she said. 'Give it to me.'

'Don't bother,' he said. 'I know you look at my work differently than I do. What's everything to me is so often nothing to you. Come on. We'll be late.'

'But I said I'd read it,' she cried, snatching the paper.

'Go ahead, then. Read it out of duty.' He sighed, shrugged his shoulders, and said, 'I can't understand you. If you're not really interested, why are you going off to Europe on a wild-goose chase? We'll have hardly any money for two, barely enough to live on. If we go broke, you'll probably want me to quit and come back and get a job.'

They were in the bedroom now and she sat down by the window to try to read the piece in the paper, but the printed letters kept dancing up and down and were lost in a mist and her veil kept dropping down in front of her eyes. She was hurt, yet she knew she had hurt him, too. 'Why didn't I read it when he first handed it to me?' she thought. 'I don't know why I didn't.'

Walter was saying moodily, 'Come on, let's go, Eleanor.'

'If you feel the way you say, I don't want to go out with you,' she said. 'If you talk like that about me, I won't go to the show.' But as she spoke, she pleaded with her eyes, wanting him to apologize and comfort her and say he had been wrong.

'Come on,' he said irritably. 'It's just a little thing. Forget it.'

'You don't think it such a little thing or you wouldn't still be so nasty, so I won't go with you while you feel that way,' she said resentfully.

'All right, don't," he said, blunt and angry. 'I can't help it if I feel that way.' He flung himself inertly on the bed and tried to show by his indifference that he was a reasonable, good-tempered fellow who was interested mainly in humouring his wife. They were both silent. Then Walter began to feel miserable and more and more bewildered. In the months before the marriage, their relationship had seemed so very simple, but already he had begun to feel a pulling and straining between them over very little things that was bewildering because it hurt so much. As he looked at Eleanor sitting forlornly by the window, he could not stand this separation and he felt his whole being drifting toward her. 'What really matters deeply to her?' he asked himself. He thought of the hours she had listened to him talking and had seemed so animated by anything that stirred him at all. 'I don't know why this has to happen,' he said mildly. 'I'm not going to sit here saying nothing. The whole thing is of no importance. I'm going downstairs.'

'Suit yourself,' she said stubbornly.

When he had gone, she tried to behave like a sensible woman who was prepared to enjoy a quiet evening by herself. She took off her coat and hat, put on a negligée, got herself an apple, and lay down on the bed to read. The window in the room looked across at another wing of the hotel, and laughter drifting across from those lighted open windows began to make her feel restless and lonesome. Very slowly she nibbled at her apple, staring at one spot on the printed page and trying to understand how Walter could speak with so much bitterness about a simple matter of having his name mentioned in the paper, and as she frowned and wrinkled her nose there grew in her a dull, heavy fear of all the trifling matters for disagreement that might arise and grow big and sharp enough to separate them. She felt even worse because her fear was so mixed up with her ache of love for him. Her mother had said, 'Eleanor, you've only known the man a year. It's very silly to get married now. You'll never have anything ahead. Just because the boy has a chance to go to Europe for a year, he wants to take you with him.' Within her grew an increasing dread of all the days ahead, days sure to be full of such abrupt, surprising disagreements . . . in the morning they were going far away to a strange country where she would have no friends, if she should find herself alone. Even in the hotel room, where she could hear the noise of laughter from open windows, she became so afraid of being alone that she felt helpless; her head dropped suddenly on the pillow and she began to cry brokenly.

She was still crying when Walter came in. He had made up his mind to come sauntering into the room smiling with tolerant good nature to conceal his awkwardness, so he got confused when he saw her and rushed across the room with a white, worried face, saying, 'What's the matter, darling?'

'I don't know,' she said, and she kept on crying. Only a little while ago it had seemed to her that the two of them were together, spinning around and around in a lump together, and she had been hurled off. It hurt her dreadfully being thrust away from him.

'Can't I do anything, darling?' he said, caressing her head.

'No. I guess I'm just lonesome, that's all. Can't I cry if I want to?'

'Why are you so lonesome? Aren't you satisfied with me?'

'I wish I were home,' she said. 'I don't want to go so far away.'

'You're afraid of how things will turn out,' he said angrily. 'When you go on like that, you make me boil.'

'Maybe I'm afraid. I don't know.'

With her black curled head pushed deep into the clean white pillow blotted by her tears, she lay there and heard him walking up and down, up and down, and at last she stopped crying.

'We're very silly,' he said finally. 'I'm ashamed. To make it worse, there was nothing to it at all. But it's my fault. Please forgive me, Eleanor.'

'All right, Walter,' she said willingly. 'Let's forget about it. Kiss me. It's just as well we're going to bed early, when we're sailing in the morning.'

He kissed her with grave tenderness, and then he said softly, almost to himself, 'We ought to feel so happy tonight. Sailing in the morning, with so much to look forward to.' He turned once to see her smiling at him, he smiled himself, then walked away restlessly, for he could not look contented, and he sat down by the window with his chin cupped in his hand.

His aloof dejection puzzled Eleanor, and after watching him for some time, she said, 'What's the matter with you now, Walter?'

'Nothing. I feel fine.'

'You can't feel fine while you look so unhappy,' she said, trying to tease him. 'Look at me and tell me what you're thinking about. Give me three guesses.'

With a bashful grin, Walter shook his head, trying to

appear offhand, then he said impetuously, 'Did you read the piece in the paper, Eleanor? Why don't you look at it now and see what you think about it?'

'You said you don't care what I think,' she answered, still teasing him with her slow smile.

'You know I care. Don't go on like that,' he said.

But she continued to shake her head firmly while he coaxed her, and as he pleaded and looked dejected, she could hardly help laughing. The more he coaxed, the more it delighted her.

'All right, then, Eleanor, don't do it,' he said humbly, and at that moment, while he spoke with such humility, she realized fully how necessary her enthusiasm was to him. She realized that there could be no pleasure even in this simple matter for him unless he shared it with her, and she was filled with wonder, and warm with joy that came from seeing how inevitably he was pulled toward her. She smiled and closed her eyes. She could hear the city street sounds far below. In the early morning, they would be hurrying to the harbour, rushing to the boat. Again she grew half timid. But even as she reached out for some slight intimation of security, she felt herself thrust so buoyantly into their life together that she sat bolt upright breathless with eagerness.

The Two Brothers

As she came along the lane in the dusk the little wind from
the lake blew back her thin dress against her body and there
was still enough light to show the eagerness that was in her
face. She came up to the fence where he was leaning so de-
jectedly, and never before had he felt so sure that she wanted
to be with him.

'You're early tonight, Peg,' he said.

'I knew you'd be waiting here, Tom. I tried to finish the
work early. I was restless. I thought we might walk.' Her
voice was very soft in her eagerness to soothe him. Tonight
she had made herself look more lovely than ever so that
when he saw her he would think only of how much he liked
her thick, light hair, her full mouth and the splendid curve
of her breast. Walking along in the dusk on the dirt road
running up from the lake they had never felt so close together. They liked this new warmth of feeling between them.
They were quiet, listening to the crickets in the grass. They
watched the darker shapes of cows moving lazily in the
pasture-land, and they knew they were having the same
thoughts: they were thinking of yesterday in town, and of the
courthouse and of his brother Frank: they were thinking of
the last thing Frank did after the white-haired judge, talking
in a measured monotone, had sentenced him to a year and
a half in jail for a drunken murderous assault on an officer.
Frank had turned, smiling reassuredly at the crowd; and
standing there in front of the big window that looked out
over the lake he was young, dark and very splendid. Through
the window behind him they could see the sweep of the blue
lake with the sun on it and the thick bank of clouds overhead. When Tom and Peg went up to shake hands sorrow-
fully, Frank had said, teasing them, 'You'd better marry

295

Peg in a hurry, Tom, because I'll be seeing you both shortly.'
He was absolutely without shame, and they led him away
laughing.

As they walked along so silently Peg wanted to show Tom
all the sympathy she felt for him. She knew that young
Frank had always spent most of his time in town with the
girls while Tom worked hard on the farm and worried about
what his brother might do, with his wild way; Tom had carried around year after year a knowledge in his heart of
something fearful impending. Peg could not bear to have
Tom walking beside her so lifelessly like that, with such
dark, sad thoughts of his brother, and she said, 'I know you'll
miss him. But a year and a half goes quickly, Tom.'

'It's what it may do to him I'm thinking of,' he said. 'We
were always together. You get used to being together no
matter what happens.' He was ashamed of the way his words
were breaking. 'I mean it doesn't matter really what he did.
We've been a long time together, that's all.'

'I've been wondering all the time what he meant when he
said, "I'll be seeing you both shortly." What did he mean?'

'I don't know,' he said uneasily.

'You don't think he'd try to get away?'

'Maybe he'd be just that crazy. It's bad enough now and
it would be worse for everybody then with everybody chasing
him. Please, Peg, let's stop talking about Frank. I want to
stop thinking about him. I seem to have been thinking about
him all my life. I want to stop.' His words came from him in
such a jerky, agitated manner that she was afraid, and she
was silent for a while, pondering, and then she brushed
close against him, patting his arm, stirring him so he would
think only of her.

His troubled thoughts made his thin face haggard and she
longed to comfort him and show him plainly that there was
a depth of love in her for him that he had never known. She
said simply, 'Let's go over there by the old elm and sit down.'

Leaving the road he helped her over the wire fence, and
when they sat in the thick grass by the tree the moon shone
out on the fields and there were hardly any sounds. Tom
began to think that the silence and the peace between them
was beautiful. Peg, who was lying full length on the grass,
was looking up at the sky with an expression of tender sad-

ness on her face, content to be there with him. As he stared down at her so solemnly he marvelled that she could have such a simple peace. After a long time he touched her thick hair timidly with his hand, brushing it back from her temple, and then he looked away over the field. 'Look at the moonlight on the buckwheat, Peg,' he said. They both looked over there at the buckwheat, which in daytime in July was like a field of separate white flowers; now with the moonlight flooding it, it glistened like a field of bright snow in the sunlight, but so much softer, more like a bank of light just on the other side of the road. They were both full of wonder and in Tom there was an unexpected elation. 'Isn't it beautiful,' he heard her saying, and then her head was sinking back and she lay with the same light shining on her face, only there was a marvellous softness and willingness in it that he had never seen before. For two years he had been wanting her for his girl, but he had always been afraid that she would never in any way show that she completely accepted him: it had been hard for him to believe that she would ever want to marry him. Yet now she was smiling up at his sober face, glad of what was so surely in him. With his heart beating heavily he bent down and kissed her, feeling her hands holding his head tenderly as she drew his face close to her. Never in his life, which had been full of hard work and laconic ways, had he felt such happiness. But he did not know what to do, he was so afraid that she might move, or that something would happen to spoil it. There was such a little shadow on her eyelids. Then her eyes were open, watching him, and she waited. After a time the clouds which were getting thicker obscured the light.

The fields were stirred by a strengthening wind from the lake. There was no longer a bank of light on the field of buckwheat.

'It's going to rain,' she said.

'I don't think it's going to rain.'

'Yes, it is. We'd better go,' she said and she got up reluctantly. As they walked along the road she was swinging her body a bit and humming. She had picked up a blade of grass and kept holding the stem to her lip.

'Would you love me, Peg? Would you love me always?' he asked.

'It's never seemed like this before, has it, Tom?'

'What does it make you feel like?'

'Just glad.'

He didn't know how to answer he was so excited, and they walked along the lane under the great elms with the leaves rustling loudly to the gate, hanging on one hinge, and there she said, 'Good night, Tom. It was lovely.' She was very quiet, almost grave now.

As he went away he felt like a happy excited child, he was so lucky. 'She would have loved me very much tonight,' he thought.

At the orchard he climbed the fence, and when he was passing under the apple trees and hearing the horses moving in the stalls in the barn, he began to think, 'Her father'll be in bed. She wanted more love than she got from me tonight. She'll still be wanting, maybe.' And for half an hour as he did whatever chores he had to do before going to bed he kept thinking of her being really alone in the house, unsatisfied with the little love he had offered. The eagerness to go back to her became too strong to resist.

Hurrying back along the lane he saw that there was no light upstairs where her father slept, just the one light downstairs where he was sure she waited. Tiptoeing to the door, he whistled softly, a signal, though he had never whistled for her before. The wind was blowing strongly from the lake now, blowing his hair back from his head, and he felt weak thinking what he might do. He tapped lightly on the door. When there was no answer he pushed the door open and looked in the big room. Near the window was a black leather couch and she was lying on the couch with her face pressed down against the leather. 'Peg,' he whispered. 'Peg.' She raised her head slowly and he saw that her face was sad and troubled, and though she was trying to smile, her eyes were wet.

'What's the matter, Peg?'

'Nothing.'

'Why are you crying?'

'I wasn't really crying,' she said. She saw how disappointed he was, she felt that he had expected to find her still full of gladness, and she tried to explain. 'I was sitting here thinking of the two of us and how everything might be.

Then I was thinking just of you because I knew how bad you were feeling over Frank. I felt blue because it all seems to go against you. I was feeling sorry for Frank too.'

'Why were you thinking of him now?' he asked irritably. 'Why do we always have to think of him?'

'It just seemed a shame. He looked like a fine fellow standing there yesterday.'

'You often think of Frank.'

'No I don't, but I've always liked him.'

'You've been feeling pretty bad about him, haven't you?'

'It's you that's been feeling bad and giving me the blues.'

He couldn't feel her compassion because of his own sharp, unreasonable jealousy. For nights he had hardly slept worrying about Frank, and now he wanted to be alone and free of him; he had been so sure he would find Peg here full of gladness for her love of him. It was hard now to believe in that love that he had felt an hour ago in the field; it was so much more than he had ever expected from her. It was so much easier to remember how Frank had always laughed and teased her just as he did the town girls he was sure of. He felt crazy with worry and weariness, wanting to shout, 'Frank spoiled everything in my life,' but he blurted out, 'Maybe with Frank being away you've found out tonight how you really feel about him.'

'It was you I was thinking of,' she whispered. 'You were so fond of him and I could watch the pain growing in you. If they were hurting you they were hurting me. Please, Tom, don't get crazy thoughts in your head.'

'Tonight it was fine,' he said quietly, talking almost to himself. 'It was all good tonight. But look how it's spoiled now. It didn't last in you at all. Everybody around here talks and worries about Frank and I'm tired, you hear, awfully tired of it. Peg, listen, he always seemed to me to have the inside track with you if he wanted it.'

'Sh, sh, you'll wake my father up.'

'You know what I'm thinking, Peg. You wouldn't bother with me if you could have him. I've often felt it.'

He seemed to be going all to pieces there at the door, jerking his hand up and down in an erratic gesture. Then he turned quickly, hurrying away from her. 'Tom, don't go. Come back, just a minute.' She ran after him begging desperately, 'You know I loved you more tonight than I ever did before,' but he was hurrying away, not hearing.

He went to bed with the wind blowing much stronger, thinking, 'It took her a long time to show much love for me. Frank always laughed at me because I was slow and fumbling with her. What got into her in the field, what made her show so much love?' He lay there holding on to his bitterness. His loneliness, the darkness and the sound of the wind began to distort all his thoughts, and though he tried to be reasonable and said, 'Maybe I was foolish with Peg,' he knew he would be afraid of Frank even if he married her. Gusts of wind sometimes hit the house and there was the sound of shingles torn from the roof spinning in the wind. He tortured himself thinking of Frank and the trouble that always pursued him. For a while he listened to the waves breaking on the shore, and then he began to torture himself deliberately with a picture of Peg and Frank living together: he saw them together in a room by themselves loving each other and maybe laughing at him. Then he fell asleep.

He woke up thinking he could hear someone moving outside on the veranda, and he sat up, listening, but he could not be sure because of the wind. There again was the sound of footsteps, and then quite clearly, a firm tapping on the door. Opening the bedroom window he called out, 'Who's there?'

'Let me in, Tom.' You could just see the side of his face in the darkness, leaning out from the veranda. 'All right, Frank. I'm coming down,' Tom said, and he hurried downstairs and opened the door. Frank was waiting there in his shirt and trousers. He was very wet, for now it was raining hard, and he was breathing so heavily he could hardly speak.

'What happened, Frank? What did you do?'

'Don't light the light, Tom. It was easy. They were driving me in the car to jail. Old Chief Fowlis was sitting with me and he always liked me so it was pretty easy and I jumped out and went off across the fields.'

'What are you going to do?'

'Cross the lake.'

'It's too rough. It'll take you all night.'

'You take an oar, Tom.'

When Frank came in and closed the door it was so fine at first to see him there, free, but that gladness went quickly, and Tom said uneasily, 'Maybe you're making a mistake, Frank. If you get away you'll never be able to come back here and you'll always be on the run, and anyway, if they catch you, they'll double your sentence. It isn't worth it. Three years would be a long time.'

Frank began to laugh, and shooting out his hand, he slapped Tom on the shoulder. 'Dear old Tom, always so cautious, what would a guy like me be doing in a jail for a year and a half?' he said. They were standing close together in the dark room with no light coming from the window and Frank's laughter sounded arrogant. When Tom didn't answer Frank said anxiously, 'What's the matter, Tom?' as if Tom was the one person in the world he was sure of.

'All right, Frank,' Tom said. 'I'd go with you anyway. You know that. It doesn't matter what I think. I'll put something on. What are you going to do on the other side?'

'Hide in the woods in the day-time and be off when night comes. Bring me some clothes. I'll look around too. Have you got any money?'

When they were ready they went down to the farm's end, carrying a bundle of clothes, and at the water's edge, though it was not so windy now, the lake looked like a restless heaving part of the immeasurable blackness overhead. They carried the rowboat down from its place at the clump of trees, and at the water, when it was tossed back by the first wave, Tom yelled, 'It'll take hours, Frank. Maybe you'd better wait,' but his words were blown away and Frank didn't answer.

Though they each pulled strongly at an oar it was very difficult getting past the point of land at the end of the farm. The wind swept around the point lashing the rain at their faces. It always seemed to blow harder at the point. Whenever they looked at the tip of land, the black shadow, measuring how far they had gone, it seemed that they had only been bobbing back to the shore, and if they rested a moment they quickly lost whatever they had gained. But they had expected this and they kept on pulling together with all their strength, their backs bending together, the same muscles aching on both of them, till they were out on the channel where it suddenly was easier. As they turned and looked back at the shore, Frank yelled, 'Good boy, Tom,' and they settled down to row steadily. They rowed perfectly together; they had been rowing on the lake in this way ever since they had been children. All their lives they might have been training for this one trip across the eight-mile lake.

During those hours of hard and silent rowing the sound of the oarlocks and the water against the boat became so regular that Tom began to repeat to himself mechanically, 'If he gets away he'll never be back around here. The people who used to like him will never see him again. I'll be alone. I'll be alone, I'll be alone.' It was such an easy thought to accept. Already he was used to never seeing Frank again, and he was contented; instead of feeling the desolation that such a notion might have brought to him, he was contented. He began to feel, too, that he was carrying Peg deep in his thoughts, but that was very secret. An immense willingness came to him to help Frank; he offered to take both oars; there was a vast gentleness within him urging him to do even more than Frank expected.

And then the hard work and the wind began to tire him, driving all the distorted night thoughts of hours ago out of his head, and soon everything that had happened earlier in the evening seemed far away, as if it had happened to some-body else. 'Frank's never mentioned Peg,' he thought. 'I've been thinking of nothing but myself for hours.' The dark blotch of the land was just ahead and they were in the shallow water, the long stretch of it in the inlet where there was a beach, and now it was easy rowing with their oars sometimes pulling out the weeds. 'We're there,' Tom said. 'I'll stay on the beach with you for a while and then you can get going. Maybe you better take some of the food and eat it now. It's stopped raining.'

'I'll eat something on the beach,' Frank said. He was resting his oars wearily as the boat pushed through the shallow water.

As soon as they pulled the boat high up on the beach they did not even wait to take out the bundle, they were so very tired; they lay down on the sand listening anxiously for any noises that might come from the trees or from out over the water. They lay close together, their bodies heavy and tired, listening to each other breathing, too, somehow being glad that they could hear each other like this. To Tom it began to seem that he had always heard it like this, years ago when he had awakened in the night and had heard Frank sleeping beside him, or maybe after he and Frank had been fighting and they had rolled over and over together: there was that time too, years ago, when they had rowed across the lake for the first time, each at an oar, and had lain maybe on this very spot to rest before going back. A bit wearily he raised himself on his arm and said, 'Frank, you're making a big mistake.'

'Mistake? What do you mean?'

'You ought to go back. You'll be on the run God knows how long, you'll never be really free and in the long run they may catch you. A year and a half now would be a little time compared with that. It would soon be over and everybody likes you around here.'

'You're talking like a fool, Tom. I got too many thoughts to bother me without listening to stuff like that.'

'You ought to go back. You'll never feel free this way. It'll spoil your whole life.'

'Shut up, Tom. If you want to talk like that, get into the boat and go back.'

Staring out across the dark water, with his wet clothes hanging on him, Tom repeated with a kind of wretched doggedness, 'Please, Frank, come back; you know I wouldn't say it if I didn't think it was best. You know how it makes me feel to have you cooped up in a rotten little jail, but I'm telling you to go back. I've always been willing to do almost anything for you . . .' He put out his hand and touched his brother's shoulder, and at that moment with the wind blowing and the water lapping on the beach, his voice faltered, for he felt a great tenderness for his brother that he could not express. He felt helpless as he said, 'Come on, Frank.'

Sitting up quick, Frank said, 'Do you really think I'd be

such a damned fool as that...after coming this far? What's on your mind?'

'Nothing but what I say.'

'I don't believe you. You've got something else on your mind.'

'It's just as I say, Frank.'

'You're getting yellow about it, that's probably it,' Frank said. He was full of contempt. They were really shouting at each other because of the sound of the breaking waves. 'I never thought you'd be so yellow, Tom. You're scared of getting caught with your finger in it, you always were such a nice respectable guy. You'd take me back now because of what the neighbours might think, wouldn't you? You're a fool. Sit here and hold your head. I'm going.' He got up slowly and started along the beach, cutting in gradually to the trees.

'Come back, Frank. Please come back,' Tom called. Frank's light shirt was moving against the dark line of the trees, going farther and farther away. Tom was frightened, he felt desperate as he used to feel years ago when Frank was in a fight with a bigger boy and getting beaten, so he started to run after him, shouting, 'Wait a minute.' He caught up and started pulling at Frank's arm. Frank shook his arm free and they both kept walking along the beach in the darkness. 'You're not going, that's settled. You've got to come back with me,' Tom said.

'Who says so?'

'I said so.'

Without even turning his head Frank said, 'Try and make me, why don't you?'

Pulling again at his arm Tom pleaded, 'If it's the last thing you ever do for me, do this, Frank. I won't ever ask you to do another thing, and if you go back everything'll straighten itself out.'

Jerking his arm free, Frank started to run, running slowly and heavily with a lurching stride because his boots sank into the wet sand, and Tom lunged after him, and the two figures were bobbing up and down against the dark background of the trees, with Tom gaining steadily because he was not so tired nor had he run so far. Once Frank looked back, then he cut in sharply towards the trees. There was a little embankment with grass on the top between the line of trees and the sandy beach, and here Frank slipped in the mud, and here Tom caught up to him, only Frank lashed out with his foot and caught Tom on the shoulder. Holding tight, though, and pulling, Tom dragged him by the leg back down the embankment, but there he could not hold him. Frank jumped up, ducked and swung both hands, hitting Tom heavily on the head. Then they clenched desperately and rolled over and over on the wet sand and closer to the line of the water till Frank's hands came loose and he flailed away frantically at Tom's head; he kept beating him wildly and when Tom would not move or let go, he suddenly quit, with Tom lying heavily on him and them both gasping for air. They lay there in this way sucking in the air. Then Frank's breathing became a kind of sob. He couldn't help it, he had run far earlier in the evening and he was weak, and without knowing why, he was crying with his face pressed in the sand.

And as he lay there, waiting, Tom was so miserable he wanted to die. He began to pray, 'Oh, God, please don't let him cry like that. Don't let him make that noise,' because he, himself, couldn't stand it there on the beach with the water lapping on the shore.

When Frank's strength began to come back he still kept quiet. There was no use moving; it was ended for him, there, with his face in the sand. Almost timidly, Tom said, 'Come on back now, Frank.'

'All right. I got to, I guess.'

They went back along the beach with Frank lurching drunkenly, with Tom longing to put his arm around him and steady him, but after the way Frank had sobbed on the sand there was a shyness between them that was hard to break.

At the boat Tom said, 'You sit there. I'll do the rowing. It's not blowing hard now,' so Frank got into the boat and huddled there with his head thrown back on one arm, his mouth still open as if he would never get enough air.

Tom began to row steadily. The wind was still strong but the water was much calmer now. Soon they were far out on the water. When he was tired Tom rested on his oars, his shoulders drooping over them, and he was looking over the water at one little path of light. The wind, scudding the clouds across the sky, had finally parted them. As the bright moonlight shone more fully on the dark water he remembered all the joy he had felt when the same light had shone on the field of buckwheat and Peg had belonged so surely to him. He could hear Peg calling, 'Come back, I loved you more tonight than ever before,' but that was just a part of his and Peg's world; it didn't touch Frank.

The oars were very heavy as he rowed, and they got heavier with each stroke, for it seemed that something was breaking inside him. 'Frank, you're not sore at me, are you? I wouldn't want to do it if it weren't for you. Can't you see that? Why don't you answer? Listen, Frank. You're not sore, are you? If you really want to I'll go back, I mean if you're sore.' Huddled there, silent and unanswering, Frank's eyes were wide open, staring up at the darkness of the night above. While he watched, Tom could still hear that desperate sob for freedom that had come from Frank back on the beach, and it brought such an ache in him that he looked around wildly. But he kept on going, one long slow stroke after another, always trying to talk softly to his brother.

One Spring Night

They had been to an eleven-o'clock movie. Afterward, as they sat very late in the restaurant, Sheila was listening to Bob Davis, liking all the words he used and showing by the quiet gladness that kept coming into her face the deep enjoyment she felt in being with him. She was the young sister of his friend, Jack Staples. Every time Bob had been at their apartment, she had come into the room, they had laughed and joked with her, they had teased her about the new way she wore her clothes, watching her growing, and she had always smiled and answered them in a slow, measured way.

Bob had taken her out a few times when he had felt like having some girl to talk to who knew him and liked him. And tonight he was leaning back good-humouredly, telling her one thing and then another with the wise self-assurance he usually had when with her; but gradually, as he watched her, he found himself talking more slowly, his voice grew serious and much softer, and then finally he leaned across the table toward her as though he had just discovered that her neck was full and soft with her spring coat thrown open, and that her face under her little black straw hat tilted back on her head had a new, eager beauty. Her warm, smiling softness was so close to him that he smiled a bit shyly.

'What are you looking at, Bob?' she said.

'What is there about you that seems different tonight?' he said, and they both began to laugh lightly, as if sharing the same secret.

When they were outside, walking along arm in arm and liking the new spring night air, Sheila said quickly, 'It's awfully nice out tonight. Let's keep walking a while, Bob,' and she held his arm as though very sure of him.

'All right,' he said. 'We'll walk till we get so tired we'll have to sit on the curb. It's nearly two o'clock, but it doesn't seem to matter much, does it?'

Every step he took with Sheila leaning on his arm in this new way, and with him feeling now that she was a woman he hardly knew, made the excitement grow in him, and yet he was uneasy. He was much taller than Sheila and he kept looking down at her, and she always smiled back with frank gladness. Then he couldn't help squeezing her arm tight, and he started to talk recklessly about anything that came into his head, swinging his free arm and putting passionate eloquence into the simplest words. She was listening as she used to listen when he talked with her brother and father in the evenings, only now she wanted him to see how much she liked having it tonight all for herself. Almost pleading, she said, 'Are you having a good time, Bob? Don't you like the streets at night, when there's hardly anybody on them?'

They stopped and looked along the wide avenue and up the towering, slanting faces of the buildings to the patches of night sky. Holding out her small, gloved hand in his palm, he patted it with his other hand, and they both laughed as though he had done something foolish but charming. The whole city was quieter now, the streets flowed away from them without direction, but there was always the hum underneath the silence like something restless and stirring and really touching them, as the soft, spring night air of the streets touched them, and at a store door he pulled her into the shadow and kissed her warmly, and when she didn't resist he kept on kissing her. Then they walked on again happily. He didn't care what he talked about; he talked about the advertising agency where he had gone to work the year before, and what he planned to do when he got more money, and each word had a feeling of reckless elation behind it.

For a long time they walked on aimlessly like this before he noticed that she was limping. Her face kept on turning up to him, and she laughed often, but she was really limping badly. 'What's the matter, Sheila? What's the matter with your foot?' he said.

'It's my heel,' she said, lifting her foot off the ground. 'My shoe has been rubbing against it.' She tried to laugh. 'It's all right, Bob,' she said, and she tried to walk on without limping.

'You can't walk like that, Sheila.'

'Maybe if we just took it off for a minute, Bob, it would be all right,' she said as though asking a favour of him.

'I'll take it off for you,' he said, and he knelt down on one knee while she lifted her foot and balanced herself with her arm on his shoulder. He drew off the shoe gently.

'Oh, the air feels so nice and cool on my heel,' she said. No one was coming along the street. For a long time he remained kneeling, caressing her ankle gently and looking up with his face full of concern. 'Try and put it on now, Bob,' she said. But when he pushed the shoe over the heel, she said, 'Good heavens, it seems tighter than ever.' She limped along for a few steps. 'Maybe we should never have taken it off. There's a blister there,' she said.

'It was crazy to keep on walking like this,' he said. 'I'll call a taxi as soon as one comes along.' They were standing by the curb, with her leaning heavily on his arm, and he was feeling protective and considerate, for with her heel hurting her, she seemed more like the young girl he had known. 'Look how late it is. It's nearly four o'clock,' he said. 'Your father will be wild.'

'It's terribly late,' she said.

'It's my fault. I'll tell him it was all my fault.'

For a while she didn't raise her head. When she did look up at him, he thought she was frightened. She was hardly able to move her lips. 'What will they say when I go home at this hour, Bob?'

'It'll be all right. I'll go right in with you,' he said.

'Wouldn't it be better...Don't you think it would be all right if I stayed the night with Alice – with my girl friend?'

She was so hesitant that it worried him, and he said emphatically, 'It's nearly morning now, and anyway, your father knows you're with me.'

'Where'll we say we've been till this hour, Bob?'

'Just walking.'

'Maybe he won't believe it. Maybe he's sure by this time I'm staying with Alice. If there was some place I could go

...' While she waited for him to answer, all that had been growing in her for such a long time was showing in the softness of her dark, eager face.

There was a breathless excitement in him and something like a slow unfolding that was all lost in guilty uneasiness. Then a half-ashamed feeling began to come over him and he began thinking of himself at the apartment, talking with Jack and the old man, and with Sheila coming in and listening with her eager face full of seriousness. 'Why should you think there'll be trouble?' he said. 'Your father will probably be in bed.'

'I guess he will,' she said quickly. 'I'm silly. I ought to know that. There was nothing . . . I must have sounded silly.' She began to fumble for words, and then her confusion was so deep that she could not speak.

'I'm surprised you don't know your father better than that,' he said rapidly, as though offended. He was anxious to make it an argument between them over her father. He wanted to believe this himself, so he tried to think only of the nights when her father, with his white head and moustaches, had talked in his good-humoured way about the old days in New York and the old eating-places, but every one of these conversations, every one of these nights that came into his thoughts, had Sheila there, too, listening and watching. Then it got so that he could remember nothing of those times but her intense young face, which kept rising before him, although he had never been aware that he had paid much attention to her. So he said desperately, 'There's the friendliest feeling in the world between your people and me. Leave it to me. We'll go back to the corner, where we can see a taxi.'

They began to walk slowly to the corner, with her still limping though he held her arm firmly. He began to talk with a soft persuasiveness, eager to have her respond readily, but she only said, 'I don't know what's the matter. I feel tired or something.' When they were standing on the street corner, she began to cry a little.

'Poor little Sheila,' he said.

Then she said angrily, 'Why "poor little Sheila"? There's

nothing the matter with me. I'm just tired.' And they both kept looking up and down the street for a taxi.

Then one came, they got in, and he sat with his arm along the back of the seat, just touching her shoulder. He dared not tighten his arm around her, though never before had he wanted so much to be gentle with anyone; but with the street lights sometimes flashing on her face and showing the frightened, bewildered whiteness that was in it, he was scared to disturb her. His heart began to beat with slow heaviness and he was glad when the ride was over.

As soon as they opened the apartment door and lit the lights in the living-room, they heard her father come shuffling from his bedroom. His white moustaches were working up and down furiously as he kept wetting his lips, and his hair, which was always combed nicely, was mussed over his head because he had been lying down. 'Where have you been till this hour, Sheila?' he said. 'I kept getting up all the time. Where have you been?'

'Just walking with Bob,' she said. 'I'm dead tired, Dad. We lost all track of time.' She spoke very calmly and then she smiled, and Bob saw how well she knew that her father loved her. Her father's face was full of concern while he peered at her, and she only smiled openly, showing no worry and saying, 'Poor Daddy, I never dreamed you'd get up. I hope Jack is still sleeping.'

'Jack said if you were with Bob, you were all right,' Mr. Staples said. Glancing at Bob, he added curtly, 'She's only eighteen, you know. I thought you had more sense.'

'I guess we were fools to walk for hours like that, Mr. Staples,' Bob said. 'Sheila's got a big blister on her foot.' Bob shook his head as if he couldn't understand why he had been so stupid.

Mr. Staples looked a long time at Sheila, and then he looked shrewdly at Bob; they were both tired and worried, and they were standing close together. Mr. Staples cleared his throat two or three times and said, 'What on earth got into the pair of you?' Then he grinned suddenly and said, 'Isn't it extraordinary what young people do? I'm so wide awake now I can't sleep. I was making myself a cup of

coffee. Won't you both sit down and have a cup with me?
Eh, Bob?'

'I'd love to,' Bob said heartily.

'You go ahead. I won't have any coffee. It would keep me
awake,' Sheila said.

'The water's just getting hot,' Mr. Staples said. 'It will be
ready in a minute.' Still chuckling and shaking his head, for
he was glad Sheila had come in, he said, 'I kept telling myself she was all right if she was with you, Bob.' Bob and Mr.
Staples grinned broadly at each other.

But when her father spoke like this, Sheila raised her
head, and Bob thought that he saw her smile at him. He
wanted to smile, too, but he couldn't look at her and had to
turn away uneasily. And when he did turn to her again, it
was almost pleadingly, for he was thinking, 'I did the only
thing there was to do. It was the right thing, so why should
I feel ashamed now?' and yet he kept on remembering how
she had cried a little on the street corner. He longed to think
of something to say that might make her smile agreeably –
some gentle, simple, friendly remark that would make her
feel close to him – but he could only go on remembering how
yielding she had been.

Her father was saying cheerfully, 'I'll go and get the
coffee now.'

'I don't think I'd better stay,' Bob said.

'It'll only take a few minutes,' Mr. Staples said.

'I don't think I'll wait,' Bob said, but Mr. Staples, smiling
and shaking his head, went on into the kitchen to get the
coffee.

Bob kept on watching Sheila, who was supporting her
head with her hand and frowning a little. There was some
of the peacefulness in her face now that had been there days
ago, only there was also a new, full softness; she was very
quiet, maybe feeling again the way he had kissed her, and
then she frowned again as though puzzled, as though she
was listening and overhearing herself say timidly, 'If there
was some place I could go . . .'

Growing more and more uneasy, Bob said, 'It turned out
all right, don't you see, Sheila?'

'What?' she said.

'There was no trouble about coming home,' he said.

As she watched him without speaking, she was not at all like a young girl. Her eyes were shining. All the feeling of the whole night was surging through her; she could hardly hold within her all the mixed-up feeling that was stirring her, and then her face grew warm with shame and she said savagely, 'Why don't you go? Why do you want to sit there talking, talking, talking?'

'I don't know,' he said.

'Go on. Please go. Please,' she said.

'All right, I'll go,' he muttered, and he got up clumsily, looking around for his hat and coat. As he started to go, his face got hot with humiliation. He longed to look back at her, and when she did not call out to him as he went, he was full of a wild resentment.

In the cold, early-morning light, with heavy trucks rumbling on the street, he felt terribly tense and nervous. He could hardly remember anything that had happened. Inside him there was a wide, frightening emptiness. He wanted to reach out desperately and hold that swift, ardent, yielding joy that had been so close to him. For a while he could not think at all. And then he felt that slow unfolding coming in him again, making him quick with wonder.

Absolution

For years Jennie Hughes had been a steady customer at Jeremiah Mallory's bar. She was a woman about forty-five years old, the wife of a lawyer who had abandoned her ten years ago, but who still sent her a little money to pay for her room and liquor. At one time she had been active and shapely; now she was rather slow and stout and her cheeks were criss-crossed with fine transparent veins. When she had first come to the neighbourhood people called her Mrs. Hughes, but now everybody just called her Jennie.

In the bar she used to sit by herself with an air of great gentility at a table opposite the bar, when she didn't have enough money to pay for a bottle to take home. Her gentility was perhaps most obvious when she was not quite sober, and if anybody in her street disturbed her at such a time, she was apt to yell and scream at the top of her voice. Neighbours, who at one time had felt sorry for her, were now anxious to have her move away. Jennie's landlady, Mrs. Turner, had been trying for two months to get rid of her, but Mrs. Turner had been unfortunate enough to try to argue the question when Jennie was tipsy.

One night Jennie was wondering if Jerry Mallory would give her any more whiskey on credit. For two weeks she hadn't paid him. She had been drinking mildly in the afternoon and now felt it necessary to have a bottle for Sunday. There were only about two fingers in the bottle left standing on the bureau. She began to put on her hat and look at herself in the mirror. Though she was aware that styles changed, she didn't seem to be able to keep up with them; now she was wearing a short skirt when everybody else was wearing their dresses long, and two years ago she had worn a long dress when other women were wearing skimpy short skirts. She was looking at herself with approval when she heard somebody coming up the stairs. Turning, and staring at the door, for she expected her landlady, Mrs. Turner, to appear, she thrust her chin out angrily. 'Come in,' she called out when there was a knock on the door.

A huge man over six feet came in, a great big serious-looking priest with thin gray hair, a large red face, and a tiny nose. 'Good evening, Mrs. Hughes,' he said politely without smiling.

'Good evening, father,' Jennie said. She had never seen the man before and she began to feel uneasy. She was actually beginning to feel nervous and ashamed of herself for some reason as she looked guiltily at the bottle on the bureau. She said suddenly, and shrewdly: 'Did somebody send you here, father?'

'Now never mind that,' the priest said sternly. 'It's enough that I'm here and you can thank God that I came.' He was an old, serious, unsentimental priest who was not at all impressed by the fawning smile and the little bow she made for him. Shaking his head to show his disgust with her, he said flatly: 'Mrs. Hughes, there's nothing more degrading in this world than a tipsy woman. A drunken man, Lord knows, is bad enough, but a drunken woman is somehow lower than a beast in the field.'

Jennie's pride was hurt, and she said angrily, without inviting him to sit down: 'Who sent you here? Who sent you here to butt into my business? Tell me that.'

'Now listen to me, Mrs. Hughes. It's time someone brought you to your senses.'

'You don't know me. I don't know you,' Jennie said abruptly.

'I know all about you. I know that you ought to be looking after your two children instead of having them in orphanages. But I'm not going to argue with you. I want to give you a very solemn warning. If you don't change your life you'll go straight to hell.'

'You leave me alone, do you hear? Go on away,' Jennie said.

'And I'll tell you this,' he said, bending close to her and

lifting his finger. 'If you were to die at this moment and I were asked to give you absolution I doubt if my conscience would permit me to do it. Now for God's sake, woman, straighten up. Go to church. Go this night to confession and ask God to forgive you. Promise me you'll go to confession. At one time you must have been a decent Catholic woman. Promise me.'

'You can't force me to do anything I don't want to do. I know. It was that Mrs. Turner that sent you here. I'll fix her. And don't you butt in either,' Jennie said.

The big priest looked at her coolly, nodded his head with a kind of final and savage warning, and went out without saying another word.

As a defiant gesture Jennie drained the last inch of whiskey from the bottle and muttered: 'Trying to drive me to confession, eh?' But she felt she was too much of a sporting lady to waste time sympathizing with herself. Making up her mind to abuse Mrs. Turner as soon as she saw her, she decided to go over to Jeremiah Mallory's bar at once.

That extra drink of whiskey had made Jennie tipsy, and as she remembered that the old priest had said she would go to hell when she died, she felt like crying. The priest, who had looked at her as if he had wanted to shake her, had half-pleased her by saying so bluntly that at one time she must have been a very good woman. With a serious expression on her face she walked along the lighted street, a stout woman in a short skirt leaning forward a bit, her wide velvet hat too far back on her head. Groping in her listless memory, she tried to remember the faces of her two children, a boy and a girl, but she hardly seemed to know them. The priest had aroused in her an uneasy longing for a time she was hardly able to remember, a time when she had dressed well, gone to church, and gone to confession too, when she was a much younger woman.

Approaching the bar, whose drawn blinds concealed the light inside, she wondered what she might say to Mallory to persuade him she intended to pay at the end of the month. The door-keeper who let her in, nodded familiarly without speaking and she went through to the lighted bar-room. No one paid any attention to her. Men and women were standing at the bar, sitting at the tables by the door, or at the small tables opposite the bar. Jennie sat down by herself at an empty table from where she could see Jerry himself, clean-shaven and neat in his blue suit, standing behind the bar, smiling affably at everybody and sometimes helping the busy young man, Henry, to pass out the drinks.

Finally Henry, looking competent with his sleeves rolled up and his bow tie, came over to Jennie and said: 'Hello, Jennie, what'll it be tonight?' He spoke as if he didn't believe there would be anything for Jennie.

'I'd like a little gin, to take out with me,' she said sooth-ingly. 'Only about a quart. And tell Jerry I'll fix it up with him next week. How are you, Henry?' She hoped he could see how nicely she was smiling.

'I don't know, Jennie,' he said doubtfully.

'Look here, you know I'll pay at the end of the month,' she said gently.

'It's like this,' Henry said pleasantly. 'I'd do it. You know that. But the boss won't let me.'

'Then let me speak to Jerry,' she said brusquely.

In a moment Henry returned and said: 'Jerry's awfully busy right now, Jennie. Maybe some other time . . .'

'I'll sit here and wait,' Jennie said firmly, folding her arms. 'I'll sit right here till doomsday and wait.'

'All right. But he's awfully busy. He may not come.'

Jennie waited and felt alone at her table, in a little alcove, and nobody paid any attention to her. She felt tired. Many thoughts and images drifted through her head. As she crossed her legs at the ankles and put her head back against the wall, she felt drowsy and dizzy. 'I oughtn't to have taken that last drink before coming here,' she thought. She tried to keep awake by muttering: 'That old priest couldn't scare me, bless him,' but she went on having the most disconnected thoughts about Eastertime and choir music. Soon she fell sound asleep, breathing steadily.

She began to breathe so heavily that customers at the bar, turning, snickered. Looking over at her, Jerry Mallory frowned irritably. She was an old, though difficult, customer, so he went over to her with a business-like air and shook her shoulder lightly. She stirred, waking. It had been very strong

in her thoughts that the old priest had wanted her to go to
confession and now, only half-awake, she mumbled uneasily: 'Bless me, father, for I have sinned.'

'Hey, Jennie, where do you think you are? Bless you, bless
you, old girl,' he said, starting to laugh.

'Eh, eh? Oh, it's you, Jerry. I forgot where I was.'

She was wide awake now, and so sober that he thought she
might have been deliberately kidding him. He laughed
loudly. 'You're a card, Jennie!' he said. 'You're a grand old
gal. And I'll get you a little gin for old times' sake.'

He turned and said to the three men at the bar who were
nearest to him: 'Did you hear what Jennie just pulled on
me?'

Jennie's face was hot and ashamed. Breathing irregularly,
she stood up, in her skirt that was too short, with her black
velvet hat too far back on her head. The men started to
laugh mildly. Then they started to laugh louder and louder.
The sound of their laughter at first made Jennie angry, with
something of a fine woman's disgust and anger, and then,
with humility, she felt herself reaching out gropingly toward
a faintly remembered dignity. Erect, she walked out.

A Princely Affair

Dogs in pursuit and red-coated huntsmen taking fences. A
statesman with a high collar and wide black tie. The calendar
huntsmen on the wall were alive and the statesman spoke
formally and coldly. Captain Bill Oakley in the barber-chair
was having a shampoo. The barber, talking respectfully, rubbed lather on Bill's head, and Bill saw faintly his image in the
mirror, his eyes half closed, thinking of the huntsmen.

The huntsmen made him think of his wife Nora. The
statesman, with the bulging forehead and long formidable
nose, belonged to the same tradition. The huntsman, his

wife, and the statesman; or his wife, the huntsman, and the statesman; or his wife, the statesman, and the huntsman, different combinations, all very good, all part of a fine tradition.

He left the barber shop. It was a spring day, a blue sky, and a strong sun. He stood on the corner opposite the city hall, looking impersonally into faces of girls passing. He held out two coppers and the newsie thrust a paper under his arm. He glanced hurriedly at headlines, then turned pages rapidly till he saw the pictures of Mrs. Oakley, the one with the turban extraordinarily clear. His Highness had danced three times with Mrs. Oakley. In the story she was called His Highness's dancing-partner and the reporter told how he had found her at home when the milkman was passing along the street. Bill, rubbing his smooth cheek, smiled to himself, then laughed excitedly, remembering clearly how he had been awake in bed till the front door had opened and he had heard Nora talking, answering questions. He had stood, in his dressing-gown, at the top of the stairs until the reporter had gone. He had hurried down and kissed her. For a long time they lay awake in bed while she talked about the ball and the Prince, and Bill kissed her passionately, then dropped off to sleep.

He was folding the paper slowly and carefully, but the city hall clock struck half past one, so he shoved it in his pocket and crossed the road, walking importantly as though many people were looking at him, a slightly stout man in light coat belted in military style, an old felt hat on the side of his head.

In the store he smiled easily at men behind the counters. He had been manager in the gents' furnishings department ever since coming back from the war, and now did the buying in London and New York. He liked knowing that store executives appreciated his energy that had made the department a distinguished haberdashery, the conservative store for men, and was quite satisfied to think the clerks didn't like him because it was much easier to fire them. He wanted other managers in the store to be respectful. He liked best his clerks who were carefully polite. Now he walked along the aisles, his belly full, his hair still damp from tonic, his hands linked behind his back, and wishing he was slightly more friendly with clerks who might mention seeing his wife's picture in the paper, but it didn't happen till John Stanley, the bald-headed clerk in the underwear, smiled and said, 'A lovely picture of your wife, sir.'

'Do you think so, John?'

'Oh, very lovely,' John said, piling up suits of underwear.

Bill leaned against the counter, pointing the toe of one shoe on the floor. He encouraged John to talk, not paying much attention to what he was saying, but liking the tone of respectful enthusiasm, and feeling generous, he casually mentioned His Highness two or three times. He didn't speak of his wife again, for John knew all about her people in England, her fondness for theatricals, and social connections in the city. John understood about Bill's wife in an entirely different manner than some of the men on the floor, who gossiped behind Bill's back, wondering how she could run around with wealthy people on his salary.

'Yes, His Highness has gone to Montreal,' Bill said, moving away.

He went upstairs to the mezzanine office and stood at the railing looking out over the main floor at all the electric globes on the ceiling, the clocks, and the clerks behind the counters. He stood there, his thumbs hooked in his vest armpit, then sat down at his glass-topped desk, inspecting with critical satisfaction three pictures of his wife pressed under the glass. He got up and took the newspaper from his pocket. The stenographer watched him spread the paper on his desk, take a knife from his pocket, and carefully clip stories of the ball, the interview with his wife, and pictures, folding them neatly and putting them in his vest pocket. He went downstairs and through the book department, the stationery, the notions to the jewellery on the other side of the store, and had a long conversation with Steiner, the manager, showing him pictures and reading aloud from clippings.

He hadn't felt so good in months but the afternoon passed slowly. He dictated a few letters, not finding words readily, and three times he stopped to ask the stenographer to phone his wife, but always there was no answer. At a quarter to five he quit work impatiently.

Nora was asleep on the chesterfield in the front room. He stood beside her, liking her face and neck. Her face always satisfied him unless she had a cold in the head. Then the whole basis of her beauty seemed to collapse. He touched her shoulder gently and her eyes opened. 'Oh, Bill,' she said.

'The little queen, the fairy princess,' he said.

She yawned: 'I could have slept for two hours yet, Bill dear, I don't feel like getting supper.'

'Not a bite, not a tiny bite?'

'Oh, heavens, Bill.'

'Tired, Nora?'

'Frightfully tired, Bill, and some silly fool phoned three times this afternoon.'

'I phoned, Nora.'

'You did? Well, I'm certainly glad I didn't bother answering.'

'If you're very tired, I'll get my own supper, Nora.'

'Oh, hell, you needn't do it. I guess I'll do it,' she said.

Disappointed, he put his hands in his pockets, for he had expected to come home and talk happily, and he was simply bothering her. She was rubbing her eyes. She said meekly: 'Kiss me, Bill.' He kissed her. 'Kiss me again, Bill, a nice kiss.' So he kissed her again.

She began lazily to get supper in the kitchen, but saw herself in the mirror, and, hastily fixing her hair and powdering her nose, she became good-humoured, humming a song. They sat down at the end of the kitchen table. She began to talk rapidly about last night and he listened eagerly, fine thoughts in his head, while she told stories about members of His Highness's party, and how she had said to His Highness that her husband was a military man and had often talked about taking up fox-hunting.

'And you have, haven't you dear?' she said.

'I sure have.'

'All you need is a horse, eh, Bill?'

'And a red coat,' he said good-naturedly.

After eating he suggested they take a walk down to the park. She had wanted a house near a park and the water, so in summer evenings she could be reminded of Old-Country beaches, but she said people would stare at her tonight, so they sat on the back porch watching kids in the yard next door pitching horseshoes. It was a new district and trees

were in most yards on the hill. The air was good, a breeze
blowing off the lake. They watched the kids pitching horseshoes till she said suddenly: 'How would you like me to go to
Montreal for a couple of days?'

'Lord, dear, what's the big idea?'

'Captain Albert suggested it last night.'

'Listen, Nora, have a heart, what about the money?'

'I said you wouldn't mind at all but would be delighted.
I said you would be honoured. Was I right in saying that,
Bill?'

'Oh, I guess so.'

'It certainly doesn't sound like it.'

'Did His Highness really suggest it, honestly?'

'He must have, Bill. I'll bet ten pounds on it.'

'That's all very well, and I might even afford it, but it's
expensive, though. No. It's too expensive.'

They talked about the trip to Montreal till it got dark and
the boys pitching horseshoes went away and the air became
chilly. Sitting on the porch in the twilight Bill felt that Nora
had become a wonderful, strange woman he had read about,
but could not expect to touch. He had thought of arguing
about Montreal, but watching her, he was in no mood for it,
and as they went into the kitchen, he took hold of her
clumsily, kissing her till she said: 'Oh, Bill, be good, heavens,
Bill.'

Before they went to bed he intended to say firmly she
should not go away, but when they got into bed, Montreal
and all his old thoughts became unimportant and he was
happy until she went to sleep finally. Then he discovered he
was not sleepy, his eyes were wide open, and he worried
about her going away. Everything had been simple and fine,
but Montreal suggested complications. He repeated that it
was for Nora, it meant a great deal to both of them, but he
had a hard time getting to sleep.

He phoned home twice from the department store next
morning, the first time to talk to her till she could honestly
convince him, the second time to tell how enthusiastic he had
become. He arranged to have dinner downtown and afterward take her to the station. He hummed a tune, after calling
her the second time, keeping time with the palms of his

hands on the desk top. Later on he talked agreeably to young Staines at the tie-counter, whom he had threatened to fire two days ago. He made snappy jokes with his assistant manager, J. C. Carlton, and in an offhand manner told him his wife was joining His Highness in Montreal. As soon as he spoke to Carlton he regretted it because Carlton had nothing whatever to say. Then he stood at the mezzanine rail, looking down at the department. John in the underwear saw him and smiled politely, Bill nodded graciously.

They had dinner at the King Edward but he didn't eat much, the curve of her white throat seemed to astonish him. They took a taxi to the station, and he carried her coat and hat box and a red-cap carried her bag. He sat in the coach with her for fifteen minutes and talked rapidly as though he had only a few minutes and some words that were difficult were essential. He said almost shyly: 'Nora, I don't know what I'll do when you're away, but I've never been so proud of you, Nora.'

'I'm happy, Bill. I'm the luckiest thing. I'm lucky beyond words.'

'No you're not, Nora, you belong, I tell you.' When he said it, he held her hand tightly, breathing slowly, and enjoying a feeling of exhilaration.

But when he stood on the platform and she waved from the train window, he felt lonesome, and jerked the brim of his old slouch hat well down over his eyes. Walking along the station tunnel and glancing at the hard smooth walls he felt utterly unimportant. No place to go. The tunnel was long and his footsteps sounded loud and made him more lonesome. He walked faster to get out of the tunnel. He was late for the show and saw poor vaudeville, but an interesting picture. At home, afterward, he sat in the front room in his stockinged feet, his collar off, and played records till he got sleepy and went to bed.

He read in the papers two days later that his wife had danced with His Highness in Montreal. In the office he clipped news stories and asked the stenographer to pin them together. The stenographer giggled when he asked her to take a wire to his wife: 'Read about it this morning. Have a good time, Bill.' He put his feet on the desk, linked his hands behind his head, seriously sober because great people in the world were entertaining his wife. He felt like talking about fox-hunting, or better still, actually trying fox-hunting.

He got a short note from Nora in which she hoped he was getting along all right. His Highness had left Montreal, but she was staying on because a man had talked to her about the stage and there was an opportunity. The note bothered him. His Highness had gone, Montreal seemed far away. He sent money and advised her to come home at once. In the evenings he walked in the park alone and sat on a bench by the water.

Waiting to hear from her he was surly in the department, and the stenographer did her work efficiently. Usually he ate in the Palm Room with managers of different departments, and a favourite sweet mustard pickle was always on the table, but now he ate over on Adelaide Street in a Chinese restaurant, saving thirty cents a day. A letter from New York surprised him, made him a little indignant, but at least it was good to hear that she hoped to get a small part in a big company, opening in New York in the fall. Her influential Montreal friends had been useful in New York, and she knew how anxious Bill was that she should be successful. He read the note in the kitchen, the envelope resting on a tin of canned food on the table, and tried to feel enthusiastic but his heart was beating too loudly.

He told John in the underwear a good story of show people and large offers made to his wife and John was so impressed Bill felt better, and thought that it was only natural her splendid success with His Highness should lead into other fields. So he wired the New York address, asking for clippings about the show. At the end of the week he got some clippings but her name wasn't mentioned. She explained that everything was satisfactory, and there was some baby talk that made him happier than he had been all week.

He expected her to write and ask for money, but days passed, and he avoided thinking about it. The last time he went over to the jewellery department to see Steiner he began by explaining pompously that his wife was having an extraordinary success and an account of it should be in the local papers. Then he talked suddenly about women who managed to live on easy street for next to nothing, arguing excitedly with Steiner about such women. He left Steiner to go down to the wash-room, and was surprised at the expression on his face in the mirror. He washed vigorously, combing his hair mechanically. Back in the department, he was caustic and critical of the clerks and fired Staines at the tie-counter. He had a suspicion Staines was talking behind his back.

He went home one evening two months after she had gone away, and found a large brown envelope in the mail-box. He tugged at his hat brim, and sat down in the front room, fumbling with the envelope. There was a picture of Nora in an ermine wrap, and a long letter, asking him if he liked her in the wrap, and calling him 'dear old Bill'. She had worn the wrap doing advertising work for a furrier, and she had liked it so much, it almost made her sick to take it off. The note was friendly, but he was disappointed, and sat back in the chair, holding the picture in both hands.

The ermine wrap was a clear picture for him, and a thought that he resolutely resisted was growing stronger, but he couldn't get rid of it, as long as he had the picture in his head. He went out on the back veranda, talked with Mrs. Johnston, next door, and was startled to realize he wasn't paying attention to words he was using, and his hands were clammy. Restless, he went into the house and stretched out on the couch, closing his eyes, dealing with the thought. He wanted to give Nora a wrap similar to the one in the picture because no one else in the world would give it to her. The notions following the thought became a repetition and monotonous. His head was tired. Such a wrap would cost at least two thousand dollars, wholesale through the store. It would take another mortgage on the house to get two thousand dollars. He lay there, exhausted mentally, thinking of Nora in the wrap till his hands began to burn and he sat up quickly, feeling feverish and unreasonable, then exultant and determined. In bed he was too tired to sleep. He couldn't find work in the office next day, his thoughts far away, so he put his elbows on the desk, assuring himself only one person could ever make him happy and nothing should prevent him getting happiness. And though it was absurd and ridiculous to send the wrap, it was tremendous.

At noontime he went to a discount company and arranged for a second mortgage on his house. He asked the man to rent the house as soon as possible, he was moving. Outside, he walked rapidly. It was a warm day, he was sweating and should have taken off his belted coat. He looked straight ahead. He thought vaguely that many girls were wearing pretty scarfs this summer, and rubbed his forehead with a big soiled handkerchief.

The manager of the fur department was impressed when Bill ordered the ermine wrap and showed the picture of his wife. Bill felt better, listening to him. He took the picture back to his office and told the stenographer to type a contract, the names to be filled in later. The contract had fine clauses such as, 'of the same quality as the one in the picture', 'of the best lining obtainable', and of course it was necessary to show the stenographer the picture.

The first week in September Bill moved from the house at the beach, and took a room in a cheap apartment house on Dundas Street. When he paid a month's rent in advance to the janitor, and sat down on the bed, looking at the oatmeal wallpaper and the thickly varnished floor, he was eager to feel he was denying himself for her, and that where he lived was unimportant. He was trying to make up his mind whether it would be better to take the wrap to New York, or simply send it. Nervously he wondered why he hesitated to go and see her, and assured himself it was because the surprise would be greater if he sent the wrap.

He carried the wrap home from the store one night and spread it out on the bed. He was excited and stroked the fur with the palm of his hand, thinking of Nora's white skin, and the wrap around her shoulders. He stood up straight, aware that the wrap was out of place in the small untidy room, and feeling strangely guilty, he went over to the window and pulled down the blind. He quickly covered the fur, and put it in the closet, his head dizzy, the room shifting. He ate very little, then hurried down town, to send it to New York.

The days passed slowly while he waited to hear from her. He avoided other managers and wasn't interested in clerks, and ate all his meals at the Chinese restaurant. When he did get the letter from Nora he was bewildered and unsure of himself because the letter read too easily. He was a dear and a darling, she said, and told him there was a splendid opportunity to go abroad. There were many kisses at the foot of the letter but nothing about coming home. She was having a good time, working hard, and she would let him know the right time to come down and see her. He went home early, telling Mr. Carlton he wasn't feeling well.

Three weeks later he was sitting in a movie near the apartment house, watching a western with good action. The show was dark, unhealthy, and smelly. He liked the movies in the neighbourhood because he couldn't be bothered getting dressed to go down town. Staring at the picture, he found himself thinking of the store. They were opening a branch in the West, and he made up his mind to suggest to the general manager that he take over the gents' furnishings in the new store.

He was surprised next day when the general manager agreed with him so readily, saying the change would do him good, he was too valuable a man to lose altogether. Bill felt uncomfortable looking at the general manager's shiny shoes and bright tie. He rubbed his hand over his face and smiled pleasantly but he didn't feel like the manager of the gents' furnishings. His suit needed pressing, and he wondered if the hole in the heel of his sock was noticeable. He thought of telling the general manager he had become poor, and needed to save money but he simply shook hands with him and said he would do much better out West.

He heard from Nora before he left the city. The letter had a Spanish postmark, and a clipping was enclosed with a picture of Nora and three fine Englishmen, and one had an arm around her waist. They were in Spain, she said. His Highness was in Spain and she knew Bill would love the country! He stared at the letter, excited inside, then tore it in two. 'To hell with His Highness,' he said.

The day before he went away he said soberly to Carlton: 'The wife is in Spain. His Highness and his party are there.'

He spoke deliberately, and didn't intend Carlton to answer him. He walked away quickly, glad that he had said it, fiercely insistent that no one should say anything to him. The department was gone. What he told Carlton belonged to a tradition. It should all go together.

Sister Bernadette

When Sister Bernadette, who had charge of the maternity ward in the hospital, wasn't rebuking a nurse in training for some petty fault, she was having a sharp disagreement with a doctor. She was a tall woman with a pale face that looked very handsome in her stiffly starched white headpiece. To her, the notion that her nun's habit might be protecting her from sharp retorts from the nurses was intolerable. But she simply couldn't hold a grudge against anybody, and if she had a tiff with a nurse she would wait till she saw the girl passing in the corridor and say innocently, 'I hear you're offended with me,' as she offered the warmest, jolliest smile. When young nurses in training, who were having a bit of idle gossip, saw the sister's tall, gaunt form, so formidable in the black robes, coming toward them, they often felt like a lot of half-guilty schoolgirls as they smiled good-naturedly. Of course Sister Bernadette had sympathy for all the women who were suffering and bearing children and she was like a mother to them, but it was the small things in the ward that were most important to her. If she saw a man in the corridor carrying a parcel carefully, she would watch him go into a patient's room, wait till he had departed, then rush into the room and look around to try and guess at once what might have been in the parcel. It was not hard for her to guess correctly, for she seemed to know every object in each private room. All the mothers liked her but were a bit afraid of her. Sometimes forgetting that women were paying expensive doctors to look after them, she would give her own instructions and insist they be carried out completely, as if she knew more about the patients than the doctors did. There was a Doctor Mallory, a short dark fellow with a broad face, a shifting, far-away expression in his eyes, and a kind of warm, earthly tenderness in his manner, who often quarrelled bitterly with Sister Bernadette because she ordered a patient of his to take a medicine he had not recommended. He did not know that Sister Bernadette loved him for quarrelling openly with her instead of being just cuttingly polite because she was a nun.

One day Doctor Mallory, looking very worried, waited in the corridor, watching Sister Bernadette's tall form with the dark robes swinging around it, coming toward him. And when he looked into her face he couldn't help smiling, there was so much fresh, girlish contentment in her expression. But this time he spoke with a certain diffidence as he said, 'Sister, I'd like to talk with you a minute.'

'Please do, Doctor,' she said. 'You're not offended again, surely.'

'Oh, no, not this time,' he said, smiling warmly. 'I wanted to tell you about a patient of mine I'd like to bring to the hospital to have her baby.'

'Now don't tell me you're so afraid of me, you have to ask my permission to bring a patient here,' she said, laughing.

'Not at all. Only this girl doesn't want to come. She's ashamed. She's of a good family. I know all about her. But she's not married and won't come here under her own name. I said I'd speak to you and you'd fix it up, Sister. Won't you?'

Sister Bernadette frowned. The doctor was smiling at her, as if he couldn't be fooled by a harsh refusal. It gave her pleasure to think that he was so sure of her sympathetic nature. But she said sharply, 'It's against the rules to register anybody under a false name, you know that, Doctor.'

'I know it, that's why I wanted to speak to you, Sister.'

With ridiculous sternness Sister Bernadette said, 'What do I care? Do what you want to do. Register the woman as Mrs. Macsorley, or anything else, it's all the same to me,' and she turned and walked away as though greatly offended. The doctor, chuckling, watched her hurrying along the corridor without looking back once.

Sister Bernadette could hardly wait to see Doctor Mallory's new patient. Five minutes after the woman was brought to the hospital, Sister Bernadette was in the room looking at her with eager curiosity and speaking in a soft reassuring voice. The patient was only a girl with big scared blue eyes and fluffy blonde hair whose confidence had been completely destroyed by her predicament. Sister Bernadette was desperately afraid that the young girl, who had been such a sinner and who was now suffering and disgraced, would be afraid of a woman like herself, a nun, who had given her life entirely to God. For some reason she wanted this scared girl to love her. That night, while the baby was being born, Sister Bernadette was in the corridor many times.

During the two weeks the girl remained at the hospital she was treated with a special attention by the nurses who thought she was an old friend of Sister Bernadette. No one suspected that Mrs. Macsorley wasn't married. Sister Bernadette got a good deal of pleasure realizing that she and the doctor were the only ones who shared the secret. Every morning she paid a visit to Mrs. Macsorley's room, talked about everything on earth, praised the baby, and tried to make the girl feel at home by strutting about like a blunt, good-natured farm woman. The fair-haired, blue-eyed girl, who was really a self-possessed, competent person, was so impressed by the sister's frank, good-natured simplicity, she sent word out to the baby's father that there was no reason why he shouldn't come to see her.

When Sister Bernadette was introduced to the father, a well-dressed, soft-spoken, tall man, she shook hands warmly, called him Mr. Macsorley and showed the baby to him. His embarrassment disappeared at once. He felt so much at ease with Sister Bernadette during that first visit that he decided to come every day at noontime. At first Sister Bernadette was delighted by the whole affair; it seemed so much like the kind of thing that was always going on in her ward, making her world seem so rich with experience that she didn't care whether she ever went outside the hospital. But when she heard that the girl's lover was a married man, it bothered her to see that he was still so attentive. Though she honestly liked the man and liked the girl too, she said to Doctor Mallory with awkward sincerity. 'I don't like to see that man coming to see the girl so much. Evidently they're still in love.'

'Does he come often?'

'Every day. And they are both so sure of themselves.'

'It isn't very nice. It isn't fair to you,' the doctor said.

'No, no, I don't mean that,' Sister Bernadette said. 'But you know that man is married and has two children. I just mean that the girl at least ought to respect his wife and children and not let him be so devoted to her.' Then Sister Bernadette began to feel self-conscious as though the doctor was misunderstanding her. 'Don't misinterpret me,' she said at once. 'The girl can run around with single men as much as she likes and come here as often as she likes as far as I'm concerned . . .'

'I'll tell them about it,' the doctor said.

'No. Please don't. You'd better not say anything,' she said.

Then it was time for Mrs. Macsorley to leave the hospital. Doctor Mallory came to Sister Bernadette and explained that he, himself, was going to find someone to adopt the baby. Coaxing and pleading, he asked if it wouldn't be all right to leave the baby in the hospital nursery for two days at the most.

Such a request didn't actually worry Sister Bernadette, but she snapped at the doctor, 'It's absolutely against the rules of the hospital to leave a baby who's in good health in that nursery after the mother has gone.' In the brief argument that followed she was short and hot-tempered, and in the end she said, 'All right, have your way, but only for one day, mind.'

She didn't think it necessary to worry till the baby had been left in the nursery for a week. Doctor Mallory was trying very hard to get someone to adopt the baby girl. Sister Bernadette began to think that the child would remain in her nursery till she, herself, did something about it. And every time she looked at the brown-eyed baby she was reminded that she had done wrong in letting the mother register at the hospital under another name. After all, it was just vanity, her eagerness to have the doctor believe her a good-natured person, that was now causing trouble. Perhaps she ought to reveal the whole matter to the Mother Superior, she thought. And in her prayers in the morning and in her evening prayers she asked that someone be found who would take the baby at once.

In the evenings, after ten o'clock feeding-time, she would go into the nursery when the lights were turned down looking at one small crib after another with an expert eye that made the nurse in charge wary. But she stood by Baby Macsorley's crib, frowning, puzzled by her own uneasiness. She lifted the baby up as though to see it for the first time. The baby was wearing a little pink sweater coat one of the nurses had knitted. Sister Bernadette knew that Baby Macsorley had become the pet of the nursery. Only last night one of the nurses had performed a mock marriage between the baby and another fine baby boy who was being taken home that day. When she put the baby back into the crib she found herself kissing her on the forehead and patting her back, as she hoped, quickly, that no one had seen her.

As soon as she saw Doctor Mallory next day she blurted out, 'If you don't get that baby out of here by tomorrow, I'll throw it in the snow bank.'

Doctor Mallory was a bit afraid of her now, for he knew that she was a determined woman, so he said, pleading, 'Wait till tomorrow. I'm trying to get one particular lady to adopt it. Wait till tomorrow. I'm working on her.'

'You'll have to work faster, that's all,' Sister Bernadette said without even smiling.

Instead of one day, she waited two days longer, but now she was so angry that whenever she went into the nursery and saw the baby, she felt herself resenting the young mother with the candid blue eyes and the baby blonde curls and the bold straight-forward lover who came so openly to the hospital and felt no shame. Once Sister Bernadette picked the baby up and then put it down hastily for she felt with disgust that the sordidness in the life of the mother and father might be touching her through the baby and disturbing her too much. 'I can't go on thinking of those people,' she muttered, 'the baby goes out of here tomorrow.'

But Doctor Mallory was avoiding her and she didn't have a chance to speak to him for three days. She saw him turn a corner and duck into an elevator. 'Doctor,' she called, 'listen to me. I'm going to put that baby in the rear seat of your car and let you drive off with it. We're through with it.'

'Why, what's the trouble now, Sister?' he said.

'It's demoralizing my nursery. I'll not have it,' she said. 'It's the pet of the whole place. Every nurse that goes in there at night picks it up. The baby's been here too long, I tell you.'

'But just thinking about it surely doesn't bother you.'

'It certainly does. It's staring me in the face every moment.'

'Here's some cheerful news then. Maybe you'll be rid of the baby tomorrow. I'm getting an answer from the lady I wanted to adopt it tonight.'

'Honestly, Doctor, you don't know how glad I am to hear that,' she said, taking a deep breath.

There was such light-hearted relief within Sister Bernadette when she entered the nursery that night that she had a full, separate smile for each baby as she moved, a tall, black-robed figure, among the cribs. And when she stood beside Baby Macsorley's crib, she began to chuckle, feeling it might now be safe to let the baby have some of the warm attention she had sometimes wanted to give. She seemed to know this baby so much better than all the other babies. Humming to herself, she picked up the baby, slapped her on the back and whispered, 'Are you really going away tomorrow, darling?'

Carrying the baby over to the window she stood there looking down at the city which was spread out in lighted streets with glaring electric signs and moving cabs, the life of a great city at night moving under her eyes. Somewhere, down there, she thought, the bold young girl with the confident eyes and her lover were going their own way. As she held their baby in her arms, she muttered, frowning, 'But perhaps they really are in love. Maybe they're out dancing.' The girl and her lover belonged to the life down there in the city. 'But that man ought to be home with his wife,' she thought uneasily.

Sister Bernadette began to think of herself as a young girl again. For the first time in years she was disturbed by dim, half-forgotten thoughts: 'Oh, why do I want so much to keep this one baby? Why this one?' her soul, so chaste and aloof from the unbridled host swarming nightly in the city streets, was now overwhelmed by a struggle between something of life that was lost and something bright and timeless within her that was gained. But she started to tremble all over with more unhappiness than she had ever known. With a new, mysterious warmth, she began to hug the child that was almost hidden in her heavy black robes as she pressed it to her breast.

It Must Be Different

Sylvia Weeks and Max Porter had known each other five months, but she never took him home to her place till that autumn evening when they had walked in the streets after the show, and the rain had begun to fall.

It had started when Max began suddenly to tell her that there was a real chance for him to get along in the radio business, and then her heart had begun to beat unevenly, for she became aware that he was getting ready to talk about wanting to marry her. He was so simple and honest about it, that she became humble and shy, and they walked along silently, both anxious about what was to be said; and then the rain began to fall in large heavy drops. Ducking their heads, they ran along the street hand in hand and stood breathless on the stoop outside her place, watching the wet pavement shining under the street light.

Sylvia could not bear to let him go as he had gone on other nights; it was as though they had looked for each other for months, and had now met suddenly face to face. That magical feeling was still flowing between them, and she couldn't bear to let him go until all the necessary words had been said, or the things done that would hold them together forever.

'Come on in for a little while, Max,' she said.

'Are you sure it'll be all right?'

'I think they'll be in bed,' she said.

They laughed a little while Sylvia fumbled in her purse for her latchkey; then they tried to go in quietly. When they were in the hall, they heard someone coughing in the living-room. Sylvia whispered uneasily: 'I thought they'd be in bed.'

'Maybe I'd better not come in,' he said.

'Come on, anyway,' she said.

In the living-room Sylvia's mother, a large woman with a face that had been quite pretty once, but which was now soft and heavy, was standing with an alarm clock in her hand. She was on her way to bed, and she had been urging her husband, who still sat in an arm-chair in his shirt-sleeves and suspenders reading the paper, to go along with her, so he wouldn't disturb her later on. When Sylvia came in with Max following shyly, the mother was flustered and began to tidy her gray hair with her hand. 'We were on our way to bed. We were just waiting for you, Sylvia,' she said reproachfully.

'We wanted to walk after the show, Mother; but it rained. This is Max, Mother,' Sylvia said.

'Oh, hello, Max. We've heard about you.'

'If it's too late, I won't stay, Mrs. Weeks.'

'So you're Max, eh,' the father said, getting up. He was a furniture-maker who worked hard all day, and who usually hurried out of the room when a visitor came in the evening; but now he stood there staring at Max as if he had been wondering about him a long time.

And Mrs. Weeks, looking at Sylvia, said: 'You must have been having a good time, dear. You look happy and kind of excited.'

'I'm not excited. I was just hurrying in the rain,' Sylvia said.

'I guess it's just the rain and the hurrying that makes your eyes shine,' the mother said; but the free ecstatic eagerness she saw in her daughter's face worried her, and her glance was troubled as she tried to make her husband notice that

Sylvia's face glowed with some secret delight that had come out of being with this boy, who was a stranger and might not be trustworthy. Sylvia and Max were standing underneath the light, and Sylvia with her flushed cheeks and her dark head seemed more marvellously eager than even before. It was easy for them to feel the restlessness and the glowing warmth in her, and the love she had been giving; and then the mother and father, looking at Max, who seemed very boyish with his rain-wet hair shining under the light, smiled a little, not wanting to be hostile, yet feeling sure that Sylvia and this boy had touched some new intimacy that night.

In a coaxing, worried voice Mrs. Weeks said: 'Now don't stay up late, Sylvia darling, will you?' Again her husband's eyes met hers in that thoughtful, uneasy way; then they said pleasantly: 'Good night, Max. We're glad to meet you. Good night, Sylvia.' And then they went to bed.

When they had gone, Max said: 'They certainly made that pretty clear, didn't they?'

'Made what clear?'

'That they wouldn't trust me alone with my grandmother.'

'They didn't say anything at all, Max.'

'Didn't you see how they stared at me? I'll bet they're listening now.'

'Is that why you're whispering?'

'Sure. They expect us to whisper, don't they?'

They sat down on the couch, but they both felt that if they caressed each other, or became gentle and tender, they were only making a beginning at something that was expected of them by the mother and father going to bed in the next room. So they were awkward and uneasy with each other. They felt like strangers. When he put his arm on her shoulder, it lay there heavy, and they were silent, listening to the rain falling outside.

Then there was a sound in the hall, the sound of shuffling slippers, and when they looked up quickly, they saw a bit of the mother's dressing-gown sweeping past the door. Then the slippers were still. In a little while there was a worried, hesitant shuffling; then they came back again past the door.

'Did you want something, Mother?' Sylvia called.

'No, nothing,' the mother said, looking in. She tried to smile, but she was a little ashamed, and she would not look directly at Sylvia. 'I couldn't get to sleep,' she said.

'Aren't you feeling well?'

'I lie awake, you know. I hear every sound in here. I might just as well be in the room with you, I guess.' And then with that half-ashamed droop of her head, she shuffled away again.

'Is she policing us?' Max asked irritably.

'I think she's just not feeling well,' Sylvia said.

They both sat stiffly, listening, though she wanted to put her cheek down on Max's shoulder. In a little while they heard the murmur of voices in the bedroom; and Sylvia knew that her father and mother were lying awake worrying about her. Out of their own memories, out of everything that had happened to them, they felt sure they knew what would be happening to her. The murmuring voices rose a little; the sounds were short and sharp as the mother and father wrangled and worried and felt helpless. And Sylvia, trying hard to recover those moments she had thought so beautiful, hurrying along the street with Max, knew that it was no use, and that they were gone, and she felt miserable.

'I think I'll get out,' Max whispered.

'Please don't go now,' she coaxed. 'It's the first night we've felt like this. Please stay.'

She wanted to soothe the hate and contempt out of him by rubbing her fingers through his hair; yet she only sat beside him stiffly, waiting, while the house grew silent, for warmth and eagerness to come again. It was so silent she thought she could hear the beating of his heart. She was ashamed to whisper. Max kept stirring uneasily, wanting to go.

Then they were startled by the father's voice calling roughly: 'Sylvia!'

'What is it?' she said.

'What's keeping you there? Why are you so quiet? What are you doing?'

'Nothing.'

'It's getting late,' he called.

She knew her father must have tried hard to stop himself calling out like that; yet she felt so humiliated she could not look at Max.

'I'm getting out quick,' Max said.

'All right. But it's nothing; he's just worrying,' she pleaded.

'They've been lying in bed all the time listening.'

'They're very fond of me,' she said. 'They'd do it, no matter what it was.'

But hating the house and her people, he snapped at her, 'Why don't they put a padlock on you.'

Then she felt that the feeling that had been so good between them, that she had tried to bring into the house and bring into her own life, could not last here, that his voice would never grow shy and hesitant as he fumbled for a few words here, that this was really what she was accustomed to, and it was not good. She began to cry softly. 'Don't be sore, Max,' she said.

'I'm not sore at you.'

'They felt pretty sure they know how it goes; that's all,' she pleaded with him. 'They think it'll have to go with me the way it went with them.'

'That's pretty plain.'

'I don't think either one of them want to see me get married. Nothing ever happened the right way for them. I can remember ever since I was a kid.'

'Remember what?'

'They never felt sure of each other. They parted once, and even now when they get mad, they're suspicious of each other and wouldn't trust each other around the block. But that was years ago, really,' she said, holding him tightly by the arm, and pleading that he understand the life in her home was not loose and unhappy. 'They're both very fond of me,' she said apologetically. 'They've had a tough time all their lives. We've been pretty poor, and – well – they worry about me; that's all.'

Her eyes looked so scared that Max was afraid to question her, and they stood together thinking of the mother and father lying awake in the bedroom.

'I guess they feel that way about people, out of what's happened to them, eh?' he said.

'That's it.'

'Their life doesn't have to be your life, does it?'

'It certainly doesn't,' she said, and she was full of relief, for she knew by his face that the things she had blurted out hadn't disturbed him at all.

'I wrote my people about you,' he said. 'They want to see you. I sent them a snapshot.'

'That was a very bad one; I look terrible in it.'

'Can you get your holidays in August, Sylvia?'

'I think so. I'll ask a long time ahead.'

'We'll go to the country and see my folks. I swear you'll like them,' he said.

That moment at the door was the one fine free moment they had had since coming in, and it did not seem to belong to anything that had happened in the house that night. While they held each other, whispering, 'Good-bye, good-bye,' they were sure they would always be gentle and faithful, and their life together would be good. Then they laughed softly, knowing they were sharing the same secret contempt for the wisdom of her people.

Without waiting to hear the sound of his footfalls outside, she rushed resolutely to her mother's bedroom and turned on the light, and called sharply: 'Mother.'

But her mother and father, who were lying with their heads together on the pillow, did not stir, and Sylvia said savagely: 'Wake up – do you hear? I was never so ashamed in my life.'

One of her father's thin arms hung loose over the side of the bed, the wrinkled hand drooping from the wrist, and his shoulders were half uncovered. Her mother was breathing irregularly with her mouth open a little, as though her dreams too were troubled. They looked very tired, and Sylvia wavered.

Then her father stirred, and his blue eyes opened and blinked, and he mumbled sleepily: 'Is that you, Sylvia?'

'Yes,' she said.

'All right. Turn out the light,' he said, and he closed his eyes.

Yet she still stood there, muttering hesitantly to herself.
'It's just that I don't want to get to feel the way you do about
people.'

Then she grew frightened, for the two faces on the pillow
now seemed like the faces of two tired people who had
worked hard all their lives, and had grown old together; and
her own life had been simply a part of theirs, a part of whatever had happened to them. Still watching the two faces,
she began to long with all her soul that her own love and
her hope would be strong enough to resist the things that
had happened to them. 'I'll be different with me and Max.
It must be different,' she muttered.

But as she heard only their irregular breathing, her fright
grew. The whole of her life ahead seemed to become uncertain, and her happiness with Max so terribly insecure.

Younger Brother

Just after dark on Sunday evening five fellows from the
neighbourhood stood on the corner under the light opposite
the cigar store. They were young and dressed carefully, all
in dark overcoats, hard hats, and white scarves, except
Jimmie Stevens, the smallest fellow without the hat, and
with black curly hair, the only one in short pants. Jimmie
was eager to please the big fellows, who did not take him
seriously because he was a few years younger. They rarely
talked directly to him. So he wanted to show off. He got a
laugh out of them the way he went whirling and twisting out
to the middle of the road, his body hunched down at the
knees, his left arm held out and his right arm moving as
though he were playing a violin, like a dancer he had seen
on the stage. In his cracked and changing voice he sang
hoarsely till one of the fellows, Bill Spiers, shouted, 'Crown

him, somebody, oh, geez, what a voice, put the skids under him!' and he ran out in the road and tackled Jimmie around the waist, though not hard enough to make them both fall on the pavement. Spiers' hard hat fell on the road as he grabbed Jimmie and the other fellows kidded him while he kept on pushing Jimmie across the street.

Then somebody yelled, 'Lay off the kid, don't hurt him!' just as Jimmie's sister, Millie, passed the cigar store, going out for the evening. She was an unusually tall, slim, blonde girl, graceful and stylish in her short beige-coloured lapin jacket with the narrow collar knotted loosely at her throat, who walked with a free, firm stride, her head held jauntily and independently on one side as she looked straight ahead, fully aware that she was admired by the boys at the corner, and at the same time faintly amused as though she knew she was far beyond them. She didn't even speak to Jimmie as she passed, for she knew he was always there on a Sunday evening. He was glad she passed so jauntily and was proud and warm with satisfaction because his sister had such fine clean lines to her body and was so smartly independent and utterly beyond any of the gang at the corner. Sometimes he felt that the big fellows let him hang around with them because they had so much admiration for his sister, who never spoke to them, though she had known them all when they were kids.

'She's a smart baby,' Buck Thompson, a thin fellow, said, looking after her. 'If I get some dough one of these days I'll take her out and give her a chance.'

'There's a fat chance for a little guy like you just up to her shoulder,' Bill Spiers said.

'Is that so?'

'Yeah, she's got too much class for you, Buck.'

'I don't know, I don't know. I guess I've known her since she was knee-high to a grasshopper, and I saw her up town a few months ago with Muddy Maguire.'

'Aw rats,' Spiers said. 'He couldn't hold a candle to her.'

Everybody knew Muddy Maguire, a tough, rough fellow, who had grown up around the street corner and had moved up town. He was just a boy from the corners who used to pick up girls under the street lights. Jimmie started to snicker: 'Say, if my old lady ever heard you say that she'd pull out your tongue, Buck.' They all knew Mrs. Stevens, a competent, practical woman, who had left her husband sixteen years ago and would never let her daughter bring a fellow near the house. Jimmie couldn't keep from grinning; he was pleased that they had all given Buck Thompson the horse-laugh for thinking he could get anywhere with Millie.

By this time Millie had passed out of sight, turning the corner by the news-stand, and one of the follows started to sing a love-song softly and the others tried seriously to croon with him, harmonizing as much as possible, all wishing they had enough money to take Millie Stevens out. For almost an hour they talked very intimately about girls, cursing each other and spitting at the sidewalk.

It was nearly eleven o'clock when Jimmie went home. The Stevenses lived in the house with the freshly painted shutters third from the corner in a long row of old three-storey brick houses with high steps and Colonial doorways. They lived on the ground floor and had the basement also. Jimmie was whistling through his teeth, a thin tuneless whistle, as he went up the steps. A light was in the big front room, shining through the shutters, and Jimmie wondered if his mother, who had been out for the evening, had brought one of the neighbours home with her. He was going along the hall to the kitchen when he thought he heard Millie's voice, then a fellow's voice. He knew at once that his mother had not come home. 'Millie's crazy bringing a guy home here,' he thought. He went through to the kitchen, but he wanted to see who was talking to his sister, so he went back along the hall and carefully and quietly opened one of the big folding doors. Millie was sitting on the sofa with Muddy Maguire. Her fur jacket and a bright scarf were tossed carelessly over the back of the sofa. 'She must have come home the other way around the block, so she would not have to pass the fellows at the corner,' Jimmie thought. Maguire was a stout, heavy fellow with small eyes, the brows meeting over them, his shiny black hair parted in the middle, a self-reliant, domineering fellow with his chest bulging under his tight vest. As soon as Jimmy saw him sitting there with his swell, unspoilt sister he felt his whole body becoming inert with disappointment. 'What can Millie see in a guy like that?' he said to himself weakly.

Jimmie tried to hear what they were saying. Millie, leaning toward Muddy, talked earnestly, her face pale, her eyes red as though she had been crying, and Muddy was leaning away from her, looking sour and ugly as though there was no mystery in her for him and he didn't want to be there at all. Millie was trying to explain something to him. Jimmie heard her say something about 'Ma', and then suddenly she must have said something nasty and insulting to him, for he straightened up quickly and slapped her lightly across the face.

Jimmie put his hand over his mouth: he expected Millie to tear Maguire's face with her nails; he couldn't imagine her taking anything from a guy like that; he wanted to yell at her and then go in and smack Maguire. But he couldn't understand it at all when she merely put her hand up to her cheek and began to cry weakly. Everything important and permanent in Jimmie's life now seemed beyond him.

Then Millie said distinctly to Maguire: 'You promised, you know you promised.'

'I was a fool,' he said.

'Then what did you come here for?'

'I don't know.'

'You were going to tell Ma.'

'Sure, I was going to tell your old lady I'd marry you.'

Millie turned her head away from him and tried to hold her lower lip with her teeth. Muddy shrugged his shoulders, then slowly and clumsily let his hands fall on Millie's shoulder. 'All right,' he said. 'I'm sorry, Millie.'

While Jimmie was waiting, trembling and angry, he heard his mother coming up the front steps. On tiptoe he hurried back to the kitchen and waited for her. When he saw her, he said, 'Sh, sh, sh.'

Mrs. Stevens, a short, stout woman, almost shapeless in her heavy cloth coat, with firm thin lips and steady pale-blue eyes, said, 'What's the matter, Jimmie?'

'Ma, Millie's in there with Muddy Maguire.'

Mrs. Stevens' face got red. She stopped taking off her coat. 'In this house?' she said.

'Go on in, Ma.'

'The vixen! I wondered who was in the front room.'

He followed his mother to the door of the front room. When Mrs. Stevens went into the room Jimmie caught a glimpse of Millie: Maguire still had his arm around her shoulder; Millie, resting her head against his chest, was crying quietly, both her arms around his neck as if he had become very precious to her. They looked up nervously when Mrs. Stevens walked into the room. Muddy, staring at her steadily, tried to conceal his feeling by an awkward indifference.

Mrs. Stevens had never wanted her daughter to belong to any man, and now she said harshly: 'Millie, what is this? What's the meaning of this?'

'We wanted to speak to you, Ma,' Millie said timidly.

Mrs. Stevens, a severe, rigid woman, had expected Millie to stand up and move away from Maguire when she spoke to her, and now she was startled to feel that Millie and this fellow were drawing closer together as they stared at her: the one emotion that held Maguire and Millie together seemed suddenly to touch Mrs. Stevens and puzzle and weaken her. She stood there, getting ready to speak roughly, yet all the severity and grimness in her own way of living seemed unimportant now. Gravely she realized why they were waiting for her, and why Millie wanted to talk to her. 'Millie, my dear,' she said, bending down to her daughter.

'We just want to have a few words with you, Mrs. Stevens,' Maguire said.

'Go 'way and close the door, Jimmie,' Mrs. Stevens said nervously, trying to conceal her agitation.

Jimmie was disgusted with his mother. When Maguire spoke to her so casually, so sure of his relation with Millie, Jimmie expected his mother to scorch him with her sharp hot tongue, and yet, as he closed the door, and bent down on one knee to listen at the keyhole, Jimmie heard his mother talking peacefully, and only at times resentfully and bitterly. For a long time he heard the mumbling and murmuring of their voices, only half hearing, till his knee was tired and stiff, and he could tell, by the few words he heard, that his mother would agree to let Maguire marry Millie. Disappointed, he went back to the kitchen and put his elbows down on the white enamelled table. 'What's the matter with Ma?' he thought. 'She should light into that guy and give him hell, she should spin that chuckle-headed sap on his ear. What's got into her?' It didn't matter what there was between Millie and Maguire, he thought. 'Ma ought to have been able to do something; why did she cave in?'

And as he sat there he remembered the jaunty aloof independence of Millie as she had passed the gang on the corner that evening, and he realized she must have known at the time that she was going to meet Maguire. He began to think of her passing the bunch at the corner: it seemed tremendously important that she should keep on passing by. The more he thought of it the more eager he was and the more pleasure he got out of thinking of her going by, always aloof and beyond them, clean, with too much class for them, leaving them nothing else to do but look after her and croon songs and wish they had enough money to take her out.

A Very Merry Christmas

After midnight on Christmas Eve hundreds of people prayed at the crib of the Infant Jesus which was to the right of the altar under the evergreen-tree branches in St. Malachi's church. That night there had been a heavy fall of wet snow, and there was a muddy path up to the crib. Both Sylvanus O'Meara, the old caretaker who had helped to prepare the crib, and Father Gorman, the stout, red-faced, excitable parish priest, had agreed it was the most lifelike tableau of the Child Jesus in a corner of the stable at Bethlehem they had ever had in the church.

But early on Christmas morning Father Gorman came running to see O'Meara, the blood all drained out of his face and his hands pumping up and down at his sides and he shouted, 'A terrible thing has happened. Where is the Infant Jesus? The crib's empty.'

O'Meara, who was a devout, innocent, wondering old man, who prayed a lot and always felt very close to God in the church, was bewildered and he whispered, 'Who could have taken it? Taken it where?'

'Take a look in the crib yourself, man, if you don't believe me,' the priest said, and he grabbed the caretaker by the arm, marched him into the church and over to the crib and showed him that the figure of the Infant Jesus was gone.

'Someone took it, of course. It didn't fly away. But who took it, that's the question?' the priest said. 'When was the last time you saw it?'

'I know it was here last night,' O'Meara said, 'because after the midnight mass when everybody else had gone home I saw Mrs. Farrel and her little boy kneeling up here,

346

and when they stood up I wished them a merry Christmas. You don't think she'd touch it, do you?'

'What nonsense, O'Meara. There's not a finer woman in the parish. I'm going over to her house for dinner tonight.'

'I noticed that she wanted to go home, but the little boy wanted to stay there and keep praying by the crib; but after they went home I said a few prayers myself and the Infant Jesus was still there.'

Grabbing O'Meara by the arm the priest whispered excitedly, 'It must be the work of communists or atheists.' There was a sudden rush of blood to his face. 'This isn't the first time they've struck at us,' he said.

'What would communists want with the figure of the Infant Jesus?' O'Meara asked innocently. 'They wouldn't want to have it to be reminded that God was with them. I didn't think they could bear to have Him with them.'

'They'd take it to mock us, of course, and to desecrate the church. O'Meara, you don't seem to know much about the times we live in. Why did they set fire to the church?'

O'Meara said nothing because he was very loyal and he didn't like to remind the priest that the little fire they had in the church a few months ago was caused by a cigarette butt the priest had left in his pocket when he was changing into his vestments, so he was puzzled and silent for a while and then whispered, 'Maybe someone really wanted to take God away, do you think so?'

'Take Him out of the church?'

'Yes. Take Him away.'

'How could you take God out of the church, man? Don't be stupid.'

'But maybe someone thought you could, don't you see?'

'O'Meara, you talk like an old idiot. Don't you realize you play right into the hands of the atheists saying such things? Do we believe an image is God? Do we worship idols? We do not. No more of that, then. If communists and atheists tried to burn this church once, they'll not stop till they desecrate it. God help us, why is my church marked out for this?' He got terribly excited and rushed away shouting, 'I'm going to phone the police.'

It looked like the beginning of a terrible Christmas Day

for the parish. The police came, and were puzzled, and
talked to everybody. Newspapermen came. They took pictures of the church and of Father Gorman, who had just
preached a sermon that startled the congregation because he
grew very eloquent on the subject of vandal outrages to the
house of God. Men and women stood outside the church
in their best clothes and talked very gravely. Everybody
wanted to know what the thief would do with the image of
the Infant Jesus. They all were wounded, stirred and wondering. There certainly was going to be something worth
talking about at a great many Christmas dinners in the
neighbourhood.

But Sylvanus O'Meara went off by himself and was very
sad. From time to time he went into the church and looked
at the empty crib. He had all kinds of strange thoughts. He
told himself that if someone really wanted to hurt God, then
just wishing harm to Him really hurt Him, for what other
way was there of hurting Him? Last night he had had the
feeling that God was all around the crib, and now it felt as
if God wasn't there at all. It wasn't just that the image of
the Infant Jesus was gone, but someone had done violence
to that spot and had driven God away from it. He told himself that things could be done that would make God want
to leave a place. It was very hard to know where God was.
Of course, He would always be in the church, but where had
that part of Him that had seemed to be all around the crib
gone?

It wasn't a question he could ask the little groups of
astounded parishioners who stood on the sidewalk outside
the church, because they felt like wagging their fingers and
puffing their cheeks out and talking about what was happening to God in Mexico and Spain.

But when they had all gone home to eat their Christmas
dinners, O'Meara, himself, began to feel a little hungry. He
went out and stood in front of the church and was feeling
thankful that there was so much snow for the children on
Christmas Day when he saw that splendid and prominent
woman, Mrs. Farrel, coming along the street with her little
boy. On Mrs. Farrel's face there was a grim and desperate

expression and she was taking such long fierce strides that the five-year-old boy, whose hand she held so tight, could hardly keep up with her and pull his big red sleigh. Sometimes the little boy tried to lean back and was a dead weight and then she pulled his feet off the ground while he whimpered, 'Oh, gee, oh, gee, let me go.' His red snowsuit was all covered with snow as if he had been rolling on the road.

'Merry Christmas, Mrs. Farrel,' O'Meara said. And he called to the boy, 'Not happy on Christmas day? What's the matter, son?'

'Merry Christmas, indeed, Mr. O'Meara,' the woman snapped to him. She was not accustomed to paying much attention to the caretaker, a curt nod was all she ever gave him, and now she was far too angry and mortified to bother with him. 'Where's Father Gorman?' she demanded.

'Still at the police station, I think.'

'At the police station! God help us, did you hear that, Jimmie?' she said, and she gave such a sharp tug at the boy's arm that she spun him around in the snow behind her skirts where he cowered, watching O'Meara with a curiously steady pair of fine blue eyes. He wiped away a mat of hair from his forehead as he watched and waited. 'Oh, Lord, this is terrible,' Mrs. Farrel said. 'What will I do?'

'What's the matter, Mrs. Farrel?'

'I didn't do anything,' the child said. 'I was coming back here. Honest I was, mister.'

'Mr. O'Meara,' the woman began, as if coming down from a great height to the level of an unimportant and simple-minded old man, 'maybe you could do something for us. Look on the sleigh.'

O'Meara saw that an old coat was wrapped around something on the sleigh, and stooping to lift it, he saw the figure of the Infant Jesus there. He was so delighted he only looked up at Mrs. Farrel and shook his head in wonder and said, 'It's back and nobody harmed it at all.'

'I'm ashamed, I'm terribly ashamed, Mr. O'Meara. You don't know how mortified I am,' she said, 'but the child really didn't know what he was doing. It's a disgrace to us, I know. It's my fault that I haven't trained him better, though God knows I've tried to drum respect for the church into him.' She gave such a jerk at the child's hand he slid on his knee in the snow keeping his eyes on O'Meara.

Still unbelieving, O'Meara asked, 'You mean he really took it from the church?'

'He did, he really did.'

'Fancy that. Why, child, that was a terrible thing to do,' O'Meara said. 'Whatever got into you?' Completely mystified he turned to Mrs. Farrel, but he was so relieved to have the figure of the Infant Jesus back without there having been any great scandal that he couldn't help putting his hand gently on the child's head.

'It's all right, and you don't need to say anything,' the child said, pulling away angrily from his mother, and yet he never took his eyes off O'Meara, as if he felt there was some bond between them. Then he looked down at his mitts, fumbled with them and looked up steadily and said, 'It's all right, isn't it, mister?'

'It was early this morning, right after he got up, almost the first thing he must have done on Christmas Day,' Mrs. Farrel said. 'He must have walked right in and picked it up and taken it out to the street.'

'But what got into him?'

'He makes no sense about it. He says he had to do it.'

'And so I did, 'cause it was a promise,' the child said. 'I promised last night, I promised God that if He would make Mother bring me a big red sleigh for Christmas I would give Him the first ride on it.'

'Don't think I've taught the child foolish things,' Mrs. Farrel said. 'I'm sure he meant no harm. He didn't understand at all what he was doing.'

'Yes, I did,' the child said stubbornly.

'Shut up, child,' she said, shaking him.

O'Meara knelt down till his eyes were on a level with the child's and they looked at each other till they felt close together and he said, 'But why did you want to do that for God?'

' 'Cause it's a swell sleigh, and I thought God would like it.'

Mrs. Farrel, fussing and red-faced, said, 'Don't you

worry. I'll see he's punished by having the sleigh taken away from him.'

But O'Meara, who had picked up the figure of the Infant Jesus, was staring down at the red sleigh; and suddenly he had a feeling of great joy, of the illumination of strange good tidings, a feeling that this might be the most marvellous Christmas Day in the whole history of the city, for God must surely have been with the child, with him on a joyous, carefree holiday sleigh ride, as he ran along those streets and pulled the sleigh. And O'Meara turned to Mrs. Farrel, his face bright with joy, and said, commandingly, with a look in his eyes that awed her, 'Don't you dare say a word to him, and don't you dare touch that sleigh, do you hear? I think God did like it.'

The Duel

In their light summer suits they kept coming up the steps from the Christopher Street subway into the warm night. Their bright faces kept coming up from the shadow into the street light. Sometimes they came slowly in groups, but those who were alone hurried when they reached the street. At first there were so many girls that Joe Simpson, standing a little piece away on Seventh Avenue, thought Inez would surely be among them. 'She'll be on the next train,' he thought. 'If she's not on that, I'll only wait three trains more.'

Waiting there, he grew more and more desolate, more uncertain and fearful, and yet, looking along the lighted avenue and remembering how often he and Inez had been among these people at this hour, there were moments when he felt eager and almost hopeful. This was his neighbourhood, here among these people; they looked just the same as they did on any other night when he and Inez were together, moving among them. At any moment she was apt to come hurrying along; she would try hard to look severe, smile in spite of herself, look very lovely, start to speak, and then maybe laugh a little instead, and then they would link arms awkwardly and walk along in silence.

But because he could not help feeling fearful, Joe started to walk along the side street toward her house, so he would be sure of not missing her. When he was nearly there a taxi came along the street and stopped a few feet away with the engine running. The driver turned around and flung open the door, and there was a little movement of his shoulders as he made himself more comfortable in his seat. Then the engine was turned off. After what seemed a very long time a big fellow in a gray flannel suit stepped out and then helped Inez to the pavement. You couldn't help hate the fellow, the way he helped her out with such special tenderness, and when he made a little bow to her the light shone on his high, handsome forehead and shiny black hair. 'Good night, Inez. You're a darling,' he was saying.

She was smiling; her face looked more lovely than Joe had thought it would look when he was thinking of her coming along and smiling at him. 'It was such a lovely time,' she said gaily.

'Dream about it,' the fellow said, grinning.

'I'll try hard,' she called as she turned, waving her hand. Her face in that light was full of a glowing excitement; there was a kind of reckless, laughing joy in it that Joe had never seen before, as if she had just come from some kind of delightful amusement she had not known for a long time, something that had left her a little breathless. The sound of her laughter scared Joe. It seemed to be the very sound he had been waiting for so fearfully. Now, in her white linen suit and white shoes, she was going across the pavement. She was taking the key out of her purse. Pausing an instant, she pulled off her hat and shook her thick, dark hair free. And then, as she opened the door, he called out sharply, 'Inez, Inez, wait a minute.'

Startled, she turned, but she did not speak. She stood there watching him coming toward her, and when he was close to her she said in a cool, even tone, 'What do you want, Joe?'

'What were you doing with that guy, Inez? Where have you been?' He took hold of her by the arm as if she had always belonged to him and now he was entitled to punish her, but when she pulled her arm away so very firmly he stopped speaking, as if he could not get his breath.

'It's none of your business where I was, Joe,' she said. 'I'm going in now, if you don't mind.'

'Who was that guy?'

'I won't tell you.'

'Was that the first time you were out with him?'

'I won't tell you,' she said wearily. 'I'm going in.'

He was trying to think of something harsh to say that would hurt her, but as he realized how aloof she was, how untouched by his presence, he grew frightened, and he said rapidly, 'Listen, Inez darling, I was only kidding the other night. I was irritable. I'm not sore now. I love you, Inez. Only you should have said you were going out with someone else when I phoned. You said you were going over to Brooklyn to see your cousin.'

'Supposing I did.'

'Well...you ought...Never mind that, Inez. Just tell me where you were now, Inez. I'm not sore. I can understand you might want to see a show sometimes like we used to. Were you at a show tonight? See, I'm not sore. Look at me, Inez.' Joe was trying to smile and look like an amiable young man who liked to see people having a good time, but when Inez finally did look up at him she wasn't reassured at all.

She grew very agitated and said angrily, 'You've got a nerve, Joe. You weren't content to leave things the way they were. Any girl would get tired of the way you go...' She didn't finish, for while he stood there, listening, she felt an ache growing in her for all the good times they had had during these last three years. Every trivial pleasure they had shared seemed to have an intense meaning now. And then she blurted out, 'I'm sick and tired of the way you've been going on, Joe. That's all over. I've made up my mind.'

'No, you haven't, Inez. I was irritable the other night,

darling. I was thinking I'd never get work. I was thinking we'd never be able to get married. I was thinking I'd be a bum all my life and go crazy. Wait a minute. Don't go.'

'Did I ever complain?'

'No. You really didn't.'

'You said yourself you were fed up. I won't go over it again.'

'I wasn't fed up with you, Inez. I was fed up with borrowing money from you and letting you do things for me. It got so it was terrible having you buy coffee and things like that for us. Don't you see?"

'I didn't say anything, but you kept shouting that I was discontented.'

'I didn't mean it, Inez. I meant only that I'd like to be able to be doing little things for you. My nerves were raw. That's why I started to quarrel and shout at you. I was the one who was discontented.'

'Well, you kept saying it so often I've come to believe it,' she said, taking a deep breath and then sighing wearily. 'Maybe I was discontented.'

'Inez, did I really make you feel it was all pretty hopeless?'

'Yes, you did.'

'Then I'm a nut. Forgive me, Inez. I love you.'

But with her face turned away from him as if she dared not listen, she started to go into the apartment house. She did not want him to see how bewildered she was. As she opened the door she said so softly that he could hardly hear, 'Good night, Joe.'

'I won't go. You can't do a thing like that. Inez, tell me where you were tonight,' he said, and he pressed his face against the glass of the door, catching a last glimpse of her ankles and then her shoes as she went up the stairs. At first he was so resentful that he wanted to pound on the door with his fist, but almost at once he felt weak and spent, and he walked away and crossed the road so he could look up at her apartment.

Standing there, Joe looked up, waiting to see her shadow pass across the lowered window-shade as she moved around the room, but there was no shadow, nothing to show she was in the room. And at last he noticed just the faintest little movement of the window drape, low down, at the corner, and then a little thin streak of light. Someone was there, peering out at the street. She was watching him, he knew, trying to hide, probably kneeling on the floor with her eyes level with the window-sill. He felt a surge of joy inside him. Inez could not leave him like that. She had to watch him. She had to kneel there, feeling herself pulled strongly toward him, unable to go while he was looking up at her window.

But it was very hard to have her up there and not be able to talk to her. He felt now a vast apology in himself for anything he might have done to destroy the tenderness she had felt for him. It was so splendid to be able to hold her there, making her watch him, that he longed to be able to do something that would coax her back to him; and he kept growing more hopeful, as if he had only to keep looking at the window faithfully for a while and the drape would be pulled to one side, the shade raised, and she would beckon to him eagerly. The same summer night air, the same murmur of city sounds, were there around them now as they had been on other nights, when they had felt so close to one another. If only she could hear him, how he would plead with her! He whispered, 'I'm not sore, Inez, only you should have said you were going out with someone when I phoned tonight.' He knew that she was kneeling there, feeling the struggle within her; all her restlessness and the bitterness of the last few days were pulling her one way, and something much deeper, that weakened her and filled her with melancholy, was resisting strongly. He said aloud, 'That guy didn't mean a thing to you, did he, Inez? You just wanted to have a little amusement with him, isn't that right, darling?'

As he kept on looking up at the window, he grew full of persuasion, full of confidence because he still held her there. All the love between them that had been built up out of so many fine, hopeful, eager moments was offering too much resistance to the bitterness that was pulling her the other way.

Knowing her so close to him, and having these thoughts

on this street where they had walked so often, he began to feel a new boldness; he felt that she must have been persuaded by this time and had yielded to him. So he began to move across the street, still looking up at the lighted room.

But when he reached the middle of the street, it was as though the struggle between them had been decided: she had left the window he knew, for in the room the light was turned out.

Running ahead wildly, he rang the apartment bell; he waited, and then rang again, and then kept on ringing. There was no answer, and he wanted to shout, 'What's the matter with her? Does she think I'm crazy? All right. All right.'

He started to run to the corner so he would hear the sound of his footfalls and be able to think of nothing, but his thoughts raced with him tumultuously: 'She thinks she won't make a mistake. She thinks I'll never get anywhere. I'm a bum, am I? I can't show a girl the town, eh, like that big guy in the swell gray suit that rides in taxicabs? Suppose I haven't had a suit in two years. Suppose I do look like a bum. Wait. It's a big town. I'll get money, I'll get clothes, I'll get girls, pretty girls.' These thoughts rushed through his mind as though he had become a buoyant, confident youth. Then he reached the corner and stood looking up Seventh Avenue. There was no breeze, and the air was warm and muggy. He looked way up the street as far as he could, and then he took a deep, tired breath.

Silk Stockings

David Monroe went into a department store to buy a pair of silk stockings as a birthday present for his landlady's daughter, Anne. Many times he hesitated as he walked the length of the hosiery counter, and he smiled shyly at the good-natured, well-powdered salesgirl who was trying to help him. He was a rather stout young man, dressed conservatively in a dark overcoat with a plain white scarf, but he had such a smooth, round, smiling face that he looked more boyish than he actually was. He blushed and kept on smiling as he tried to look at many pairs of stockings very critically while he wondered whether it would help if he explained to the lady that he was getting the stockings for a girl who was very dainty and stylish, and as smart as any girl anyone ever saw hurrying along the street in the evening. But all he said was: 'I wonder if these mesh hose would look good with a black seal jacket and a little black muff? She has so many different dresses that you can't go by them. I want something good. I don't care whether they're expensive.'

At last he paid three dollars and fifty cents for a pair of gun-metal mesh stockings that were so fine he could squeeze them into a ball and conceal them in his hand. When he went out to the lighted streets that were crowded with people who were hurrying home, he began to scrutinize all the well-dressed women to see if one of them had on a pair of stockings as nice as those he had in his pocket for Anne. He was anxious about the way the stockings would look on her because he had been wondering for a week what he could give her that would suggest his intimate interest in her, that would indicate he didn't want to be just a pal. David began to hurry, for he had to cross over to Brooklyn and he wanted to get home to the boarding-house before Anne did.

His boarding-house was like most of the other boarding-houses in the quiet neighbourhood except that the wood-work always looked clean and freshly painted. As soon as he opened the door he bumped into Anne's mother, Mrs. Greenleaf, a steady-eyed widow with a gentle nature, who had always been motherly and patient with David. They spoke cheerfully, as if they liked each other. The only time David ever saw a harsh, stern expression on Mrs. Green-leaf's face was in the evenings at eleven-thirty when she was walking up and down in the hall waiting for Anne to come home. If Anne happened to be only a few minutes late, her mother argued with her bitterly, as if she alone understood there was a nasty blemish in the girl's nature. The trouble was that Mrs. Greenleaf was a prude and didn't want Anne to go out with fellows at all, and every time David heard her arguing with her daughter in the hall, he thought: 'What does she think the girl's doing, punching a time-clock or something?'

'Is Anne home yet, Mrs. Greenleaf?' he asked.

'Not yet, but she'll be here in a minute. I've got something nice to eat because it's her birthday. Goodness, it must be crisp out; you're just bursting with good health. And here I am driven to bed with my neuralgia all down the side of my face!'

'It's nippy out, but it makes you feel good. It's a shame about that neuralgia,' he said. When Mrs. Greenleaf suffered from neuralgia she used to take many aspirin tablets and try to sleep. As David went upstairs he wondered why it was that two people like Anne and her mother, who were so fine and so sympathetic to each other in many ways, were never able to understand each other. In his own room he put the stockings carefully under his pillow and sat down on the bed to wait. But he couldn't help thinking of the stockings on Anne's ankles; in his head he was making little pictures of her hurrying along the street, a slim, stylish girl with tiny feet wearing expensive fashionable hose that any-one ought to notice, especially when she passed under a street light. Then he heard Anne coming upstairs. He could imagine her running with her coat open and billowing back, her toes hardly touching the steps. She seemed to be in a great hurry, as if she wanted to get dressed before dinner so she could go out right after eating. David, standing at his open door, said: 'Just a minute, Anne, here's something for your birthday. And Anne, would you ever go out with me some night?'

Pulling off her hat, she held it in her left hand. Her black hair was parted in the middle and pulled back tight across her ears. She dangled the silk stockings in one hand, her expression quite serious. Then her face lit up eagerly and she said: 'Oh, aren't they lovely! And I may have them? They're just what I wanted. Would I go out with you? I certainly would!'

'They're yours. I hoped you'd like them.'

'You're a dear, Dave. I'm crazy about them. I'll wear them tonight. I could kiss you.' She almost seemed ready to laugh, but her eyes were soft as she looked away bashfully. Then she crimsoned, hesitated, stood up on her tiptoes, took his head in her hands and kissed him, and then ran along the hall, leaving him standing there with a wide grin on his face. 'Jiminy Christmas!' he said. 'By Jiminy Christmas!'

And before she went out that night she came upstairs and called to him: 'How do you like them, Dave?' She was standing under the hall light, holding her dress up a few inches so he could see the stockings. She was wearing her seal jacket and carrying her little black muff in one hand, and she looked so smart he was delighted to think that the stockings seemed to belong to her costume. 'You look like a million dollars, Anne,' he said.

'Don't the stockings look swell?' she said. 'Bye-bye, Dave.'

He would have liked to ask her where she was going, but the main thing was that wherever she went that night, she would be wearing silk stockings that were his, and for the first time, as he thought of her, he had a feeling of ownership.

That night he went to the armoury to see the fights. On his way home he went into the corner cigar store to get a tin of cigarettes. When he came out he stood on the sidewalk, lighted a cigarette, and as he looked across the street he thought he recognized the girl with the little black muff who was talking to a fellow wearing one of those absurdly long, straight dark overcoats with wide padded shoulders. A small light-gray hat was pulled down over one eye. He looked like a foreign tough guy who has made good and bought himself some snappy clothes. 'What's Anne doing with a mug like that?' Dave thought. He felt like going across the street and pushing the man away. Anne and the fellow moved under the light by the news-stand and he could see the man's swarthy, bluish face that looked as if it had to be shaved every four hours. Anne was holding his arm loosely as they talked and argued with each other. Twice she turned to leave and each time went back and said something to him. Dave didn't actually feel angry till he saw the light shining on her silk stockings, and then he remembered the way she had kissed him and he wanted to shout across the street at her and insult her. But Anne was leaving the man, who was patting her shoulder. Instead of going away himself, the fellow turned, bought a morning paper at the news-stand, put a cigar in his mouth, and leaned against the post.

Dave, who was following Anne along the street, let her go into the house without catching up to her. In the hall upstairs he heard Anne answering her mother, who was calling sleepily.

'Are you in for the night, Anne?'

'Yes. I'm in, Mother,' Anne said.

In his room, Dave sat on the bed, rubbing his face with his hand and trying to figure out what Anne would be doing with a guy who looked like a gangster. 'Lord, no wonder her mother tries to keep an eye on her!' he thought. He felt both jealous and humiliated, and the only thought that comforted him was that she had promised to go out with him, too. Then he heard someone moving softly outside in the hall, tiptoeing downstairs. As he pulled his door open, he saw Anne, who still had on her fur jacket, half-way downstairs. With one hand on the bannister she looked up at him, blinking her scared eyes. He walked down toward her.

'Where are you going, Anne?' he said.

'Out for a little while,' she whispered, putting her finger up to her lips. 'Please be quiet, or Mother will hear you.'

'You're going back to that guy you left down at the corner, I know,' he said stubbornly. 'Why can't you bring the fellows you go out with to the house?'

'Mother wouldn't let me anyway. You know that. She never would.'

'I didn't think you ever sneaked out this late at night.'

'Well, only a few times when Mother's had neuralgia and put herself to sleep.'

'Listen, Anne, please don't go back to that corner.'

'Go on, Dave, please; I'm in a hurry.'

He stared at her, shaking his head; all evening while he had been at the armoury watching the fights, he had been dreaming of the way she had kissed him. Now he felt that her delight at his birthday gift meant nothing, her kiss was just a casual incident, and that she was hurrying out, wearing the stockings he had given as a first intimate gesture, to meet the fellow on the corner. She tried to push him aside. Stuttering with rage, he said: 'I know all about that guy without even speaking to him.' When she didn't answer, he grabbed hold of her arm and pulled her back from the door. He was so full of jealous rage he tripped her and pushed her back on the stairs and tried to hold her there with a forearm across her chest.

'Dave, Dave, you're hurting me! What are you trying to do?' she gasped.

'I'm going to pull those stockings off you,' he said, pushing her back roughly. Then she started to cry, the tears running down her cheeks as if he had hurt her badly. 'Oh, gee, Anne, what's the matter?' he said, and all the energy went out of him. She was sitting on the stairs, swaying back and forth with one hand on her breast as she tried to get her breath.

'You hurt me, you hurt me,' she whispered, biting her lip.

'Oh, I'm so sorry, Anne.'

'You've got to watch how you push a girl. You can't be that rough with a girl.'

'I'm sorry, awfully sorry,' he said, helping her up and patting her gently as if she had become so fragile he hardly dared touch her.

'I know you didn't mean to hurt me, Dave,' she said, wiping her eyes. 'I know you like me.'

'I've always liked you, Anne.'

'I like you, too,' she said, taking a deep breath and looking as if she might cry again as she began to powder her nose.

'Anne, why is a girl like you going out at this hour with that tramp?'

'He's all right. I've been going out with him for two years. He's been good to me. He loves me. I've got so I love him.'

'Is he waiting for you at the corner?'

'Yes.'

There was a sudden fear in his heart and he wanted to say: 'Where are you going?' but he said, haltingly: 'If you want me to, I'll leave the latch off the door, Anne.'

'If you want to, Dave,' she said, looking away. 'Don't tell Mother, will you?'

'No, I won't.'

She went out. For a moment he waited, then he hurried up the stairs to put on his hat and coat. Mrs. Greenleaf must have wakened suddenly, for she called: 'Did I hear you talking to somebody, Dave?' Reassuringly, he said: 'I guess you heard me coming in, Mrs. Greenleaf. It's all right.' Then he tiptoed downstairs and went out to the street. Anne was quite a way ahead. By the time she reached the corner, he was almost up to her, but on the other side of the street. Seeing her coming, the man who was waiting, leaning against the post, tossed his paper into a refuse can, and without saying a word, took hold of her arm possessively. They went walking along the street. Dave stood there, watching with increasing resentment the man's long, straight, wide-shouldered overcoat. Then he saw the light flash on Anne's stockings. At first he felt glad to think that something of his was going with her. The two, who were walking ahead, turned a corner, so Dave hurried after them. He followed them for three blocks till he saw them turning into a brownstone rooming-house. There was only one hall light in the house. Anne was standing about a pace behind the man while he bent down and fumbled with a key in the lock. As Dave stood there, clenching his fists and not knowing whether to be angry at Anne or her mother, he was desperately uneasy, for he remembered he had called out: 'It's all right, Mrs. Greenleaf.' Then he saw the man against the hall light holding the door open, and Anne went in, and the door was shut.

Magic Hat

It was not true that Jeannie Warkle had been too easy for
Joe Stanin. It was no truer than saying Joe had been too easy
for her. It had worked both ways, and that was how they
wanted it. She had known she belonged to him the first time
she had met him, at the end of the summer when she had
been modelling sports clothes for Wentmore, who had given
a party in his show-rooms for the visiting professional tour-
nament golfers. Joe was there because he was a commercial
artist with the agency that handled the Wentmore account
and he wanted to meet some of the big-name golfers, but
instead, he had met her modelling that gray flannel ski suit
with the ridiculous plunging neckline. The first thing she had
said to him was that she, herself, wouldn't dream of wearing
it skiing without a handkerchief around her neck.

A few nights later he, too, had known that in some way
they were committed to each other, but he had said frankly,
'I don't want to settle down. Not for years. I know it's a
crazy independence in me, but at least I like a girl to feel the
same way. We must never feel we have any strings on each
other, Jeannie. And anyway, they're moving me to New
York in the winter. I'm a bad lot, Jeannie, and I can't do you
any good.'

Knowing there could be nothing in it for her but the
happiness they got out of being together made her love for
him seem like a gift more precious than if she had demanded
some security, and anyway, no promise he could have given
her would have been as good as his free and happy gentle
love-making.

When January came and it was time for Joe to go away,
she knew she was expected to act like a good sport with no
regrets and no complaints, but it was very difficult. She felt

she belonged completely to him. To have wailed that he was abandoning her would have cheapened her. His last week in Montreal was very hard on her, because she had to hide her dread of the loneliness she would feel when he had gone. What made it worse was that in that week he couldn't spend much time with her; he was having conferences with his advertising colleagues that lasted until late in the evening, and she had to sit around at home under the eyes of her father and mother and sister Alma, looking pale and distracted.

Her father, putting down his newspaper, would look at her and say, 'Why wait around for that fellow to call you, Jeannie? I'll be glad when you've seen the last of him.' And her mother, looking up quickly, her plump face indignant, would chime in, 'I should say so. He took up all your time, and there was never anything in it for you.'

They didn't know she felt she belonged to Joe and couldn't go out with anybody else. It was humiliating. She knew she would have to find an excuse for keeping in her own room until Joe went away. In a fashion magazine she had seen a picture of a Chinese coolie hat, a gay foolish hat with a pink and black silk sectional crown. At the time she had seen it she had no intention of making it, but she had to appear to be busy, and she decided to copy the hat.

The night she came home with the materials, she had a purposeful air that impressed her family. After dinner she went to her own room and began to shape the buckram for the crown. Again and again she put it on her head. Then she cut a paper pattern for the silk sections that were to cover the crown completely. There was to be a corded silk tassel hanging from the point of the crown. As soon as she sat down and started sewing, she felt much happier. She felt she was absorbed in her work, although she was hoping of course that the telephone would ring and sometimes imagined she heard it, but now it was a more peaceful kind of waiting.

She found a consolation in the work she was putting on the hat; she found that the pattern she was making with the pink and black silk segments took on in her thoughts the pattern of the happy months she had spent with Joe. While she cut the silk segments according to the pattern she had made and smoothed them on her knee, she would pause and ponder and believe that Joe needed her without knowing it, and even when he went away sooner or later he would realize he needed her. She could tell this to herself over and over again while she sewed, and as the hat took the colourful shape she had planned, so her desperate hope took a real shape, too, and she couldn't bear to stop working. She worked at the hat until her eyes ached, and she knew she was making it for Joe.

But there were only three evenings left, evenings she had counted on having with him, and he had telephoned to tell her that some work in the office had to be cleared up. He was in on the planning of the layouts for an account. The conference would go on into the night, he said. And she was left at home again working on the hat in her own room, wondering if she would have even one date with him.

Then Alma came into the room. 'I thought you were to go out with Joe,' she said.

'He's tied up. It's those silly conferences.'

'Tied up, eh? You know, Jeannie, the trouble with you was that when Joe whistled you always ran.'

'I could whistle when I wanted to. I did my share of whistling.'

'You don't fool me, Jeannie,' Alma said. Then she looked at the hat. 'Why are you in such a hurry to finish that hat? Here – let's see it.'

Taking the hat from Jeannie's knee, she put it on her own head and looked at herself in the mirror. She had a round, plump face like her mother's. The hat made her look like a peasant. 'I don't like it at all,' she said, adjusting it at another angle.

'Take it off, then,' Jeannie said quickly, for she couldn't bear to see the hat on anyone else. By this time it seemed to her to belong to all that had been good for her and Joe. She took the hat from Alma.

'Let's see it on you then,' Alma said.

It looked like a different hat on Jeannie, for she had a narrow, oval face, and she knew how good it looked on her and she smiled brightly at Alma.

'Just the same, I don't think you'll wear it much. It's too gaudy. You'll throw it away. When does Joe go?'

'In a couple of days. Why?'

'A smooth operator, isn't he?'

'How so, Alma?'

'I know the type,' Alma said, and she looked wise. She was buxom and sure of herself. 'They tell you from the beginning you can't have them, and then they're in the clear.'

When Alma had gone, Jeannie had to put down the hat. Her hands were trembling and she couldn't sew. She got up and walked around the room restlessly, asking herself if it could possibly be true that she had only been a cheap soft touch for Joe, and if he were deliberately keeping away from her now to make it easy for himself at the end. It was an unbearable thought, and her head ached and she felt sick. She began to loathe herself. To distract herself, she picked up the hat again. She sewed at it blindly. It was too late now for Joe to phone, but she knew where he was, and while she sewed she seemed to see him sitting in the LaSalle bar with his colleagues. A few months ago she would have thought nothing of going to the LaSalle looking for him. She would have felt as free and independent as he did. Breaking the thread with her teeth, she put down the needle, looked at the hat, and suddenly realized it was finished. It was there on her knees, and as she stared at it, all the hope she had felt while working on it returned. 'How do I know he isn't cornered by his colleagues and can't get away, no matter how much he's longing to see me?' she asked herself.

If she put on the hat and went down to the LaSalle and met Joe, mightn't she look so new and strange to him that he would be unable to leave her, she asked herself, and the thought enchanted her. She tried to hold back and feel ashamed of herself for running after him possessively and seeking humiliation. No, he's there, and he'll be glad, she thought. As soon as he sees me he'll be glad. And she got dressed quickly and put on the hat.

It was cold and snowing a little, with a wind from the

mountain, and when she got out of the taxi her cheeks were glowing. She sauntered into the bar, tall and elegant, with her well-cut muskrat coat that looked like mink wrapped around her, and though her thumping heart cut off her breath, her manner was what she wanted it to be – easy and untroubled.

Joe was sitting at the corner table with three red-faced advertising men. He looked thinner and younger than the others. 'Hi, Joe,' she called brightly. He was surprised, of course, but then he grinned and stood up, and she felt weak with relief. 'See, I really must –' he said to the others. Joining her, he whispered, 'I'm going to miss you, baby. Where am I going to find a girl who'll know when to come along and rescue me?'

'You won't have much trouble, Joe,' she said lightly. 'Not when you can grin like that.'

'But I've got in a rut with you, Jeannie,' he teased her. 'It'll take a while to get you out of my eyes.'

'You'll do all right, Joe.'

'Just the same, I had a good girl in Montreal, Jeannie.'

'You'll have a good one in New York, Joe,' she said gaily. 'You always get the girl who's good for you.' But she was waiting for him to say something about her hat.

'Let's go down to Charlie's bar and see what's doing,' he said. The hat wasn't going to do her any good. It didn't matter what she wore or how she looked – he had made the separation from her in his mind and by this time had accepted it, she thought miserably. She was bewildered, then bitter. All she could think of was: I don't even look any different to him in this hat. No! He's deliberately refusing to notice it.

They went along St. Catherine to Charlie's bar, and Joe talked about his big plans for New York. He wasn't aware that she was too bright, too gay, too sympathetic. Afterward, just as if it were any other night, they went to his little apartment on Bishop Street. She took a long time taking off her hat. She put it on the bookcase. But he flopped down in the chair, loosened his collar, and talked and talked. 'Please, please stop talking!' she wanted to cry out. But her cry would have been a wail of protest at being left behind and a cheapening of what was left to her of her self-respect.

She was simply there, and he was at home with her; he was used to her, and foolishly at ease with her. Her hat, on the bookshelf, caught her eye. It reminded her of her blind hopefulness. She kept staring at it with a blank concentration even when his arms were around her, so she would not cry out, 'How can you be so completely self-centred?'

'I should go home. It's awfully late,' she said finally.

'No, let's go somewhere on the way,' he said. 'It's the last chance we'll have.' So they stopped somewhere else and found his friend Lou. He got very sentimental with Lou, talking about how happy he had been in Montreal. There were only three cities on the continent with any real colour of their own, Lou said, and they agreed enthusiastically that Montreal was one of them. But Joe did not see that he was breaking Jeannie's heart, telling how happy he had been in Montreal. It was almost dawn when they left Lou, and it was snowing hard.

'Let's walk,' he said taking her arm. 'I feel like walking for hours.'

'It's pretty wet,' she said, looking at the snow streaming across the street lights. She was going to say, 'What about my hat?' but she no longer cared about it.

The snow was wet and three inches thick, but she had on her galoshes, and he walked her west on Dorchester and they both had their heads down against the snow. He talked about writing letters to her. Whenever he thought of Montreal he would think of her, he said; in fact, when he thought of home she would be there, and he wanted her to promise to write to him.

Her flat hat caught the snow like a plate, but he walked her along, talking eloquently, and they turned up the hill to her street. At the corner under the light he stopped as he turned to speak, and he started to laugh. The heavy, wet snow crown had melted through the silk and the buckram, and the water, in two little rivulets, beginning at her ears, was trickling down her cheeks.

'What's the matter?' she asked.

'Your hat's leaking,' he said solemnly.

'What does it matter?' she asked indignantly. 'It's ruined anyway, isn't it?'

'Here. Let me shake the snow off it,' he said.

Lifting the hat from her head, he shook off the big blob of snow, and while she watched him with blank resentment, he held the hat by the tassel and spun the brim like a wheel, and the spraying drops of water made a circle in the light. While the hat was still spinning, he held it high and let it settle at a crazy angle on her head. He started to laugh; then he stopped, looking at her with wonder. 'You know something, Jeannie?' he said earnestly. 'At that angle on you it looks like a circus hat – sort of crazy and black and pink and shining in the snow.'

'Yeah – like a clown's hat,' she whispered. 'And why not?'

'I'm sorry, Jeannie,' he said. 'I shouldn't have walked you. I should have noticed.'

'Should you?' she blurted out. 'Why should you notice?'

'Why shouldn't I?' he asked innocently.

'Because you don't notice anything that's happening.'

'I don't get it,' he said.' 'You don't want to quarrel about a hat. Not tonight, Jeannie. Not about a hat.'

'I took a lot of time with that hat,' she said fiercely.

'All right. It was a fine hat,' he said impatiently. 'So it's ruined and it's my fault. I'll get you a new one.'

'A new one,' she said bitterly. 'Sure. Go ahead. Get everything new.'

'I can do that, too,' he said quickly.

'And I can get myself a new hat,' she said, her voice breaking. She tried to stop herself; she didn't want to make the wild protest that would humiliate her, and she told herself desperately it would be all right and unnoticed if she protested fiercely only about the hat. 'I sit up at night,' she said angrily. 'I sew till my eyes ache –' But he grabbed at her arm, and she jerked away and went running up the street.

Her galoshes sloshed through the snow, and she ran as fast as she could. 'Jeannie!' she heard him call, but she knew he still stood there, because there was only the sound of her own footsteps and it was a terrible sound. Yet when she heard his longer, heavier step and the sound of his curse, as he slipped and fell, she wanted frantically to go faster, to fly far beyond his reach and hear him thudding after her and never able to catch up to her; she wanted the wild happiness of being beyond him.

She stumbled up the steps to her door just as his big hand grasped at her shoulder. Whirling around, exhausted, she gasped fiercely, 'Leave me alone. You don't own me.'

'All right, you little fool,' he said angrily. 'And you don't own me.'

'That's the way we've played it. Now go away.'

The melting snow from his hat dripped on her face as he held her hard against his wet coat.

Struggling with him, she repeated, 'Go away. Go away.'

'How can I go away?' he asked angrily. Then he softened and got mixed up. 'All evening I've known I didn't want to go away, and I didn't know why. I didn't know I couldn't go without you. But when we stopped under the street light and I happened to look at you – that hat stuck on your head at that crazy angle –'

'Just happened to look. Just happened to look,' she repeated.

'Yeah. Like I said.'

'Just a whim. Just an accident,' she protested. 'Oh, it's unfair.'

'What's unfair?' he asked, growing bewildered.

'It couldn't be like that with me.'

'Sure it could,' he insisted, but he sounded surprised, himself. Then she knew that in the silence he was sharing her apprehension that the course of their lives could change as a result of a little thing like an unpremeditated glance at a hat. 'Maybe that's the way it goes,' he said awkwardly. 'Maybe there's always one moment – everything can look different at one moment. Yeah, that's it,' he said, confused now himself. 'Maybe that's always how it happens, maybe that's how a guy knows he wants to marry,' he added helplessly.

But she was sobbing softly, and he couldn't console her. All she said was: 'It's just that you're like you are and I'm like I am, and it gets so hard waiting for – for the right moment – with nothing to fall back on but a home-made hat.'

'Well, now that we know, Jeannie –' From then on she wasn't sure what they said except that she was agreeing to go away with him and saying how soon she could be ready; but she wanted to close her eyes and hear again the sound of his footsteps thudding after her.

When he had kissed her and gone, she took off her shoes and went in quietly. But her mother, hearing her, called out anxiously, 'Is that you, Jeannie? It's nearly dawn.'

In her own room she stood in a trance, her shoes in her hand, thinking. I'm really going to marry him. Then she took off the wet hat and put it carefully on the radiator. While it dried, she undressed. The pink and black silk on the hat wrinkled up in the heat. The crown, as it dried, was twisted out of shape. She would never wear the hat again, but it didn't matter. Picking it up carefully, she smoothed it and put it on the bureau, and she sat down on the bed and looked at it for a long time with profound surprise.

Rigmarole

After they had come in from the party, Jeff Hilton, the advertising man, looked up and saw his young wife, Mathilde, standing there beaming at him. She seemed to him to be glowing from the memory of many whispered conversations with young men who had been anxious to touch her hand or her arm; she smiled and went on dreaming and her wide dark eyes grew soft with tenderness. She began to hum as she walked over to the window and stood there looking down at the street in the early winter night; and as Jeff went on watching her he kept resenting that she should have had such a good time at a party that he had found so dull. She had left him alone a lot, but he had always remained aware of the admiration she aroused in the young men around her. And now she turned, all warm and glowing, and burst out, 'Didn't you like the party, Jeff?'

'It was a lousy party,' he said vindictively. 'I'm fed up with that crowd. No one ever has anything new or bright to say. They've all gone a little stale.'

Mathilde tried to stop smiling, but her dark, ardent face still glowed with warmth as she stood there with her hands clasped in front of her. Though Jeff went on talking with a kind of good-humoured disgust his earnest face began to show such a desolate loneliness that she suddenly felt guilty; she longed to offer up to him all the tenderness, all the delight it had been so enchanting to have in her since the party. 'I had an awfully good time,' she said. 'But I kept my eye on you. I know who you were with. Were you watching me, Jeff?' and she rushed over to him and threw herself on his lap and began to kiss him and rub her hand through his hair, laughing all the time like a little girl. 'Did you think I was flirting? Did you think I laughed and whispered too much? Don't you love people to think I'm pretty?'

But Jeff who had had such a dull time felt only that she was trying to console him and make him feel good so he said irritably, 'You don't need to feel you neglected me. Don't feel guilty. Nobody ever has to worry about me trailing you around. You can feel free.'

'Jeff,' she said, very softly. 'I don't want to feel free. I don't feel free now.'

'Sure you do. You'd be the first to complain if you didn't.'

'Didn't you worry a little about me once tonight, Jeff?'

'Listen here, Mathilde,' he said shortly, 'jealous men are the greatest bores in the world.'

'Jeff, put your arms around me.'

'What's the matter with you? You don't need to mollify me or feel guilty because you had a good time. Surely we've got beyond that.'

'I wasn't trying to mollify you,' she said, looking quite lost, and she began to show in her face much of that curious discontent he had felt growing in her the last three months. She was pouting like a child and she had the shame of one whose innocent gift has been rejected curtly, and then she went away from him awkwardly and curled herself upon the couch, almost crouching, her eyes hardening as she stared at him.

After a while he said, 'You're childish, Mathilde. Why are you sitting there as if you hate me?' But he began to feel helpless against her silent, unreasonable and secret anger. 'These last few months you've become about as unreasonable as a sick woman. What on earth is the matter with you?' he said. And he got up and paced up and down and his voice rose as he went on questioning her, but every time he passed the couch where she was crouching he became more disturbed by the passionate restlessness he felt in her.

So he tried to laugh and he said, 'This is a lot of nonsense, Mathilde,' and he sat down beside her. In a rough, good-natured way he tried to pull her against him. When she pushed him away he stared at her for a long time till at last he began to desire her, and again he put his arm around her, and again she pushed him away. Then he lost his temper; he threw his arms around her and held her down while he tried to caress her. 'Stop it, stop it Jeff,' she cried. 'Haven't you got any sense at all? Doesn't it mean anything to you that you didn't want me near you a few minutes ago? What do you think I am?' As she pulled away roughly she was really pleading with him to see that she was struggling to hold on to something he had been destroying carelessly month after month. 'Doesn't it mean anything?' she asked.

'There you go,' he said. 'Why can't you be direct about things instead of sentimental.'

'Because I don't want things that way,' she said. And then she cried passionately, 'You can't touch me whenever you like. You can't do that to me just when you feel like it,' and her eyes were full of tears as if at last she had touched the true source of all her disappointment.

But he grabbed hold of her, held her a moment to show he could possess her, then pushed her away. 'I'm not a little boy playing that old game,' he shouted. 'We've been married three years. Why all the rigmarole?' and he expressed the rage that was growing in him by banging her on the knee with his fist.

'Oh, you've hurt me,' she said, holding the spot. 'Why did

you do that?' and she began to cry a little. 'That ends·it.
You'll never hit me again,' she said.

'Damn it all, I didn't hit you.'

'You did. Oh, dear, you did. That settles it. I'll not stay
around here. I'll not stay another night. I'm going now.'

'Go ahead. Do what you want to.'

'Don't worry. I'll soon be gone,' she said, and with tears
streaming from her eyes she ran into the bedroom. He stood
gloomily at the door with his arms folded across his chest.
He watched her pull out drawers, toss dresses into a suit-
case, sweep silver at random from the top of the dresser.
Sometimes she stopped to press her fists against her eyes.
He began to feel so distressed, watching, that he shouted at
last, 'I won't stand for this stupid exhibition,' and he jumped
at her and flung his arms around her and squeezed her as
though he would crush forever the unreasonable revolt in
her soul. Then he grew ashamed and he said, 'I won't stop
you, and I won't stay and watch this stupid performance
either. I'm going out.' And when he left her she was still
pulling out dresser drawers.

As soon as Jeff walked along the street from the apartment house on that early winter night he began to feel that he
really had not left that room at all, that wherever he walked,
wherever he went, he would still be pulled back there to the
room to watch her, and when he went into the corner tavern
to have a glass of beer he sat there mopping his forehead
and thinking, 'Not just what I want, not just when I feel like
it! I can't go on with that stuff when we're so used to each
other. I'd feel stupid.'

In the crowded tavern men and women leaned close together and whispered and while he listened Jeff kept hearing her voice beneath the murmuring voices and the clink
of glasses and seeing her face in the smoke of the tavern,
and as he looked around a dreadful fear kept growing in him
that whatever was warm and vital among people was being
pushed out of his reach; and then he couldn't stop himself
from getting up and hurrying back to the apartment house.

He saw her coming out wearing her brown coat, and her
felt hat was pulled down over her eyes. She was carrying
her bag. A taxi was waiting. In a foolish way, to hide his

eagerness, he smiled and said, 'May I take the bag for you, madam?' He even made a little bow.

'No thanks,' she said, and she swayed the bag away from his outstretched hand, looking at him in that shy pleading way.

'Are you sure you wouldn't like me to take it?'

'Quite sure,' she said.

'All right,' he said politely, and he stood there trying to smile while she got into the cab, and when the cab actually moved off along the street, he stood there, worried and unbelieving, feeling there was no place to go.

But he went into the apartment and as he wandered aimlessly into the bedroom and looked at the empty dresser drawers his loneliness deepened, and he thought, 'I tried to use some common sense anyway. She'll come back. If I went on struggling with her like that all the time I'd never be able to hold my job. I'll bet a million dollars she'll be back.'

And he waited and was desolate remembering the shy pleading look in her eyes as she swayed the bag away from him on the sidewalk, and he listened for every small sound from the street, the stairs and the door; and when at last he heard the key turning in the lock he jumped up triumphantly and rushed to meet her.

She came in quietly with a timid, apologetic smile, and as she pulled off her hat she said in a bantering tone, 'What were you doing, Jeff? What was keeping you up till this hour?'

'Waiting for you, of course.'

'You mean you missed me?'

'Sure I missed you. You know I did, too,' he said. He helped her off with her coat, begged her to sit down, rushed to the icebox to get a snack for them and his face kept showing all of his childish triumph. She was delighted to be waited on in this different way. Every time the broad smile came on his face she asked, 'What are you laughing at, Jeff?'

'How does it feel to be free?' was all he said.

But when they were going to bed and she had buried her dark head in the pillow she began to cry brokenly, and no matter how he coaxed her, or how gently he spoke she would not be quiet. 'Aren't we happy now, Mathilde? Isn't it all over now,' he kept saying.

'No, I'm not happy. I can't bear it,' she said.

'You can't bear what?'

'The way you let me go. No matter what happened I didn't think you'd ever let me go. You wouldn't have done it two years ago.'

'But you wanted to go, Mathilde, and if I thought you wanted to . . .'·

'Two years ago you would have made me come back. You would have been afraid of losing me.'

'I knew you'd come back like a homing pigeon.'

'Yes, you were so sure of it. You were so very sure,' she said, and then she put her hands over her face and she turned her head away, mumbling, 'I'm silly. I guess I sound silly. I guess I don't know what I want,' and he could only see the back of her neck and her hand moving over her cheek.

As he walked around the bed, looking at her, he thought, 'Why didn't I stop her? Why can't she see that knowing we love each other is better than worrying that we don't?' but he began to feel terribly afraid. 'Nobody loves insecurity,' he said, knowing his words sounded weak and apologetic. For a while he watched her, then went to speak, but he found himself shyly fumbling what seemed to be old words, so he stood there, silent, with his love becoming an ache, for it seemed a terrible thing that such words should sound strange just because they had grown used to each other. Then he knew that his fear had been that he would never be able to express all the feeling he had for her. And all he said was, 'I had a glass of beer at the corner and I began to feel terrible.'

'Did you?' she said without looking up.

'I think I know what you've been missing,' he said.

'Yes,' she said.

'I couldn't stay away from here,' he said. 'I felt you'd be pulled back too.'

She looked up at him timidly for though the words he used were neither new, nor warm, nor strange, she began to feel his awkward shyness, she began almost to hear him thinking, 'What happens that you can't keep showing your love when it's so strong in you?' She just waited there and grew shy too, and the feeling between them at that moment seemed so much deeper than any earlier time of impulse and sudden joy.

It Had To Be Done

On the drive out to the country that night to get the suits Chris had left at Mrs. Mumford's place, he kept telling Catherine she shouldn't have come. He was only going because he needed the suits. It didn't matter whether or not Mrs. Mumford only wanted him to be wearing something she had once bought for him. 'She knows I'm going to marry you,' he said.

'That's why I should meet her. Then maybe she'll believe it,' Catherine said. 'You're not ashamed of me.'

They were crossing the Delaware and driving through the soft rolling hills, and it seemed to Catherine that they never would be able to stop talking about Mrs. Mumford. He had met Mrs. Mumford five years ago when he was broke and wanted to be an architect, and she was rich and believed in his talent. She had so much enthusiasm he had thought he might be in love with her, even if she was five years older. She got him one job, then another, then had him quit the jobs and go to Europe with her to study. There never was a chance for him to worry about anything. But when he woke up and found she wanted to marry him and had taken charge of his life, he hated himself for getting into it and left her. But she kept track of him and still kept trying to look after him. When she heard he was with Catherine she wrote him that maybe a girl like Catherine whom he had met at a dance and who worked in a department store would be good for him for a while. Then she asked him why he didn't come out and get the suits he had left at her place: she said she knew he needed them.

They had turned off the highway and were going up the side road past the little lighted store, and then Chris stopped the car. 'Here we are,' he said.

'I'll go up with you, Chris.'

'I know,' he said, getting out of the car. 'But it can't do any good, see. I'll only be gone twenty minutes.'

'But she'll wonder why you didn't bring me.'

'She'd certainly be surprised if I did,' he said, pulling his bag out of the back seat.

'That's just it,' she said eagerly. 'She's sure you wouldn't, no matter how often you write her that we love each other.'

'Look, honey,' he said, patting her arm. 'I don't want to make a visit out of this. I want to get out quick, isn't that right? I'll only be gone twenty minutes.' Then he kissed her and went on up the slope, swinging the bag, and his shadow got longer in the moonlight and broke over the car.

When he was out of sight she got out of the car and stood in the road looking around nervously. She had her hands deep in the pockets of her belted coat, and she pulled off her little blue hat and shook her long-bobbed fair hair. She was twenty-one, fifteen years younger than Mrs. Mumford, and as she stood looking back at the light in the little store and then at the way the moonlight touched the stone fences as they curved up over the meadow-land on Mrs. Mumford's property, she felt like a timid child. She was thinking that as soon as Chris opened the door Mrs. Mumford would say, 'Why, darling, where's your girl?' and no matter what excuses he made she would know that he was ashamed to bring her.

In spite of herself she started to go up the road after Chris, but when she got to the little rippling stone-banked creek she grew afraid. She could go no farther. Staring at the big white house and the lighted windows and the dark high hill behind it, she sat down weakly in the grass. When a cow-bell tinkled in some nearby pasture-land and she heard the swishing sound of the cow moving in the grass and then settling down again by a fence, she felt suddenly lost in a country that belonged to a rich woman, a country

where Chris had lived and that was so beautiful and peaceful that surely as he walked up the road he would be remembering how he had wanted to hear all these little sounds
again. Maybe he was remembering and hearing these
sounds every time Mrs. Mumford wrote him offering to
loan him money and giving him advice about little things
and wishing him great happiness like a very noble woman.

'Oh, Chris, we've had such good times. You've said you
felt free for the first time in your life,' she was whispering
to herself, looking up at the house. He had got a job in an
architect's office. He seemed to feel like a kid with her. He
said he wanted to work and make something out of himself.
He said that she would never understand what it was to
have someone own your life and smother you and never
give you a chance to be yourself. She was trying hard to
remember these things, but if he was ashamed of her, then
nothing she had given him was good. While he felt that he
did not want Mrs. Mumford to see her, he could never
really belong to her.

As she got up and began to go slowly toward the house
she was frightened. She felt she had to do it, and the loud
beating of her heart could not stop her. At the door she
faltered, then she rapped weakly. 'I was waiting,' she said
to the maid. 'Mrs. Mumford will know me.' Then she went
into the old white colonial living-room, trying to smile and
walk lazily.

Chris and Mrs. Mumford were standing together at the
long pine table. The open bag was on the table, and Chris
was packing his suits in it. As Catherine came in they both
turned, startled. Mrs. Mumford was a large handsome woman with jet-black hair drawn back tight from her bold
and vivid face, and the white part in her hair was shining
in the light. If Chris had only smiled naturally, or come to
her to welcome her she would have felt immense relief,
but his face reddened as Mrs. Mumford stared at Catherine,
then turned, wondering, to him.

'It got chilly outside,' Catherine said. 'I thought I might
as well come in.'

'You're Catherine, aren't you?' Mrs. Mumford said.

'Yes.'

'Why, Chris,' she said, 'you said you came alone.'

'I didn't want to stay more than a minute,' he explained awkwardly. 'It wasn't like a visit, see. I mean, I knew you'd want us to stay.' But out of the corner of his eye he glanced at Catherine savagely and she felt panicky.

'Please sit down,' Mrs. Mumford said, and she smiled and nodded sympathetically, and it was terrible for both of them because she made them feel that she understood their embarrassment and only wanted to help them. So Catherine sat down by herself with her toes close together. After that one appraising glance, Mrs. Mumford turned away and tried to help Chris with the straps on the bag. His hands were pawing at the lock. His head was down and his ears were red as he fumbled with it. 'If only you both had come for the evening we could have had such a lovely chat,' Mrs. Mumford was saying. It seemed to Catherine, praying that Chris hurry, that the woman was mocking her. Beneath Mrs. Mumford's simple calmness she felt a vast assurance and aggressiveness that terrified her. If Mrs. Mumford had offered her suddenly to take a walk around the house, she felt she would get up meekly and do it. She began to long to find something within herself that Mrs. Mumford would see she could never touch.

Chris was still having trouble getting the edges of the bag together, and as he bent over the bag, muttering, Mrs. Mumford bent over, too, to help him. Their heads were close together. 'What's the trouble?' she asked. 'Let me try.'

She jammed the edges together suddenly when Chris had his finger against the edge of the metal lock. 'Ouch. Damn it, my finger!' he said.

'Why, it's your nail,' she said. 'Oh, dear. That's terrible. Let me see it.' She took his hand and lifted it close to her face. 'Why, it's bleeding.'

'It's nothing. It doesn't hurt at all,' he said uneasily.

'It'll turn black. I'll get some ointment,' she said. 'Maybe I should put a piece of cloth around it,' and suddenly she seemed to enfold him. Her face lit up with an energetic warmth. She seemed to be ministering to someone she possessed. It was only a little thing, but Catherine stood up, frightened. It seemed to her that if she let Mrs. Mumford do one thing more for Chris he could never really belong to her.

'Why don't you leave him alone?' she whispered.

'Why, his finger's hurt,' Mrs. Mumford said, startled.

'That isn't it,' Catherine said breathlessly as she took a step toward Mrs. Mumford.

'Catherine, please – ' Chris begged her.

'It's just a little thing, I know,' Catherine went on doggedly.

'What's the matter with her, Chris?' Mrs. Mumford asked.

'This is the matter,' Catherine blurted out, white-faced. 'Somebody's got to tell you. Why don't you leave him alone? Leave him alone. You don't own people. Stop trying to boss him around.'

But the contempt she saw in Mrs. Mumford's eyes suddenly silenced her. She turned helplessly to Chris.

'I'm sorry,' he was saying to Mrs. Mumford. 'I didn't want this to happen.'

'I understand, Chris,' she said calmly.

But she kept looking at Catherine. Her long appraising look made Catherine feel she had to hurt her. 'Come on, Chris,' she said. 'Come on, let's go. The lady doesn't think much of me.'

Then her heart was pounding wildly and she didn't care what she did. And she swung her coat back and put her hand on her hip, showing the fine curve of her breast and her slimness and her young body. As she moved she swaggered a little, swaying her hips, her eyes mocking Mrs. Mumford and seeming to say, 'Go on, take a look at me. You haven't got everything.'

But Mrs. Mumford only turned to Chris, trying to get him to look at her. He was staring at Catherine, pain and surprise in his eyes. Then the shame and humiliation Catherine had been dreading ever since she came there flooded through her. She looked scared.

'Don't you think you made a mistake?' Mrs. Mumford said, turning to Chris.

'The mistake I made was in coming here,' he shouted at her. And he swung away from her and grabbed the handle of the open bag and jerked it off the table. It flopped open and the suits spilled out on the floor. Then he and Mrs. Mumford looked down at the suits. 'She's right,' he said to her. 'And you remember it.'

Hoisting the empty bag under his arm he grabbed Catherine by the shoulder and pushed her toward the door, and he kept pulling her out and down the path of light from the open door.

'I'm sorry, Chris. I'm sorry,' she began to sob.

'Why did you have to come in?' he shouted.

'I acted like a cheap little chippie,' she wept. 'I didn't want to. I guess I had to.'

'I told you to stay out and you didn't,' he said. He was rushing her down the road and she could hardly keep up to him. 'Maybe you should stay with her. Maybe she's right. You shouldn't be with me,' she said. Her face kept turning to him, pleading, apologetic and ashamed. 'That's it.' Without stopping, he turned, stricken, as if scared she was going to deny him suddenly everything that had built his life up. His hand tightened on her arm. She felt a furtive leap of joy; they were going down the road faster, and he seemed to be holding her to him tighter than ever before.

The Homing Pigeon

When the fifth day passed and still his father, the doctor, didn't return to Frenchtown, Dick started out looking for him. He went over to Charlie's barber shop and sprawled in the chair. He was seventeen, big for his age, and he looked at the barber a long time with a serious, worried face before he spoke to him.

'How do you want it, same as usual – use the scissors at the sides?' Charlie asked, taking the scissors off the glass ledge.

'I don't want a haircut, I just want to ask you something.'

'Go ahead, Dick.'

'You know my old man hasn't shown up yet.'

'That's bad, that's bad, that's getting worse.'

'You know he stayed away before, and I figured you'd know where he was.'

'Me?'

'Sure. You're the only one around here that knows he gets drunk.'

As he took off his glasses and began wiping them with the hem of his white coat, the barber started to splutter, 'I didn't think you'd be worrying much about the doctor, Dick. I mean the two of you didn't get along very well – everybody knows that. There's things you've got to make allowances for. When a man's wife dies it upsets the swing of his life a little, don't you see?'

The doctor's son took an envelope from his pocket, showing it to the barber. On the back of the envelope there was a Twenty-eighth Street, New York, address.

'Do you think he might be at this address?' he asked. 'Have you been there with him?'

'Now, now, Dick. I wouldn't go there looking for him.'

'Would he be there?'

'I'd let him look after himself if I were you, Dick. He'll come home when he's ready,' the barber said.

The doctor's son went out and along the street to the garage where Williams' truck was waiting, and he yelled up to the driver. 'Are you going right into New York, Bert?'

'That's right.'

'Can I come?'

'Looking for your old man?'

Dick was a little ashamed and only said, 'It's time I had a look at the big town, isn't it?'

But when he was sitting on the big high seat with Bert Williams, the round-faced, rosy-cheeked grocery boy who had grown up in the town with him, and the truck was swinging him around the bends in the road in the late afternoon and swinging them close together, he found himself talking eagerly about his father.

It was true he and his old man had never got along very well – they just didn't seem to have any affection for each other, but there were times when he thought his father missed this affection; little things he said, ways he had of looking at him; and he himself was often puzzled and felt maybe their natures were just antipathetic. A few months ago, when his mother died, it got worse between them. Perhaps she had been all that held them together – held them with her soft, gentle way and the little bits of encouragement she was always giving him to be friendly with the old man. She had made him feel that he simply had to like his father and that his love for her even was spoiled and no good unless he was willing to share it with his father. 'There's just the two of us in the house now, and I got the idea today that's maybe one reason why he stays away. He's got an idea I've no use for him. What do you think? Maybe he'd like it if he saw I really wanted him back. We might start being good friends. What do you think?' he asked.

'It's very likely,' Bert replied, 'I always liked him.'

'I figure my mother would certainly want me to dig him up no matter where he is,' said Dick, and he lay back on the seat with his eyes half closed, watching the darkness creep over the low Jersey hills and thinking of the way his mother used to laugh. He had always felt that it was a secret between them that he knew she wanted most to be a gay, carefree, laughing woman, because she was always grave and polite when his father and other people were around the house.

Soon they were crossing the flat lands of Jersey, then crossing the great bridge and going through the tunnel, and as he looked at the lights of the city he felt an indescribable elation, a puzzled breathlessness, and exclaimed, 'Gee, why do I feel like this?'

'What do you mean?'

'I don't know, it just seems pretty exciting to be going into the town,' he said. 'Maybe it's because I'm doing the right thing and I feel good about it.'

'I thought you said you'd been here often.'

'Not at night, just a few times when I was a kid with my mother,' he said.

He got off the truck at Seventh Avenue and Twenty-eighth Street and Bert Williams yelled, 'Here's hoping you find your old man, kid.'

'I'll find him,' replied Dick.

'Sure you got the address?'

'I know it by heart.'

'Supposing you don't find him, or he don't want to see you?'

'I got a couple of bucks, Bert. Don't worry about me.'

'Okay, lots of luck,' yelled Bert, and the engine roared and he was gone, and Dick was left there with his heart beginning to beat heavily as he looked up Seventh Avenue toward the rash of fire in the sky over Times Square.

There were four apartments in the house on Twenty-eighth Street, and when he stood in the dimly lit hall he was in a panic. He began to wish he hadn't come. The woman in the lower apartment said, 'Dr. Harvey? No, I don't know no Dr. Harvey.' On the second floor a man in his shirt-sleeves with his collar off, said, 'You got the wrong number, son.' He began to wish that he actually had the wrong number; he didn't want to find his father there. On the third floor a plump, red-faced, blonde woman in a green dressing-gown opened the door and said, 'Dr. Harvey? Who wants him?'

'I do.'

'What do you want?'

'I want to talk to him.'

'Who are you?'

'I'm his son,' he said.

The woman hesitated, and half turning her head looked back into the room, and Dick knew his father was in there. He was terribly disappointed. In Frenchtown everybody respected him and he was a good country doctor. But this soft, blowsy-looking woman with the mouth that was heavy and cruel in spite of the way she laughed so easily, half closed the door, and looking at him a long time grinned and said, 'He isn't here.'

'I know he's here.'

'Look,' she said, tapping his arm as though he were a little kid. 'You go home, and if I see him I'll tell him you were looking for him. See what I mean?' Her face was soft and warm and smiling as she whispered, but her hard eyes were worried. He hated the way she was trying to tell him she knew what was good for him.

'I'm going to talk to him,' he said, pushing her away.

'Hey, stop pushing me!'

'Leave me alone, that's all,' he said.

With one hand on her hip she stepped back and screwed up her eyes and made him feel young and unimportant by the way she sized him up. Unsmiling, she said, almost to herself, 'I've heard about you.' The knowing, reflective way she said it made him feel sure she not only knew all about him, but about his family, his mother, the way they lived. His resentment against his father mounted as he strode past her into the apartment that smelled of beer, food and cheap perfume.

On the round table there were glasses and a trayful of cigarette butts. A bedroom door was open. He took a couple of steps toward the bedroom, and then stood still, suddenly afraid. The woman watched thoughtfully.

'Is he in there?' he asked.

'It's your party,' she said, shrugging.

'Who's that, Tony; who's there?' his father called.

'A kid who says you're his old man,' she called, and laughing in a soft, indolent, mocking way, she sat down lazily and linked her plump arms behind her head.

'This is going to be funny,' she said.

There was the sound of the creaking of bed springs, of feet hitting the floor, and Dr. Harvey came slowly into the room. He was a big, powerful man. His collar was undone, his short, tightly clipped, stiff, gray hair was tousled and the big veins on the side of his head were blue and swollen against the ashen colour of his face. He stumbled a little, then he stiffened when he saw his son, and his hand went out to the door-post for support. He was still a little drunk, and when he saw Dick staring at him in a kind of desolate wonder, he shook his head and lurched toward him.

'What do you want?' he asked. 'Where did you come from?'

'I've been worried. I wanted you to come home.'

'Missing me, eh? Look, Tony, he missed me. You didn't think anybody would miss me.'

'Yeah, I've been worrying,' Dick said.

Rubbing his hands across his face, the doctor sat down, and you could see he wanted to appear calm and reasonable. Then he turned to Tony and smiled cynically, 'Why does he want to spy on me, Tony?'

Shrugging, she said, 'Why don't you give the kid a break? Maybe he means what he said.'

An idiotic laugh that made his face suddenly red came from the doctor, and then he couldn't stop laughing. His head kept dropping down to the table as if his neck were too weak to support it, then he would jerk it back and the crazy laughter kept pouring out of him. Dick felt sick with shame. He had never before seen his father like this.

'Shut up, shut up,' the big blonde woman said. 'Stop that crazy laughing or get out of here. Do you want all the neighbours in?'

'You've done this to him. Leave him alone,' Dick said to her.

'I ought to throw the both of you out of here,' she said. 'What's the matter with me?'

'Wait a minute, wait a minute,' the doctor said. 'Why did he come here? He doesn't like me. He never did.'

'I wasn't thinking of just you.'

'You bet your life you weren't. There, didn't I tell you, Tony?'

'I was thinking of Mother.'

'What about her?'

'How do you think she would feel if she saw you here like this?'

'What's the matter with it?'

'Here, with her,' he said, nodding at Tony.

'He doesn't like me, George,' she said, laughing. 'Your wife wouldn't like me, he says.'

'Come on and get dressed,' Dick said, and he tried to take his father under the arm, but his father pushed him away heavily.

'Take your hands off me,' he said. 'You know what your mother would say? Nothing, absolutely nothing. What do you think of that? So don't lecture me. Leave me alone. I always left you alone, didn't I?'

'I don't care what you think about me,' Dick said, and then he said desperately to Tony, 'Why don't you help me to get him out?'

'I don't think he wants to get out,' she said, and she grabbed the doctor by the shoulder, gave him a couple of stiff slaps on the forehead and shook him and pushed him around a bit.

But the sight of his father, a respectable man, an educated man, a man who could walk down the street with great dignity on Sunday afternoons, letting himself be pushed around by such a cheap, blowsy woman enraged Dick, and he cried out, 'You ought to be ashamed! Why don't you get up and come home? Wherever she is now, she's ashamed of you and I am, too.'

'Ashamed of me,' the doctor shouted, and he jumped up and shoved Dick toward the door. 'Neither she nor you have any right to be ashamed of me, so don't come around here insulting my friends.'

'I'm ashamed because you're my father, that's all,' Dick whispered.

'My God, listen to him,' the father cried.

'That's the only reason,' Dick said, refusing to budge.

'It is, eh?' the doctor said savagely. 'Beat it, beat it, do you hear? I'm not your father.'

'What do you mean?'

'You heard me, didn't you?' the doctor said, glaring at him. Then the puzzled wonder in the boy's eyes made him turn away.

Like a bewildered child, Dick rubbed his hands over his face, and while they watched him and he tried to smile his eyes grew full of terror. He looked helplessly at Tony, wanting her to say something to him. When she didn't speak he pleaded with her very softly, 'He doesn't know what he's saying, does he?'

'He's crazy,' she said. 'He's been like that for days.' The doctor was walking up and down rubbing his forearms as if they were cold and mumbling, 'She's dead now. You can't say I said anything while she was alive. It's better for him to know. There never was any good feeling lost between us.' And while he was walking up and down mumbling this justification to himself, Dick grabbed him by the arm and cried, 'You're crazy, you're a crazy fool,' shouting imprecations in a young wild voice. Then, as though he realized he had been pushed away from all living things, he looked around helplessly and whispered to the doctor, who looked scared now.

'Would you mind telling me something?'

'I don't mind, Dick. You know I don't mind,' the doctor said. 'It just burst out, see? I didn't mean to say it. I thought maybe you'd felt it for years. I didn't think it would hit you like it did.'

'Who's my father?'

'Don't keep at it. Don't keep at me,' the doctor said.

'I've got to know, can't you see?'

'A man named Page.'

'Where did he live?'

'Around here. I think he's dead now. Cut it out. Let it rest, can't you?'

'Where was I born?'

'Around here. What's the use of going into it?'

'He's right. Come on, son,' the big blonde woman said, and she took Dick by the arm in a comforting way and led him out to the hall. 'You shouldn't pay no attention,' she said. 'He talks a little crazier every day and most of the time he takes it out on me. You just happened to be around.'

But Dick was so bewildered he began to go down the stairs without answering; down, down slowly, as if there was nothing in the world for him but the terror of the sound of his own footfalls, and feeling of descending into the dark, further and further away from his own life.

'Son, hey, son,' the big blonde woman was calling to him from the top of the stairs. She was leaning over the bannister, worried, her dressing-gown flopping over loosely, and when he looked up, white-faced, she called, 'Go home and forget it. I'll send him home.'

'I'm not going back there,' he said simply.

'Where are you going?'

'I don't know,' he said, going on down and out.

Outside the wind struck his face and he began to feel alive again. He went slowly along the street and stood a while by the lamp-post on the corner looking up at the glow of lights up there high over Time Square. Every time a man passed him he stared at his face. He stared eagerly at each passing face as if searching for some sign of recognition, something that would pull him into place and time and life again. 'My father and mother lived here. My mother used to be happy when she lived here with my father,' he kept saying over and over. 'And I was born here and maybe a part of such happiness.'

He started to walk along the street, feeling that he would walk all night, that all the past, all the future was here for him, that he must let the sights, the sounds, the smell of the place seep into him, and maybe as he walked he would feel again that eagerness he had felt coming along the highway when he saw the sweep of the lights and felt as if he had been away for a long time and was coming home.